# About the Authors

**Miranda Lee** is Australian, and lives near Sydney. Born and raised in the bush, she was boarding-school-educated, and briefly pursued a career in classical music before moving to Sydney and embracing the world of computers. Happily married, with three daughters, she began writing when family commitments kept her at home. She likes to create stories that are believable, modern, fast-paced and sexy. Her interests include meaty sagas, doing word puzzles, gambling and going to the movies.

**Michelle Douglas** has been writing for Mills & Boon since 2007 and believes she has the best job in the world. She lives in a leafy suburb of Newcastle, on Australia's east coast, with her own romantic hero, a house full of dust and books, and an eclectic collection of '60s and '70s vinyl. She loves to hear from readers and can be contacted via her website, michelle-douglas.com.

**Kandy Shepherd** swapped a career as a magazine editor for a life writing romance. She lives on a small farm in the Blue Mountains near Sydney, Australia, with her husband, daughter and lots of pets. She believes in love at first sight and real-life romance—they worked for her! Kandy loves to hear from her readers. Visit her at kandyshepherd.com.

# Australian

## AFFAIRS

# Australian Affairs:
# Taken

MIRANDA LEE

MICHELLE DOUGLAS

KANDY SHEPHERD

**MILLS & BOON**

First Published in Great Britain 2019
By Mills & Boon, an imprint of HarperCollins *Publishers*
1 London Bridge Street, London, SE1 9GF

AUSTRALIAN AFFAIRS: TAKEN © 2019 Harlequin Books S.A.

*Taken Over By the Billionaire* © 2014 Miranda Lee
*An Unlikely Bride for the Billionaire* © 2016 Michelle Douglas
*Hired by the Brooding Billionaire* © 2015 Kandy Shepherd

ISBN: 978-0-263-27525-4

0119

MIX
Paper from
responsible sources
FSC® C007454

This book is produced from independently certified FSC™ paper
to ensure responsible forest management.

For more information visit: www.harpercollins.co.uk/green

Printed and bound in Spain
by CPI, Barcelona

# TAKEN OVER BY
# THE BILLIONAIRE

## MIRANDA LEE

# CHAPTER ONE

MURPHY'S LAW STATED that if anything could possibly go wrong, then eventually it would.

Jess did not subscribe to this theory, despite the fact that her surname was Murphy. But her father was a firm believer. Whenever anything annoying or frustrating happened, such as a flat tyre when he was driving a bride to her wedding—Joe owned a hire-car business—then he blamed it on Murphy's Law: bad weather at the weekends; down-turns in the stock market. Recently, he'd even blamed the defeat of his favourite football team in the grand final on Murphy's Law.

Admittedly, her dad was somewhat superstitious by nature.

Unlike her father, Jess's view of unfortunate events was way more rational. Things happened, not because a perverse twist of fate was just waiting to spoil things for you without rhyme or reason, but because of something someone had done or not done. Flat tyres and stock-market crashes didn't just happen. There was always a logical reason.

Jess didn't blame Murphy's Law for her boyfriend suddenly having decided last month that he no longer wanted to drive around Australia with her, having opted instead to go backpacking around the whole, stupid world for the next year! With a mate of his, would you believe? Never mind that she'd just gone into hock to buy a brand-new four-wheel drive for their romantic road trip together. Or that she'd started thinking he might be Mr Right. The truth, once she'd calmed down long enough to face it, was that Colin had caught the travel bug and obviously wasn't ready to settle down just yet. He still loved her—he claimed—and had asked her to wait for him.

Naturally, she'd told him what he could do with that idea!

Neither had Jess blamed Murphy's Law for recently having lost her much-loved part-time job at a local fashion boutique. She knew exactly why she'd been let go. Some cash-rich American company had bought up the Fab Fashions chain for a bargain price—Fab Fashions was in financial difficulties—and had then sent over some bigwig who had threatened the managers of all the stores that, if they didn't show a profit by the end of the year, all the retail outlets would be closed down in favour of online shopping. Hence the trimming of staff.

Actually, Helen hadn't wanted to let her go. Jess was an excellent salesgirl. But it was either her or Lily, who was a single mother who really needed her job, whereas Jess didn't. Jess had a full-time job during the week working at Murphy's Hire Car. She'd only taken the weekend job at Fab Fashions because she was mad about fashion and wanted to learn as much as she could about the industry, with a plan one day to open her own boutique or online store. So of course, under the circumstances, she couldn't let Helen fire poor Lily.

But she'd seethed for days over the greed of this American company. Not to mention the stupidity. Why hadn't this idiot they'd sent over found out why Fab Fashions wasn't making a profit? *She* could have told him. But, no, that would have taken some intelligence. And time!

Before she'd been let go last weekend, she'd asked Helen if she knew the name of this idiot, and she'd been told he was a Mr De Silva. Mr Benjamin De Silva. Some searching on the Internet just this morning had revealed a news item outlining the takeover of several Australian companies—including Fab Fashions—by De Silva & Associates, a private equity firm based in New York. When she looked up De Silva & Associates, Jess discovered that the major partner and CEO was Morgan De Silva, who was sixty-five years old and had been on the Forbes rich list for yonks. Which meant he was a billionaire. He was divorced—surprise, surprise!—with one son, Benjamin De Silva: the idiot they'd sent out. A clear case of nepotism at work, given his lack of intelligence and lateral thinking.

The office phone rang and Jess snatched it up.

'Murphy's Hire Car,' she said, trying not to let her irritation show through in her voice.

'Hi, there. I have a problem which I sure hope you can help me with.'

The voice was male, with an American accent.

Jess did her best to put aside any bias she was currently feeling towards American males.

'I'll do my best, sir,' she said as politely as she could manage.

'I need to hire a car and driver for three full days, starting first thing tomorrow morning.'

Jess's eyebrows lifted. They didn't often have people wanting to hire one of their cars and drivers for that length of time. Mostly, Murphy's Hire Car did special events which began and ended on the one day: weddings; graduations; anniversary dates; trips to Sydney airport; that sort of thing. Based on the central coast a couple of hours north of Sydney, they weren't an overly large concern. They only had seven hire cars which included three white limousines for weddings and other flash events, two white Mercedes sedans for less flash events and one black limousine with tinted windows for people with plenty of money who wanted privacy.

Recently her father had bought a vintage blue convertible Cadillac but it wouldn't be ready for hiring till next week, having needed new leather seats. Jess knew without even looking up this weekend's bookings on the computer that she wouldn't be able to help the American. They had several weddings on. Not uncommon given that it was spring. 'I'm sorry, sir, but we're fully booked this weekend. You'll have to try someone else.'

His weary sigh elicited some sympathy in Jess. 'I've already tried every other hire car company on the Central Coast,' he said. 'Look, are you absolutely certain you can't wangle something? I don't need a limo or anything fancy. Any car and driver would do. I have to be in Mudgee for a wedding on Saturday, not to mention the stag party tomorrow night. The groom's my best friend and I'm the best man. But a drunk driver ran into me last night, wrecked my rental and left me unable to drive myself. I've a bunged up right shoulder.'

'That's terrible.' Jess hated drivers who drank. 'I truly wish I could help you, sir.' Which she genuinely did. It would be awful if he couldn't make it to his best friend's wedding.

'I'm prepared to pay over and above your normal rates,' he offered just as she was about to suggest he try one of the larger hire car firms in Sydney. They could surely send a car to him lickety-split. He might even have success hiring an ordinary taxi.

'How much over and above?' she asked, thinking of the hefty repayments she had to make on her SUV.

'If you get me a car and driver, you can name your own price.'

Wow, Jess thought. This American had to be loaded. He could probably afford to charter a helicopter—not that she was going to suggest such a thing. Jess wasn't about to look a gift horse in the mouth.

'Okay, Mr...er...?'

'De Silva,' he said.

Jess's mouth dropped open.

'Benjamin De Silva,' he elaborated.

Jess's mouth remained agape as she took in this amazing coincidence. With his being American and having such a distinctive name, he *had* to be the same man!

'Are you still there?' he finally asked after twenty seconds of shocked silence.

'Yes, yes, I'm still here. Sorry, I...er...was distracted for a moment. The cat just walked onto my keyboard and I lost a file.' In actual fact, the family moggie was sound asleep on a sun-drenched window sill, a good ten metres away from Jess's desk.

'You have a *cat* in your office?'

He actually sounded appalled. No doubt there were no cats allowed in the pompous Mr De Silva's office.

'This a home-run business, Mr De Silva,' she said somewhat stiffly.

'I see,' he said. 'Sorry. No offence intended. So, can you help me or not?'

Well, of course she could help him. And it was no longer just a question of money. For how could she possibly give up the opportunity to tell the high and mighty Mr Benjamin De Silva what was wrong with Fab Fashions?

Surely there would be plenty of opportunities somehow to bring up her lost job during the course of their very long drive together. Mudgee was a long way away. She'd never actually been there but she'd seen it on the map when she and Colin had been planning their trip. It was a large country town in the central west of New South Wales, a good five- or six-hour drive from here, maybe longer, depending on the state of the roads and the number of times her passenger wanted to stop.

'I can take you myself, if you like,' she offered. 'I am well over twenty-one, a qualified mechanic and an advanced driving instructor.' She only helped out in the office on Mondays and Thursdays. 'I also own a brand-new four-wheel drive which won't have any trouble negotiating the roads out Mudgee way.'

'I'm impressed. And extremely grateful.'

And so you should be, she thought a little tartly.

'So where exactly are you now, Mr De Silva? I'm presuming you're on the Central Coast somewhere.'

'I'm staying in an apartment at Blue Bay.' He gave her the address.

Jess frowned as she tapped it into the computer, wondering why a businessman like him would be staying up here instead of in Sydney. It seemed odd. Maybe he was just doing the tourist thing whilst he was in the country. Combining business with pleasure, as well as going to his best friend's wedding.

'And the address in Mudgee where I'll be taking you?' she asked.

'It's not actually *in* Mudgee,' he replied. 'It's a property called Valleyview Winery, not far from Mudgee. It's not difficult to find. It's on a main road which connects the highway to Mudgee. After you drop me off, you could stay at a motel in Mudgee till I need you to drive me back here again on the Sunday. At my expense, of course.'

'So you won't actually need me to drive you anywhere on the Saturday?'

'No, but I'll pay you for the day just the same.'

'This is going to be ridiculously expensive, Mr De Silva.'

'I'm not worried about that. Name your price and I'll pay it.'

Jess pulled a face. It must be nice never having to worry about money. She was tempted to say some exorbitant amount but of course she didn't. Her father would be appalled at her if she did such a thing. Joe Murphy was as honest as the day was long.

'How about a thousand dollars a day, plus expenses?' Mr De Silva suggested before she could calculate a reasonable fee.

'That's too much,' she protested before she could think better of it.

'I don't agree. It's fair, under the circumstances.'

'Fine,' she said briskly. Who was she to argue with Mr Moneybags? 'Now, I will need some other details.'

'Like what?' he demanded in a rather irritated tone.

'Your mobile phone number,' she said. 'And your passport number.'

'Okay. I'll have to go get my passport. I won't be long.'

Jess smiled whilst he gathered the information he wanted. Three thousand dollars was a very nice sum.

'Here we are,' he said on returning, and read out the number.

'We also need a contact name and number,' she said as she typed in the details. 'In case of an emergency.'

'Good grief. Is all this strictly necessary?'

'Yes, sir,' she said, wanting to make sure he was the right man. 'Company rules.'

'Fine. My father will have to do. Mum's on a cruise. But Dad does live in New York.'

'I did assume he'd be American, Mr De Silva. You have an American accent. His name and number, please?'

'Morgan De Silva,' he said and Jess smiled. She'd *known* it had to be him!

He rattled off a phone number which she quickly typed in.

'Do you want to pay for this via your credit card or cash?' she asked crisply.

'Which would you prefer?'

'Credit card,' she said.

'Fine,' he said, a decided edge creeping into his voice. 'I have it here.'

He read out the number. American Express, of course.

'Okay. That's all done. We'll deduct one thousand dollars in advance and the rest on completion.'

'Fine,' he bit out.

'What time would you like me to pick you up tomorrow morning, Mr De Silva?'

'What time do you suggest? I'd like to be out there by mid-afternoon. But first, could we dispense with the "Mr De Silva" bit? Call me Benjamin. Or Ben, if you'd prefer.'

'If you like,' she said, slightly taken aback by this offer. Australians were quick to be on a first-name basis but she'd found people from other countries weren't quite so easy going. Especially those who were wealthy. Maybe Mr De Silva wasn't as pompous as she'd originally thought.

'As to time,' she went on with a little less starch in her own voice, 'I would suggest that I pick you up at seven-fifteen. That way we'll avoid the worst of the traffic. Any earlier and we'll run into the tradies plus Sydney commuters. Any later and it'll be the people going to work at Westfield's, not to mention the mothers taking their kids to school.' Lord, but she was babbling on a bit. She could almost hear him sighing down the line.

'Seven-fifteen it is, then,' he said abruptly as soon as

she gave him the opportunity to speak. 'I'll be waiting outside so we don't waste time.'

Jess's eyebrows lifted. She'd picked up a few well-heeled tourists in her time and they rarely did things like that. They always made her knock, were often late and never helped her with their luggage—if it was a trip to the airport, that was, and not just a day out somewhere.

'Excellent,' she said. 'I won't be late.'

'Perhaps you should give me *your* mobile phone number, just in case you don't show up for reasons outside your control.'

Jess rolled her eyes. It sounded like he was another subscriber to Murphy's Law. But what the heck? She was used to it.

'Very well.' And she rattled off her number.

'And what should I call *you*, Miss...er...?'

'Murphy. Jessica Murphy.' She was about to say he could call her Jess—everyone else did—but simply couldn't bring herself to be that friendly to him. He was still the enemy, after all.

So she said a businesslike goodbye instead and hung up.

# CHAPTER TWO

BEN SIGHED AS he flipped his phone shut and slipped it into his jeans pocket. The last thing he wanted to do was be driven all the way to Mudgee tomorrow by Miss Jessica Murphy, qualified mechanic and advanced driving instructor, he thought grumpily as he headed for the drinks cabinet. She'd declared herself well over twenty-one. More likely well over forty. And plain as a pikestaff to boot!

Still, what choice did he have after that doctor at Gosford hospital had declared him unfit to drive for at least a week? Not because of the excuse he'd given over the phone just now. His right shoulder *was* stiff and bruised but quite usable. It was the concussion he'd suffered which was the problem, the doctor having explained that no insurance company would cover him till he had a signed medical clearance.

Stupid, really. He felt fine. A little tired and frustrated, maybe, but basically fine.

Ben scowled as he sloshed a good two inches of his mother's best bourbon into one of her crystal glasses. He supposed he should be feeling grateful he'd found a hire car at all, not irritated. But Miss Jessica Murphy had got right up his nose. There was a fine line between efficient and officious and she'd certainly been straddling it. He half-regretted making the offer for her to call him Ben, but he'd had to do something to warm the old tartar up, otherwise the drive tomorrow would be worse than tedious.

If only his mother had been here, Ben thought as he headed for the kitchen in search of ice. She could have driven him. But she wasn't. She was off on a South Pacific cruise with her latest lover.

Admittedly, this one was older than her usual. In his mid-fifties, Lionel was only a few years Ava's junior. And he was currently employed—something in movie production—so he was a big improvement on the other fortune-hunting toy-boys who'd graced her bed over the years since his parents' divorce.

Not that his mother's affairs bothered him much these days. Ben had finally grown up enough to know his mother's personal life was none of his business. A pity she didn't return the favour, he thought as he scooped a few cubes of ice from the fridge's automatic ice-dispenser and dropped them in his glass. She was always asking him when he was going to get married and give her grandchildren.

So maybe it was better she wasn't here right now. The last thing he wanted was outside pressure about his relationship with Amber. He was having enough trouble as it was, deciding whether he should give up the romantic notion of marrying for love and settle for what Amber was offering. At least if he married Amber he wouldn't have to worry about her being a fortune hunter, which was always a problem when a man was heir to billions. Amber was the only daughter of a very wealthy property developer, so she didn't need a meal ticket in a husband.

In all honesty, Ben hadn't been under the impression that Amber wanted a husband at all yet. She was only twenty-four and was clearly enjoying her life as a single girl with a glamorous though empty job at an art gallery, a full social calendar and a boyfriend who kept her sexually satisfied. But, just before his trip down under, Amber had suddenly asked Ben if he was ever going to propose. She said she loved him, but she didn't want to waste any more time on him if he didn't love her back and didn't want marriage and children.

Of course he hadn't been able to tell her that he loved her back, because he didn't. He'd said that he liked her a lot but did not love her. Ben had been somewhat surprised when she'd replied that she would be happy enough with his liking her a lot. He'd assumed—wrongly, it seemed— that a woman genuinely in love would be more heartbroken by his own lack of love. Apparently not! She'd given him till Christmas to make up his mind. After that, she would be looking elsewhere for a husband.

Ben lifted the bourbon to his lips as he wandered back into the living room and over to the glass wall which overlooked the beach. But he wasn't really looking at the ocean view. He was recalling how he'd told Amber that he would think about her offer whilst he was in Australia and give her an answer on his return.

And he *had* been thinking. A lot. He did want marriage and children. *One* day. But, hell, he was only thirty-one. On top of that, he wanted to feel more for his future wife than he currently felt for Amber. He wanted to fall deeply in love, and vice versa, the kind of love you had no doubts over. The kind which would last. Divorce was not on his agenda. Ben knew first-hand how damaging divorce was to children, even when the parents were civilised about it, as his own parents had been. His workaholic father had sensibly and generously given Ben's mother full custody of Ben, allowing her to bring him back to Australia, with the proviso that Ben spent some of his school holidays with him in America.

Ben had still been devastated to find out that his parents

no longer loved each other. He'd only been eleven at the time, and totally ignorant of the circumstances which had led to the divorce. It was testament to his parents' mutual love of their son that they'd never criticised each other in front of him, never blamed each other for the break-up of the marriage. They'd both just said that sometimes people fell out of love and it was better that they live apart.

Ben had hated coming to Australia at first, but he eventually grew to love this wonderful laid-back country and his life out here. He'd loved the school he'd been sent to and the many friends he'd made here. He'd especially loved his years at Sydney University, studying law and flat-sharing with Andy, his very best friend. It wasn't till he'd graduated that his father had finally told him the ugly truth: that his mother had trapped him into marriage by getting pregnant. She'd never loved him. She'd just wanted a wealthy husband. Yes, he'd also admitted to having been unfaithful to her, but only after she'd confessed the truth to him one night.

His father had claimed he hated hurting Ben with these revelations but believed it was in his best interests.

'You are going to inherit great wealth, son,' Morgan De Silva had said at the time. 'You need to understand the corrupting power of money. You must always keep your wits about you, especially when it comes to women.'

When a distressed Ben had confronted his mother, she'd been furious with his father, but hadn't denied she'd married the billionaire for his money, though she'd done her best to explain why. Born dirt-poor but beautiful, she'd had a tough childhood but had finally made it as a model in Australia and then overseas, having been taken on by a prestigious New York agency. For several years she'd made very good money but just before she'd turned thirty she'd discovered that her manager hadn't invested her money wisely, as she'd believed, instead having wasted it all on gambling.

Suddenly, she'd been close to broke again and, whilst she'd still been very beautiful, her career hadn't been what it once was. So, when the super-wealthy Morgan De Silva had come on the scene, obviously infatuated with the lovely Australian blonde, she'd allowed herself to be seduced in more ways than one. She'd been attracted to him, she'd insisted, but had admitted to Ben that she didn't love his father, saying she doubted he'd loved her either. It had just been a case of lust.

'The only thing your father loves,' she'd told Ben with some bitterness, 'is money.'

Ben had argued back that this wasn't true. His father loved *him*. Which belief had prompted his move to America shortly after his graduation from university.

Not that he'd cut his mother out of his life altogether. She'd been a wonderful mother to him and he still loved her, despite her faults and flaws. They talked every week or so on the phone, but he didn't visit all that often, mostly because he rarely had the time.

Life since going to the States had been full-on. An economics post-graduate degree at Harvard had been followed by an intense apprenticeship in the investment business. There'd been a few snide remarks when he'd made his way quickly up the ladder at De Silva & Associates, but Ben believed he'd earned his promotion to an executive position in his father's company, along with the seven-figure salary, the sizeable bonuses, the flash car and the equally flash New York apartment. Along the way, he'd also earned the reputation for being a bit of a playboy, perhaps because his girlfriends didn't last all that long. Invariably, after a few weeks he would grow bored with them and move on.

Never once had he fallen in love, making him wonder if he ever would.

It was a surprise to Ben that his relationship with Amber had lasted as long as it had—eight months—possibly because he didn't see all that much of her. He was working very long hours. He'd never thought himself in love with her. She was, however, attractive, amusing and very easy to be with, never fussing when he was late for a date or when he had to opt out at the last minute. Never acting in that clinging, possessive way which he hated.

She'd also never once said she loved him in all those months, so her recent declaration had come out of the blue.

Ben had been startled at first, then flattered, then tempted by her proposal, possibly because of his father's mantras, on marriage.

'Rich men should always marry rich girls,' he'd said more than once, along with, 'Rich men must marry with their heads. Never their hearts.'

Sensible advice. But it was no use. Ben knew, deep down in *his* heart, that marriage to a girl he didn't love would be settling for less than he'd always wanted. A lot less.

So his answer had to be no.

Ben considered ringing Amber and telling her so immediately, but there was something cowardly about breaking up over the phone or, God forbid, by text message. She'd already asked him not to call or text her whilst he was away, perhaps hoping that he would miss her more that way.

Frankly, just the opposite had happened. Without phone calls and text messages, the connection between them had been broken. Now that he'd made his final decision, Ben felt not one ounce of regret. Just relief.

When his phone suddenly vibrated in his pocket, Ben hoped like hell it wasn't Amber. But it wasn't her, the caller

ID revealing it was his father. Ben frowned as he lifted the phone to his ear. It wasn't like his father to call him unless there was a business problem. Morgan De Silva wasn't into social chit-chat.

'Hi, Dad,' Ben said. 'What's up?'

'Sorry to bother you, son, but I was thinking about you tonight and decided to give you a call.'

Ben could not have been more taken aback.

'That's great, Dad, but shouldn't you be asleep? It must be the middle of the night over there.'

'It's not that late. Besides, you know I never sleep much. What time is it where you are?'

'Mid-afternoon.'

'What day?'

'Thursday.'

'Ah. Right. So you'll be off to Andy's wedding in a couple of days.'

'I'm actually driving up to his place tomorrow.' For a split second Ben contemplated telling his father about the accident and his fiasco about finding a hire car, but decided not to. Why worry him unnecessarily?

'Nice boy, Andy.'

His father had met Andy when Ben had brought him to America for a holiday. They'd gone skiing with Morgan and had a great time.

'So, when do you think you'll be back in New York?' his father asked.

'Probably not till the end of next week. Mum's away on a cruise and doesn't get back till next Monday. I'd like to spend a day or two with her before I fly home.'

'Of course. Why don't you stay a little longer? Have a decent holiday? You deserve it. You've been working way too hard.'

Ben stared out at the beach and the ocean beyond. In

truth, it had been a couple of years since he'd had more than a long weekend off, his mother recently having accused him of becoming a workaholic, just like his father.

'I might do that,' he said. 'Thanks, Dad.'

'My pleasure. You're a good boy. Give my regards to your mother,' his father said abruptly, then hung up.

Ben stared down at his phone, wondering what in the hell that had been all about.

# CHAPTER THREE

JESS WAS GLAD to get out of the house the following morning before her parents were up and about. Her mother had started going on and on the night before about her taking a risk, driving some stranger all the way out to Mudgee and back.

'He might be a serial killer for all you know,' she'd said at one stage.

She hadn't stopped with the doomsday scenarios till Jess had told her everything she knew about Mr Benjamin De Silva, including his being the son of a super-rich American businessman whose company had taken over several Australian firms, including Fab Fashions.

'He's not a serial killer, Mum,' she'd informed her mother firmly. 'Just a man with more money than sense.'

To Jess's surprise, her sometimes pessimistic father had taken her side in the argument.

'Jess knows how to look after herself, Ruth,' he'd said. 'She'll be fine. Just give us a call when you get there, love, and put your mother's mind at rest. Okay?'

She'd happily agreed to do so, but hadn't trusted her mum not to start up again this morning, so she'd packed an overnight bag the night before, then risen early, giving her time to take some extra care getting ready. Under the circumstances, she didn't want to look like a dag. Or a chauffeur, for that matter—so she'd already dismissed the idea of wearing her usual driving uniform of black trousers with a white shirt which had *Murphy's Hire Car* emblazoned on the breast pocket.

She did wear black trousers. Rather swish, stretchy ones which tapered in at the ankles and made the most of her long legs, combining them with a V-necked white T-shirt topped with a floral jacket which she'd made herself. Jess was an excellent dressmaker, having been taught how to sew by her gran. She dithered a bit over how much make-up to wear, opting in the end to play it conservative, using just a bit of lip gloss and a light brushing of mascara. Her clear olive skin did not really need foundation, anyway. She then scooped her thick, black hair back up into a ponytail, wrapping a red scrunchie around it which matched the red flowers in the jacket. Finally, she pulled on a pair of very comfy black pumps before bolting out of the house by six-thirty, a good twenty minutes before she needed to leave.

The drive from Glenning Valley to Blue Bay would take fifteen minutes at most. Probably less at this time of day. She filled in some time having breakfast at a local burger bar, after which she drove leisurely towards the address she'd been given. Jess knew the area well. Whilst there were still lots of very ordinary weekenders around, any property on the beach front was worth heaps. Most of the older buildings which had once graced the shoreline had been torn down, replaced by million-dollar units and multi-million-dollar homes. Over the last decade, Blue Bay had become one of *the* places to live on the coast.

It wasn't till she turned off the Entrance Road into the long street which led down to Blue Bay that Jess felt the first inkling of nerves. Though normally a confident and rather outspoken girl, she suddenly realised it wasn't going to be easy bringing up the subject of Fab Fashions with the man responsible for taking over the company. If truth be told, he would probably tell her to mind her own business. He also wouldn't be pleased with the fact that she'd looked him up on the Internet.

Maybe she should forget about the probably futile idea of trying to save Fab Fashions and just do what Mr De Silva had hired her to do—drive him out to Mudgee and back. Alternatively, maybe she would wait and see what kind of man he was; if he was the kind to listen or not. He hadn't sounded too bad over the phone. Maybe a little frustrated, which was understandable, considering he'd just had a car accident and all his plans had gone awry. And he *had* asked her to call him Ben, which was rather nice of him. She almost felt guilty now that she hadn't asked him to call her Jess in return.

Jess wondered how old he was. Probably about forty, she guessed. If he looked anything like his father—there'd been a photo of Morgan De Silva on the Net—then he'd be short, with a receding hairline and a flabby body from a sedentary lifestyle and too many long business lunches.

'Oh, dear,' she sighed.

Jess was no longer looking forward to today in any way, shape or form.

After letting out the breath she'd been unconsciously holding, she started scanning the numbers on the post boxes, soon realising that the number she was looking for would be on the left and right down the end of the street. Truly, what else had she expected? The son of a billionaire wouldn't be staying anywhere but the best.

The sun was just rising as she approached a block of apartments which carried the right number and which, yes, of course, overlooked the beach. A man was already standing on the pavement outside the building. Beside him sat a black travel case on wheels, across which was draped a plastic zip-up suit bag.

Jess tried not to stare as she pulled into the kerb beside him. But it was difficult not to.

He wasn't short with a receding hairline and flabby body. Hell, no. He was anything but. He was very tall and slim, with broad shoulders and the kind of well-chiselled face you saw on male models in magazines advertising aftershave or expensive watches. High cheekbones, a strong, straight nose and a square jawline. His hair was a light sandy colour, cut short at the sides and slightly longer on top, brushed straight back from that oh, so handsome face. His skin was lightly tanned, his eyes blue and beautiful. His clothes were more what she'd been expecting. Sort of. Dark-grey trousers and a long-sleeved blue business shirt which was open at the neck and which had a pair of sunglasses tucked into the breast pocket.

Jess dragged her eyes away from him, switched off the engine, then climbed out of the car, her thoughts somewhat scattered. Who would have imagined he would be so good-looking? Or so *young*? He couldn't be more than early thirties. Maybe even younger.

'Mr De Silva, I presume?' she asked as she stepped up onto the pavement less than a metre from him. Up close, he was even more attractive, if that were possible.

'You can't possibly be Miss Murphy,' he returned, the hint of a wry smile teasing one corner of his nicely shaped mouth.

She bristled at his comment. 'I don't see why not.'

He shook his head as he looked her up and down. 'You're not what I was expecting.'

'Oh?' she returned stiffly. 'And what were you expecting?'

'Someone a little older and a little less…er…attractive.'

Jess thanked the Lord she wasn't a blusher. For if she had been she might have gone bright red under the openly admiring gaze of those beautiful blue eyes.

'That's nice of you to say so, Mr De Silva. I think,' she added, wondering if she'd sounded old and ugly on the phone.

'I told you to call me Ben,' he said, and smiled at her, a full hundred-watt smile which showed perfect American teeth and a charm which was just as dazzling.

Oh my, Jess thought, trying not to be too dazzled.

Not without much success, given she just stood there staring at him whilst her heartbeat did the tango and she forgot all about Fab Fashions.

'Perhaps we should get going,' he said at last.

Jess gave herself a mental shake. It wasn't like her to go ga-ga over a man, even one as impressive as this.

'Yes. Yes, of course,' she said, still far too breathlessly for her liking. 'Do you need help with your bags?' she added, recalling what he'd said about having a banged-up right shoulder.

'I can manage,' he returned. 'Just open up the back for me.'

He managed very well. Managed the passenger door without any help either.

By the time she climbed into the driving seat and belted up, Jess had taken control of her wildly dancing heartbeat, having told herself firmly to get a grip and stop acting like some awestruck schoolgirl. She was twenty-five years old, for pity's sake!

Taking a deep breath, she reached for her sunglasses and put them on.

'Would you mind if I called you Jessica instead of Miss Murphy?' he said before she could even start the engine.

Jess winced. She hated being called Jessica. 'I'd rather

you call me Jess,' she replied, and found herself throwing a small smile his way.

'Only if you promise to call me Ben,' he insisted as he snapped his seat belt into place.

Jess suspected that women—no, people in general—rarely said no to Ben De Silva. His combination of looks and charm were both seductive and quite corrupting. Already she wanted to please him. Yet she wasn't, by nature, a people pleaser. Jess had always had a mind of her own and a mouth to match. Suddenly, however, all she wanted to do was smile, nod and agree with everything Ben said. Already he was Ben in her head.

'Okay. Ready, Ben?' she said as she reached for the ignition and glanced over at him again.

Dear heaven but he *was* gorgeous! He smelt gorgeous too. She did like men who wore nice aftershave.

'As soon as I put these on,' he replied, pulling his own sunglasses out of his pocket.

They were very expensive looking. God, now he looked like a movie star, a very sexy movie star, the kind a girl fantasised over in the privacy of her bedroom.

Jess's susceptibility to this man was beginning to annoy her. Next thing she'd know, she'd start flirting with him. Which wasn't like her at all! Gritting her teeth, she checked her rear and side mirrors, executed a perfect three-point turn, then accelerated up the street. Neither of them said anything for a full minute or two, Ben being the first to speak.

'I must thank you again, Jess, for doing this for me.'

'You don't have to thank me. You're paying for the privilege.'

'Still, I can see you probably had to put yourself out to do this. I would imagine a girl as attractive as yourself would have better things to do over the weekend than work.'

'No, not really.'

'You didn't have to break any dates?'

'Not this weekend.'

'That surprises me. I would have thought you'd have a boyfriend.'

'I did,' she bit out. 'Till recently.'

'What happened?'

She shrugged. 'We were going to go on a road trip together around Australia. That's why I bought this four-wheel drive. Anyway, at the last moment he decided he didn't want to do that. Instead, he took off backpacking around the world with a mate.'

Jess felt, rather than saw, Ben's startled look. When driving a client, she rarely took her eyes off the road.

'He didn't ask you to go with him?' he quizzed, his shocked tone soothing Jess's still lingering hurt over Colin's defection.

'No. He did ask me to wait for him, though.'

'I hope you said no.'

She laughed as she recalled her quite volatile reaction. 'I said a little more than just no.'

'Good for you.'

'Perhaps. Colin said I have a sharp tongue.'

'Really? I find that hard to believe.'

Was he mocking her?

A quick glance showed a perfectly straight face. A perfectly straight, very handsome face. Jess decided he was just making conversation, which was better than sitting there saying nothing all the way to Mudgee.

'He also said I was bossy and controlling.'

'No!'

He *was* mocking her. But not unkindly.

She sighed. 'I suppose I am a bit controlling. But I just like things to be organised. And to be done properly.'

'I'm somewhat of a perfectionist myself,' Ben said. 'Ah, there's Westfield's. Not far to the motorway now.'

Jess frowned. 'How come you know Westfield's? I thought this was your first visit to Australia.'

'Not at all,' he said. 'I've spent a lot of time here. Well, in New South Wales, at least. My parents are divorced, you see. You already know my father's American, but my mother's Australian. She owns the apartment in Blue Bay. I actually went to boarding school in Sydney. That's where I met Andy—he's the one who's getting married.'

'Goodness!' she exclaimed. 'I had no idea.'

'Well, why would you?' he said, sounding puzzled.

Jess suppressed a groan. As the saying went, *oh, what a tangled web we weave when first we practise to deceive.*

It actually went against Jess's grain to be less than honest with people. But her intentions had been good. Hopefully, Ben wouldn't be too annoyed with her if she told him the truth. She really didn't want to drive all the way to Mudgee watching what she said and didn't say. And, yes, she supposed she did still hope to discuss the future of Fab Fashions with him. He seemed very approachable and a lot smarter than she'd given him credit for. But that didn't make the act of confessing any easier.

'Oh gosh, this is just so awkward. I suppose I simply *have* to tell you now. I…I just hope you won't be too annoyed.'

# CHAPTER FOUR

BEN HAD NO idea what she was talking about. 'Tell me what?' he asked.

'The thing is, Ben...' she started, obviously with great reluctance.

'Yes?' he prompted when she didn't go on.

She pulled a face. 'I just hope you understand.'

'Understand *what*?' he demanded to know.

'Just wait, will you, till we're safely on the motorway?'

Jess turned right onto the ramp which took them down to the highway, heading north.

'I have a confession to make,' she said at last, then hesitated again.

'Go on,' Ben said with more patience than he was feeling.

'The thing is... I knew who you were yesterday on the phone once you said you were Benjamin De Silva.'

Ben tried to assimilate what Jess was actually saying, but failed.

'What exactly do you mean by who I was?'

'I mean, I knew you worked for De Silva & Associates and that you were Morgan De Silva's son.'

Ben could not have been more taken aback.

'And how come you knew that?' he said, sounding more confused than angry. 'I wouldn't have thought my father

was all that well known in Australia. He keeps a low public profile. Same with myself.'

Her sigh was heavy. 'You might understand better if I
tell you I used to have a part-time job at a Fab Fashions
boutique in Westfield's till last weekend, when the manager had to let me go.'

'Ah,' Ben said, light dawning. Though what she was
doing working part-time in a fashion boutique at all was a
mystery. She'd said she was a mechanic, hadn't she? And
an advanced driving instructor.

There was no doubt that Jess was a surprising girl in
more ways than one. You could have knocked him over
with a feather when she'd turned up, looking nothing like
the middle-aged battle-axe he'd been envisaging. Not
only was she young—surely no more than mid- to late-
twenties—she was also hot looking. Normally he went
for blondes, not brunettes. But he found Jess quite delicious with her full lips, flashing dark eyes and seriously
great legs. She also had an engaging and rather amusing
personality. That boyfriend had been a fool, letting her go.

'Yes, ah…' Jess said somewhat sheepishly. 'I asked
Helen…she's the manager…what the problem was and
she told me about this American company taking over Fab
Fashions and threatening them with closure if they didn't
make a profit before the end of the year. I was so mad I
found out what your name was and looked you up on the
Internet. Not that I found out much about you,' she added
hastily. 'Mostly it was about your father and the company
he founded. Anyway, when an American chap rang yesterday and told me his name was Benjamin De Silva, I
nearly fell off my chair.'

Ben didn't doubt it.

'So why on earth did you agree to drive me anywhere?'

he asked her. 'I would have thought you would have told me to drop dead.'

'Good heavens, no. What would have been the point of that? Look, the truth is that I had this crazy idea that during our long drive out to Mudgee I could somehow bring Fab Fashions into the conversation. I imagined you'd be surprised at the coincidence that I'd once worked for them but that you wouldn't be suspicious. I'd then tell you what I thought could be done to make Fab Fashions more profitable. I know that sounds terribly arrogant of me but I do know fashion. It's a lifelong passion with me. My grandmother was a professional seamstress and she taught me everything she knew. I've also done a design course online and I make a lot of my own clothes.'

'I see,' Ben said slowly. She was serious, he realised, but truly there was probably no saving Fab Fashions. Retail was in a terrible shape worldwide. He'd only given them till the end of the year because he hadn't wanted to play Scrooge. His father had wanted him to shut them down straight away, having bought them only because it came as a package deal along with other companies which had much better prospects and assets.

But Ben wasn't about to tell Jess that. Not yet, anyway.

'So why did you look so surprised when we first met today?' he asked, trying to get the full picture.

Jess frowned.

'You did stare at me, Jess,' he went on when she didn't say anything.

'Yes… Yes, I did, didn't I?' she said, seeming a little flustered. 'The thing is…there was a photo of your father on the Internet and…well…you don't look much like him, do you?'

Ben had to smile. She really didn't have a tactful bone in her body. Or maybe he meant artful. Yes, that was it. Jess was not, by nature, a deceiver. She was open and honest. He suddenly wished that something could be done with Fab Fashions, just to please her.

'No,' he agreed. 'I take after my mother.'

'She must be very beautiful.'

Ben suppressed another smile with difficulty. Lord, but she was quite enchanting. And totally ingenuous in her honesty. She wasn't trying to flatter him, or flirt with him. Which was a change. It was years since Ben had encountered a girl who did neither in his company.

'Mum was very beautiful when my father married her,' he said. 'She still is, despite being over sixty. She was quite a famous model in her time. But that came to an end when she married Dad. After their divorce, she came back to Sydney and started up a modelling agency. Did very well too. Sold it for heaps a couple of years back. But perhaps you already knew all that, did you? From the Internet?'

'Heavens, no. The only personal information was that your father was divorced with one son, Benjamin. The article was all about business. It didn't say a word about your mother.'

Ben imagined that was his father's doing. He was a powerful man and still very bitter about the divorce. He rarely spoke of his ex-wife, which made his parting words on the phone last night extremely surprising.

*Give my regards to your mother...*

Odd, that.

'Ben, I'm really very sorry for prying into your life like that,' Jess suddenly blurted out, perhaps interpreting his thoughtful silence for annoyance. 'I realised as soon as I met you that I shouldn't have done it. But I didn't mean any harm. Truly.'

'It's all right, Jess,' he said reassuringly. 'I haven't taken offence. I was just thinking about Fab Fashions,' he invented. 'And wondering what we could do about it. To-gether.'

'Oh,' she said, and fairly beamed over at him, her smile lighting up her face in a way which went beyond beauty.

It was a force of nature, that smile. He felt it deep down in his gut. Very deep down.

His flesh leapt and he thought, *Uh-oh. This is not what I need right now.*

And then he thought…why not? He'd finished with Amber. What was to stop him from exploring this attraction further?

Ben almost laughed. Because this wasn't just attraction he was suddenly feeling down south of the border. This was lust, an emotion he was not unfamiliar with. But this time it felt stronger. Much stronger.

Impossible to ignore.

Impossible not to pursue.

Though not too seriously. He'd be going back to America soon. All he could fit in was a short fling.

His conscience pricked him. Jess didn't come across as the kind of girl who indulged in short flings. Though, maybe he was wrong. Maybe she'd be only too willing to go along with whatever he wanted. After all, he was the son of a billionaire, wasn't he? That made him super-attractive to women. On top of that, she already thought him very beautiful.

'You'd honestly listen to what I have to say about Fab Fashions?' she asked him eagerly.

'I'd be mad not to,' he replied, since this would give him a viable excuse to spend more time with her whilst he was in Australia. 'You're obviously a clever girl, Jess, with lots of smarts.'

'I'm not all that smart,' she said with delightful self-deprecation.

'I don't believe that.'

'Look, there's smart and there's smart. School smart, I wasn't. But I've always been good with my hands.'

Ben wished she hadn't said that, his eyes drifting over to where her hands were wrapped around the steering wheel. Hell, but he wanted those hands wrapped around *him*. Caressing him, stroking him, teasing him, whilst she did delicious things with her mouth. Such thoughts sent hot blood roaring through his veins, giving him an instant and quite painful erection.

Ben gritted his teeth as he tried to will his aroused body back into line. He was not a man who liked tipping out of control, even sexually. *Especially* sexually. Ben liked to be the boss in the bedroom, or wherever it was he chose to have sex. He enjoyed having total control of the action, along with his partner, which meant he had to have total control over himself, something which he'd practised and perfected over the years.

'Is that why you became a mechanic?' he asked, pleased with how normal he sounded despite his wayward flesh continuing to defy him.

Her shrug showed surprising indifference to her choice of career. 'Before Dad started up his hire car business, he owned a garage. Not up here. Down in Sydney. Anyway, all my brothers became mechanics and I just followed suit.'

'So when did you move up to the Central Coast?'

'A good few years back now,' she replied. 'I'd just finished my apprenticeship. I know I had my twenty-first birthday party up here so I must have been nineteen or twenty. I'm not sure of the exact year. Why?'

'Just making conversation, Jess,' he said, searching his mind for more safe topics. He could not believe that he still had an erection. 'You're not using your GPS, I see. So I guess you know the way to Mudgee.'

'It's pretty straightforward. We stay on the motorway till we reach the New England Highway, heading for Brisbane. But we turn off onto the Golden Highway just before Singleton. Then we don't get off that road till the turn-off to Mudgee. Easy peasy.'

'You sound like you've been this way a dozen times before.'

'I've driven to Brisbane via the New England Highway once or twice but I've never been along the Golden Highway before. Or to Mudgee, for that matter. I checked it up last night on the Internet.'

'I've never been this way before either,' he admitted.

Her glance carried curiosity. 'You've never been to your best friend's place before?'

'Yes, of course I have. Several times. But you take a different route when you're driving from Sydney.'

'Oh yes, of course. I didn't think of that. You said you went to boarding school in Sydney, is that right?'

'Yes. Kings College. It's near Parramatta. Do you know it?'

# CHAPTER FIVE

A MOMENTARY FLASH of pique had Jess's hands tightening around the steering wheel. Just because she'd said she wasn't school smart didn't mean she was ignorant. Of course she knew of Kings College. It was one of the best private schools in Sydney. Despite it being located in the western suburbs, it was a far cry from the humble high school she'd gone to only a few miles away.

'Yes. I know it,' she said, thinking how way out of her league this man was. 'It's a very good school.'

'That's where I met Andy.'

'Your best friend?'

'Yes. We went on to study law together at Sydney Uni as well.'

Oh, Lord. Now he'd studied law at Sydney University, another prestigious establishment. Jess knew what it took to get into law. Which showed Ben was very school smart. But then, she'd guessed that already.

What next? she wondered. He probably wintered in the ski fields of Austria every year. And took his girlfriend to Paris for romantic weekends.

This last thought gave her a real jolt. Jess hadn't thought of Ben as having a girlfriend, which was very stupid of her. Of course he must have, a man like him. Not a wife, though.

When she'd asked him for a contact name and number yesterday he hadn't mentioned a wife.

A fiancée was still on the cards, however.

'And now your best friend is getting married,' she said, trying to make her voice cool and conversational, not like she was dying of curiosity. 'Are *you* married, Ben?' she asked.

'No,' he said.

'Engaged?'

'No.'

She'd gone too far now to stop. 'You must have a girl-friend back home.'

'Not any more. I did have a girlfriend. But, like yours, that relationship has now gone by the board.'

'She *dumped* you?' Jess said with total disbelief in her voice.

'Not exactly…'

'Sorry. I'm prying again.'

'I don't mind,' he said. 'I enjoy talking to you. Actually, *I'm* the one who decided to call it quits. I just haven't had the opportunity to tell Amber yet. I only decided last night.'

*Amber*, Jess thought with a curl of her top lip. A typical name for the type of girl he would date. She sounded beautiful. And rich. Jess hated her, till she remembered Ben was breaking up with her. Since that was the case, she could afford to be less bitchy. But she was still curious.

'What went wrong?'

'She wanted marriage and I didn't.'

'I see,' she said. What was it with men these days that they shied away from commitment?

When Jess found herself surrendering to a sinking feeling, she decided a change of subject was called for. She thought of returning to the problems with Fab Fashions but for some strange reason her enthusiasm for that project had lost some of its appeal. It was probably a waste of time, anyway. So she turned to that old favourite to fill awkward moments in a conversation. The weather.

'I'm so glad it's a nice sunny day,' she said with false brightness. 'There's nothing I hate more than driving in the rain. Though the recent rain was greatly appreciated. We had a terribly dry winter. Now everything's lovely and green.'

Ben turned his head to gaze at the countryside. 'It does look good. I can't say the same for this road, though. It's deplorable for a main highway. All cracked and patched up.'

'That's because it's built over the top of coal mines,' Jess explained. 'It suffers from subsidence. Still, that's Australia for you. We're notorious for our dreadful roads.'

'That's because the country is too big for your population. Not enough taxes for proper infrastructure.'

'Not enough taxes!' Jess exclaimed, putting aside her uncharacteristic desire to please and giving vent to her usual outspokenness. 'We're one of the highest taxed countries in the world!'

'Not quite. Australia's only number ten. Most European countries pay higher taxes.'

'Not America, though,' Jess argued. 'People can become rich in America. It's hard to become rich in Australia unless you're a crook or a drug dealer. Though, come to think of it, bankers are doing pretty well at the moment,' she added a touch tartly. 'My dad works his bum off and still only makes a living. Mum and Dad haven't had a decent holiday in years.' She didn't call five days in Bali last year a decent holiday.

'That's a shame. Everyone must have holidays these days or stress will get you in the end.'

'That's what I keep telling them.'

'How old are they?'

'Dad's sixty-three. Mum's fifty-nine.'

'Close to retirement age, then.'

'Dad says he'd rather die than retire.'

'My dad says the same thing,' Ben said. 'He loves working.'

*Loves making money, you mean*, Jess thought but didn't say.

'You mentioned brothers earlier,' Ben said. 'How many do you have?'

'What? Oh…er…three.'

'I always wanted a brother. So, Jess, tell me a bit about these brothers of yours.'

Jess shrugged. There seemed no point not telling him about her family. They had to talk about something, she supposed.

'Connor's the oldest,' she said. 'He's thirty-six. Married with two boys. Then there's Troy. He's thirty-four and married too, with twin girls. They're eight,' she added, smiling as she thought of Amy and Emily, who were the sweetest girls. 'Then there's Peter, who's closest to me at twenty-seven. He's not long married and his wife is expecting a bub early next year.'

'No sisters?'

'No, no sisters.'

'So you're the baby of the family.'

'Not a spoilt one, I can assure you,' she said, though this was a lie. Her brothers had indulged her shamelessly. And had been very protective of her when the boys had started hanging around. They were the reason she hadn't had a boyfriend till she'd left school. Because they kept frightening them off. Peter, especially. Jess had been a virgin till she was close to twenty.

'I suppose you want kids as well. I saw you smiling when you talked about the twin girls.'

'I'd love at least two children,' Jess admitted. 'But getting married and having children is not high on my list of wants right now. I'm only twenty-five. First, I'd like to travel all around Australia. That's why I bought this little darling,' she added, tapping the steering wheel. 'Because it can cope with whatever terrible roads Australia can throw at me.

'Oh look, there's the turn-off to the Hunter Valley vineyards,' she pointed out. 'If you're staying up on the Central Coast for a while after you get back from your friend's wedding, then that's one of the places you should visit. It's lovely at this time of the year. Lots of great places to stay and terrific wine to taste. You can even go up in a balloon. Colin and I did that not long ago and it was fantastic.'

'Had you been going out with this Colin fellow for long?'

'Just over a year.'

'And you were serious about him?'

'Serious enough,' she admitted. 'To be honest, I thought I was in love with him. But I can see now that I wasn't.' How could she have been? Colin had been gone from her life less than a month and she already had the hots for another man.

'For what it's worth, Jess,' that other man said, 'I think this Colin was a total idiot, leaving a girl like you behind.'

Jess could not help glancing over at Ben. His head turned her way and their eyes would have met if they hadn't both been wearing sunglasses. Even so, something zapped between them like a charge of electricity, taking Jess's breath away. And suddenly she knew, as surely as she knew that she should get her eyes back on the road ahead quick smart, that Ben fancied her as much as she fancied him. And, whilst the realisation of his sexual interest was exciting and flattering, it also terrified the life out of her.

# CHAPTER SIX

BEN COULD HARDLY contain the burst of triumph he experienced when he heard her sharply indrawn breath, then watched her reef her eyes back on the road like the hounds of hell were after her.

Perhaps they were, he thought darkly. Be damned with his conscience. Be damned with common sense! He had to have this girl. And soon.

Jess was annoyed with herself for feeling flattered by Ben's interest. Why shouldn't he fancy her? she reasoned with more of her usual self-confidence. She was an attractive girl, with a nice face and figure. And, yes, super legs. Okay, so she probably wasn't a patch on this Amber female, but *she* was over in New York and Jess was right here. On top of that, he didn't want Amber. *No, no, be honest here, Jess, it wasn't Amber he didn't want, just marriage.* No doubt he would have continued their sexual relationship if she hadn't put the hard word on him. The truth was he was out here in Australia, probably feeling a bit lonely, and suddenly there she was, with no boyfriend and availability written all over her stupid face!

Jess was dragged out of her frustrating train of thought by the sudden end of the motorway. She hadn't even seen the signs to slow down. Rolling her eyes at herself, she made a careful left at the roundabout onto the New England Highway and set sail for the Golden Highway. Thankfully, Ben had fallen silent. No doubt he was working out when to make a pass whilst she was working out how she was going to act when that happened.

As Jess drove on silently, she wondered why she couldn't be like other girls—the ones who could sleep with guys on a first date, or even on meeting them for the first time at a pub, or club, or disco or whatever. She could never do that. She found the idea repulsive. And dangerous. She had to get to know the guy first. And like him. Had to see that he liked her too. Liked her enough to wait for her. Till she felt ready to go all the way.

She'd made Colin wait for weeks. Jess suspected Ben wouldn't wait weeks for her.

Not that she wanted him to. Lord, what was happening to her here? This wasn't like her at all! But Ben wasn't like any man she'd ever met before. It wasn't just a question of his movie-star looks, although they were hard to ignore. There was something else. A cloak of confidence which he wore without effort and which she found incredibly attractive. And very sexy. He would be a fantastic lover, she was sure. Very experienced. Very…knowledgeable. He would know exactly what to do and how to do it to make sure she always came.

A shiver rippled down her spine at this last thought. She didn't always come during sex. But she would like to.

'When are we going to make our first stop?' Ben suddenly piped up. 'I'll need to have a coffee fairly soon.'

Jess suppressed a groan as she realised that she'd once again become distracted from her driving. It took an extreme effort of will to drag her overheated mind away from those corrupting thoughts and put it to the task of estimating exactly where they were, quickly realising that they couldn't be far from the turn-off onto the Golden Highway.

'Denman is about half an hour from here,' she said, having studied the route and memorised all the towns and services on the way. 'I checked it up on the Internet. It's a small historic town down in a valley with a nice pub and a couple of cafés. If that's too far off for you, we could drive into Singleton, but then we'd have to double back.'

'No. No doubling back. Denman sounds fine. You wouldn't happen to have any pain killers with you, would you? I should have taken a couple this morning but forgot.'

Jess only then remembered his bad shoulder. 'There's some in the glove box,' she said. 'And a bottle of water in your door, if you want to take the tablets straight away.'

'Thanks.'

'How bad is your shoulder?' she asked, happy to have something safe to talk about.

'It's a bit stiff and sore this morning, but honestly it's fine. I could have driven, but the doctor at the hospital said no. Not because of the shoulder—I had a mild concussion as well.'

'Best you didn't drive, then.'

'I'm glad I couldn't—I wouldn't have met you.'

Jess could not stop her heart swelling with pleasure. Yet she knew what he was about. She'd seen how her brothers had acted with girls whose pants they wanted to get into. She'd watched them lay the compliments on thick and fast. And she'd watched those silly girls lap them up, then give her brothers what they wanted in no time at all.

Maybe that was why *she'd* acted differently with boys who came onto her. Or she had, till this handsome devil had come along.

He'd thrown a spanner in her works all right. Jess

could not believe she was thinking of having a one-night stand with him. Or that just the thought of it made her heart race faster than a Formula One car on the starting blocks.

# CHAPTER SEVEN

'WHAT A LOVELY little town this is,' Ben said.

They had stopped and were sitting at a table on the ve-randa of an old farmhouse which had been converted into a café, sipping their just-delivered coffee and looking out onto a quite lovely garden full of flowering shrubs. Ben knew nothing about gardening and plants but he knew what he liked. It was the same way with art. He never bought art on the so-called reputation of the artist. He only bought what he liked.

He glanced over the table at Jess and thought how much he liked her too. Maybe that was why his desire for her was so strong. During the last half-hour of the drive, he'd been thinking how he could be alone with her this weekend in a place suitable for seduction. And he'd finally come up with a plan which would work, provided she went along with the idea.

'So, Jess,' he said. 'I think it's about time you started telling me what's wrong with Fab Fashions. I didn't want to talk business during the drive; I just wanted to drink in the wonderful scenery. But now that we've stopped...'

She put down her cup, then looked up at him with those big brown eyes of hers, the kind of eyes a man could drown in. He almost wished she'd put her sunglasses back on. But she'd left them hooked over the sun visor in the four-wheel drive. Lord, but they were expressive eyes. He could only hope that his own didn't give away his innermost thoughts, since he'd removed his sunglasses a couple of minutes earlier and popped them back into his shirt pocket.

'You honestly want to hear my ideas?' she said, sounding somewhat sceptical.

*Not really*, he conceded privately. They were a waste of time. But it was part of his plan.

'But of course,' he said.

Her face lit up and, yes, so did her eyes. Guilt threatened, but he pushed it firmly aside. Guilt, Ben conceded, was no match for lust.

'Okay. Well, for starters there's its name. "Fab Fashions" implies it caters for the young where in fact most of the stock in Fab Fashions is targeted towards the more mature woman. Either change the name or change the stock. I would suggest change the name; there are enough clothes around for teenagers.

'Then you should change your buyers. Get people in who aren't just buying to price. Someone who knows what's in fashion and what is comfortable to wear. The more mature lady wants comfort as well as style. Also, it might be a good idea to stock more of the most common sizes instead of just buying across the board. Most women over forty are not size eight! And of course you *should* have an online store too. To fall behind the times is stupid.'

Ben was surprised and impressed. All her suggestions made sense. They might even work. 'You really know your stuff, don't you?'

'I told you…fashion is a genuine passion with me. On top of that, I hate to think of all those people losing their jobs. If every owner shut their stores during a down-turn in the economy, the country would go to the wall. Surely it's not always about profit, is it, Ben? I mean…everyone has to take the bad times with the good, especially big companies like yours.'

'It's not always quite as simple as that, Jess.'

She bristled. 'I knew you'd say that.'

'I didn't say I wasn't prepared to do what you suggested. What say we have a think over the weekend and see if we can find a fab new name which would lend itself to a successful marketing campaign?'

Jess's frown was instant. 'But we don't have any spare time this weekend. You have to go to a stag party tonight and the wedding's tomorrow. I suppose we could talk on the drive home.'

'We could,' he said. 'But when I'm excited about something, I like to get straight to it,' he added with considerable irony and another tweak to his conscience. 'How about I give Andy a ring and organise for you to stay at the winery over the weekend instead of some motel in Mudgee? They have a small cottage on the property away from the main house which is very comfy. We could stay there together.'

'Together!'

'There's two bedrooms, Jess. Of course, there won't be much time for talking tonight, since I'll be at Andy's bachelor party. But the wedding's not till four the next afternoon. That should give us plenty of time to talk. And, speaking of the wedding, I'm sure I could wangle you an invitation.' If she didn't have a suitable dress, he would take her into Mudgee and buy her one.

Wariness warred with temptation in her eyes. 'Won't Andy think it odd, you asking him to invite a virtual stranger to his wedding?'

'But you're not a stranger, Jess. I already know more about you than most of my past girlfriends. On top of that, we're now business colleagues. I'll tell Andy you're a marketing consultant I've hired to help me with Fab Fashions and who kindly offered to drive me up here after I had that unfortunate car accident. There's no need to mention anything about you working for a hire car company, is there?'

Jess shook her head. Did he honestly think she didn't know what he was doing? She wasn't a fool. But there was simply no saying no to him.

'You do like to take over, Ben, don't you?'

His smile was both charming and sexy at the same time. 'What can I say? People tell me I'm bossy and controlling.'

Jess laughed. He was a clever devil. But totally irresistible.

'I'm sure Andy's folks will still think it odd, you asking for us to stay together in that cottage.'

'In that case, I'll say we're dating.'

'But we're not!'

'We will be, come Sunday. I have every intention of asking you out once we get back to the coast.'

'I might say no.'

'Will you?'

'No.'

He grinned at her. 'Great. No problems, then. I'll tell Andy you're my new girlfriend.'

Jess sighed. 'You are incorrigible.'

'I'm smitten, that's what I am.'

She just stared at him. *She* was the one who was smitten. *He* just wanted to get into her pants.

'I think you should know in advance, Ben, that I don't sleep with a guy on a first date.' Or she hadn't, till he'd come along.

There was that hint of a smile again. 'Who said anything about sleeping?'

'Very funny. You know what I mean.'

'Yes, of course I do. Let me assure you, Jess, that I would always be respectful of your wishes.'

Mmm…meaning he was very confident that he could seduce her in no time flat. Which he could, of course. But she had to make some kind of stand. Her pride demanded it.

'Fine,' she said. 'Just so you understand my feelings in advance. I don't want to have to fight you off at the end of the night.'

'I appreciate you being straight with me, Jess. I admire honesty.'

Oh, dear. She hoped she didn't look too guilty. Because of course she was probably going to sleep with him. How could she possibly say no? He was the sexiest man she'd ever met.

'Soon as I finish this coffee, I'll ring Andy,' Ben said, looking very pleased with himself.

He made the call out of earshot, walking around the garden as he talked. Jess wondered what he was telling his friend. She hated to think it was one of those 'nudge-nudge, wink-wink, say no more' conversations where Ben and his best friend were becoming co-conspirators in her supposed seduction. She would hate that. Still, Andy had already to know that Ben hadn't been out here in Australia for long. So how could she possibly be a proper girlfriend? She was just someone he'd met and fancied, but who would be quickly forgotten once he flew back to America.

Now that she was thinking straight, Jess also doubted Ben would really do anything about Fab Fashions. His interest in her ideas was just a ploy to keep her sweet. It also crossed Jess's mind as she watched Ben chatting away to his friend that she wouldn't be the first girl he'd installed in that cottage for the weekend. He was the sort of guy who would always have a willing girl on his arm. And in his bed. Jess would just be one in a long line of conquests.

She didn't like that thought, or the other thoughts she'd been having since he'd left her at the table.

Feeling decidedly disgruntled, Jess stood up, thanked the lady who ran the café and marched back to her four-wheel drive.

# CHAPTER EIGHT

AFTER BEN FINISHED his call to Andy, he went back to the table on the veranda, only to find it empty. He glanced around and saw that she was out by the SUV, standing with her arms crossed and her face not at all happy. Ben wondered what had gone wrong during the last ten minutes. And there he'd been, thinking all his plans for the weekend were on track. Andy had accepted his entire story about Jess and agreed to put them both in the cottage. He'd also said there would be no problem with her coming to the wedding tomorrow.

Her body language worsened as he walked towards her, her manicured but unvarnished fingertips digging into the sleeves of her floral jacket.

'What's wrong?' he asked straight away.

Her mouth tightened. 'I don't like lies, that's what's wrong! I'm not your girlfriend, Ben. Not really. Not yet, anyway. Why, you haven't even kissed me yet!'

Jess could not believe she'd just said that. It sounded dreadful, like she was *asking* him to kiss her.

'Well, that can be easily fixed,' he returned, his eyes dropping to her mouth as he reached out and took firm possession of her shoulders.

Oh, Lord, she thought as panic set in.

He didn't rush anything; her arms dropped to her sides

long before he actually kissed her. He gathered her against him very slowly, his eyes holding hers captive as easily as he was holding her body. The descent of his head was just as slow, Jess's heart pounding against her ribs by the time his lips made contact with hers. Even then, he didn't kiss her properly, just brushed his mouth over hers. Once. Twice. Three times. Finally, her tingling lips gasped apart, desperate for more.

But he denied her desire. And, in doing so, deepened it. She moaned when his head lifted, her eyes glazed as they stared up at him.

'Will that do for now to raise your status to girlfriend?' he said, shocking her with his cool manner. She was on fire inside. Yet he seemed totally unmoved.

'Like I said, lovely Jess,' he went on, 'I'm smitten with you. Seriously smitten. I'm already planning on extending my stay here in Australia to spend more time with you. And, since you don't like lies, let me say right here and now that I doubt very much if I can fix Fab Fashions, even with your very excellent ideas.'

He was a wicked devil, she decided shakily, using honesty now to seduce her.

'But I'm willing to give it a try,' he added, 'if it makes you happy.'

What to say to that? She could hardly admit that Fab Fashions wasn't high on her personal agenda right at this moment. All she could think about was being with this man.

At the same time, she didn't want Ben thinking he could play her for a fool.

Pulling herself together, Jess did her best to imitate his controlled demeanour.

'It would be nice to try to turn things around,' she said. 'So, yes, it would make me very happy.'

'Good. And, whilst I'm in the mood for confession,' he

went on, 'my reason for organising for us to stay together at the cottage was something far more...intimate.'

Ben was watching her eyes closely and decided she wasn't upset by his admission. Just the opposite, in fact. There was a glittering of dark excitement in their gorgeous depths. She was trying to act cool with him but her eyes gave her away. Besides, he'd felt her tremble in his arms just now. And that frustrated moan of hers had been very telling. She wanted him as much as he wanted her. He hadn't dared deepen that kiss for fear of losing it himself. Jess really did have a powerful effect on him. Much more than Amber ever had.

'Not tonight, unfortunately,' he said with true regret, 'Since I'll be otherwise occupied. But I thought by to-morrow night, after the wedding, I'd be in with a chance.'

'Did you now?' Jess threw at him, desperate to find some composure, not to mention her pride.

His beautiful blue eyes glittered with amusement, not to mention supreme confidence. 'Let's just say I was hopeful.'

'You'll need to improve your kissing technique.'

'Really? And there I was, thinking you'd enjoyed being teased.'

Jess shook her head in defeat. He was just too clever for her. And way too knowing. 'You are incorrigible.'

'And you're irresistible.'

Jess said nothing to that, but her mind kept ticking over. Oh yes, he was a wicked devil all right, with all the right words and all the right moves. She wondered how many women he'd had in his life.

Lots, she supposed.

And she would be just one more.

Not the happiest of thoughts.

'I think we should get going now,' she said abruptly. It

was almost ten; it had taken them longer to get to Denman than she'd estimated.

'Good idea,' he said.

They climbed in and belted up, both of them reaching for their sunglasses at the same time, Jess careful not to look over at him lest she give away even more of her vulnerability to this man. She hated Ben thinking he was onto a sure thing tomorrow night. Though, of course he was. No point in denying it to herself. But that didn't mean she had to act like some gushing nincompoop who was overwhelmed by his attentions.

'I thought we'd stop at Cassilis for lunch,' she said matter-of-factly as she started the engine. 'Sandy Hollow is the next town but it's too close. After that, it's straight to your friend's place.'

'Sounds like a good plan.'

'We should easily arrive by mid-afternoon, depending on how long you want to stop for lunch.'

'I guess that would depend on how quickly we get served.'

Very quickly, as it turned out. They settled on a pub lunch, eaten out in the very pleasant beer garden. Jess ordered just the one glass of white wine with her steak and salad, since she was driving, whilst Ben decided on a schooner of beer with his. But they ate slowly and talked a lot. And, whilst the conversation was very superficial, all the while Jess was aware of a dangerous excitement growing deep inside her. Every time she looked at Ben a sexual image jumped into her head. When he forked some food into his mouth, she found herself staring at that mouth and thinking of how it would feel kissing, not her mouth so much, but other more intimate parts of her body. His hands brought similar sexy images. They were rather elegant hands. Well-manicured with long fingers and rounded tips. Jess imagined them doing darkly delicious things to her.

Her bottom tightened with shock at her thoughts, for Jess was not that sort of girl. Or so she'd imagined up till now. Her boyfriends so far had been rather lacking in imagination when it came to foreplay, which was perhaps why she hadn't come every time. Not that she hadn't enjoyed herself. She liked male bodies, especially well-built ones. Sex with Colin had been somewhat better, perhaps because he liked her being on top. Which she liked too. Perhaps because of that controlling nature of hers, or because she always came that way.

Jess glanced over at Ben and wondered again how many women he'd had in his life. Which sent Amber into her mind.

Jess wished Ben had already broken up with her. She wanted to tell him to ring her and do it, right now! But she didn't have the courage—or the gall—to say so. It would be a waste of time, anyway. For what would it matter in the end? The cold, hard truth was that eventually he would leave her and go back to America anyway. He didn't want marriage. She was just a girl he'd met out here whom he fancied and whom he meant to have.

A part of Jess was flattered by his determined passion for her. But she didn't deceive herself into thinking this would ever be a serious romance. They were just ships passing in the night. She decided—perhaps in protection of her fluttering female heart—that she would think of him as an experience. An adventure. Possibly even an education. For Jess knew, as surely as she knew the house wine she was drinking was rubbish, that sex with Ben would be unlike anything she'd ever experienced before.

Falling for a man like Ben, however, would be a stupid thing to do. *Very* stupid.

'You've gone quiet on me,' Ben said.

Jess perked up immediately. She didn't want Ben to think she was worried about anything. Which she was, somewhat. But forewarned was forearmed. Now that she'd decided to go down this road, she was determined to do so in a positive state of mind. There were worse things that could happen to a girl than an affair with the handsome son of a billionaire. Not that Ben's having money mattered to her. Jess had never been overly impressed by wealthy people. They never seemed all that happy, for one thing. But Ben's privileged background had given him a confidence and polish which was very attractive.

'I was thinking I should ring Mum soon,' she said with a quick smile. 'And reassure her that I'm still alive.'

'What? Surely she wasn't worried about you driving? You're an excellent driver.'

'No. Mum has every faith in my driving abilities. She was worried that you might be a serial killer.'

The shock on his face was classic.

'I assured her that you weren't. You were just a rich businessman with not an ounce of intelligence to save your soul.'

He pretended to look offended. 'You *do* have a sharp tongue, don't you?'

His eyes narrowed as men did when they were challenged. 'I'm actually quite intelligent.'

'I've yet to see evidence of that fact.' Lord, but she was actually loving this. She'd never sparred verbally with Colin, or any of her other boyfriends. She'd never flirted like this either. But it was such fun.

'I'll have you know that I was dux of my school.'

'Yes, but that's just school smart, Ben, which is a lot different from street smart. How can you possibly be street smart when you were born with a silver spoon in your

MIRANDA LEE 61

mouth?' It was a lovely mouth, though. The more she studied it, the more she liked it. His bottom lip was full and
sensual, whilst his top lip was thinner and harder. She suspected Ben could be stubborn as well as arrogant. Maybe
even a little ruthless. But there was something decidedly
sexy about a man being ruthless. You wouldn't want to
marry a ruthless man, but having an affair with him was
a different matter entirely.

'Keep that up and your mother might have something to
worry about,' he quipped, his beautiful blue eyes sparkling
with good humour. 'Women have been strangled for less.'

She smiled, and was still smiling when they left the
hotel and set off again. It wasn't till they were well down
the road to Mudgee that she realised she *hadn't* rung her
mother.

'Is this the road Andy lives on?' she asked.

'Yes, I'm sure it is.'

'Are we nearly there yet?'

'I think so. It's been a while since I've been up here but
I'll recognise the place once I see it.'

'In that case I'd like to stop for a sec and make that
phone call to Mum,' she said, pulling off the road and
parking under the shade of a tree.

Her mother answered on the second ring.

'Jess?'

'Yes, Mum.'

'Are you okay? Are you there yet?'

'Yes, Mum, I'm almost there and I'm fine. Mr De Silva
wasn't a serial killer after all,' she added, at which Ben
shook his head at her. 'He's really quite nice,' she added,
and pulled a face at him.

He smiled a crooked smile.

'That's a relief. A girl can't be too careful, you know.'

'Mr De Silva's friend lives at a winery along this road.

After I drop him off, I'll head into Mudgee and book into a motel. Look, I'd better go. I'll give you another call later tonight. Bye for now. Love you.'

'Why didn't you tell her you were staying at the winery?' Ben asked as she gunned the engine and pulled out onto the road. 'I thought you didn't like lies.'

'Don't be silly, Ben. She's my mother. All girls lie to their mothers. We do it to protect them from worry.'

He laughed. 'That's a good one. But I suppose it would be a bit hard to explain.'

'Very. Now, how far along this road is Valleyview Winery?'

'Not too far now. I recognise that place over there. I'm sure it's just along here on the left. Yes, there it is now.' And he pointed high up to the left.

Her eyes followed the direction of his finger, landing on an impressive federation-style homestead built on the crest of a hill so that its wraparound verandas could take advantage of the valley views.

'The driveway is not far now,' Ben added. 'Yes, there it is.'

Jess slowed, then turned into the driveway, passing through widely set stone gateposts, one of which doubled as a post box, the other having the name 'Valleyview Winery' carved into the stone and painted black so that it stood out. The driveway was relatively straight and nicely tarred, bisecting gently sloping paddocks which held rows and rows of grapevines.

'So, does this place belong to Andy or his parents?' she asked, Jess only then realising they hadn't really talked about Andy, or the upcoming wedding, at all. They'd been totally taken up with each other.

'His parents. And the house is actually not as old as it looks. His folks built it while we were at boarding school together. His dad was a stock broker in Sydney but made enough money to retire early, so he decided to indulge his hobby and start up a winery.'

Jess suppressed a sigh. She should have known Ben's best friend would be rich.

'And what does Andy do?'

'He's now the official wine-maker here. He did law like me when he first left school, but decided after we graduated that it wasn't for him, so he went to France and studied wine-making with the masters. Then he came back and took over. Till then his dad hired a professional wine-maker. Apparently, it's not an art you can learn from a how-to book.'

'I dare say.'

As they drew near to the house, three people emerged onto the front veranda. Two men and a woman. Jess presumed it was Andy and his parents. The younger of the two men separated himself from the others and hurried down some side steps which led to a large tarred area at the side of the house where she was about to park.

'This do?' she asked Ben as she pulled to halt.

'Perfect,' he said, already unclicking his seat belt. In no time he was out and hugging his best friend with a big bear-hug.

Andy wasn't as tall as Ben, she noted as she climbed out from behind the wheel, but he was nice looking, with dark hair, brown eyes and even features.

'Long time no see, bro,' Andy said, finally disengaging from the hug.

Ben shrugged. 'Been busy in the Big Apple.'

'You know what they say, mate, about all work and no play. Still, you're in Australia now, the land down under where the weather is hot and so are the girls. Speaking of hot girls, I presume this is Jess,' he added, giving her the once-over with appreciative eyes.

'How intuitive of you,' Ben mocked. 'Jess, this smart Alec is Andy.'

'Hi, there, Jess,' he said, and came forward to give her a peck on the cheek. 'Lovely to meet you.'

'Are you sure it's all right for me to stay here?' she said in reply. 'I wouldn't like to put your mother to any extra trouble.'

'No, no, she's fine with it. The cottage is always ready for guests and Mum's very easy going. Come inside and have some afternoon tea. And some of Mum's blueberry muffins—the ones you like, Ben. You know, Jess, I'm not sure what it is about Ben here, but women fuss over him like mad.'

'Search me,' she returned with a straight face. 'It's not as though he's handsome or charming or anything like that.'

Andy stared at her for a second, then laughed a big belly laugh. 'Oh, that's priceless. You can keep this one, Ben, if you like.'

'I do like,' Ben whispered in her ear as he slipped a possessive arm around her waist and steered her towards the house.

But, even as she quivered inside with delicious pleasure at his touch, Jess knew Ben had no intention of keeping her. They would be together whilst he was here. And then he would go back to America and it would all be over.

# CHAPTER NINE

ANDY'S PARENTS WERE as lovely as their home. Jess had been half-expecting that they would be snobbish, since they were wealthy and owned a winery. But they were anything but. Whilst obviously well-educated and well-spoken, both of them were very down to earth and welcoming, insisting immediately upon introduction that she call them Glen and Heather.

Afternoon tea had been set up in the main living room which had French doors leading out onto the veranda. Heather explained that it was a little too breezy today to have it out there, a wind having sprung up seemingly out of nowhere.

Jess had just finished her cup of tea and was popping a second delicious mini muffin into her mouth when a nearby phone rang. Not the ring tone of a mobile. The unmistakable sound of a landline.

'Do excuse me,' Heather said, moving over to a long sofa table which rested against the wall and on which sat a phone, along with some very nice pieces of pottery.

Jess tried not to listen but it was impossible once she heard Heather make a sound which was halfway between a gasp and a groan.

'Oh, my dear, that's most unfortunate,' she said to whoever she was talking to. 'So what are you going to do? Yes, yes, I'll get Andy for you right away.'

Andy's attention must already have been grabbed because he jumped up immediately and rushed to take the phone from his mother. It didn't take Einstein to realise he was talking to his fiancée and that something had gone wrong. Heather, thank God, quickly enlightened the rest of them.

'Catherine's matron of honour has been rushed to hospital with a threatened miscarriage. Anyway, she's okay, but she has to stay in bed for at least a week and can't be at the wedding tomorrow. She's naturally very upset. Catherine is too. I suppose she'll just have to move the other bridesmaid up to be opposite you, Ben. It means it will be a very small bridal party, but what else can she do?'

Murphy's Law had struck, was Jess's immediate thought. And cruelly. She felt terribly sorry for them all, but especially the bride.

'She could always put Jess in her place,' Ben suddenly suggested.

Jess threw him a horrified look. 'Don't be ridiculous, Ben. Andy's fiancée doesn't even *know* me.'

'In that case, we'll take you over to her place and she can meet you,' he said in his usual taking over fashion. 'She only lives next door. It's not an ideal solution, Heather,' he said, turning his attention to Andy's mother, 'but it *is* a solution.'

'Well, yes, I...I suppose so,' Heather said before Jess could object again. 'It would also make Krissie feel better. She thinks she's spoiled her best friend's wedding. Not to mention the wedding photos. Catherine was only having the two bridesmaids and now she's down to one.'

'It's a perfectly sensible solution,' Glen said with typical male pragmatism. 'Andy!' he called out. 'Ben here said Jess would be willing to take Krissie's place, if it's all right with Catherine.'

Jess held her breath whilst Andy explained Ben's suggestion to his bride.

'She's Ben's new girlfriend,' Andy went on when he was obviously asked for further explanation. 'Her name is Jess. They only met recently. Over some business deal in Sydney. Anyway, Ben got his rental car totalled by some drunk and Jess offered to drive him out here... She'll look great in the wedding photos.'

Jess cringed, not sure now if she wanted the bride to say yay or nay. Still, it wasn't as though she wouldn't have been at the wedding anyway. And if it made everyone a bit happier... After all, weddings were supposed to be happy occasions.

Andy turned to face Jess. 'She says thanks heaps for the offer. Says you've really saved the day, but she would still have to see you asap. Something about whether the dress would fit you or not. It might need altering. Krissie was pregnant, after all.'

'Fine,' Ben said, standing up. 'Tell Catherine we'll be over straight away.'

After Andy relayed Ben's message, he shot his friend a droll look. 'She says *I'm* not allowed to come. Something about my not being allowed to see any of the dresses before the big day.' He rolled his eyes and placed his hand over the phone. 'Women! *Truly.*'

'No sweat, Andy. Tell Catherine we're on our way.' Taking Jess's hand, Ben pulled her to her feet, made his excuses to an understanding Glen and Heather, then steered Jess from the room.

'Make sure you're back for tonight, Ben,' Andy threw after them.

'Will do,' Ben threw back.

Jess resisted resorting to belated objections on the way out. What was done was done.

'Don't be angry with me,' Ben said as they climbed into their respective seats in the SUV.

'I'm not,' Jess said with a somewhat resigned sigh, then started the engine. 'But it might be an idea if you didn't always presume I would do whatever you wanted. A girl likes to be consulted first.'

He seemed startled by her stand. Clearly, he was used to women kow-towing to him all the time.

'Sorry,' he said. 'I was just trying to fix things for Andy.'

'Yes, I know that. That's why I'm not angry.'

'Good. But I will try to be more thoughtful in future. Right, you just turn left when we hit the main road and it's the next driveway along. Catherine's parents own a horse stud. Racehorses.'

'So they're rich too?'

'Not as rich as Andy's folks. But, yes, they're well off.'

'Do you have any poor friends?'

Ben hesitated before answering.

'Not many,' he said.

'I thought not,' she said drily. Rich people mixed with rich people. She was the odd one out here.

'There's the driveway,' he said, pointing.

This one was more impressive than Andy's driveway, with a huge, black iron archway connecting the tall brick gateposts with the name 'Winning Post Stud' outlined in red. The road itself—which was concreted rather than tarred—was lined with white-painted wooden fences behind which grazed the most beautiful horses Jess had ever seen, some of them with foals at foot. She wasn't a horse person herself but her father liked a flutter on the races and she always had a bet on the Melbourne Cup every year. Often won too, which piqued her dad considerably, since she knew next to nothing about form. Mostly she just picked names that she liked.

The house itself was similar in style to Heather and Glen's but genuinely old, made of stone rather than wood. It was also two-storeyed with iron lacework on the verandas and lots of chimneys.

Jess parked outside the large shed behind the house.

'Before we go in, exactly what did you tell Andy about me?'

'I said you were a marketing consultant I'd met connected with Fab Fashions. But I did let him think we'd met a week or so back, not this morning.'

His reminding her that they'd just met today startled Jess. It underlined just how far they'd come in a few short hours. She should have been more shocked, she supposed. But she was beyond shock. When she shook her head in a type of confusion, he leant over and brushed his lips over hers.

'Don't stress the small stuff, Jess,' he murmured against her quivering mouth. 'Just go with the flow.'

When his head lifted she blinked up at him. He wasn't a flow, she realised. He was a raging current which threatened to carry her out to sea and leave her there, like so much flotsam.

'Ah, here's Catherine, and presumably the other bridesmaid, come to meet us,' Ben said and reached for the door handle.

With an effort, Jess pulled herself together.

Catherine turned out to be a right sweetie. Late twenties, Jess guessed. Above-average height, with an athletic figure and blonde hair. Possibly not a natural blonde, but it suited her. She was very attractive with blue eyes and a warm, friendly manner. Nothing bitchy or snobby about her at all. Jess didn't like her bridesmaid nearly as much, perhaps because she made eyes at Ben from the moment she made an appearance. Her name was Leanne and she and Catherine had gone to boarding school together at some college in Bathurst, along with Krissie, who was the only one of the three friends who'd married so far.

'The teachers at school called us "the unholy trinity",' Catherine said, smiling.

'We *were* a bit naughty,' Leanne trilled.

'I can't believe that,' Ben said, annoying Jess with his flirtatious tone. If he was trying to make her jealous, then he was being successful!

After a little more idle chit-chat, Jess and Ben were led inside the house, where they refused offers of another afternoon tea from Catherine's harried-looking mother. Her name was Joan, a handsome woman, but way too thin, with anxious eyes.

'We just had afternoon tea at Andy's place,' Ben explained.

'I see,' she muttered, then gave Jess a frowning once-over. 'You're a lovely looking girl, dear, but I don't think you're going to fit into Krissie's dress.'

'I don't think so either,' Catherine agreed. 'Luckily, she's about the same height as Krissie, but I'd say she's a good size smaller. Krissie's put on some weight since getting pregnant. But no worries, Mum. At least she's not too big. There's nothing Doris could do to make the dress bigger, but making it smaller is not so much of a problem.

'Doris is a lady in Mudgee who does alterations for Mum and me,' she explained to Ben and Jess. 'I'll give her a call once I know what needs to be done. Meanwhile, we should go upstairs and try the dress on post haste. Then I'll ring her. No, no, you stay down here, Ben,' Catherine added when he went to follow them. 'You're not allowed to see the dresses either. You might tell Andy about them and that's bad luck. Mum, take Ben into the living room and put the TV on.'

It rather amused Jess to see the look on Ben's face. Clearly, he wasn't used to being told what to do, especially by women. Most of them probably said yes to him all the time. Jess realised it would do Ben good if she rejected him tomorrow night. But she couldn't see that happening. She would kick herself if she let him go back to America without spending at least one night with him.

Not knowing what it would have been like would haunt her for ever!

'Don't worry,' Catherine said in a conspiratorial whisper as she led Jess up a large, curving staircase, a reluctant Leanne in their wake. 'He won't go anywhere whilst we're gone.'

Jess laughed. 'Well, he can't, can he? He can't drive.'

'Gosh, that must be hard for him. I know Andy would die if he couldn't drive. Is Ben badly hurt?'

'Only his ego,' Jess replied.

'He's very sweet,' Leanne defended from behind them. 'And very rich.'

'Is he?' Jess said casually.

'You said his dad was a billionaire, didn't you, Catherine?'

'That's what Andy told me,' Catherine confirmed.

Jess shrugged. 'Well, that's his dad, not him.'

'But he's an only child,' Leanne persisted as Catherine led Jess into her bedroom, which was huge.

'I'm not interested in Ben for his money,' she said a bit sharply.

'Are you serious about each other?' Catherine asked.

'We've only just met, but we like each other a lot I think...' Jess replied. She didn't want anyone thinking she was that easy. *She* didn't like thinking she was going to be that easy.

Catherine smiled over her shoulder. 'Well, let's get this dress on and see what has to be done.'

The dress was pale-pink chiffon lined with satin, strapless in style with a seam straight under the bust from which the skirt fell in feminine folds to the floor. It was a sweet dress—not Jess's usual style, but surprisingly it looked good on her, the pale pink suiting her strong colouring. It was not a colour she ever chose for herself, thinking she needed bolder colours.

The dress was too large in the bust line, however. The bodice was just too wide. It needed to be taken in at the side seams which would be a time-consuming job; both the chiffon and the lining would have to be carefully unpicked before being resewn. Thankfully, it was the right length, Krissie obviously being of a similar height to Jess. And, whilst the matching shoes were half a size too large, it was better than them being too small.

Catherine tipped her head to one side as she looked Jess over. 'It actually looks better on you than it did on Krissie. But I won't be telling her that,' she added with a quick smile. 'She feels bad enough as it is. Anyway, I'll just give Doris a call. She altered my wedding dress for me a couple of weeks ago when I lost weight. I'm sure she won't mind, since it's an emergency.'

But as it turned out Doris was in Melbourne visiting her sister.

Murphy's Law at work again, Jess thought silently as she took off the dress and put her own clothes back on again. But at least she could do something about the dismay which had already entered the bride-to-be's face.

'It'll be all right, Catherine,' she said soothingly. 'I can fix the dress. I know exactly what to do. And, before you ask, I have my trusty sewing machine sitting in the back of my four-wheel drive.'

Both Catherine and Leanne gaped at her.

'But…but…' Catherine stammered, not looking too certain about Jess's offer.

Jess smiled reassuringly. 'You don't have to worry. I'm a very experienced dressmaker. It was my profession before I went into marketing,' she added, backing up Ben's little white lie. 'I made this jacket myself, you know, and I think it's a pretty good design.'

'You can say that again!' Catherine exclaimed. 'I've been envying it ever since you arrived.'

'Me too,' Leanne gushed. 'Floral jackets are very *in* this spring.'

'But tell me something, Jess,' Catherine said, looking puzzled. 'Do you *always* travel around with your sewing machine?'

Jess realised immediately she could hardly say that, until fate had stepped in and changed everything, she'd been going to do some sewing whilst she was stuck in a motel room for most of the weekend.

'Lord, no,' she said, laughing. 'I simply forgot to take it out of the car after I did some sewing at a girlfriend's place last weekend. How lucky is that?' As little white lies went, it wasn't too bad, except that it made Jess realise she didn't have girlfriends the way Catherine did. When she'd left Sydney to come live on the Central Coast she'd drifted away from all the female friends she'd made at school. She did see a couple of them occasionally but they weren't in her life on a regular basis. In truth, she didn't actually have any female friends now that Colin had debunked, her recent social life having been more his mates and *their* girlfriends.

Jess had never thought of herself as being lonely before. She did have a large family, but suddenly she envied Catherine her girlfriends.

Still, she didn't entertain her negative feelings for long, vowing instead to do something about her lack of girl-friends once she got back home. Maybe she would join a gym. Or a sports club of some kind. She'd been good at basketball at school, her above-average height giving her an advantage. Yes, she'd join a basketball club. For females only. Jess suspected that after Ben went back to America she would want a spell away from male com-pany for a while.

Her heart lurched at this last thought but she stead-fastly ignored it.

'How about I drive Ben back to Andy's place?' she sug-gested. 'Then come back and get stuck into the dress? It could take a couple of hours. I don't want to rush things. I want to get it right.'

Catherine beamed at her. 'Jess, you are a life saver! You must stay here for dinner,' Catherine added. 'Then after-wards we can have a little hen party of our own. I mean, there's no point in your returning to Andy's place. He and Ben are going out on the town in Mudgee tonight. A few of their mates from uni are staying at a motel there, so they're having a big get-together. I did tell Andy not to stay out too late or do anything seriously stupid, but you know Aussie men when they get a few beers into them. Ben might sound like an American these days, but he's an Aussie boy through and through.'

Jess didn't agree with Catherine on that score. Ben was nothing like any Aussie boy she'd ever met.

'At least the wedding's not till four-thirty,' Catherine added. 'So they have time to recover.'

'Where is the wedding, Catherine?' Jess asked.

'We're having it outside in Mum's rose garden, with a

celebrant officiating. And the reception will be in a marquee set up on the back lawn. It's due to go up first thing in the morning. Once that's done, the wedding planner and her lot will swoop in and set everything else up.'

'You booked a wedding planner?' Jess said, surprised. She would want to plan her own wedding right down to the last detail.

'Gosh, yes. I knew it would be a nightmare if I did it. Mum would want to help, but the poor love gets in a flap over the least little thing. The lady I hired has been fantastic. She's arranged everything, right down to the cars and the flowers. She even took me down to Sydney and helped me choose the dresses. Not that it's a large wedding. Only about a hundred guests. This business with Krissie and her dress is the first hiccup there's been.'

'Is the weather forecast good for tomorrow?' Jess asked, worried that Murphy's Law might raise its ugly head again at the last minute. She was beginning to be a serious believer.

'Perfect. Warm, with no rain in sight. Okay, let's get ourselves downstairs and I'll reassure Mum whilst you drop Ben back at Andy's. But don't be away too long,' she added, flashing Jess a knowing smile. 'No hanky panky, now. Keep that till after the wedding.'

# CHAPTER TEN

'ARE YOU SURE you can do this, Jess?' Ben said as Jess sped down the driveway. 'I mean, altering a dress can't be the same as making one from scratch.'

'It won't be any trouble. Gran did a lot of alterations and I used to help her. I earned my first pocket money that way.'

'You are full of surprises, aren't you?' he said, smiling over at her. 'A good person to have around, I would imagine. I dare say you can cook as well.'

Jess shrugged. 'I'm not bad. Mum's better, though. Can you cook? Or is that a silly question?'

'Not at all. I think all men should be able to cook a bit, especially ones who live alone. I can make a mean omelette, and my mushroom risotto has received several compliments.'

Jess laughed. 'I dare say it has.' She could imagine Amber gushing over every single thing he did. She could hear her now: *Oh, Ben, darling, you are so clever. And talented. And handsome. And rich.*

No, no, Amber wouldn't actually say that last bit. She would not be as obvious as Leanne. Or as envious. Because Amber would have money of her own. Jess was sure of it.

His sideways glance was sharp. 'Do I detect some sarcasm in that remark?'

Her returning glance was brilliantly po-faced. Or so she thought.

'Not at all.'

He chuckled. 'You little liar, you. You enjoy taking the Mickey out of me.'

'That's a very Aussie saying. Maybe you're not as American as you sound.'

'What's wrong with being American?'

'Absolutely nothing.' It was his being a *filthy rich* American that was the problem.

'You're not going to sleep the night at Catherine's place, are you?' he asked abruptly.

Jess frowned at this question. 'I wasn't planning to, but what difference would it make if I did? You're going out and from what I gather you'll be home very late.'

'I just want you to be there in the morning. I want to have breakfast with you and talk to you some more.'

'Okay,' she agreed. 'But do try to be quiet when you get in. I'm going to be tired after doing that dress. I don't want to be woken by drunken revellers.'

'I have no intention of getting drunk tonight,' he surprised her by saying. 'I don't want to be hung-over tomorrow, thank you very much. I have plans for tomorrow night which require me to be fit and well.'

'Oh,' she said, and for the first time in her life Jess blushed. But it wasn't the blush of embarrassment, it was the blush of heat. Sexual heat.

'Don't miss Andy's place,' he said.

'What? Oh, God, I forgot where I was for a moment.' She glanced in the rear-view mirror as she braked sharply before turning into Andy's driveway.

'Thinking of tomorrow night?' he asked in a low, oh, so sexy voice.

Jess refused to act rattled by him, even though she was.

'But of course,' she said, her cool tone a total contrast to the inferno raging inside her.

Ben should not have been surprised by her bald honesty. Jess didn't play games. But Ben had games very much in mind for tomorrow night. He didn't want sex with her to be over quickly. He wanted to savour it. To savour her. He also wanted the love-making to last and last and last.

'How many lovers have you had, Jess?'

'Not as many as you've had, I'll bet,' she countered, thinking he had a hide to ask her that. 'Now, could we stop talking about sex?' She reefed the car to a ragged halt. 'You sit here whilst I go get Andy, and I'll explain things, then find out where this guest cottage is. And, before you object, you're not fooling me by pretending you can get in and out of your seat without some pain in your shoulder because I know differently. So just be a good boy and sit still for a while.'

She didn't give him a chance to come back with some witty riposte because she was off in a flash, running up the side steps of the house, leaving Ben to ponder just how good a boy he was going to be tonight. And he wasn't talking about at the stag party.

The temptation to come home early was acute. He could easily make some excuse pertaining to his car accident— claim a crippling headache from the concussion, or an appallingly painful shoulder. It *was* sore, but nothing to write home about.

No, he decided in the end. He would wait. Waiting often made the sex better. And Jess would be even more inclined to be thoroughly seduced.

Tomorrow night would be a first for him in more ways than one. His first wedding. His first brunette. The first girl in a decade who didn't seem overly impressed with his being Morgan De Silva's son and heir.

Now, that really would be a first!

# CHAPTER ELEVEN

THE GUEST COTTAGE was cute and quite a long way from the main house, set on a smaller hill and surrounded by trees. Made of weatherboard, it had a pitched iron roof, covered porches front and back and a hallway which cut the cottage in two. On the left on entering was a lounge followed by a dining room and then the kitchen. On the right were two bedrooms separated by a bathroom, followed by a utility room and walk-in pantry. All the rooms were delightfully furnished in comfy, country-style furniture which was probably newer than it looked. Apparently, it had once been a miner's cottage, and had been on the property when Andy's parents had bought the place.

Andy had shown them the way to the cottage personally, which was a relief to Jess. Nothing like a third person being present to prevent Ben doing something which she didn't want him to do. Not yet, anyway. If truth be told, she was terrified of that moment when he would stop the talk and walk the walk, so to speak. She'd always thought herself quite good at sex but, on a scale of one to ten, she doubted she came much above a five. She would hate it if he found her a disappointment.

She quickly put her overnight bag in the smaller of the two bedrooms, insisting that Ben have the front room with the queen-sized bed, since he was too big for a single bed.

He didn't argue, just sat down on the side of the bed and bounced up and down, as though testing it for comfort. Andy carried Ben's things into the room whilst Jess hovered in the doorway.

'I'll come back with some more provisions shortly,' Andy told them. 'Some stuff for breakfast. There's already white wine in the fridge, and red wine in the cupboards, along with coffee, tea and biscuits, etc. But I'll bring down some fresh bread, eggs and bacon.'

'Well, I won't be here,' Jess returned before he could escape. 'I have to get back to Catherine's. I won't be back till late tonight.'

'Oh, right. I forgot. I also forgot to thank you for what you're doing, Jess. Catherine rang me and told me about the dress. You are one clever girl, isn't she, Ben? Fancy being able to sew like that.'

'She's amazing,' Ben said.

Jess just smiled, awake to his many compliments.

The moment they were alone Ben gave her a narrow-eyed look. 'You won't be staying in that bedroom tomorrow night.'

She glowered at him, never being at her best when men started ordering her around. 'Maybe I will,' she bit out. 'If you start acting like some jerk.'

That sent him back in his heels. 'What do you mean?'

'I run my own race, Ben. I don't like men telling me what to do and when to do it.'

'Is that so?'

Ben stood up and strode over to her, taking her firmly by the shoulders and pulling her hard against him. She didn't struggle, or protest. Just stared up at him with wide, dilated eyes. Ben could actually feel her galloping heartbeat. She thought she didn't like to be ordered around, but he knew that a lot of strong-minded women liked their lovers to take charge.

It came to him that she'd probably never had a dominant lover before. What an exciting thought!

He could hardly wait for tomorrow night to come.

'When the time is right, Jess,' he said quietly, his eyes intense on hers, 'you *will* like me telling you what to do. Trust me on this. But, for now, perhaps you should get going. Because if you stay I won't be responsible for what might happen.'

Jess left the cottage in a fluster, her body cruelly turned on and her thoughts totally scattered.

*Trust* him, he'd said. To do what? Turn her into some kind of mindless sex slave?

At this moment she didn't doubt he could do it. If she let him.

Did she want that to happen?

The answer to that question lay in her thudding heart and rock-hard nipples.

Suddenly, Jess was overwhelmed by a wave of desire so strong that she almost ran off the road. Giving herself a savage mental shake, she slowed down to a crawl, then turned shakily into Catherine's driveway, proceeding very carefully up the cement road, grateful now that she had a job to do which would take her most of the evening; *very* grateful that she had no reason to go back to that seductive cottage till well after Ben had left with Andy for their night on the town. Thank heavens he wouldn't get home till the small hours of the morning. By which time she would be sound asleep.

Jess had to laugh over that one. There would be no sleeping for her tonight.

But at least she could pretend she was asleep.

Things didn't turn out quite like that, however. Jess finished the dress around nine-thirty, after which she refused all offers of wine, saying she was tired, then drove back to the cottage. In actual fact she'd only just remembered that she'd promised to give her mother a ring. This she did whilst she opened a bottle of the white wine resting in the door of the fridge. She poured herself a large glass, sipping it as she sat at the kitchen table, and gave her mother an edited version of what had happened, telling her the truth about the dramas over the wedding and how she'd fixed the dress tonight, plus the plan for her to be a substitute matron of honour the next day. Naturally, she didn't mention anything about her being thought of as Ben's girlfriend or that she was staying with him, alone, in this cottage. She admitted staying as a guest at the winery but that was all.

'It sounds like it's been a rather surprising trip so far,' her mother said.

'It certainly has,' Jess agreed with considerable irony as she poured herself a second glass of wine.

'You'll have to ring me tomorrow night and tell me all about the wedding.'

Jess winced. She could hardly tell her mother why that wasn't going to happen.

'Mum, the wedding's not till late in the afternoon. By the time the reception is over and I get to bed, it's going to be very late and I'm going to be exhausted. I'll call you on Sunday morning. But not too early, mind. I might sleep in.' Jess was grateful that her mother couldn't see inside her head at this moment, as the images in there were not fit for a caring mother's consumption.

'Oh, all right,' her mother said. 'But don't forget to take some photos. I'd love to see what you looked like. What you *all* looked like, actually. Which reminds me. What does this Ben fellow look like? You said he was nice but I have a feeling he's good-looking, am I right?'

'Yes, he's very good-looking,' she admitted, struggling to keep her voice calm in the face of a looming panic attack over her sexual inadequacies. 'And very tall.'

'Tall, dark and handsome, eh?'

'No, he's actually fair-haired, with blue eyes.'

'And how old, did you say?'

'I don't know. Early thirties, perhaps.'

'And rich?'

'Filthy rich, Mum. His father's a billionaire.'

'Goodness. And did you tell him that you lost your job at Fab Fashions because of him?'

'I did mention it. And he promised to see what he could do.'

'Well, that was nice of him. But did he mean it?'

The jury was still out on that score. 'Maybe. I guess we'll have to wait and see, Mum. Now, I really must go. I'm tired.' That was a lie. She had so much adrenaline flowing through her body at the moment that she had no hope of sleeping. That was why she was downing all this wine; sometimes wine made her sleepy. Unfortunately, it didn't seem to be working.

'Driving can be very tiring,' her mother said. 'Good-night, darling. Sleep tight. Love you.'

Jess suddenly came over all emotional.

'Love you too, Mum,' she choked out, then hung up.

Jess decided after her third glass of wine that it definitely wasn't working. So she put the half-drunk bottle back in the fridge and headed for the bathroom. A long, hot bath filled in another hour but didn't relax her one iota. She'd just emerged from the bathroom, dressed in a nightie, when she heard a car screech to a stop in front of the cottage. Running to the front living room, Jess peered through the curtains in time to see Ben climb out of the back of a taxi.

Flustered—what on earth was he doing home this early?—she whirled to make a dash for the bedroom, in her haste catching her left foot under the curled up corner of a rug. She cried out as she fell, her hands bracing themselves to protect her face whilst her knees hit the wooden floorboards with a painful thud.

Ben heard Jess cry out as he made his way up onto the front veranda. He dashed inside, switching on the hall light and calling her name at the same time.

He found her sitting back on her haunches in the semi-dark on the living-room floor, dressed in a red satin nightie with spaghetti straps which showed off her gorgeous figure. Her lovely hair was down, spread over her shoulders in dishevelled disarray, adding to the criminally sexy picture she presented.

'What happened?' he asked, and held out his left hand to help her up.

'I fell over,' she said, but made no move to take his hand, her eyes on her ground. 'My foot got caught under the rug.'

'I see,' he said, not seeing at all. What was she doing in this room, anyway? The lights weren't on. Neither was the television. 'Well, do you want to take my hand or are you going to stay there all night?' he said, his tone betraying his inner frustration.

She glanced up at him.

Jess only just managed not to groan out loud. God, but he looked utterly gorgeous dressed in grey stone-washed jeans, an open-necked white shirt and a fabulous looking charcoal-grey jacket.

Finally, she placed her hand in his, his fingers closing tightly around hers as he pulled her to her feet.

'What on earth are you doing home *this* early?' she asked whilst she tried to ignore the direction of his gaze. Right where her erect nipples were poking against the red satin. Maybe he would think she was cold. Though she wasn't, having turned off the air-conditioning when she'd got home. The temperature had dropped considerably once the sun had gone down but it was a nice twenty-three degrees inside the cottage.

'Do you want the truth?'

'Of course.'

'I told Andy I had a vicious headache and that if he wanted me on deck tomorrow, then I should go home.'

'And do you? Have a vicious headache?'

'No. I simply couldn't stop thinking about you.'

Jess tried not to let his flattering words seduce her but it was way too late for such a futile struggle.

'I've been thinking about you too,' she admitted somewhat shakily.

'So do I still have to wait till tomorrow night?'

She shook her head.

She half-expected him to kiss her then but he didn't. Instead, he just smiled.

'I need a shower,' he said. 'I smell of beer. Can I tempt you to join me?'

The desire to lick her suddenly dry lips was intense but somehow she resisted. Jess swallowed instead, putting some moisture into her mouth. 'I...I've just had a bath,' she said, her voice thick and throaty.

'Then you can come and watch.'

Jess blinked at him, her mouth falling open briefly before snapping shut again.

'All right,' she said, wondering if this was what he'd meant earlier about her liking him telling her what to do.

She did. Which was weird. If Colin or any of her other boyfriends had suggested the same thing to her, she would have told them to get lost. Bathrooms were private places, in her opinion. They weren't places where you *watched*. Yet she wanted to watch Ben shower, didn't she? She wanted to see him naked. Wanted to do all sorts of things she'd never done before.

Her head spun at the thought.

When she didn't move, he frowned at her. 'You've changed your mind already?'

*Changed her mind?* Was he insane? How could she possibly change her mind when she'd already lost it?

She shook her head.

'Good,' he said, and held out his hand to her again.

# CHAPTER TWELVE

BEN LIKED THE way Jess let him lead her meekly into the bathroom. He could tell she was turned on, the same way he was. Even the slightest touch turned him on with her. It was quite incredible, the effect she had on him. But nothing he couldn't control, now that she was being deliciously cooperative.

He settled her, somewhat stunned-looking, on the side of the claw-footed bath, then started undressing.

Jess could not believe she was doing this, sitting there watching whilst Ben took all his clothes off in front of her. But, dear heaven, it was exciting!

After he kicked off his shoes, he removed his jacket and then his shirt, revealing an upper half which didn't look like it spent all day seated behind a desk. He must work hard in a gym, she decided, or go swimming a lot. His light tan suggested this might be the case. He had broad shoulders, one of which carried a nasty bruise. But it didn't seem to stop his arm working. His chest muscles were wide and well-toned, his stomach a surprising six-pack. Very little body hair, she noted, and liked.

Jess held her breath when he whipped the belt out of his jeans, but he just dropped it on the floor, then ran the zipper down. When his hands hooked under the waist band

and pushed down, she finally let go of the air trapped in her lungs.

He was wearing black underpants, made out of a silky material which hid nothing.

She wondered if he was as big as he looked. Jess had always believed that size *did* matter. To a degree. She liked a man to be well built in that area.

He was. Bigger than her previous boyfriends. And magnificently erect. Circumcised, with only a smattering of fair hair at the base. She knew he would feel—and taste—fantastic.

He stood facing her, a golden Adonis in every way.

'Now you, Jess,' he commanded. 'Stand up and take that nightie off. I want to see all of you.'

She stood up onto shaky legs, utterly compelled to obey him. Her belly tightened as she slowly slipped the straps off her shoulders, first on, then the other. She wasn't wearing any undies. She never wore undies to bed. The nightie slid down her body with a whoosh, pooling around her feet on the tiled floor.

His gaze dropped down to those feet first, then gradually travelled upwards, lingering on the neatly waxed V of curls between her thighs, before lifting to her breasts.

'Beautiful,' he said.

Jess knew she was attractive, but she'd never considered herself beautiful. She had physical flaws, like most people. Couldn't Ben see that her nose was too big for her face? So was her mouth. The back of her thighs had some dimples of cellulite which no amount of massage or cream could remove, though he wouldn't see that unless he ordered her to turn around.

Jess suspected Ben wasn't about to do that. He was enjoying looking at her breasts too much. Admittedly, they were the best feature of her figure. Full and high, with perky pink nipples that grew astonishingly in size when they were played with. Or when she was excited. Which she was right now. God, yes. Her whole breasts seemed to be swelling under his hot, hungry eyes, though perhaps it was just Jess's ragged breathing.

'No more arguments or excuses, Jess,' he said thickly. 'You're coming into that shower with me and then we're going to bed. Together.'

Once again, she obeyed him, blindly and without protest, letting him pull her with him into the shower cubicle. And it was there, as the hot jets of waters did dreadful things to her hair, that he cupped her face and finally kissed her properly.

Jess had been kissed many times in her life. And by men who were quite good kissers. But Ben kissing her was a once-in-a-lifetime experience. She felt its effect through her whole body right down to her toes. It overwhelmed her. Then obsessed her. She could not get enough of it. And of him. When at last his head lifted, she sank against him in total surrender, her arms wrapping tightly around his waist.

'Are you on the pill, Jess?'

She pulled back enough to glance up at him. 'What?'

'Are you on the pill?'

Her mind cleared a little. 'Well…yes…but…'

'You still want me to use protection.'

'Please,' she said, despite being tempted to say no. *Just do it to me. Right here and now.*

'In that case, I think we should cut this shower short this time.'

Again, no protest from her. She just stood there whilst he switched off the taps, then reached for one of the towels hanging on the rack, rubbing rather roughly at her dripping hair before giving himself a brisk rub down. Then he scooped her up in his arms and carried her back to his bedroom.

Jess shivered as he laid her gently down on top of the bed, goose bumps springing up over her body.

'Are you cold?' he asked as he lay down next to her, propping himself up on his left side.

'A little,' she lied.

'Do you want to get under the covers?'

She shook her head.

'I've been wanting to do this all day,' he said, and bent his lips to hers once more, his right hand sliding up into her still damp hair.

His return to gentle kisses surprised her at first, then entranced her. She sighed under their soft sweetness. Gradually, however, the pressure of his mouth grew stronger. When his teeth nipped at her lower lip, she gasped, and his tongue slipped inside once more, Jess moaning softly as it explored the sensitive skin of her palate. She gasped again when a hand covered her right breast, playing with her nipple in ways she'd definitely never experienced before: soft rubbing with his palm interspersed with quite painful pinching till it was on fire.

And all the while he kept on kissing her, his tongue alternately snaking deep, then withdrawing before plunging in again. When his hand moved across to her other nipple, she felt momentarily bereft for the abandoned one. If he could have played with both at the same time, she would have been in heaven. Or hell. Jess could not work out if she was in agony or ecstasy. Not that she cared, as long as he didn't stop.

He stopped, both the kissing and the nipple pinching, leaving her moaning in dismay till she realised why he'd stopped. Already he was down there with that knowing mouth and tongue of his, making her groan and squirm as he licked and sucked and showed her that all her other lovers had been seriously ignorant of a woman's body. Ben knew exactly what to do to bring her to the brink of coming, not once but several times. How he knew when to back off, she wasn't sure. Maybe it had something to do with his fingers being deep inside her all the while. Maybe he could feel the way her muscles tightened when she came close to coming.

His head lifted at last. 'Enough, I think,' he muttered, then collapsed on his back beside her, breathing very heavily.

She levered herself up onto her elbow and stared over at him. 'You're not stopping, are you?'

'Just for a few seconds. I need a breather, and then I have to get a condom on. I put two in that top drawer this afternoon,' he said, nodding towards the bedside chest next to her. 'Get one for me, would you, Jess?'

Jess wondered if Ben always used protection, even when his girlfriends were on the pill. She had a feeling that he did. Maybe he was worried that one of them might try to trap him into marriage. Seriously rich men would have to worry about such things, she imagined. If this Amber wanted to marry him enough, it wouldn't be beyond her to do such thing.

'Put it on for me,' he said after she extracted one from the drawer.

Oh, Lord, Jess thought as she opened the foil packet and turned back to him. She *had* put a condom on before. Just not whilst she was in such an excited state. She found it extremely difficult with her hands shaking so much. When Ben groaned, she shot him a worried look.

'Am I hurting you?'

His smile was both tortured and wry. 'Oh, honey, you're killing me. But not in the way you think. Would you mind being on top?'

'You want me on top?' she echoed. Whilst it was her favourite position, she hadn't imagined it would be Ben's. Earlier on, he'd seemed keen to be the one in control. And whilst it had turned her on, being ordered around, she was happy to have their roles reversed for a while. Though the position had been *his* idea, come to think of it.

'I would have thought you'd like being on top,' he said.

'I do quite like it,' she confessed.

'Then what are you waiting for?'

What, indeed?

Ben's stomach tightened when she moved to straddle him, his heart thundering in his chest when she took hold of him and presented the bursting tip against the entrance to her body. He could feel the heat and the wetness of her, but he couldn't see it. She wasn't one of those girls who totally denuded herself of body hair, her sex protected by a smattering of soft dark curls. Ben rather liked that. It was different. She was different. In every way. There was no pretence about her. She was sweet and very natural, and he wanted her as he'd never wanted any woman before. His excitement was so great that he had no patience with playing games tonight. He wanted her now!

A groan escaped his lips as she pushed him inside, her flesh slowly swallowing his with a silky snugness which was incredibly pleasurable. He braced himself mentally against what it would feel like when she moved. He didn't want to come too soon. Hell, no. That would never do!

Jess had been right. It felt incredible with him deep inside her, filling her totally. He obviously liked it too, judging by the look on his face. Though was it rapture she was seeing, or torture? A mixture of both, she imagined. Men could be very impatient at this stage. So she kept her movements slow and gentle at first, lifting her hips only slightly before lowering herself down again. But it wasn't long before her own desire for satisfaction took over, urging her to lift her hips higher, then to plunge down harder. She tried not to think about anything but her sexual pleasure, valiantly ignoring the emotional responses which hovered at the edges of her brain. This wasn't love, she told herself firmly. This was just sex. Great sex, yes, with an utterly gorgeous man. But still just sex. *Enjoy it, girl. Because you could go the rest of your life without finding a lover like Ben.*

Their coming together distracted her totally from any thought of love, her own orgasm so intense that all she could think about were the physical sensations. The electric pleasure of each spasm, plus the wonderful relief from the tension which had gripped her all evening. Finally, when it was over, every pore in her body succumbed to a huge wave of languor. She collapsed across him, totally spent, sighing a long, sated sigh when he wrapped his arms around her, his lips in her hair.

'That was fantastic,' he whispered. '*You're* fantastic.

'No, don't move,' he said when she tried to lift her head. 'I want to fall asleep like this, with me still inside you. My only regret is that we can't do it again. I'm just too damned tired all of a sudden. But I'll make it up to you tomorrow. I promise. Just stay where you are, you delicious thing. Stay,' he repeated, his voice slurring a little.

Within thirty seconds, he'd fallen asleep.

Less than a minute later, she followed him.

# CHAPTER THIRTEEN

BEN WOKE TO the smell of bacon cooking, plus no Jess in bed with him. Hell, he'd really passed out last night. And slept for a good ten hours, he realised with amazement as he glanced at his watch. And whilst he regretted not waking—he hadn't intended sex with Jess to be so short and swift—the long sleep had done him a lot of good. His shoulder was one hundred percent better and he felt marvellous.

Ben fairly leapt out of bed, calling a hurried, 'Good morning,' out to Jess before bolting for the bathroom. After a very quick shower, he wrapped a towel around his waist, then made his way to the kitchen, anxious to see Jess again. She glanced over her shoulder as he walked in, her lovely eyes lighting up at the sight of him.

'You look good in a towel,' she said, smiling.

'And you look good in anything,' he returned, his gaze raking over her from top to toe. She was wearing the same fitted black trousers again, but her top was different, a simple scoop-necked sweater in a bright-green colour which suited her dark hair and olive skin. She wasn't wearing any make-up and her hair was up, secured on top of her head in a rather haphazard fashion. On closer inspection, he could see she'd wrapped it around itself in a knot, a few bits and pieces already escaping. Her lack of artifice continued to enchant him. Amber was always fully made up and her hair groomed to perfection before showing herself in the morning.

Jess made Amber look terribly shallow. And impossibly vain.

'Flatterer,' she said, laughing, then turned back to the stove.

'That smells good,' he said, coming up behind her to slide his arms around her waist.

Jess tried not to stiffen at his touch, having determined to act naturally with him. It had been difficult not to ogle his beautiful body when he'd come into the kitchen just now, but she'd managed, telling herself all the while that a sophisticated New York woman wouldn't ogle. She would sail through the morning after the night before with style and panache. She wouldn't ask for reassurances that he wanted more from her than sex. She would be pleasant and easy going. Slightly flirtatious, yes, but nothing heavy.

So, when Ben placed a hand under her chin and turned her face towards his, she hid her momentary panic and let him kiss her. Fortunately, it wasn't too deep, too long a kiss. But, oh…how her heart raced, her head instantly filling with images of him scattering everything off the kitchen table with one sweep of his arm and taking her on it then and there.

His eyes were glittering when his head lifted. 'If that bacon wasn't already cooked,' he said, 'I'd have *you* for breakfast.'

'Really,' she replied with superb nonchalance. 'I might have something to say about that.'

His eyes carried the knowledge she was bluffing. 'Come now, Jess, let's not play games this morning. You and I both know that what we shared last night was something special. And highly addictive. But you're right. We should eat first.'

'Your bruise looks much better,' she said, turning her attention back to the breakfast. 'When bruises start going all the colours of the rainbow, it usually means they're on the mend. Now, sit down, for Pete's sake, and let me get on with this.'

'You sound like you're familiar with bruises,' he said, pulling out a chair at the kitchen table and sitting down.

'I have three brothers,' she reminded him. 'There wasn't a day that they didn't come home from school with bruises.'

'Habitual fighters, were they?'

'No. Just physical.'

'Like you. You're very physical. And very sexy.'

Jess felt some dismay—and irritation—that Ben's focus seemed to be all about sex. She was more than that… wasn't she?

Somehow, she managed to serve up toast, bacon and eggs without burning anything. Ben ate his with relish, Jess just picking at hers. She'd always been a girl who lacked appetite when she was upset about something. She tried telling herself she was foolish to expect anything more than sex from Ben, but it was a losing cause.

'You didn't eat much,' Ben remarked after he finished his breakfast.

'I'm not very hungry. I had some coffee before you got up.'

'You're not one of those girls who lives on coffee, are you?'

'Not usually.'

'You don't need to lose weight, Jess. Your body is absolutely gorgeous just the way it is.'

Jess struggled not to show her feelings on her face. But did he *have* to concentrate on her body?

'I'm glad you think so. By the way, you said yesterday we could have a talk about Fab Fashions this morning.'

He seemed genuinely taken aback. 'Yes, I know I did. But that was before last night.'

Jess glared at him across the table. 'You mean you don't have to pander to me any more because we've already had sex.'

Ben hid his guilt well. Because she was right, wasn't she? But, damn it all, he wasn't about to waste time talking about business when he could be having sex with her again.

'No,' he said carefully. 'That's not true. Though what we shared last night does change things, Jess. It was so very special. We can talk about Fab Fashions during the drive home tomorrow. And every day next week. Meanwhile, we probably only have a couple of hours to ourselves before we both have to get ready for the wedding this afternoon. What time do you have to be over at Catherine's?'

She seemed mollified by his explanation. 'I said I'd be there at three. But I have to do my hair first. Catherine and Leanne are having their hair done at a hairdresser's in Mudgee this morning, but I prefer to do my own hair. I'm better at it than the hairdresser.'

He smiled. 'I have no doubt you are. Okay, Andy said he's going to collect me around two-thirty. We're all getting ready together up at the house before heading over to Catherine's around four. Apparently, it doesn't do for the groom's party to be late arriving.'

'You haven't been in a bridal party before?'

'Actually, no, I haven't. Have you?'

'I was a bridesmaid at all of my three brothers' weddings.'

'Maybe next time you'll be the bride.'

'I doubt it,' she said, her voice sharp.

'Don't you want to get married?'

'Well, yes, I do. Eventually. That's what we do in our

family. But I'm prepared to wait till the right man comes along. After Colin, I'm not in any hurry.'

Ben wasn't in any hurry either. But it did cross his mind that Jess would make some man a wonderful wife.

'And what would make him the right man?' he asked.

Jess shrugged. 'That's a difficult question. For starters, he'd have to be reasonably successful in whatever he's chosen to do in life. I like men who are confident.'

'Would he have to be rich?'

'Not rich like you, Ben De Silva. I would never marry a man as rich as you.'

Ben felt perversely offended. 'Really? A lot of women would.'

'Yeah. Silly, greedy ones like Leanne. And already rich ones like your Amber.'

Ben frowned. 'Why makes you think Amber's rich?'

Jess stood up and started clearing the breakfast things away. 'Am I wrong?' she threw at him.

'No. She *is* rich. Or, her father is.'

'I thought as much.'

Ben laughed. 'You're not jealous, are you, Jess? You have no reason to be. Amber's history.'

His accusing her of jealousy was very telling. Because she was. Horribly so. Jess turned her back on him and walked over to the sink. She'd be history too one day soon. It was just a matter of time. And geography.

His suddenly taking firm possession of her shoulders startled her. She hadn't even heard him get up.

'Don't be angry with me, Jess. Come back to bed. We can talk about Fab Fashions there, if you like. We can multi-task.'

She couldn't help it. She laughed. 'Men can't multi-task.'

'Don't you believe it,' he said as he pulled her back hard

against him. 'I can talk and get an erection at the same time. See?' he said and rubbed himself against her bottom. 'There's proof.'

She laughed some more.

'I love it when you laugh,' he murmured as he nuzzled her neck. 'But I love it more when you come. The sounds you make, the way your insides squeeze me like a vice… You drove me crazy last night. Drive me crazy again, lovely Jess. With your mouth this time. And those hands you're so damned good with.'

She was the one who was being driven crazy. No man had ever said things like that to her. He made her want to do *everything* with him. Oh, God…

She didn't say a word, just whirled in his arms and kissed him. And he kissed her back, a long, wet wildly passionate kiss which scattered her brainwaves and turned her body to liquid.

'Come on. Back to bed,' he said when he finally came up for air.

'Bed?' she echoed, dazed.

His smile was wry. 'Yeah. You know. The furniture thingy with sheets and pillows where you go to sleep at night. But we're not going to sleep in it today, beautiful,' he added. 'Not even for a single second.'

# CHAPTER FOURTEEN

'Do you think I'm doing the right thing?'

Jess almost shook her head at the bride in exasperation. After all, why ask *her*? She knew next to nothing of Catherine's relationship with Andy. It was also rather late to have second thoughts with the bridal party about to make its way over to the rose garden where the groom would be impatiently waiting. They were already twenty minutes behind schedule. At the same time, Jess did feel some sympathy for the girl. Her mother was not the most reassuring of mothers—the woman had spent the last two hours in tears—and marriage *was* a big step, especially in this day and age when divorce was rife and the 'for ever' kind of love seemed like a pipe dream. But, as they said in the classics, better to have loved and lost than never to have loved at all!

'Do you love Andy, Catherine?' Jess asked quickly.

'Yes, of course.'

'There is no *of course* about it. Lots of girls marry for reasons other than love.'

'Not me.'

'Nor me. And does Andy love you?'

'Yes, I'm sure he does.'

A sudden thought crossed Jess's mind. 'You're not pregnant, are you?'

'Lord, no. No. But we do plan on having children.'

'Sounds like you don't have any reason for last-minute doubts, Catherine. Now, come on, girl, we're already running late. Though, before you go, let me say you look absolutely gorgeous!' Which was true. Her dress was a bit OTT in Jess's opinion, but it suited Catherine's feminine blonde beauty.

'Oh.' The bride fairly beamed. 'You look gorgeous as well. And you too, Leanne.'

Leanne preened whilst Jess just smiled. Yes, they did all look very nice.

'Aren't you girls ready yet?' Catherine's father snarled at them.

Jess had disliked the man within seconds of having met him. He was one of those larger than life men who was absolutely full of himself. Jess decided with sudden insight that his bombast could explain why Catherine's mother was a nervous wreck and why perhaps Catherine was afraid of marriage. If Andy had been anything like her father in character—which fortunately he didn't seem to be—then she would have every right to be hesitant.

Jess decided to put him on the spot. 'Don't you think your daughter looks absolutely divine?'

'What? Oh, yes, yes. Very nice. Now, let's go.'

Jess and Leanne exchanged rolling eyes which told it all. Jess decided if her father ever said she just looked *nice* on her wedding day she would throttle him.

Thinking of her own future wedding day thoroughly distracted Jess as they made their way from the house over to the rose garden, making her only dimly aware of her surrounds. She'd done her best to put a halt to her escalating feelings for Ben during the hours she'd spent with him earlier on, focusing on the physical and not the emotional. But her heart had been as impossible to control as her body. It had soared every time she'd touched him. But it had been performing oral sex on him which had been the killer. She had loved the way he'd lost control under her mouth and hands. He hadn't wanted to, she was sure. But he'd seemed as powerless to stop himself as she'd been. Not that that meant anything. She wasn't that naïve.

They'd used the only remaining condom in no time, with a still turned-on Jess eventually offering to go and get the condom she kept in her bag which was in the other bedroom. Ben had followed her there, pulling her down onto the rug by the bed where he'd taken her on all fours, squeezing her nipples as she came. It was the first time in her life that she'd had sex that way and she'd loved it, giving rise to the hope that she wasn't falling in love, just suffering from an intense case of lust.

Ben had been wrong about their not actually sleeping. When he'd carried her back to bed after that rather rough mating on the floor, she'd passed out, not waking till Ben had started shaking her shoulder.

'Oh, Lord!' she'd exclaimed, sitting bolt upright and pushing her tangled hair out of her eyes. 'What time is it?' Ben was dressed, she'd immediately noted. Not in what he would be wearing at the wedding. Just jeans and a top.

'Shortly before two-thirty. Andy will be here any moment. You said you had to do your hair.'

Jess had grimaced. 'I'll have to shampoo it again. It's a mess.'

Just then there'd been a knock on the front door, Andy calling out as he'd opened it and walked into the hallway. Panicked, Jess had grabbed a sheet to cover herself, Ben unable to get to the open doorway in time before Andy had been standing in it.

'Oh, sorry,' Andy had said hurriedly on seeing an obviously naked Jess in the bed. 'I'll…er…wait for you out-side, Ben.'

'No sweat.' He'd turned to throw Jess an apologetic glance. 'Sorry about that, my darling. See you at the wed-ding.'

Jess recalled that her heart had turned over at his call-ing her his darling. It turned over again when she caught sight of him standing with Andy at the end of the strip of red carpet which had been rolled out between the rows of decorated seats. No doubt the groom and the other grooms-man looked almost as good as Ben in their black dinner suits. But Jess didn't see anyone or anything else but him, smiling at her. Talk about tunnel vision!

Some taped wedding music started up and she floated down the makeshift aisle, unaware of the admiring whis-pers from the guests, aware of nothing but Ben's eyes upon her.

*Bloody hell*, Ben thought as Jess walked slowly towards them. *She is just so damned desirable!*

'You are one lucky guy, mate,' Andy murmured out of the side of his mouth. 'That is one hot babe.'

'You ought to talk,' Ben managed to whisper back when the bride finally came into view. But he hardly noticed Catherine or heard the ceremony. He just went through the motions, producing the rings on cue, thankful that it was a relatively short service. He could not wait to be alone with Jess again.

His first opportunity to speak to her was at the signing of the register which they did to one side after Catherine and Andy had been declared man and wife.

'You look very pretty in pink,' he whispered as he passed her the pen. 'But I prefer you in nothing.'

He noticed her hand trembling as she signed her name. It excited him, the way he could turn her on like that. She wasn't like other girls he'd slept with. She seemed less experienced and more capable of being surprised. That, in itself, was very arousing. The temptation to push her sexual boundaries was acute, especially since she was obviously a highly sexed girl. She'd loved going down on him. He'd loved it too. It worried Ben, though, the tendency he had to lose control with her on occasion.

Next time, he would not let that happen. Ben had a penchant for erotic fun and games, first sparked when he'd had an affair with an older woman during his university days. She'd been a mature student who liked being dominated in bed, teaching Ben all there was to know about such role playing. Ben had enjoyed playing lord and master to the hilt. He still did. Ben already had an idea in mind for tonight, an idea which he hoped Jess would go along with. He felt pretty sure that she would.

Damn, but it was going to an excruciatingly long evening!

Jess could not believe how long the evening proved to be. The photos had been tedious, as had the serving and eating of the three-course meal. It wasn't till coffee and cheeses were served that Ben finally stood up to make the best man speech.

He didn't look at all nervous. Which irritated her. Perhaps because it underlined how confident a person he was. Which was perverse. Hadn't she told him she liked confident men?

She actually didn't mind *liking* Ben. She would never have had sex with him if she hadn't liked him. She just didn't want to fall in love with him.

'Ladies and gentlemen,' Ben began. 'Firstly, let me thank you all for coming here today to celebrate Andy's marriage to Catherine who, might I say, is the most beautiful bride I have ever seen.'

Not just confident, Jess thought ruefully, but a silver-tongued charmer.

'For those who don't know me personally, you might be wondering what a chap with an American accent is doing as Andy's best man. Trust me when I say I might sound like a Yank, but if you scratch the surface you will find an Aussie through and through.'

Cheering from the guests.

'Andy and I go way back. He was my best friend all through boarding school and then through law school. He was always there for me. Always. And I love him. Sorry, Andy, I know you don't like mushy. Now, I know it is traditional to embarrass the groom by telling stories of things he got up to in his pre-wed life, but I have struggled to think of anything which Andy ever did which was stupid or reckless. Of course, I have been living in the US of A for the past ten years, so perhaps a few potential slip-ups have eluded me. I did hear a rumour that when he was in France he burnt the candle at both ends, so to speak.'

Laughter from the guests.

Ben smiled. 'But I do not believe a word of it. From what I saw last night at Andy's stag party, his candle is still in full working order.'

More laughter from the guests. And a horrified glance from the bride.

'Just kidding, Catherine. Andy's was the best behaved stag party I have ever attended. On a serious note, folks, believe me when I say that Andy is the most sensible, smartest man I have ever known. It's testimony to his brain power that he has chosen such a lovely girl as Catherine as his life partner. They are a well-matched couple who love each other dearly. Such love is a precious gift, one which should be treasured. And protected. And toasted. So, will you please all be upstanding and charge your glasses…'

Everyone obeyed, especially Jess, who had been moved by the last part of Ben's speech. Love was indeed precious, especially true love. Colin hadn't truly loved her. As for Ben… No point in going there!

'To Andy and Catherine,' Ben said loudly as he held up his own glass.

All the guests repeated his words as they clinked glasses and drank.

Jess did likewise, then sat back down, feeling suddenly drained. More speeches followed and, finally, Andy stood up to speak. He did not have Ben's gift of the gab, or the same smooth delivery, but what he said was sweet and touching. It actually brought tears to Jess's eyes, which she had to blink back swiftly when he proposed a toast to the bridesmaids, explaining how Jess had had to step in at the last moment and how grateful they were to her.

Jess sat there, her right hand fingering the lovely silver and diamond pendant Andy had given the bridesmaids earlier. Catherine had received a magnificent pair of diamond-drop earrings. When Jess had insisted to Catherine that they give her pendant to Krissie afterwards, Catherine had said no, she and Andy would buy Krissie something special for the baby when it came.

They really were a very nice couple. And, yes, very much in love. Jess couldn't help envying them their happiness. She was no longer pleased that Ben planned to stay in Australia a little longer. She knew the score. He wanted hot sex with her after which he would wing his way back to New York and forget she ever existed. And by then, she could very well be left behind with a broken heart.

Common sense demanded she have no more to do with Ben after this weekend was over. But common sense was no match for the sexual heat which had been charging through her veins ever since they'd signed the marriage certificate together. A few hot words whispered in her ear and she had almost combusted on the spot. Her still-erect nipples burned as they pressed against the satin lining of her dress, her belly tight with sexual tension. She couldn't wait for this reception to be over so she could be with Ben again. She could not wait!

But she *had* to wait, she accepted wretchedly. Dear God, but she was in over her head here with this man.

At last they moved along to the cake-cutting part. Soon would come the bridal waltz, after which the serious partying would begin. Though tempted, Jess decided not to drink too much, so there wouldn't be a problem with driving back to the cottage as soon as they could leave.

Which wouldn't be any time soon, Jess realised with some dismay. No way could the best man leave till the bride and groom had gone—only a couple of hours to go, but it seemed like an eternity.

'Care for a dance, ma'am?' asked a voice with a thick, southern accent.

Jess's head jerked around to find Ben standing behind her chair with a goofy smile on his face.

'They say a fella's best chance to get lucky at a wedding is with one of the bridesmaids,' he added, acting like some redneck out of the hills.

Jess had to smile. *He* obviously hadn't been sitting there, all churned up. This was all just fun and games to him!

'Well, I sure wouldn't want to disappoint a fella as handsome as you,' she returned saucily. There was no point in being a wet blanket. Though dancing with him was going to be sheer torture.

'Aw, shucks, ma'am,' Ben returned, twisting his hands

together in fake embarrassment. 'You shouldn't say things like that to a shy boy from Alabama.'

Jess laughed as she stood up. 'Now you sound like a character from one of those Doris Day, Rock Hudson movies.'

'Yeah, I know,' he said, dropping the fake southern accent as he steered her onto the dance floor. 'Those old movies have a way of drawing you in. I gather you like them too,' he added, and pulled her into his arms.

Jess melted into him and closed her eyes, savouring the feel of his body against hers whilst trying to contain her ever-increasing excitement.

'Mum does,' she said. 'I sometimes watch one with her. She likes happy endings.'

'And you? What kind of movies do you like?'

Oh, Lord, now he wanted to chat! She tried not to sigh. 'I guess something which is both entertainment and escape. I don't go to the movies to watch things that are too real. I can't stand stories about drug dealers or war or people who are mean and cruel.'

'You like reading?'

'I'm not as avid a reader as Mum. I spend a lot of my spare time sewing. But I do like a good thriller.'

'Romances?'

'One or two. I did read a certain erotic romance which swept the world by storm.'

'And did it give you a few delicious ideas?' he murmured against her ear.

She shivered as his lips made contact, his tongue tip dipping inside. But only for a split second.

She groaned softly when his head lifted, suppressing another groan when the other groomsman, Jay, tapped Ben on the shoulder and suggested they change partners.

Ben no more wanted to dance with Leanne than fly a

kite, but what could he do? He'd been brought up to be polite, to have proper manners. So he smiled and handed Jess over to Jay whilst he did his duty and danced with the very silly Leanne.

'So, how long have you known Jess?' was the first thing Leanne said, her voice as curious as her eyes.

'Not that long,' he replied, his own eyes drifting over to where Jay was holding Jess too darned close, in his opinion.

'She's very attractive, isn't she?' Leanne went on.

Ben agreed.

'Girls like that can get any man they want,' she said with an envious sounding sigh.

Ben thought of Colin doing a flit but didn't mention him.

Leanne fluttered her eyes up at him. 'It must be difficult for a really rich man like you to know if a girl likes him for himself or his money.'

Ben was astonished at the sly bitchiness behind Leanne's remark. 'I'm not that rich, Leanne.'

Leanne smiled a knowing smile. 'Maybe not now but you will be one day. I mean, your daddy's a billionaire, according to Catherine. Not that I think Jess is a gold-digger. She's a very sweet girl.'

'You're certainly right there,' Ben stated, thinking to himself that Leanne was a nasty piece of work. Of all the girls he'd ever been with, Jess was the *least* likely to be with him for his money. If anything, his wealth was a mark against him. Hadn't she said she would never marry a man as rich as he was?

It was a relief when Andy tapped him on the shoulder and handed him over to Catherine. Let *him* put up with Leanne's malicious prattle. He'd had enough of her for one night. Ben had to smile, however, when within less than a minute Andy whirled Leanne over to Jay and gave her back to him, happily dancing with Jess instead.

Which made Ben happy as well. He didn't mind Jess dancing with Andy. He certainly hadn't liked her dancing with Jay. Hadn't liked another man holding her that close and possibly trying to crack onto her.

Ben frowned as he realised just how possessive he was beginning to feel about Jess. It wasn't like him to be jealous. He'd always despised that kind of self-destructive emotion. But with Jess he just didn't have the control over his emotions that he usually had. He didn't have as much control over his body either.

It had been a battle to stop himself from having an erection all evening, finally losing the war when he'd taken her in his arms just now. Not that anything showed. His dinner jacket covered the evidence of his almost obsessive desire. But he could *feel* it, damn it. Not just in his flesh, but in his mind. Never had he wanted a woman as much as he wanted Jess. He could not wait to strip that infernal dress off her and do all the things he wanted to do to her.

# CHAPTER FIFTEEN

'THANK GOD THEY'RE GONE,' Ben muttered under his breath as Andy and Catherine drove off in their much-decorated car. The happy couple were spending their wedding night in a nearby, very swanky guest house, which was fortunate, given Andy had imbibed quite a lot of champagne. Ben hadn't touched a drop; he needed a clear head and an un-intoxicated body for the games he had in mind for Jess tonight. It possibly would be the last opportunity to indulge himself with her in such a fashion. He did have full access to his mother's apartment at Blue Bay tomorrow night—she didn't get back till Monday—but Jess might not be willing to stay the night with him there. It was obvious that she still lived at home and still had to answer to her parents. Her mother, anyway.

Meanwhile...

Jess spotted Ben standing at the edge of the throng of guests who'd gone outside to watch the bride and groom depart. He'd been in a distracted mood the last hour or so. Not talking much. Not drinking either. She'd kept her consumption to a minimum, but then she had to drive. He didn't.

When she came up to him, he was frowning.

'Why are you frowning like that?' she asked him. 'Is your shoulder aching?' She wouldn't put it past him to have lied to her about his arm. Men hated to admit to any weakness, especially physical ones.

'No,' he said, giving her an odd look. 'It's fine. And more than capable of giving you a good spanking when the time comes.'

Jess sucked in sharply. 'Spanking?' she repeated in shocked tones even as the picture of her being bent naked over his thighs zoomed into her mind.

She stared up at him, her whole head whirling as she tried to work out if the idea excited or repulsed her.

'I think you might enjoy the experience. But only if you want me to, Jess,' he continued in that soft, seductive voice he often adopted. 'I would never force you to do anything you didn't want to do.'

But that was the problem, wasn't it? Once he started on her, she wanted to do whatever he wanted to. Already she was wondering what it would feel like to be spanked.

Jess struggled to act cool when she was anything but. 'I...I'll think about it,' she said. And of course that was another problem. Thinking about doing sexual things with him invariably turned her on. She was already turned on. Had been all evening. Now, her body temperature and her desire metre were zooming off the charts.

'Come on,' he said brusquely. 'Let's get out of here.'

Jess hesitated. 'But shouldn't we say goodbye to people first?'

'Who do you have in mind? We'll see Glen and Heather in the morning before we leave. We can say goodbye to them then.'

'But we won't see the bride's parents in the morning. We should say goodbye to them. It's only polite.'

Ben grimaced. 'You can, if you like. I can't stand either of them. I'll wait here for you. Don't be long.'

She whirled away from him and raced back into the

marquee, taking less than five minutes to say the appropriate goodbyes and collect her bouquet. He was still looking impatient when she returned to his side.

'What took you so long?' he growled as he steered her in the direction of the main house and her parked SUV.

She could not contain a surge of exasperation, shrugging off his bruising hold and grinding to a halt. 'For pity's sake, Ben, what's got into you all of a sudden? You're acting like a jerk.'

He sighed. 'Sorry. Just impatient to be alone with you, that's all.'

'Oh.' Trust him to say the one thing guaranteed to defuse her anger.

'Do you have your keys with you?' he asked when they approached her vehicle.

'Yes, of course.'

'Good. Now, get in and drive.'

She got in, tossed her bouquet in the back, then drove, all conversation between them ceasing during the five minutes it took to negotiate the short trip back to the cottage. By the time she pulled up in front of the small porch, her stomach was churning and her heart was pounding behind her ribs.

Was she really going to let him spank her?

Oh, Lord, she thought, and let out a panicky rush of air.

Ben heard her ragged sigh and recognised the reason behind it.

'Don't be nervous,' he said gently.

'I am a bit. I've never been spanked before.'

'I gathered that. Have you ever been tied up before?'

Her eyes went like saucers. 'No. I…I thought they only did things like that in books and in brothels.'

'Lots of real people like to play erotic games. Which is all I'm suggesting. Nothing serious. I'm not into humiliation or pain. I just want to give you pleasure, Jess. You can say no at any stage to anything you don't like.'

'But…but I might not know that I don't like it till you've done it.'

'I see.' God, but she was delightful. And delicious. And he wanted her like crazy. 'I promise to take things slowly, then. Give you time to say no before things go too far.'

'Oh. All right.'

'Let's go.'

He took her into the bathroom first where he undressed her—slowly, as he'd promised. The sight of her fiercely erect nipples revealed that she was genuinely enjoying herself. So far. She gasped when he tweaked one of the pink peaks, then groaned when he did the same to the other one.

'Still a little tender?' he enquired as he quickly disposed of his own clothes.

'A little,' she confessed shakily.

'But not too tender,' he said, and she shook her head.

'Good. Here, I think I should take off that diamond pendant as well. We wouldn't want it to get broken, would we?'

Her head whirled whilst he undid the clasp, then placed the pendant on the vanity along with his expensive looking wrist-watch. He hadn't taken his watch off last night, she recalled. But then he hadn't spanked her last night.

*Oh, God.*

Her heartbeat went up another notch.

'We'll have a shower together first,' he said. 'But no touching from you, beautiful. You are *way* too good with your hands.'

Ben turned her back to him whilst he washed her, making her moan when he rubbed the soapy sponge back and forth between her legs, her peach-like buttocks clenching tightly together when he moved his attention to them. By the time he switched off the water and turned her to face him, he knew she was ready for him to do whatever he wanted. Her eyes were glazed over and her lips had fallen apart as she panted for breath.

Ben thought she had never looked more beautiful or more desirable. He almost decided to bypass the foreplay in favour of straightforward sex but he suspected Jess was by now looking forward to the experience. Ben could only hope that he would be able to control himself during what was usually a lengthy game.

He stepped out of the cubicle and reached for the two white towelling robes which were hanging on the back of the door. After putting one on, he handed the other robe to Jess.

'Put that on,' he ordered.

When she did so without question, he wanted her all the more.

'No, don't do it up,' he said, and reached for the sash, sliding it through the side loops before wrapping it around his left wrist.

He had to take her hand and lead her back to the bedroom. By the time they got to the side of the bed, she was trembling. But he felt certain it was no longer from nerves.

'You should be dry by now. So you won't be needing that robe.'

'But you've still got yours on,' she protested.

'That's the idea.'

When she hesitated, he bent and whispered in her ear. 'Yours is not to reason why, Jess. Yours is just to lie back on that bed and let me give you pleasure.'

His breathing quickened as she obediently took off the robe and lay down on the bed, her head on the pillows.

'No, not that way,' he said and she just stared at him, sucking in sharply when he turned her over onto her stomach.

'Just say no if you want me to stop,' he said.

She didn't say no, but she did bury her face in the pillow.

Gently, he took both her hands and placed them in the small of her back, then looped her wrists together with the sash from the robe. Not tightly, but enough so that she would feel bound and helpless. Which was the point, of course. That was what would excite her to fever pitch. Finally, he removed the pillow from under her face and slid it under her hips, raising her buttocks in the most erotic and inviting fashion.

When Ben stepped back to examine his handiwork, the sight of her like that took his breath away. Dear God, she was just so sexy looking. And totally at his mercy! It was a heady combination. And, whilst he was fiercely erect, all of a sudden Ben wasn't so concerned about his own satisfaction but how Jess was feeling. He hated to think she might be afraid to say no at this stage.

'Are you all right, Jess?' he asked softly. 'Do you want me to continue?'

# CHAPTER SIXTEEN

WAS HE INSANE? She would die if he didn't continue. She'd never been so excited in her whole life!

'I'm fine,' she said, her voice high-pitched and raspy. 'Please don't stop.'

He laughed a short, sexy laugh. 'Your wish is my command.'

Now *that* was a laugh, Jess thought. *He* was the one doing the commanding. But didn't she just love it!

*No touching from you, beautiful... Put that on... You won't be needing that robe.... Just lie back on that bed and let me give you pleasure...*

'It's just a game, Jess,' he said. 'You can stop me at any time. Okay?'

'Okay,' she mumbled.

The first crack of his hand on her right buttock brought a gasp of shock, rather than pain. Though it did sting. Jess buried her face into the quilt, determined not to cry out again. Another slap followed. Then another, his hand moving from left to right in a slow, relentless rhythm till both her buttocks were burning. And red, no doubt. Yet despite her discomfort—oh, yes, her whole bottom was stinging like mad—she didn't want to tell him to stop. There was something exquisitely pleasurable in the whole experience. She held her breath between slaps in anticipation of his large palm making contact with her soft skin, biting her bottom lip each time it happened. The slaps began coming at a slower interval now, her time of waiting extended till she almost pleaded for more. When he finally stopped altogether, she groaned in frustration.

'That's enough,' she heard him say.

But he didn't untie her. Instead, the bed dipped as he lay down beside her. She saw he was naked now when she twisted her head to look at him.

'So what did you think?' he asked her.

'I think,' she choked out, 'that if you don't have sex with me in the next ten seconds, then you're a dead man.'

He smiled. 'You're not really in a position to give orders right now, are you, darling Jess?'

'Ben,' she said pleadingly. 'Please.'

'If you insist.'

She couldn't believe it when he didn't untie her first, just spread her legs wide and moved around between them. She moaned when he rubbed his tip against her, her teeth digging into her lower lip to stop herself from screaming.

'So wet,' he muttered.

Ben was close to losing it. Time to get a condom on, he realised, before things got out of hand.

Thank God Andy had given him a good supply so he had one at the ready.

She cried out when he entered her, her bottom moving frantically against him with an urgency which betrayed a cruel level of frustration. He wasn't much better, grabbing her hips with bruising fingers and setting up a savage rhythm, forgetting everything but what his flesh was feeling at that moment. The heat. The urgent need. The madness of it all. Her stunningly violent climax only preceeded his by a second or two, Ben thrilling to the way she cried out as she came.

Jess lay there afterwards, stunned yet totally sated. A draining languor started seeping into her limbs, her eyelids growing heavier and heavier. Ben was lying across her back, his own breathing now slow and heavy. She desperately wanted to stay awake. But sleep would not be denied. It came quickly, with Jess's wrists still bound.

Ben fell asleep too, still slumped across her back.

He woke first, momentarily confused by where he was. And then he remembered. Everything.

He groaned as guilt consumed him. How could he possibly have left her that way? She didn't wake as he carefully withdrew, then even more carefully untied her. She stirred slightly when he slid the pillow out from under her hips, but she didn't wake, thank God, though she did curl herself up into a semi-foetal position. After throwing a sheet over her far too delicious derrière, he headed for the bathroom.

A quick shower later and he was back in the bedroom, standing at the side of the bed and staring down at her still body. Ben supposed he really had nothing to be guilty about; Jess had obviously enjoyed herself. Ben was never absolutely sure if his girlfriends went along with his demands because they were genuinely on the same sexual wavelength or because he was Morgan De Silva's son and heir. He definitely had no such doubts with Jess. Damn it, but he wished she lived in America.

Maybe he would ask her to go back with him. He could get her a job and lease her a nice little apartment. Or she could even move in with him.

Ben frowned at this last thought. His father had warned him never to do that: have a woman move in with him. Not unless they were married. As much as Jess claimed she would never marry a rich man, she hadn't seen his New York lifestyle. His thirty-square apartment overlooking Central Park had a lap pool on the roof plus a fully equipped gym and spa room. He had a wardrobe full of designer suits and hand-made shoes, a Ferrari in the underground car park and an expense account which allowed him to dine at all of New York's finest restaurants. He also had access to the company's private jet which flew him to Acapulco for weekends in the summer and Aspen in the winter.

That kind of lifestyle could corrupt even the nicest girl, especially if she'd never experienced such luxury. Which Jess obviously hadn't.

No, best not ask her to go back to America with him. Best he do what he'd originally intended: have a holiday fling with Jess, then leave it at that. It wasn't as though he was in love with her. He just liked and admired her a lot. And wanted her like mad. Already he had another erection, tempting him to climb back into bed and wake her. He didn't think she'd mind.

Ben sensibly armed himself with protection first, then climbed in under the sheet and curved his body around hers, spoon fashion. She stirred immediately, stiffening against him when he began to caress her breasts. Obviously they were still sensitive from all the attention he'd been giving them, so he moved lower, stroking her stomach, then her thighs.

'Yes please,' she choked out when he pressed himself against her still-wet sex.

A wave of tenderness engulfed Ben as he slid into her. God, but he'd never felt anything like this for a girl before. She was just so sweet, yet so sexy at the same time. A girl in a million.

He took his time, setting up a gentle rhythm, loving the sounds she made, loving the way she wriggled against him as her excitement grew. And, when he knew he was close to coming himself, he touched her in a way that would guarantee her release as well.

They came together, Ben startled as another wave of emotion hit him. Not just tenderness this time, but something deeper. Much deeper. He held her tightly in his arms afterwards and wondered if he was finally on the verge of falling in love.

# CHAPTER SEVENTEEN

Jess was woken by Ben shaking her shoulder again, plus the sound of her phone ringing.

'I was in the kitchen making coffee when it rang,' he explained as he handed it to her.

Jess tried to take the phone, sit up and cover her bare breasts at the same time, but failed.

What the heck? she thought despairingly. It wasn't anything he hadn't seen before. Yet, strangely, she felt shy in front of Ben all of a sudden. Jess supposed it wasn't every day that one woke to such memories. In a way, it didn't seem real. Had she really let him tie her up and spank her? Obviously she had, if her still-tender bottom was anything to go by.

'It's my mother,' she said, trying to look and sound cool. 'Would you mind?' She waved him away.

He smiled, turned and left the room. Thank God. The infernal man was stark naked. Obviously, he never suffered from shyness.

'Hello, Mum,' she said into the phone. 'It's a little early, isn't it? I've only just woken up. Can I tell you all about the wedding when I get home?'

'I guess so. But, before you go, I was also ringing to remind you that today is family barbecue day. I thought you might have forgotten.'

She had, actually. It was a once a month tradition where the family got together at her parents' place.

'I was thinking that you could ask Ben to come along. Your father and I would love to meet him.'

Meaning *she'd* like to see what he looked like. Her mother was a very intuitive woman and had probably picked up something from Jess's voice.

'I'll ask him, Mum,' she said. 'But I won't guarantee that he'll say yes. He might just want to get home after such a long drive.'

'I see. Well, how about you call me when you stop and tell me if Ben's coming or not?'

'Will do. Now, I must go, Mum.'

'Before you go, did the wedding go off all right yesterday? No other Murphy's Law disasters?'

'Everything was perfect, Mum,' she said. 'I'll ring you later. Bye.'

Rising, Jess dashed for the bathroom, where the sight of her pink bridesmaid dress draped over the bath reminded her of the submissive scenario Ben had insisted upon in there. That was where her loss of will-power had all started, of course. In that shower. By the time he'd turned off the water, she'd been so excited that he could have done anything to her and she would not have objected.

The speed with which he'd turned her into a submissive sex slave was quite shocking. So why wasn't she more shocked this morning? Maybe it was because underneath all that S&M role-playing Ben was a nice man. A decent man. She felt confident that he would never hurt her for real. Look at the way he'd made love to her later in the night, so gently and rather sweetly. She'd enjoyed that time even more than all the other times so far. And there'd been quite a few already, Jess thought ruefully. Ben couldn't seem to keep his hands off her. In more ways than one!

After a rather quick shower, Jess rubbed some of the body lotion she found in the vanity into her buttocks. They were still a little on the tender side, but nothing major. Once her teeth were cleaned and her hair up in a pony-tail, she hurried into the other bedroom where she took out some fresh clothes: a pair of three-quarter length white trousers and a navy-and-white striped top. Slipping white sandals onto her feet, she headed for the kitchen where Ben was thankfully now wearing the white bathrobe which had been on the bedroom floor earlier. He was sitting at the kitchen table with some toast and coffee in front of him.

'I think your mother's checking up on you,' he said.

'Possibly. It's hard to put anything past my mum.'

'Not for the want of your trying, though,' he said, smiling at her.

Lord, but he was devilishly attractive when he smiled like that, even with slightly bleary eyes and a stubbly chin.

'She wanted to know how the wedding went. And to invite you to our family barbecue tonight.'

His eyebrows lifted, then fell. 'Do *you* want me to go, Jess?'

She shrugged. 'I doubt you'll enjoy it much. Mum will give you the once-over, then Dad'll probably give you the third degree, if he thinks you're interested in me.'

'Which I am.'

It annoyed Jess, his saying that. Because he wasn't re-ally interested in her in that way. He just wanted to have more sex with her whilst he was here in Australia. Okay, so Ben was basically a good man, but he was also spoiled and selfish. It wasn't all his fault, of course. He'd been born beautiful and into great wealth: both very corrupting fac-tors. He'd probably developed his liking for kinky sex be-cause he'd had so much sex in his life he'd got bored with straightforward love-making. Which was a pity. Because he did straightforward love-making very well indeed.

Jess sighed. 'I honestly don't think you should go.'

'Why not?'

'For the reasons I just told you.'

'But I want to meet your parents.'

Jess rolled her eyes. 'For pity's sake, *why*?'

'Because I want to ask them to give you this week off so we can go to Sydney and work together on Fab Fashions. I thought we might stay down there instead of driving up and down the motorway every day. Mum has a flat in Bondi we could use.'

Jess didn't know what to say. She wanted to go, of course. Wanted the opportunity to do something about Fab Fashions. And, yes, she wanted to spend more time alone with Ben, especially some more of his very exciting brand of sex. She'd be lying if she didn't admit that, especially to herself. But at the back of her mind, in that place reserved for difficult decisions, she knew if she did this, then she was sure to become even more emotionally involved with him.

'I…I don't know, Ben,' she said hesitantly, turning away to make herself some coffee. 'Like you said, there's probably no fixing Fab Fashions. We'd just be wasting our time.'

'I don't agree. We'll have that chat on the drive home and come up with a new name, one which will lend itself to a successful marketing strategy. Because you're right, Jess. Companies like ours shouldn't just bail out when things get tough. We can afford to ride some losses for a while, especially when the alternative means that people will lose their jobs.'

Jess wanted to believe he meant it. But she didn't. Companies like De Silva & Associates were all about making profits. They didn't give a damn about the little people. Which was what she was. One of the little people.

Jess finished making her coffee, then carried it over to the table. 'I'm sorry, Ben,' she said, pulling out a chair and sitting down, 'but I'd rather not. I'm a mechanic, not some marketing expert.'

'So you're giving up on Fab Fashions?'

'I've told you what's wrong with the business. You're an intelligent man. I'll put my thinking cap on during the drive back and come up with a name which might suit. Then it's up to you to do something with it.'

He looked at her long and hard, then shrugged. 'Okay. If that's the way you want it.'

What she wanted at that moment was never to have met Ben De Silva.

'I still wouldn't mind coming to that barbecue, Jess.'

'No, Ben. I'd rather you didn't.'

He frowned at her. 'Why is that?'

'I don't want my parents knowing what we've been up to this weekend. And they will. Mum will take one look at us together and she'll know.'

'We're consenting adults, Jess. Our having sex isn't a crime.'

'No, but it's very unlike me, Ben, to hop into bed so quickly. Mum's sure to jump to the wrong conclusion.'

'Which is?

'That I've fallen madly in love.'

Again, she was on the end of another long, thoughtful look.

'I take it that hasn't happened?'

'You know it hasn't. We've been having a dirty weekend, Ben. That's all.' It went against her grain to describe their weekend in such a crude fashion, but it was the truth after all.

'I don't see it that way, Jess. I like you. A lot. And I want to see more of you.'

'You mean you want to have more kinky sex with me whilst you're in Australia.'

He pursed his lips in obvious annoyance. 'You make it all sound so tacky. Yes, of course I want to have more sex with you, but not just kinky sex. I enjoy making love to you in more traditional ways as well. I also want to spend time with you out of bed.'

Jess's laugh was a little bitter. 'Yes, I noticed you like having sex out of bed too.'

His blue eyes flashed with frustration. 'Very funny. Just remember, you're the one who knocked back my offer of our working together on Fab Fashions.'

'I can live with that. I can't live with you taking me for a fool.'

He sat bolt upright in his chair, his face furious. 'I would never do that. I think you're one of the smartest girls I've ever met. And the most stubborn. I suppose if I asked you to go back to New York with me, you'd say no to that as well!'

Jess could not have been more taken aback. Or more speechless.

'Well?' he snapped when she said nothing. 'What *would* you say to such an offer?'

Jess gathered in a deep breath, then let it out slowly. 'I would say thank you very much, Ben, but no thank you. My life is here, in Australia. I wouldn't be happy in New York.'

'How do you know?'

'I just know.'

His eyes carried exasperation. 'Most girls would jump at the chance. For Pete's sake, Jess, you wouldn't have to pay for a thing. You could stay in my apartment and have the holiday of a lifetime.'

The word 'holiday' reaffirmed what Jess already knew. He wasn't seriously interested in her. Not the way she would have liked. But then, that was never going to happen. He'd already said he didn't want to get married. She was just a passing amusement, one which he hadn't grown bored with yet.

'Couldn't we just leave things the way they are, Ben? I'm happy to go out with you whilst you're staying up on the coast. I like you a lot, but I don't want to go to America with you.'

Ben should have been relieved, he supposed, that she hadn't jumped at his somewhat impulsive offer. But he wasn't. He was bitterly disappointed. He'd wanted to show her New York, wanted to give her the time of her life.

'Fine,' he bit out.

'Please don't think me ungrateful, Ben,' she went on, her eyes softening on him. 'It was a very generous offer. But it's best I stay here in Australia.'

He sighed, then smiled at her. 'So we're still on for dinner tomorrow night?'

Jess smiled back at him. 'Of course. Where are you going to take me?'

'I have no idea. I'll ask Mum when she gets back tomorrow. She knows all the best local restaurants. But you'll have to pick me up. I'm not allowed to drive till I get that stupid medical clearance. Hopefully by Tuesday that'll be done and I can drive Mum's car.'

'So your mother will be there when I pick you up?' she said, sounding a bit panicky.

'Yes, but you don't have to worry. Mum's really quite nice, despite everything.'

'What do you mean by that?'

'I'll explain on the drive back,' he said, thinking he shouldn't have made such a leading comment. But it was too late now. Besides, it would give them something to talk about. Telling Jess all about his mother's exploits over the years would take some time. 'I'll go shower and shave whilst you have breakfast. Then we should get going.'

# CHAPTER EIGHTEEN

By THE TIME they stopped at Sandy Hollow for lunch, Jess had a much better understanding of why Ben wasn't interested in marriage. To find out that your mother had married your father for his money must have come as a bitter blow. Still, it had been good of his father not to say anything till Ben had turned twenty-one. That way, Ben had been able to grow up loving his mother who, though materialistic, had obviously been a good mother to him.

Despite that, Jess could just imagine how Ben had felt when his mother had admitted she'd trapped his father into marriage with a pregnancy and had never loved him. His money was what she'd loved. Yes, there were reasons for her materialism, but the bottom line was still not very nice. Her actions certainly wouldn't have engendered faith in her son's own relationships with the opposite sex. Given he would one day be as rich as his father, Ben would always be on the lookout for signs that his girlfriends were gold-diggers. Which was an awful way to have to live.

But it did also explain why Ben concentrated on sex when he was with a girl he liked. Sex was safe, especially the kind of sex he indulged in. Such goings-on kept his girlfriends at a distance, both physically and emotionally. Jess realised that the only time he'd had sex face to face with her had been when she'd been on top. But even then he'd adopted the role of voyeur rather than that of a loving partner.

'Neither of your parents have married again,' she remarked once they sat down to another pub lunch. Different pub but similar food. A steak sandwich and salad. 'Why is that, do you think?'

Ben shrugged. 'Mum always said she would marry again if she ever fell in love. But that's unlikely to happen, given the type of man she usually dates—all young, handsome studs without much between their ears. Mum does like intelligence when she's out of bed.'

Jess tried not to look shocked at his talking about his mother's sex life in that fashion.

'But who knows? This fellow she's gone on the cruise with seems a different kettle of fish. Not so young and he actually works. I'll find out more when she gets home tomorrow. As far as Dad is concerned… This might sound silly but I think Mum was the only woman Dad ever truly loved. Though don't get me wrong. He was unfaithful to her during their marriage. Had several mistresses going at once, apparently. He still has women running after him, despite being sixty-five and not the best-looking man in the world. Money is a powerful aphrodisiac,' he added drily.

Jess sighed. 'I can understand now why you don't want to get married.'

'What?' Ben said, almost knocking his drink over. 'I never said I didn't want to get married.'

Jess frowned. 'But you did. When I asked you why you broke up with Amber you said she wanted marriage and you didn't.'

'Not with *her* I don't. I don't love her. That doesn't mean I wouldn't consider it with anyone else at some stage.'

'Oh,' Jess said, startled by this turn of events. Not that

it changed anything. Ben might want marriage at some stage, but it wouldn't be to an ordinary girl like her.

Ben stared across the table at Jess and wondered if that was why she'd refused to come to New York with him. Because she wanted marriage and she thought he didn't. Not that he was about to propose. He did, however, feel more strongly about Jess than any girl he'd ever met.

He decided then and there that he would ask her to come to New York with him again later in the week. Meanwhile, he'd show her the time of her life every night. And, yes, behind the scenes he'd even do something about that damned Fab Fashions.

'Are you absolutely sure you don't want me to come to your family barbecue?' he asked coolly before picking up his steak sandwich and taking a big bite.

She was tempted. He could see she was tempted.

'I promise to be on my best behaviour,' he added once his mouth was temporarily empty.

She laughed. 'It's not you I'm worried about. It's my mother.'

Ben didn't give a damn if her mother realised they were sleeping together. Mothers had never been a problem to him. They usually liked him a lot. 'I can handle your mother,' he said.

Lord, but he was an arrogant devil. But she did so like him. And she wanted him like mad. Already she was regretting not going to New York with him, even if it *was* only for a holiday. Still, she suspected Ben hadn't totally given up on that idea. Jess wondered what she would say if he asked her again.

Hopefully, she would have the courage—and the common sense—still to say no. But, dear Lord, she did have a lot of trouble saying no to him.

'I'm coming to that barbecue,' he announced firmly,

'And that's final. Now, about that new name for Fab Fashions; I've given it some thought. What do you think of Real Women? It would lend itself to a good advertising campaign. Clothes for real women, et cetera, et cetera.'

The take-over man in action again, Jess thought. Telling her he was coming, then changing the subject.

She had to smile. He was clever all right.

'I think it's a great name,' she said. 'I love it.'

He beamed across the table at her. '*Finally* she agrees with something I've suggested!'

'I can be agreeable,' she said. 'When it's a sensible suggestion.'

'Coming to New York with me is just as sensible.'

'Ben,' she said with a warning look. 'Just leave it, will you?'

'Okay. I will. For now. But I make no promise to do so indefinitely.'

They both fell to eating their meals, Jess doing her best to stop thinking about her potentially dangerous feelings for Ben. Once again she wished she could be like other girls. Most would jump at the chance of going to New York with him, even if it didn't lead to anything permanent.

But maybe it would; she started hoping as she ate. How would she know unless she agreed? She'd gone to bed with Ben initially because she knew she'd regret it if she didn't. Maybe she'd regret not going to New York with him and not giving their relationship a chance.

But it *wasn't* a relationship, her more pragmatic side argued. It was just a fling, or an affair, for want of a better word. Ben had never said he loved her. Not that he would. It was way too early for a man of his natural wariness to make such a declaration. She certainly wasn't about to tell him she was close to falling for him either. That would only give him power over her. He had enough of that already.

No, she wouldn't be foolish enough to admit that. But she would think about going to New York with him and, when he asked her again, she probably would say yes.

'That steak was quite good,' Ben said, wiping his mouth with a paper serviette.

'My dad cooks much better steak on the barbecue,' Jess told him. 'And Mum's salads are way better.'

'In that case, I'm in for a treat later today.'

'Just don't let my brothers give you too much beer.'

'Why? You're worried I might not be able to perform when you take me home?'

'What? No, of course not! Ben De Silva, haven't you had enough sex for one weekend?'

'There's no such thing as too much sex.'

'There is if it involves getting your bottom spanked,' she whispered so that the people at the next table couldn't hear.

He frowned. 'Sorry. I did get a little carried away last night. In that case, you can have today off.'

She tried to be annoyed with him but she simply couldn't. Instead, she smiled. A slightly wry smile, but still a smile. 'One day, some woman is going to tell you where to go, Ben De Silva.'

He nodded. 'You could be right there. And I have a feeling she's sitting across the table from me.'

*I wish*, Jess thought. But she just laughed, then finished off her coffee. Ten minutes later, they were back on the road and heading for home, turning off the motorway just after three-thirty.

# CHAPTER NINETEEN

JESS'S HOME WAS bigger than Ben had expected, a two-storeyed, family-sized house in blond brick, with the biggest shed that Ben had ever seen sitting in a nearby paddock. A workshop, obviously, plus garaging for the hire cars. Two of the three massive roller doors were open and Ben could glimpse several cars within. The land around the house was bigger than he'd expected too, at least five acres. It was a lovely looking property with well-tended gardens, rolling lawns and enough trees to give privacy and shade.

Jess drove her SUV off the driveway onto a large square of gravel by the side of the house, the clock on her dash showing five to four as Ben climbed out. Jess had explained on the way that the barbecue wouldn't start till five-ish, so they had some time before her brothers and their families descended upon them.

'What a lovely place,' he said straight away.

Jess smiled. 'We like it. Mum will be in the kitchen, preparing the salads. You can meet her first. This way...'

'I presume that's the office,' he said as he walked past a converted double garage which had sliding glass doors at the front with 'Murphy's Hire Car' in big, black letters engraved on it.

'Yes,' she said. 'That's mostly Mum's domain. I help out when Mum's shopping or plays bowls or just needs a break. Mum, we're here,' Jess called out as she opened the front door.

A woman appeared at the end of the hallway, light behind her forming the silhouette of someone much shorter than Jess, and somewhat plumper.

'Goodness, but you made good time. I didn't expect you till four-thirty at least.'

When she came forward, Ben saw her more clearly. She looked nothing like Jess, being short, with ash-blonde hair and blue eyes. Attractive for her age, though.

'Hello, there,' she said, smiling as she looked him up and down. 'You must be Ben.'

'And you must be Mrs Murphy,' he replied, stepping forward to give her a kiss on the cheek. 'Lovely to meet you.'

Jess could not believe the look on her mother's face. It was the kind of look you saw on the face of a female fan of a rock star. Truly!

'Oh, don't call me that.' Her mother fairly simpered at him. 'Call me Ruth.'

Jess gained some satisfaction in the thought that he wouldn't charm her father so easily. Joe Murphy was a tough nut to crack. He wasn't going to be impressed by a New Yorker who'd never had dirt under his fingernails in his life.

'In that case, Ruth,' Ben said, flashing those brilliant white teeth of his, 'would you kindly point me to the nearest bathroom?'

Her mother didn't point. She escorted Ben herself to the small powder room next to the family room, leaving Jess standing there in the hallway like some shag on a rock.

Jess sighed, then trudged upstairs to use the toilet in the main bathroom. By the time she made it downstairs, Ben was ensconced on one of the kitchen stools, chatting away happily to her mother whilst she worked on the various salads.

'That's a terrific new name Ben's come up with for Fab Fashions, isn't it?' she directed at Jess as she joined them.

'Fantastic,' Jess agreed, at which Ben slanted her a narrow-eyed glance. Had he heard the slight sarcasm in her voice?

'You might get your job back there soon,' Ruth rattled on.

'You never know, Mum. I presume Dad's in the shed working on that blue Cadillac?'

'Yes, the seats finally came yesterday. He's been working on them all day.'

'I think I should take Ben out to meet Dad before the others get here, don't you?'

'Oh, but I just put the kettle on for a cup of tea. Ben says he likes tea more than coffee. Same as me.'

'We won't be long, Mum,' she said, then gave Ben a look which brooked no protest.

He slid off the stool and followed her back down the hallway and out of the front door.

'You *are* bossy and controlling,' he said as she marched in the direction of the shed with him in her wake.

'And you're a serial charmer,' she snapped.

He laughed. 'Better than being a serial killer.'

'I suggest you curtail that silver tongue of yours with my sisters-in-law. The Murphy men are known to be extremely jealous.'

'What about the Murphy women?' he threw at her.

'Them too. So watch yourself.'

'I like your being jealous.'

'Of course you do. It suits your male ego, which is insufferably large.'

'So will something else be if you keep that up. I get turned on by feisty women.'

She gave up at that point, throwing her hands up in the air in defeat.

She was glad that her father chose that moment to walk out of the shed, wiping his hands on a towel as he did so.

'I thought I heard someone,' he said, coming forward. 'You must be Ben,' he said, and held out his hand.

Ben shook it, thinking that this was where Jess got her striking looks. Joe Murphy was one handsome fellow, with thick black hair sprinkled liberally with grey and the deepest, darkest brown eyes, which at that moment were surveying him with considerable thoughtfulness.

'So, how did your weekend go?' he asked Ben, not Jess. 'The wedding go off okay in the end?'

'It was close to perfect,' Ben said. 'Jess here was marvellous, the way she stepped in. You heard about what happened, did you?'

'Oh yes, Ruth told me all about it. Look, I just have to finish a job here and I'll be over to clean up and get the barbecue ready. You ever cook on a barbecue, Ben?'

'Lots of times,' he said. 'I was brought up here in Australia.'

'No kidding; I didn't know that. So that's how your best friend turned out to be Australian.'

'Yep,' Ben said, sounding more Ocker by the minute. 'We went to school together in Sydney.'

'Fancy that.'

'So, what's this job you're doing, Mr Murphy? Can I help?'

'I doubt it. I'm just putting some new seats into an old Cadillac convertible I bought. The kids like to hire cars like that for their graduation night.'

'My dad collected vintage cars at one stage. Which model Cadillac is it?'

Jess could not believe it when they went off together, talking cars. Spluttering, she whirled and stormed back to the house, only just managing to have her exasperation under control by the time she reached the kitchen.

'Where's Ben?' her mother asked straight away.

'Helping Dad with the Cadillac, would you believe? I'll have tea, though, if you're making it.'

'Can you get it yourself, dear? I really need to go spruce myself up a bit. I can't wear this old thing when we have a guest like Ben.'

'He's just a man, Mum, not some movie star.'

'Well, he looks like a movie star. I know you said he was handsome, Jess, but he's beyond handsome, with that smile and those eyes. I've never met a man quite like him. I dare say you haven't either. He makes Colin look very ordinary. And I thought *he* was good-looking.'

When Jess sighed, her mother gave her a sharp look.

'Did something happen with Ben over the weekend that I should know about?'

Jess kept a straight face with difficulty. 'Like what?'

'You know what, girlie.'

'I think, Mum, that my sex life is my private business, don't you?'

Her mother looked at her for a long moment before smiling an understanding smile. 'Of course it is. You're a grown woman. But let me just say that I don't blame you, love. If I were thirty years younger I would have done exactly the same thing.'

Jess stared after her mother as she walked off. She'd been expecting the third degree, or disapproval, or something! She certainly hadn't expected her mother's reaction to Ben to be so blindly approving. Couldn't she see that her daughter's leaping into bed with such a man was fraught with danger to her happiness? She should have been warning her off him, not saying she would have done exactly the same thing!

Jess sighed. The man was a devil all right. With way too much sex appeal. And way too much charm. Even her father liked him. No doubt her whole family would fall under his spell in no time flat.

Still, if they did, she would at least be able to relax a bit and enjoy the barbecue instead of being on tenterhooks all the time. This last weekend might have been exciting but it hadn't exactly been relaxing!

# CHAPTER TWENTY

BEN WAS HELPING Joe with the barbecue when Jess joined them, a huge black-and-white cat in her arms.

'You haven't been plying Ben with too much beer, have you, Dad?' Jess said in a teasing but loving voice which Ben could never imagine using with his own father. Or his mother, for that matter. He'd thought he had a good relationship with both his parents but seeing Jess interacting with her parents was a real eye-opener.

So was her interaction with the rest of her family. She was so warm with them, caring and considerate, asking after their well-being when they arrived with real interest, not just giving lip-service. He could see how much they loved her back as well. The children had flocked around her, vying for her attention. Even the damned cat loved her, yet he'd been warned by Joe not to touch Lazarus, as he was known to scratch. When he'd commented on the cat's name, he'd been told that Lazarus had been stillborn but Jess had resurrected him with the kiss of life.

Ben didn't doubt it. She was a girl of many talents, and a wealth of stubbornness. He still could not believe she'd refused to come to New York with him. But he had no intention of giving up on that score.

'The boys want Ben to go play cricket with them and the kids,' Jess said. 'I'll take over for him here,' she offered before dropping the cat gently onto the paved pergola which stretched across the back of the Murphy house.

'Can you play cricket?' Joe asked as Jess took the fork Ben had been using to turn the steak and sausages. 'I gather it's not a popular sport in America.'

Ben grinned. Could he play cricket or what? He'd been captain of his school's A-grade cricket team. But best not mention that. That would be bragging.

'Don't forget, Joe,' he replied, still smiling. 'I went to an *Australian* school. A *boy's* boarding school, where sport was compulsory. We played footie in winter and cricket in summer.'

'Right. Off you go, then. Just don't go hitting the ball into that thick bush over there. Can't count the number we've lost in there over the years.'

Ben resolved to peg back his batting ability a bit. No need to be a smart Alec.

Jess watched Ben stride off, a wry smile on her face. If she knew Ben, he would be anything but an ordinary cricket player. He wasn't ordinary at anything he did. He was an exceptional man, with exceptional abilities and exceptional social skills.

She was still amazed at how he instinctively knew what to talk about with every member of her family. He talked cars with her father, sport with her brothers and the advances in technology with her very smart sisters-in-law. He didn't mention his wealth when he was introduced, or sit back and play the role of honoured guest. He was happy to help with the food and very happy to drink beer. She imagined that over in New York his social life was very different. He'd go to fancy restaurants and fancy parties where they'd eat caviar and drink the most expensive champagne.

Jess frowned at this last thought. She would be uncomfortable with that kind of life. It was shallow, in her opinion. And snobbish. And way out of her league. She was a simple girl at heart with simple wants, like love, marriage and a family. She wasn't cut out for the high life.

Such thoughts renewed her resolve not to go to New York with him, if and when he asked her again. Jess suspected she would not enjoy the experience. The sex part, yes. And possibly some of the sightseeing. New York was a fabulous city, she was sure. But she shrank from the idea of meeting any of Ben's American friends or ex-girlfriends; shrank from being looked down upon by the type of people he mixed with.

The barbecue finished early, as the younger children got tired and the older ones had to go to school the next day. Ben seemed reluctant to leave, however, staying to help clear up and to have a final beer with her father. It was after ten before Jess could drag him away.

'You have a wonderful family, Jess,' was the first thing he said on the way back to Blue Bay. 'You're very lucky.'

'Yes, I am,' she agreed. 'By the way, my mother knows about us.'

His head jerked her way. 'You *told* her?'

'No, she guessed. Like I said, she's very intuitive.'

'How much does she know?'

'No details. Just that we've had sex.'

'That's good, then. She won't worry if you get home late.'

'She'll still worry. That's a mother's job. Frankly, I was surprised at how calm she was over my sleeping with you.'

'That's because she knows I'm one of the good guys.'

'Hmm. I doubt that's the reason. Now, I'm not coming

inside with you tonight, Ben,' she went on firmly, determined not to weaken and be seduced by him. Again. 'I'm
dropping you off and going straight home.'

'Fair enough.'

She blinked her surprise at his easy acceptance of her
stance. Maybe he was tired. Yes, that was probably it. He'd
had a very tiring weekend.

In no time she was pulling into the kerb. She did get
out to open the boot and, yes, she let him give her a kiss
goodnight after he'd placed all his things on the pavement.
Not too long a kiss, as it turned out, both their heads lifting when his phone rang. Frowning, Ben rifled the phone
out of his pocket and stared at the ID.

'Damn,' he said. 'It's Amber.'

'Aren't you going to answer it?' Jess asked, trying not
to sound as sick as she was suddenly feeling.

'I might as well,' Ben said. 'She has to know sooner or
later that it's over between us.'

He put the phone to his ear. 'Hello, Amber. I thought
you said we weren't to contact each other till I got back.'

Jess just stood there, listening to a one-sided conversation, her stomach tight with tension.

'What?' he suddenly snapped. 'Say that again?'

Jess watched as Ben suddenly lost all his normal glow,
his face going a ghastly ashen colour. Whatever Amber
was telling him had to be dreadful.

'No, no,' he choked out. 'I'll come home straight away.
Tell the funeral home to delay things till I can be there to
make the arrangements.'

Jess's heart sank. She could think of only one person's
funeral which would make Ben look this way. His father
must have died. Oh, dear God, poor Ben...

'No, I don't want you to help,' he was saying, his voice
under control again. 'No, Amber, I don't want to marry you

either. I'm sorry but I've met someone else... Yes, an Australian girl... Yes, yes, I do,' he said and looked a startled Jess straight in the eye. 'I'll be bringing her back with me.'

Jess's mouth fell open. It was still open when Ben put his phone back in his pocket.

'Please don't say no, Jess. My father died of a massive coronary last night. I can't bury him alone,' he said brokenly.

Jess's heart turned over at the raw grief in his face. Even if she had decided not to go to New York with him if he asked again, she would say yes to this. How could she turn her back on the man she loved when he was at his most vulnerable? Because, of course she loved him. She couldn't deny it any longer. Not to herself, anyway.

'Yes, of course I'll come with you,' she said gently.

'Thank you. I don't know what I would have done if you'd said no. I need someone I care about by my side, Jess. If you're there, I'll make it through.'

Jess's breath caught at his words. 'You really care about me, Ben?'

'Yes, of course I do. You care about me too, don't you? I refuse to believe you're just with me for the sex.'

'Of course I'm not!' she blurted out, shocked that he would think such a thing.

He sighed a deep sigh. 'That's a relief. Let's go inside and start making plans.'

His mother's apartment was as she'd imagined it to be. Very spacious and modern with large windows, polished wooden floors and Italian leather furniture.

'I'll get onto the airline,' Ben said, 'whilst you ring your parents. You do have a current passport, don't you?' he added sharply.

'Yes,' she answered.

'Good. I'll make my calls from the kitchen. You stay here.'

Her mother answered on the second ring, her voice anxious.

'What is it, Jess? Have you had an accident?'

'No, Mum,' she said, then launched into an explanation of events.

'And you're going to go back to New York with him?' her mother said, sounding shocked.

'Yes, Mum.'

'When?'

'As soon as possible. Ben's on to the airline now.'

'But you hardly know the man, Jess.'

'I know him better than I ever knew Colin.'

'You love him, don't you?'

'Yes, Mum. I do.'

'Does he love you back?'

'I'm not sure.'

'You do realise that with his father dying he'll be a very rich man.'

'Yes, Mum. I'm not stupid.'

'But…'

'We'll talk more when I get home, Mum,' she said as Ben walked back into the room. 'Gotta go.'

'Well?' she asked Ben straight away.

'Our flight leaves first thing in the morning. We'll have to leave here around four to be there on time. But we can sleep on the plane. We're flying first class.'

First class, Jess thought with less enthusiasm than most girls would have had. She'd never flown first class before. But that was what Ben probably did every time.

'What clothes will I need?' she asked, trying to be practical in the face of her mounting concern.

'Something black for the funeral, I guess. It's cool in New York so make sure you have a jacket. Other than that, just trousers and tops and a dress for going out at night. I can buy you anything else you might need.'

Jess conceded that he could certainly afford to buy her anything she needed, now that he was a billionaire. But she didn't want him to do that. She didn't like him thinking he could buy her as well if he wanted to.

Just what was she supposed to be by his side? Girlfriend or mistress?

She doubted he had fiancée in mind. But who knew? Love did make one hope.

'How long will you want me to stay?' she asked, doing her best to sound nonchalant.

For ever, Ben thought. But he knew it was too soon to say that. Too soon to tell her that he loved her. He wished now he hadn't said as much to Amber. She was sure to be at the wake and she might say something.

Well, too bad if she did. It was the truth.

'As long as you like,' he answered. 'It's up to you.'

# CHAPTER TWENTY-ONE

THEY BOTH MANAGED to sleep on the very long flight to
New York, which was just as well, because as soon as
they landed and were allowed to use their mobile phones
again it was all systems go. Ben didn't stop making phone
calls during the rather long, slow drive from the airport
to wherever his apartment was located. Jess did send her
mother a text saying they had arrived safely but her attention was more on her surrounds. She had never seen so
many tall buildings, so many people or such thick traffic.
Sydney was small compared to New York. She stopped
herself just in time from gushing when she spotted the
Empire State Building. She wasn't there as a goggle-eyed
tourist but as Ben's support system during this very difficult time for him.

Jess remained discreetly silent in the taxi. Though, they
weren't called taxis here, were they? They were called
cabs. When they finally pulled up outside a swish looking
apartment building, she did her best not to do or say anything gauche which would embarrass Ben. But she was seriously impressed, both by the uniformed porter who took
care of their luggage, and the doorman who said hello to
Ben in a very deferential manner. Inside, the lobby was
just as impressive, with marble floors and a huge, fresh
flower arrangement sitting on a circular table underneath

a massive chandelier. The security guard behind the desk in the corner nodded to Ben as he steered Jess over to the bank of lifts against a side wall.

'Everything's arranged,' Ben said briskly once the lifts doors closed and they were alone. 'The funeral will be at two tomorrow afternoon with the wake afterwards at Dad's apartment. My apartment's not large enough to cater for so many people.'

*Not large enough?* Jess thought in amazement when she walked into his apartment. The main living room was ginormous with ten-foot ceilings and tall French doors which opened out onto a very large balcony. All the walls were white, which only added to the feeling of space. On them hung some of the loveliest paintings Jess had ever seen. She hardly knew which one to look at first. Or where to look at all. The furniture was obviously very expensive, an eclectic mix of modern and antique.

'Goodness, Ben,' she said. 'How many people are you expecting at the wake if this place isn't big enough to house them?'

'Two hundred, at least,' he replied. 'Dad had a lot of business colleagues.'

'What about friends and relatives?'

'Not too many of those. Dad was an only child and his parents are long gone. So are his aunts and uncles. He possibly has a few cousins somewhere but he never kept in touch with them.' Ben gave a crooked smile. 'There might be the odd mistress or two attending, wondering if he's left them anything. But I fear they'll be disappointed. Dad told me not long ago that he left everything to me.'

Ben watched Jess's eyes when he said this, wondering if his being a billionaire would make any difference to her. Quite frankly, he didn't care if it did. He loved her and he had every intention of marrying her. He understood now how his father had felt when he'd proposed to his mother. Love did have a blinding effect on one.

But Jess was nothing like his mother. Ben felt sure of that.

'Amber might be there,' he said, feeling that he should warn Jess in advance. 'Her father was a close business associate.'

'That's okay,' she said. Though it wasn't. Not really. Jess supposed there was a small part of her which was curious to meet this Amber. But she could have managed well without the experience.

The doorbell rang. It was the porter delivering their luggage.

'Leave it just inside,' Ben directed, getting out his wallet and handing the man a note.

'I'd forgotten you have to tip everyone here,' Jess said after the porter had left. What a different country America was from Australia.

'You'd better believe it,' Ben said. 'No tip, no service.'

She didn't much like that, but didn't say anything.

'Will you be staying with me in the master bedroom?' he asked her. 'Or do you want one of the guest rooms?'

'Where do you want me to stay?' she returned, suddenly feeling nervous. Realising that she loved him seemed temporarily to have banished any desire for the exciting love-making they'd shared. Now, she just wanted him to hold her in his arms and make love to her like they were normal people.

'With me, of course.'

'Okay. As long as you don't...you know...'

His eyes clouded over. 'You needn't worry. I'm not in the mood for fun and games at the moment, Jess.'

'No, no, of course not. I just...' She stopped, then let out a long sigh. 'I'm sorry. That was insensitive of me. Of course you don't want to do things like that at the moment. I know exactly how you must be feeling. When my grandmother died last year, it felt like someone had taken a huge jagged spoon and scraped a great big hole out of my heart. I'm sure that's how you're feeling at this moment. Maybe even worse. He was your father.'

He looked at her with such sad eyes. 'I think he knew something was wrong with him. They say sometimes people have a premonition of their death from a heart attack, even when there are no actual symptoms.'

'Yes, I've heard that's true,' Jess said.

'He rang me, you know. On the night before we drove out to Mudgee. It wasn't like him to ring unless it was to discuss business. But he just chatted away. And then, right before he hung up, he said, "give my regards to your mother". I thought that was a bit odd at the time. Now I think it was because he knew he was going to die and he wanted to put all that old bitterness behind him.'

Ben gave an unhappy sigh. 'I did send Mum a text in the taxi about Dad dying and she answered me; said how sad it was for me but not to expect her to fly over for the funeral. I knew she wouldn't come, that's why I went ahead with the arrangements for tomorrow. She believed Dad hated her. But she's wrong about that. I think he actually loved her.'

'Yes. Of course he did,' was all Jess could think of to say.

Just when Ben looked as though he was going to burst into tears, he dragged in another deep breath, then straightened his spine.

'Dad would expect me to be strong,' he said.

Jess wanted to tell him that tears didn't make a man weak but she knew it would have been a waste of time.

Her father had never cried in front of her, neither had her brothers. It was just the way lots of men were.

'I'll put these in the bedroom,' he said as he picked up their bags and headed down a hallway.

Jess followed him with a heavy heart.

The master bedroom was magnificent, of course. Lavishly furnished with a king-sized bed and everything anyone could possibly want, including a huge flat-screen TV built into the wall opposite the bed. Ben opened the door of a walk-in dressing room which proved bigger than her bedroom back home. She tried not to gape as she hung up her outfit for the funeral, but the extent of Ben's wardrobe was mind-boggling. How could one man wear so many suits?

She unpacked the rest of her things silently, thankful that she'd thought to bring her newest and best nightie. To wear something cheap in this place wouldn't seem right. It was made of white satin, adorned with white lace. The colour would even match the room, which was mainly white and grey, not a single piece of dark wood in sight.

'I dare say you'd like to freshen up after that very long flight,' Ben said. 'And no, I won't be joining you in the shower, so you don't have to worry. I also don't want to go out to dinner tonight. I'll order something in for us. Will Chinese do, or would you prefer something else?'

'No, no. I love Chinese food,' she said.

'Good. Take your time in the bathroom. Have a bath, if you'd prefer.'

Jess hated how sad he looked. She instinctively walked over and put her arms around him, hugging him tightly. 'It's going to be all right, Ben,' she said as one did when one didn't know what else to say.

He hugged her back for a long moment before extricating himself from her arms and giving the weariest sigh.

'Dear, sweet Jess,' he said and laid a gentle hand against her cheek. 'Maybe it will be all right. In time. Meanwhile, tomorrow is going to be hell.'

# CHAPTER TWENTY-TWO

IT WAS WORSE than hell, Jess decided by five the following afternoon. Firstly, it had rained overnight and she'd frozen to death, both in the church and at the cemetery. She did have a jacket, one which matched her black crepe skirt, having chosen to wear the black Chanel-style suit she'd made to attend her grandmother's funeral. But even though it was lined it wasn't a warm outfit. Everyone else, she saw, was wearing overcoats. Some were wearing hats. She didn't even own a hat!

She'd warmed up a little during the drive from the lawn cemetery back into the city, though Ben hadn't said a word. Obviously, he'd been in a pretty bad place in his head after having to deliver the main eulogy, then watch his father's coffin being lowered into the ground. He'd held her hand so tightly whilst that had happened, she'd thought her fingers would break. She hadn't known what to say to make him feel any better so she'd said nothing.

But none of that compared to the hell the wake proved to be. Jess had felt intimidated from the moment she'd set foot in that mausoleum of an apartment Ben's father had owned. Maybe if she'd been able to stay by Ben's side she would have been able to cope better. But people kept taking him away from her, smarmy men in black suits with sucking-up manners and ingratiating voices. Everyone seemed to want his ear now that he was no longer the heir but the man himself. It was all quite sickening. And depressing.

Time ticked away very slowly spent with people she didn't know, making conversation with her about things she knew nothing about. When one particularly snobbish woman asked her what she did for a living, Jess rather enjoyed telling her that she was a mechanic. The expression on her snooty face was horrified. Anyone would have thought she'd said she was a garbage collector.

Finally, just after the grandfather clock in the main hallway struck five, an exasperated Jess scooped up a glass of white wine from a passing waiter and slipped out onto one of the many balconies, hopeful of finding some solitude and peace.

But she wasn't about to be so lucky. A svelte blonde who'd been at the funeral, and who'd stared daggers at Jess across the graveside, followed her out onto the balcony.

'Well, hello there,' the blonde said. 'You must be Ben's new girlfriend, the one he told me about over the phone.'

It didn't take a genius to conclude who the blonde was.

Amber wasn't beautiful, Jess decided. But she was attractive, and she shouted money with her super-sleek hairdo, her shiny complexion and her expensive-looking black sheath dress. No doubt they were real diamonds twinkling in her ears, Jess wished that she was wearing the diamond pendant Andy had given her at the wedding. But she'd left it at home in her jewellery case.

Despite knowing that her own outfit didn't look homemade it suddenly felt home-made. And dated. Which was silly.

'Hi,' Jess returned, refusing to feel intimidated any more today. 'I presume you're Amber. Ben told me all about you too.'

Amber's smile was not at all nice. 'Did he, now? I'll bet he didn't tell you what he and I used to get up to.'

Jess hated to think of Ben doing with this creature what he'd done with her. But there was no use pretending that some of it wouldn't have happened. Ben obviously had a penchant for erotic fun and games.

'I wouldn't dream of questioning Ben over what he did with his previous girlfriends,' she said coolly. 'What's past is past.'

The blonde laughed. 'In that case, you might be in for a few surprises, sweetie. But let me warn you...if you've set your cap at marrying the dear boy, then it might be wise to play a more conservative role. I tried to accommodate his kinky little demands and it didn't get me anywhere in the end. Not that I enjoyed any of it, but a girl will do just about anything, won't they, when there are billions at stake.'

'So it seems.'

Jess and Amber whirled at the sound of Ben's voice.

Amber went a guilty shade of pink whilst Jess just stared at him.

'Amazing what you learn after a relationship is over,' he said, still glaring at Amber. 'If I'd known your father was on the verge of bankruptcy, then I'd have better understood your sudden declaration of love. Not to mention your timely proposal.'

'Ben, I...I...'

'Save it, Amber,' he snapped.

'*She* doesn't love you,' Amber retaliated spitefully. 'She just wants your money, the way your mother wanted your father's money. For God's sake, just look at her. She's a nothing from down under. A nobody!'

Jess stepped forward and slapped Amber's face before she could think better of it. 'I do so love him,' she spat at the stunned blonde. 'And I am *not* a nobody!'

All of Amber's face went bright red, not just the palm print on her cheek. 'I'll sue you for assault, you bitch. And you too, you bastard—for breach of promise. I'll make you pay for wasting all that time on you.'

Ben's look in return was chillingly cold. 'Give it your best shot, sweetheart. I have billions at my disposal and you've got what? A dead-broke father and a dead-end job, working for peanuts in an art gallery.'

Amber opened her mouth to say something, then just whirled and stormed off.

Ben stared at Jess who was feeling somewhat shattered by the nasty incident.

'Did you mean it?' he asked her. 'Do you really love me?'

Tears pricked at her eyes. 'Of course I do. Why do you think I'm here?'

'Amber just said it's for the money.'

'Amber's a fool. And so are you, if you think that.'

'I don't think that. That's why I love *you*.'

Jess gaped at him then burst into tears. He gathered her close and pressed his lips into her hair. 'I love you,' he murmured. 'And I want to marry you.'

Jess wept all the harder. Because how could she marry this man and live this life with him? She would hate it. And soon she would hate him.

Finally, when the crying had stopped and she could gather enough courage, she pulled back from him and lifted still, wet eyes to his. 'I do love you, Ben,' she said shakily. 'Very much. But I can't marry you. I'm sorry. I just can't.'

# CHAPTER TWENTY-THREE

'I DON'T UNDERSTAND why you won't marry me,' Ben raged when he finally got Jess back to his apartment. 'If you love me the way you say you do, then what's the problem? Hell on earth, Jess, I can give you anything you want.'

'That's the problem, Ben. I don't want what you can give me. I don't want to live this kind of life,' she said, sweeping her right arm around at his apartment. 'It's too much. We wouldn't have any real friends. Neither would our children.'

'That's ridiculous. I have real friends.'

'No, you don't. There wasn't a single person there to-night who was a real friend. The only real friend you have is Andy in Australia, and that's because you met him when you weren't so rich. Being a billionaire means you can't live an ordinary life, Ben. As your wife, I won't be able to live an ordinary life either. You'll want me to go to toffee-nosed dos and dinner parties all the time with people that I despise. You'll want me to stop making my own clothes. You'll insist I have a stylist and a designer wardrobe. Our children will have nannies and bodyguards and be sent to snobby boarding schools whilst we stay at home and *entertain*. I'm sorry, Ben, but that's not what I want for my children. That's not what I want for *me*.'

He stopped pacing around the living room and sent her a disbelieving look. 'You really mean this, don't you?'

'I do,' she said, even though her heart was breaking.

He swore, then strode over and yanked her hard against him. 'I could make you change your mind,' he ground out darkly.

'No, Ben,' she said firmly. 'You couldn't.'

'Even if I promise you the world?'

'Especially if you promise me the world.'

'Then you don't really love me,' he growled and threw her from him.

When she almost fell over he grabbed her again, but not so roughly this time, his expression both apologetic and desperate. 'I'm sorry. God, I'm sorry. I would *never* hurt you, Jess. But please, don't do this. I beg of you. Stay with me. I need you. I love you. I won't let you go!'

Jess was not at her best when cornered. 'You can't stop me, Ben.'

'Then go, damn you.' And, before she could say another word, *he* was gone, slamming the front door behind him.

She waited for hours but he didn't come back. She tried his phone but it was turned off. Clearly, he didn't want her contacting him. She couldn't rest, just paced the apartment, her mind awhirl with regrets and recriminations.

It had been cruel of her to reject Ben's proposal like that on the same day that he'd buried his father. It was no wonder he'd lost his temper with her. She'd hurt him. Terribly. At the same time, Jess could not deny that what she'd said had been true. She knew she wouldn't be happy living this kind of life. And he wouldn't be happy with her as his wife. They lived in different worlds. She had always led a simple life whereas Ben lived like *this*, she thought, her gaze once again taking in the sheer luxury of her surrounds.

In the end, Jess made an agonising decision. She packed,

then went downstairs and got the doorman to summon a cab for her.

'JFK airport,' she told the driver in a broken voice.

She cried all the way to the airport where she had to wait some time before she could get a flight out. Just before she boarded, she sent Ben an explanatory and deeply apologetic text message. She didn't want him to worry about where she was, but she also didn't want him to follow her. The plane she caught set down in San Francisco, where she changed planes for the long flight back to Sydney. When she checked her messages, there wasn't one from Ben.

Jess didn't sleep much on the plane—she was travelling economy—so by the time she reached Mascot she was very tired and seriously depressed. She caught the bus over to the long-distance car park where she'd left her four-wheel drive, then literally had to force herself to drive home. Fortunately, it wasn't peak hour in Sydney, so it only took her a couple of hours. Even so, by the time she pulled into the driveway at home, she was totally wrecked.

Her mother must have heard a vehicle pull up outside; the front door was flung open just as Jess staggered up to it.

'Jess!' she exclaimed. 'Good heavens. I didn't expect it to be you. I was just having morning tea when I heard a car. What are you doing back so soon?'

'Mum, I can't talk now. I have to go to bed.'

'Can you just give me a clue as to what's happened?' Ruth asked as she followed her weary daughter up the stairs.

Jess stopped at the top step. 'If you must know, Ben told me he loved me and wanted to marry me.'

'He did?'

'I turned him down.'

'You turned him down?' Ruth repeated, somewhat stunned.

'Mum, he's too rich. I would have been miserable.'

'It wouldn't have been an easy life,' her mother said, feeling terribly sorry for her obviously heartbroken daughter. But she was proud of her too. Jess had a very sensible head on her shoulders. There weren't many girls who could turn down a man like Ben.

'Mum, I have to go to bed,' Jess said, tears threatening once more.

'You do that, darling. I'll go tell your father that you're home.'

*'What?'* was Joe's first reaction. 'She turned him down, did you say?'

'Yes,' Ruth said with a sigh.

'Ben won't take that lying down,' Joe said. 'He'll come after her.'

'Do you think so, Joe?'

'You mark my words. That man's crazy about our Jess. He'll be on our doorstep in less than a week.'

But he wasn't.

A week went by. Then two weeks. Then three.

Still no contact from Ben, either by phone, email or in person.

Joe couldn't believe it. Ruth wasn't quite so surprised. Maybe it was a case of out of sight, out of mind. Men, she believed, fell out of love more quickly than women.

On the following Sunday, Ruth did suggest Jess ring *him*, but this was vehemently rejected.

'No, Mum, there's no point. He's not going to give up his lifestyle for me and I'm not going to give up mine for him. That's the bottom line. So he's being sensible, not contacting me. It would only delay the inevitable. And make it even harder for me to move on.'

'But you're not moving on,' Ruth pointed out, frustrated. 'You're not even sewing any more!'

'Give me time, Mum. It's not even been a month.'

It had been, in fact, three weeks, four days and five hours since she'd last seen Ben, Jess thought bleakly. And even longer since she'd slept in his arms. Which she had the night before the funeral. It had been quite wonderful to have Ben make love to her, face to face, then to fall asleep with her head on his chest and her arms around him. She would remember the way that had felt for ever.

That Sunday night, Jess dreamt a futile dream where she and Ben got married somewhere overlooking a beach. An Australian beach. Shelley Beach, she recognised after she woke. It was an upsetting dream because that was only what it would ever be. A stupid dream! God, was she ever going to get over that man? Maybe she should have said yes and been miserable in New York, for this was just as bad, living life without him. Maybe worse!

She had to work in the office that day. Unfortunately, it turned out not to be a busy day for Murphy's Hire Car with hardly any phone calls or bookings coming in. She had way too much time to twiddle her thumbs, drink endless cups of coffee and think depressing thoughts. By the time twelve o'clock came, Jess had had enough. She stood up from her desk, deciding that she needed distraction or she'd go stark, raving mad. She would go to the movies, find herself a silly comedy. Or an action flick. Putting on the answering machine, she made her way from the office over to the house where she found her mother in the kitchen, packing away the food shopping.

'Mum, I think I'll go to the movies this afternoon. Do you mind?'

'Not at all. I'll look after the office.'

'Thanks, Mum.'

Ruth Murphy watched her daughter walk off slowly, thinking to herself that it would take Jess a long time to get over Ben. A small, selfish part of Ruth was glad that nothing had come of their relationship. She could not bear to think of her only daughter going off and living in America. At the same time, she could not bear to see her so unhappy.

Sighing, she finished putting away the shopping, made herself a sandwich and coffee, then toddled over to the office. After checking the answering machine—there'd been no calls—she ate her lunch, then picked up the book she kept there for reading when the office was slow. But she'd only finished a few pages when the phone rang.

'Murphy's Hire Car,' she said brightly.

'Hello, Ruth.'

Ruth sat up straight once she detected the American accent.

'Is Jess there?'

'No,' she said, feeling both anxious and defensive at the same time. 'Jess isn't here at the moment. Are you calling from New York?'

'No, Ruth. I'm parked just down the road from your place.'

Oh, dear Lord, he *had* come after her, like Joe had said.

'I tried Jess's phone several times but it's turned off.'

'She's at the movies.'

'At the movies?' He sounded puzzled, as though he couldn't imagine why she would be at the movies at this time of day.

'She needed to get out of the house, Ben. She's been very down since she came back from New York.'

'Did she tell you what happened?'

'Yes, she did. We're a very close family. There are no secrets between us.'

'I love your daughter, Ruth. And I mean to marry her.'

Ruth was taken aback by the fierce determination behind his words.

'In that case, what took you so long to come after her?' she couldn't help throwing at him.

'I needed time to change my life so that she would accept my proposal.'

'What do you mean? How have you changed your life?'

'I would rather discuss that with Jess, if you don't mind. Though, there is something I'd like to ask her father first, if he's here.'

'Well, yes, he is. He's working on one of the cars.'

'I'll be there shortly.'

When Ben hung up, Ruth just sat there in a total panic. Clearly, Ben meant to ask Joe for Jess's hand in marriage. What else could it be? She should have warned Ben that he might not get so civil a reception from Joe. He was mad as a hatter with Ben. Alternatively, she could race down to the shed and warn Joe that Ben had come to win Jess over.

But she'd dithered too long, Ruth realised when she saw a white sedan speed past the office on its way to the shed.

Joe heard a car pull up outside, but he was underneath one of the limousines when the driver walked in, so all he saw was a clean pair of trainers and some bare legs under cream shorts.

'Are you there, Joe?' Ben called out.

Joe's temper had already flared by the time he slid out from under the limo and stood up to face his visitor. 'You took your bloody time, didn't you?' he snarled. 'My girl's been in a right state over you.'

'I'm sorry about that, Joe. To be honest, I was in a right state myself when she turned me down. Took me a day or two to see sense after she left, but then I got to thinking more rationally and I realised she was right. We wouldn't have been happy living in New York. But it took some time to fix things so that we would be happy.'

'What kind of things?'

'I would prefer to discuss that with Jess first. Let me just say that I think she'll accept my proposal after I tell her what I've done. But I guess there's no harm in you knowing that I've come home to Australia to live. Permanently.'

Joe was both stunned and relieved. 'That's good news, Ben. Really good news. Ruth will be especially thrilled. So you're going to ask my girl to marry you again, is that it?'

'That's the plan. But I want to do it right, Joe, so I'm asking you first for your daughter's hand in marriage. I know that your approval would mean a lot to her.'

Joe could not have been more pleased. Or more proud.

'You have my full approval, Ben. But I sure hope you haven't bought the ring yet.'

Ben's heart plummeted at this statement. 'You think she might still say no?'

'Hell, no. But she'll want to pick the thing herself, if I know my Jess. That's one strong-minded girl.'

'Tell me about it.' Ben laughed. 'Now, I'd better get going.'

'Good luck,' Joe shouted as Ben made his way back to the car. 'You're going to need it!' he chuckled to himself.

# CHAPTER TWENTY-FOUR

Nausea swirled in Ben's stomach as he headed for West-field's and the movie theatre. A lack of confidence was not something he was familiar with. Admittedly, his ego had been brutally crushed by Jess's refusal to marry him back in New York. He had, in fact, lost a day or two indulging his sorry self in a serious drinking binge, which was most unlike him. But once he'd sobered up, and realised a future without Jess was unthinkable, he'd attacked all the changes necessary to his lifestyle in a very positive state of mind. Not once had he entertained the thought that he would not succeed in winning Jess over.

But now, suddenly, he wasn't so sure.

Maybe, during these last few weeks of silence, Jess had decided that she didn't love him after all. Maybe it was a case of out of sight, out of mind, rather than absence making the heart grow fonder. Her being 'in a right state', as her father had described, could have been her realising that it wasn't love she'd been suffering from but lust. Maybe she even regretted letting him do the things he'd done to her. Though, damn it, he was sure she'd enjoyed everything at the time. She wasn't like Amber, just doing what he wanted in the bedroom with an eye on his money. Hell, Jess was nothing like Amber at all. He really had to stop thinking all these negative thoughts. Negativity never achieved anything!

By the time Ben pulled into the large car park, he'd regained some of his confidence and composure. Once parked, he quickly checked Jess's mobile; it was still turned off. Climbing out from behind the steering wheel, he locked the car, then hurried into the shopping centre, heading through the food court and stopping at a spot where Jess would have to pass by as she exited the cinema complex.

Jess stood up as soon as the credits started coming up. The movie had been quite funny in parts. She'd managed to laugh once or twice. But the moment she exited the cinema her depression returned. What on earth was she going to do? Sit and have a coffee, she supposed wearily. No way was she going home yet. It was only just three.

She wandered slowly along the carpeted hallway which separated the numerous theatres, her blank eyes not registering the few people who passed her. Monday afternoon—especially on a warm spring day—was not rush hour at the movies. She did not bother to look at the advertisement posters on the walls like she usually did, not caring what blockbuster movies were about to hit the screens. Her mind was filled with nothing but one subject. She'd almost reached the food court just outside the cinema when someone called her name.

Her eyes cleared and there he was, standing right in front of her.

'Oh, my God,' was all she could say. 'Ben.'

When he smiled at her, she almost burst into tears. But she caught herself in time.

'What are you doing here?' she said, her sharp tone a cover for her confusion. She wanted to believe that he'd come for her, but it seemed too good to be true. And yet here he was, looking as handsome as ever.

'Your mother said you were at the movies. So I came and waited for you to come out.'

'You rang my *mother*?'

'I tried your mobile first, but it was turned off, so I rang Murphy's Hire Car and your mum answered.'

'Oh…'

'Is that all you've got to say?'

'Yes. No. What do you expect me to say? I'm in shock. I mean, you haven't rung or texted me at all. I thought you were finished with me.'

'It was you who finished with me, Jess.'

Her grimace carried true pain. 'I did what I thought was right. For both of us. So why *have* you come, Ben? Please don't ask me to go back to New York with you and marry you. That would just be cruel. I gave you my reasons for saying no and they haven't changed.'

'But you're wrong there, Jess. Lots of things have changed.'

'Not really. You're probably richer than ever now.' Hadn't she read somewhere that billionaires earned thousands of dollars a day from their many and varied investments? Or was it thousands every minute?

'What say we go have a coffee somewhere a little more private and I'll explain further?'

'There is nowhere here more private,' Jess said, waving at the open-plan and rather busy food court. People might not be flocking to the movies on a Monday but, since October had tipped into November, Christmas shopping had begun.

'I seem to recall there was a small coffee shop down that way on the right,' Ben said. 'Come on, let's go there.'

Jess didn't say a word as he led her away. She was still trying to work out what could possibly have changed.

The café he was referring to was half-empty with tables and booths to choose from. Ben steered her to the furthest booth where a sign on the back wall said you had to order at the counter.

'Would you like something to eat with your coffee?' he asked.

'No thanks.'

'Fine. What would you like? Flat white? Latte? A cappuccino?'

'A flat white,' she answered. 'No sugar.'

'Right.'

Jess tried not to ogle him as he got their coffee, but he looked utterly gorgeous in cream cargo shorts and a black polo shirt. His hair had grown a bit, she noted. It suited him longer. But then, he'd look good no matter what he wore or how long he grew his hair. Fate was very cruel to have her fall in love with a man with so many temptations.

As Jess waited for him to come back with the coffee, she tried to get her head around him suddenly showing up like this. Obviously he thought he *could* get her to change her mind. And maybe he was right. She'd been so miserable. And she'd missed him so much. Missed his love-making as well. Seeing him again reminded her of what an exciting lover he was. Exciting and dangerous and downright irresistible!

In the end, she looked down at where her hands were twisting nervously in her lap, not glancing up till he put her coffee in front of her, then sat down with his.

'Thank you,' she said politely, not really wanting coffee at all. Her stomach was in a mess. But she picked it up and had a small sip before putting it back down again. 'Now, would you mind telling me what's going on?'

He looked deep into her eyes. 'What's going on is that I still love you, Jess. And, yes, I still want to marry you.'

Oh, God, he *was* cruel.

'I don't doubt that, Ben, since you're here,' she replied. 'But sometimes love isn't enough.'

He reached over and touched her on the hand. 'You might change your mind on that when you hear what my love for you has achieved.'

It was hard for Jess to think straight when he was touching her. 'What are you talking about?'

'Well, first of all, I've come home to Australia to live.'

Her heart leapt. 'You *have*?'

'Yep. I knew you would never live with me in New York so I quit my job, then sold my majority interest in Dad's company to his partners.'

Jess just stared at him.

'After that, I used the money from the sale to set up a charity trust fund that gives financial assistance to people affected by natural disasters. We do seem to have a lot of them nowadays. Dad always gave lots of money to whatever disaster relief effort was going on, but he often worried if the money actually made it to where it was meant to go. I took this on board, so I'm the CEO of the fund. *I* decide when and where the money goes. The capital is safely invested so it should last for yonks. I don't take a salary or expenses myself, but I had to employ a couple of professional charity workers to oversee the day-to-day transactions and they do get paid. Other than that, all the money earned by the trust will go where it should go.'

Jess could only shake her head at him. 'You gave *all* your money away to charity?'

'Not all of it. Just what I inherited from the sale of Dad's company. Which, admittedly, was the majority of his estate. I still have his cash account—which was considerable—plus the money from the sale of his real-estate assets. When they're finally sold, that is. This includes his furnished apartment in New York and another one in Paris. They should bring in about twenty to thirty million each. If you include all the artwork he invested in over the years, you can add several more million. Though, I might donate them to various museums around the world. Yeah, I think I'll do that. The upshot is I'm still a multi-millionaire, Jess. Just not a billionaire. I knew you wouldn't marry a billionaire, but there's nothing attractive about poverty either.'

Jess's shock was beginning to change to wonder. 'You did all that for me?'

'The strange thing is, Jess, even though I initially gave away most of my money to win you back, after I actually did it, it felt good. Very good. They say there's more pleasure in giving than receiving and they're darned right. Anyway, as you can imagine, all that organising takes some considerable time, even when you're doing your own legal work. Which is why it took me this long to get here. I still might have to fly back occasionally, to attend to fund business, but Australia will be my permanent home from now on. It has to be, since I'm going to have an Australian wife. One whom I can't bear to live without.'

'Oh, Ben,' she said, the tears coming now. 'I can hardly believe it.'

Ben was struggling now to retain his own composure. 'Then your answer is yes this time?'

'Yes,' she choked out as she dashed away her tears. 'Of course it's yes.'

'Thank God,' he said, slumping back against the seat. 'I was worried you might still say no. And so was my mother.'

Jess blinked in surprise. 'You told your mother about us?'

'But of course. She's been at me to get married and have children for years. She'll be over the moon when I tell her.'

'You want children as well?' Jess said, still in a state of shock.

'Hell, yes. As many as you want. And if I know you, Jess, that will be more than one or two.'

'Yes, I'd like a big family,' she confessed. 'So when did you tell your mother about us?'

'Last night. I stayed at her apartment in Bondi. I flew in late, you see, too late to come up here. Though in the end, I stayed up even later, telling Mum everything. Then, would you believe it, I slept in. Didn't make it up to the coast till after lunch. Like I already told you, when you didn't answer your phone I rang Murphy's Hire Car and your mum answered.'

Jess was still a bit dumbstruck by everything Ben had done for her. 'I hope Mum was nice to you.'

'Very nice. So was your dad, after I asked him for your hand in marriage.'

'You actually asked Dad for my hand in marriage?'

'I wanted to do everything right, Jess. I didn't want anything to go wrong this time.'

'Oh, Ben, you make me feel awful.'

He frowned. 'Why awful?'

'Because you've done everything for me and I've done nothing for you.'

Done nothing? Ben looked at this wonderful girl whom he loved and he thought of all the things she'd done. Firstly and most importantly, she'd loved him back, not for his money but for himself—Ben the man, not the heir to billions. She'd also made him see what was important in life. Not fame and fortune but family and community. Not a high-flying social life but a simpler life, full of fun and friends and children. Oh yes, he couldn't *wait* to have children with Jess. What a lucky man he'd been the day he'd rung Murphy's Hire Car and met her.

But Ben knew if he said all that she'd be embarrassed. So he just smiled and said, 'Happiness is not nothing, Jess. You make me happy, my darling.'

'Oh,' she said, and looked like she was going to cry again.

'No more tears, Jess. You can cry on our wedding day, if you like, but not today. Today is for rejoicing. Now, drink up your coffee and we'll go buy you an engagement ring. There must be a decent jewellery store here somewhere.'

Half an hour later, the third finger of Jess's left hand was sporting a diamond solitaire engagement ring set in white gold, not as large and expensive as one Ben would have chosen.

'It's not how much it costs, Ben,' she'd told him firmly when she'd made her choice. 'But the sentiment behind it. Besides, I wouldn't like to make my very nice sisters-in law envious. They don't have engagement rings with diamonds the size of Ayer's Rock.'

Ben lifted his eyes to the ceiling. 'Fine. But don't go thinking I intend to buy a house with any constraints on it. I aim to have everything you and I want in it.'

'Fair enough,' Jess said, thinking to herself that that was fine by her. She wasn't a jewellery person but she'd always wanted a truly great house.

'Okay,' Ben said. 'Now that the ring business is all sorted out, take me along to that Fab Fashions store you used to work in.'

'But why?' she asked, puzzled. 'You don't own it any more.'

'Ah, but you're wrong there. When I sold Dad's company, that's the one asset I arranged to keep—the Fab Fashions chain. Dad's partners were only too happy to let me have it for nothing. They all consider it a right lemon, but I reckon that with your advice we could make a go of it. So what do you think, Jess? Can you help me out here?'

Jess's heart swelled with happiness. What an incredibly thoughtful man Ben was! And very clever. He knew exactly the way to her heart. And she told him so.

He grinned. 'Andy always said that no one should get between me and the goal post.'

She smiled. It wasn't every day that a girl liked being called a goal post.

'Does Andy know about your dad dying?' she asked on a more serious note.

'Not yet. They're still on their honeymoon. But they get back next week. Perhaps we could drive up and visit them one weekend soon, now that we're engaged. Stay in that nice little cottage for a night or two before they knock it down. Andy's planning on building a family home on that site in the New Year. Till then, they're living in the main house.'

Jess's heartbeat had quickened at the mention of the cottage, which immediately evoked the most wickedly exciting memories.

'That would be nice,' she said rather blandly. Wow, what an understatement! She could hardly wait.

He gave her a narrow-eyed look. Then he laughed. 'You don't fool me, Jess Murphy. You liked those fun and games as much as I did.'

'Yes,' she admitted. 'But I think they should be kept for special occasions, not an every-day event. I like the way you made love to me that night in New York, Ben. I thought you liked it too.'

'I did. Very much so. Okay, we'll keep the fun and games for special occasions, and weekends in nicely private cottages. Now, take me to Fab Fashions.'

\* \* \*

Helen was surprised when Jess walked in on the arm of the most handsome man she'd ever seen. He reminded her of a young Brad Pitt.

'Hello, Helen,' Jess said, looking oddly sheepish. 'This is Benjamin De Silva, the American businessman who took over Fab Fashions.'

'Please call me Ben,' the American said and extended his hand. 'Jess has been telling me about the difficulties you've encountered since my order came through for you to make a profit before Christmas or be closed.'

Helen shook his hand whilst wondering what on earth was going on here.

'I just wanted to personally deliver a new order to you. There will be no closing down, and come the New Year there will be huge changes to Fab Fashions. A new name and brand-new stock, plus an extensive advertising campaign to go with it. Till then, I'd like you to put all of your current stock on sale at fifty-percent off. Get rid of it all. Oh, and one more thing—Jess has just agreed to become my wife.'

Jess was still smiling when Ben steered her out of the shopping centre ten minutes later.

'Did you see the look on Helen's face when you said we were engaged?' she said.

'She did seem a little shocked.'

'Shocked? She couldn't speak for a full minute and that's not like Helen at all.'

'Well, she soon made up for it. What do you think of her idea of stocking more accessories for the clothes?'

'It's a good one. Ladies love accessories. We already had a few bits of jewellery, but that could be increased, and I think some scarves, handbags and even shoes could do well.'

'We'll have to invite her to the wedding,' Ben said. 'She's nice.'

'She is. And so is her husband.'

'Then we'll invite them both.'

Jess's heart swelled with pride at the man by her side. He'd changed in so many ways. Still a 'take charge' kind of man, but she liked that about him. Still charming too. But there was more sincerity behind his charm. More depth of feeling.

'So, where have you parked your car?' she asked once they were out on the pavement. 'You do have a car this time, don't you?'

'Yes, I rented one till I knew whether I was going to actually buy a car or a plot in Wamberal Cemetery in anticipation of my throwing myself off a cliff after you turned me down again.'

Jess sucked in sharply. 'You wouldn't have done that, would you, Ben?'

'Nah. I would have gone back to New York, become a movie producer and made millions.'

'You're not going to become a movie producer here, are you?' Jess said, horrified at the thought.

'Are you kidding me? I'm going to buy myself a place on the beach, have half a dozen kids and take up golf.'

'You're not going to work?'

'Well, I do have Fab Fashions to sort out. I also might go into business with your dad, doing up vintage cars. I was very impressed with what he's done with that Cadillac. I could be the money man and he could do the actual work.'

'Sounds good to me, provided you've got enough money left to support me and all those children.'

'I have more than enough. Now, whilst we're making serious plans here, when can we actually get married? I'd like to do it asap.'

'Ben De Silva, I'm going to have a proper wedding. And I aim to plan it all myself. That takes time.'

'How much time? It only takes a month to get a licence.'

'It'll be Christmas in just over a month, which is a big celebration in our family. No way can our wedding be organised before then.'

'What about January? Or February?'

'I don't like January or February for weddings either. It's way too hot. How about March?'

'I can live with March,' Ben said. 'Just.'

'March it is, then,' Jess said happily. 'Now, let's go and tell Mum and Dad the good news.'

# EPILOGUE

*March, four months later...*

THE LIGHTNING AND thunder started around ten in the morning. Jess and her parents rushed out onto the back veranda and stared up at the suddenly leaden sky, which had a rather ominous green colour.

'Murphy's Law,' Joe grumbled. 'You'd think it would leave me alone on my only daughter's wedding day.'

'It's not Murphy's Law, Dad,' Jess said, despite feeling disappointed. They'd been going to have the wedding ceremony at a picturesque open-air spot overlooking Toowoon Bay. 'It's just a storm.'

'No, it's bloody Murphy's Law!' he growled.

'I'm not going to let a little bit of rain spoil my big day, Dad. We have Plan B, don't we, Mum? We decided when we booked the Shelley Beach golf club for the reception that if it rained we could always have the ceremony there. They have some lovely balconies with nice views of the ocean and the golf course. If needs be, I'll give the club a call later. Everything will work out, Dad.'

It was at that point that it started to hail, denting even Jess's positive spirit.

'The wedding's not till three,' Ruth pointed out. 'It will probably have passed over by then.'

The hail was gone quite quickly but heavy rain continued all morning, resulting in several panicky phone calls
from Jess's bridesmaids, who were all at the hairdresser's.
None of them had stayed at Jess's place overnight, but were
due out there as soon as they'd had their hair and make-
up done. Jess reassured them that they had a Plan B, and
told them to stop worrying, after which she went upstairs
to do her own hair and make-up.

Just after midday, the rain finally stopped. The girls
arrived around one, looking gorgeous, the sun making its
appearance shortly before the bride and her four bridesmaids were due to leave.

Jess beamed her happiness at Catherine, whom she'd
asked to be her matron of honour. They'd become good
friends over the last few months. Andy, of course, was
Ben's best man. Catherine was pregnant, but only two
months gone, so hopefully there would be no last-minute
dramas. Jess's three sisters-in-law were her other bridesmaids, thankfully none of them pregnant at the moment.
Pete's wife, Michelle, had given birth to a baby girl two
months earlier but had got her figure back very quickly.
Jess had made the dresses for the wedding party, all of
them strapless and full-length. Jess's bridal gown was in
ivory silk and the bridesmaids' in a pale-yellow shantung.

The bride's bouquet, made from yellow and white roses,
reached from her waist to just above the hem of her dress.
The other bouquets were smaller with just white roses.
Jess had chosen a white rose for Ben's lapel and yellow
ones for the other men.

Ruth hadn't let Jess make *her* dress, however, choosing
a lovely blue mother-of-the bride outfit from Real Women,
which now had an excellent range of elegant clothes for the
more mature lady. After an Australia-wide marketing cam-

paign during January, the chain of stores was beginning to do quite well. No great profit as yet, but it was early days.

'See, Joe?' Ruth said a little smugly. 'I knew the sun would shine on our daughter's wedding. She's a lucky girl. Now, I must get going. See you all soon at Toowoon Bay.'

Jess watched her mother drive off in the family sedan whilst her father escorted her over to the first of the gleaming white wedding cars.

'Your mother's right,' he said to Jess once they were settled in the roomy back seat. 'You *are* a lucky girl to snare yourself a man like Ben. But then, he's a lucky guy to have a girl as special as you for his wife. Not to mention so exquisitely beautiful.'

'Please don't say things like that to me, Dad,' Jess said, her eyes pooling with moisture. 'I don't want to cry and ruin my make-up.'

'You won't cry, darling daughter. You're too sensible for that.'

But he was wrong. Jess almost cried as soon as she saw Ben standing there waiting for her with a look of such wonder and love in his eyes. She came even closer to weeping when he promised to love her till his dying days. She definitely would have cried when the celebrant announced that they were husband and wife, but Ben saved the day by kissing her with such passion that she forgot all about tears.

After that she didn't think about crying, being swept along with all the things which had to be done—first the photos at Toowoon Bay, then more at the golf club, followed by the greeting of the guests, pre-dinner champagne on the balconies and then the official part of the reception.

She smiled her way through all the speeches. Andy was suitably funny and Ben wonderfully complimentary about his beautiful bride. She smiled during the cake-cutting and the bridal waltz. She smiled and laughed with

Catherine whilst she changed into her going-away outfit, a chic white linen dress with red accessories. She and Ben planned to spend their wedding night at the Crown Plaza at Terrigal and the following day they were setting off on that long-awaited road trip around Australia; Jess's trusty four-wheel drive was already parked at the hotel. Not only was it parked but packed with every provision they could possibly need.

It wasn't till Jess was saying her goodbyes to her parents that tears suddenly flooded her eyes.

'Come now, Jess,' Joe said in a choked up voice as he hugged her. 'You don't want to spoil your make-up, do you?'

Jess laughed, then wiped away her tears. 'Absolutely not,' she said. 'But they aren't unhappy tears. I was just thinking what wonderful parents you and Mum are.'

'Oh, go on with you,' Joe said, though he seemed pleased. Ruth, however, started to look a bit weepy.

'Jess is right,' Ben said, stepping forward from where he'd been saying goodbye to his own mother. 'You are both wonderful. So we got our heads together and decided to give you both a little personal something. Here…' And he handed Joe a rather large envelope which had a well-known travel agency's logo on the outside.

'What on earth have you done?' Joe said as he opened the envelope and pulled out the printed itinerary of a very extensive trip around Europe.

'Now, we don't want to hear any objections,' Ben went on as a very wide-eyed Ruth looked over her husband's shoulder and read where they would be going. Knowing that they weren't seasoned travellers, Ben and his mother had booked guided tours as well as a long cruise down the Rhine. It would take them a good four months to do it all, the various tours taking in almost every country in Europe, finishing in Italy.

'Your departure date is not till late April. It's not a good idea to holiday in Europe in the dead of winter if you don't have to,' he added. 'As for Murphy's Hire Car…Jess's brothers will look after that till you get back. They assured me it's not a busy time of the year, anyway.'

'But it says we'll be travelling first class,' Ruth said, amazed.

Ben's mother, who'd been standing nearby, suddenly came forward, her arm linked with Lionel's. 'Please don't worry about the cost,' Ava said. 'I have more money than I need. Besides,' she added, smiling coyly at her partner, 'Lionel has decided to make an honest woman out of me and he has buckets of money himself, haven't you, darling?'

Darling Lionel just smiled.

'Now,' Ava raced on, 'I've been to all those places in Europe and it would be a real shame for you not to go whilst you're young enough to enjoy it. Oh, and Ruth, you and I are going clothes shopping in Sydney before you leave. I know exactly what you'll need.'

Ruth beamed at her. 'I'd love that, Ava.'

'And Lionel can take Joe clothes shopping at the same time,' Ben suggested.

'I'd be only too happy to,' Lionel agreed. 'If Joe wants me to, that is.'

Joe grinned. 'Sounds good to me. Can't have Mother showing me up, can I?'

'That's all settled, then,' Ben said, looking pleased with himself. 'Then, when we both get back from our holidays, Joe, we'll get right to work on that vintage car idea I told you about.'

'Too right,' Joe said, clapping Ben on the back.

'Hey!' Jess exclaimed, pretending to be piqued. 'Where does that leave me?'

'You can stay at home and clean that big house I bought you,' Ben said.

'But I didn't want such a big house. That was your idea.'

'You didn't say no.'

The three parents rolled their eyes at each other.

'Are these two having their first marital spat?' Andy said on joining them.

'I hope not,' Joe said.

Jess and Ben looked at each other, then laughed. 'We're just kidding. We both love our house.' It wasn't on a beach; Ben had decided he needed more room if and when he had sons. Their new purchase sat on a five-acre lot at Matcham, a rather exclusive rural enclave not far from the coast. The house was huge with six bedrooms, three bathrooms, a four-car garage, a tennis court and, of course, a solar-heated pool. They had already planned to have Christmas there the following year, Jess aiming to make it a very special occasion.

Thinking this last thought sent another thought into Jess's mind.

'Is a wedding night a special occasion?' she whispered to Ben once they'd said their final goodbyes and climbed into the back of the waiting limousine.

His eyes widened in mock horror. 'Are you suggesting what I think you're suggesting?'

'Not quite. I don't want to have to drive all that way to-morrow with an iffy bottom.'

'Hush up, wife. The driver might hear.'

'You're no fun any more,' she said sulkily.

Ben had actually refused to make love to her all week, saying she had to learn to wait.

'No fun!' Ben exclaimed. 'Might I remind you what we got up to just last month in Andy's cottage?'

'Hush up, husband. The driver might hear.'

Ten minutes later, they were safely alone in the bridal suite, which was beautifully furnished and quite seductive, with its big bed and mounds of pillows.

'If you must know,' Ben said as he busied himself with the waiting champagne bottle, 'I packed a little box of surprises which might come in handy during our rather elongated honeymoon.'

Jess's heart leapt. 'What kind of surprises?'

'Just a few naughty little items which I found on a website. You'll find out if and when required. But we certainly don't need anything like that tonight. Tonight is meant for more romantic sex. Though even romantic sex requires that clothes be removed. Why don't you get naked, my lovely wife, whilst I pour us some of this splendid champagne?'

'Aren't you going to get naked too?' a fiercely turned-on Jess asked after she'd complied.

He walked over to her slowly and handed her a glass. 'All in good time, my darling,' he murmured with wicked lights dancing in his beautiful blue eyes. 'All in good time.'

\* \* \* \* \*

# AN UNLIKELY BRIDE FOR THE BILLIONAIRE

## MICHELLE DOUGLAS

To Amber and Anthony, and Jessica and Tim, who are raising the next generation of heroes and heroines with grace and style...and a splendid sense of fun!

# CHAPTER ONE

'BUT—' MIA STARED, aghast, at Gordon Coulter '—that's not my job!' She was a trainee field officer, not a trainee event manager.

Her stomach performed a slow, sickening somersault at the spiteful smile that touched his lips. Gordon was the council administrator in charge of Newcastle's parks and wildlife—her boss's boss and a petty bureaucrat to boot. Plum Pines Reserve fell under his control. And he'd made no secret of the fact that he'd love to get rid of her—that he was simply waiting for her to mess up so he could do exactly that.

She did her best to moderate her voice. 'I'm in charge of the weed extermination project that's to start on the eastern boundary. Veronica—' the reserve's ranger '—insists it's vital we get that underway as soon as possible. We're supposed to be starting today.'

'Which is why I've handed that project over to Simon.'

Every muscle stiffened in protest, but Mia bit back the objections pressing against the back of her throat. She'd worked ridiculously hard on fine-tuning that project, had gathered together an enthusiastic band of volunteers who didn't care one jot about her background. More exciting still, she and Veronica had planned to take a full botanical inventory of the area—a comprehensive project that had filled Mia with enthusiasm. And now she was to have no part in it.

'This isn't up for debate, Mia.'

Gordon pursed his lips, lifting himself up to his full paunchy height of five feet ten inches. If it was supposed to make him look impressive, it failed. It only drew her attention to the damp half-moons at the armpits of his business shirt.

'You have to understand that teamwork is vital in an area as poorly funded as ours. If you're refusing to assist the administrative team in their hour of need then perhaps this isn't the right organisation for you.'

She wanted to know where Nora was. She wanted to know why Simon hadn't been given *this* job instead of her.

'The Fairweathers will be here at any moment, so if you *are* refusing to assist...'

'Of course I'm not refusing.' She tried to keep her voice level. She couldn't afford to lose this job. 'I'm surprised you'd trust me with such an important assignment, that's all.'

His eyes narrowed. 'If you screw this up, Maydew, you'll be out on your ear.'

She didn't doubt that for a moment.

'Naturally Nora will take over once she returns.' His lips tightened. 'She assures me you're the only one who can possibly deputise in her stead.'

She bit back a sigh. Nora wanted her on the events team, claiming she was wasted as a field officer. Mia had plans, though, and they didn't involve being part of the events team.

*Where was Nora?*

She didn't ask. She refused to give Gordon the satisfaction of telling her it was none of her business. She'd ring Nora later and make sure she was okay.

The receptionist knocked on the office door. It was Nora's office, but Gordon co-opted it whenever he decided to work from Plum Pines rather than his office at Council Chambers.

'Mr Coulter? Mr Fairweather is here.'

'Send him in.'

Mia moved to the side of the desk—she hadn't been invited to sit—fighting the urge to move to the back of the room, where she'd be able to remain as unobtrusive as possible.

'Mr Fairweather, it's delightful to meet you!' Gordon moved forward, arm outstretched, greasy smile in place.

Mia repressed a shudder.

And then she glanced at Dylan Fairweather—and had to blink, momentarily dazzled by so much golden…*goldenness*. Dear Lord, the papers did Dylan Fairweather no justice whatsoever. Not that Mia spent much time reading the society pages, but even *she*—hermit that she was—knew that Dylan Fairweather was considered one of Australia's bright young things. Earlier in the year he'd been named one of Australia's Top Twenty Eligible Bachelors.

If steal-your-breath sex appeal was one of the criteria then Dylan Fairweather had that in spades! Too-long dark gold hair and sexy designer stubble coupled with a golden tan had Mia's fingers curling into her palms. At six feet two he towered over Gordon, his pale blue business shirt and sand-coloured chinos achieving a casual elegance Gordon had no hope of matching.

Nor did his clothes hide the breadth of his shoulders or the latent strength of powerful thighs. All that power and flaxen golden brilliance should have made him look terrifying—like a prowling lion. But it didn't. He looked…he looked like a prince out of a fairytale.

Mia tried to tear her gaze away, but couldn't. Never, in all of her twenty-five years, had she been in the presence of someone so physically perfect.. She remembered one of the women in prison describing how she'd felt when she'd first laid eyes on Vincent van Gogh's painting *The Starry Night*. That was how Mia felt now.

Swallowing, she shook herself, appalled at the way her heart raced, at the craving that clawed at her belly. Pulling in a breath, she reminded herself that she wasn't some primitive savage, controlled by greed and impetuous impulses. Not any more.

When Gordon had said she'd be taking care of the Fair-weathers today, she'd been expecting a blushing bride and her aunt, maybe an attendant or two. She hadn't been expecting the bride's *brother*.

His pleasantries with Gordon exchanged, he turned to her and offered his hand with an easy, 'Dylan Fairweather.'

She took it automatically, appreciating the just-firm-enough grip and almost melting under the unexpected warmth of his smile.

*You're not the melting type.*

'Mia Maydew. It's nice to meet you. Carla is taking a call. She should only be a moment.'

'That's no problem at all.' Gordon ushered Dylan to a chair, frowning at Mia over his head.

Dear God! Had her paralysing preoccupation been evident for all to see? Heat climbed into her face. Brilliant. Just brilliant.

Gordon took his chair. He still didn't invite Mia to sit. 'Unfortunately Nora can't join us today. She sends her apologies. She was involved in a car accident on her way to work this morning.'

Mia couldn't prevent her involuntary intake of breath, or the way her hand flew to her abdomen, just below her breasts, to counter the way her stomach jumped. Startlingly brilliant blue eyes surveyed her for a moment, and while the brilliant colour might have the ability to distract a mere mortal, Mia sensed the shrewdness behind them.

Dylan Fairweather shifted ever so slightly on his chair. 'I hope she's okay.'

'Yes, yes, she's fine, but her car is apparently a write-off. I insisted she go to the hospital for a thorough examination, though.'

Mia closed her eyes briefly and let out a breath.

'Wise,' agreed Dylan—*Mr Fairweather*.

'In her stead—as a temporary measure, you understand—you'll have Mia here to run you through wedding options.

Anything you'd like to know—ask her. Anything you'd like to see—she'll show it to you. I promise that nothing will be too much trouble.'

*Easy for him to say.*

She straightened. It wasn't the Fairweathers' fault that Gordon had thrust her into the role of Assistant Events Manager. She'd helped Nora out before with weddings and corporate events. She'd do everything she could to answer the Fairweathers' questions and help Carla plan the wedding of her dreams.

'If you'd like to take it from here, Mia?'

'Certainly.' She forced a noncommittal smile to her face. 'If you'd just hand me the Fairweather file from the top drawer of the desk, I'll take Mr Fairweather through to the meeting room.'

She was tempted to laugh at the disgruntled expression that flitted across Gordon's face. Had he really thought she didn't know about the file? She'd helped Nora compile parts of it earlier in the week. Did he hate her so much that he'd risk a lucrative account, not to mention some seriously good publicity, to undermine her? The thought killed any urge to smile.

She had to counsel herself to take the file calmly, before leading Dylan Fairweather out of the office to the meeting room. Her pulse skittered and perspiration gathered at her nape. She preferred working with animals to people. Better yet, she liked working with plants. With over one hundred and seventy hectares of natural bushland to its name, it should have been relatively easy to avoid human contact at Plum Pines Reserve.

'Can I get you tea or coffee…maybe some water?' She gestured for Dylan to take a chair at the table, doing what she could to stop her fingers from shaking. This account had excited Nora enormously and, Gordon aside, Mia wanted to do her best for her boss.

From across the table Dylan eyed her closely, a frown in

his eyes, although his lips remained curved upwards in a pleasant smile. 'I think a carafe of water and three glasses would be an excellent idea.'

He thought *she* needed a drink of water? Dear Lord. She scurried away to fetch it. Did her nerves show that badly? She usually came across as a difficult study. She took a couple of deep breaths to compose herself before returning to the meeting room.

'Nora is a friend of yours?' he asked when she was seated, taking charge of the carafe and pouring a glass of water before pushing it across the table to her.

It hit her then that he'd misread her nerves as worry for the other woman. She hesitated. Would Nora consider Mia a friend? 'Nora is a close colleague. I like her a lot.'

'The news of her accident was a shock?'

She wasn't used to anyone being interested in her reactions. 'It was. I'm relieved it's not too serious.' When he continued to stare at her—which did nothing to slow her heart-rate—she forced her lips upwards. 'I'll call her later to check if there's anything she needs. It's kind of you to be so concerned. Now, let me show you the material Nora and I have gathered in relation to Ms Fairweather's wedding.'

'Please—you must call us Carla and Dylan.'

Must she? There was a certain protection afforded by the formality of Mr and Ms.

*The customer is always right.*

She bit back a sigh. If that were the case…

'Dylan.' She tested the name on her tongue. It emerged without any effort at all and tasted like her favourite brand of dark chocolate—flavoured with a bite of sea salt. His smile was her reward, making her forget the rest of her sentence.

'See…it wasn't so hard, was it—Mia?'

He made her name sound like a song.

He smiled. 'I can see why Carla requested you work on her wedding'

She opened her mouth and then closed it, blinking. 'I

think you've mistaken me for someone else. I'm afraid I don't know your sister, Mr Fair—uh… Dylan.'

He stared across at her, but in the end he merely nodded and let it go without challenge. It was as if someone had cut a string and released her.

She glanced down at the folder in an effort to collect herself. 'Do you know…?' She cleared her throat. 'Do you know where Carla would like the ceremony to take place?'

He glanced towards the door, as if hoping his sister would magically appear. 'Beside some lily pond. It's apparently where she and Thierry met.'

*Right*. Mia jotted a note down on her pad.

Blue eyes twinkled across the table at her when she looked up at him again. 'Aren't you going to gush about how romantic that is?'

Should she? Was gushing part of the job description?

He laughed as if he'd read that thought in her face, pointing a lean tanned finger at her. 'You, Ms Maydew, are *not* a romantic.'

He stared at her as if he knew her. It was utterly disconcerting. She had no intention of letting him know that, though.

She pointed her pen back at him. 'I *am*, however, an excellent worker.'

'Perfect.' His grin widened. 'You'll at least provide a port of sanity amid all the craziness.'

That made her lips twitch. She'd watched TV programs about Bridezillas. Was that what they had on their hands with Carla?

'Hallelujah!' He raised his hands heavenwards.

'What?'

'I finally managed to get a proper smile out of you.'

She stared at him, nonplussed. Why should he care one way or the other whether she smiled or not? Was smiling also part of the job description?

Darn it—it probably was! Give her animals and plants any day.

She forced her lips to curve upwards.

'Oh, dear me, no! On a scale of one to ten, that's not even going to score you a three.' He donned a mock commentator's voice. '*And Mia's smile has only scored a two point one from the Romanian judge!*'

She had to choke back a laugh.

He leant his elbows on the table. There was the whole width of the table between them, but somehow he seemed to bridge that distance without any effort at all. Maybe it was a combination of his height and breadth? She could make out the tiny laughter lines that fanned out from his eyes. She suspected Dylan laughed a lot. She noted the dusky eyelashes…ridiculously long and tipped with gold…and the firm fullness of his bottom lip. She'd bet he kissed a lot too. A pulse started up in the centre of her chest.

'I suspect, Mia Maydew, it'd be really something to make you laugh.'

She couldn't explain why, but she found herself jerking back as if he'd just propositioned her.

To cover her confusion, she folded her arms and narrowed her eyes. 'I have your number, Dylan Fairweather.' She used his full name in the same way he'd used hers. 'You're an incorrigible flirt. I suspect you can't help yourself.'

He raised his hands. 'Guilty as charged! But it's flirting without intent…just a bit of frivolous nonsense.'

His smile made her stomach tumble. 'Then why…?'

'Because it's fun.' His grin widened and she swore he had the devil in his eyes. 'Aren't you going to flirt back?'

She couldn't help it. She laughed.

Thank heavens! The woman *could* laugh.

Dylan sat back and let out a breath when the rather plain and schoolmistressy Mia momentarily transformed from uptight and ordinary-looking to mischievous imp. His gaze lingered on her mouth. He hadn't noticed how wide and generous it was earlier.

Since he'd witnessed her shock at learning of Nora's accident, and sensed her nerves at being thrust into the role of wedding co-ordinator, he'd wanted to put her at ease. Putting people at ease was his stock in trade. Mia might call it flirting, but it was nothing more than a bit of harmless fun designed to make her laugh and loosen up. And it had half worked—she'd laughed.

Having now seen Mia smile for real, though, he could see that she was neither plain nor schoolmistressy. It was just an attitude she cultivated. Interesting...

Nora had been ecstatic yesterday when he'd mentioned that they'd like Mia as part of their wedding team. Nora mightn't have known it, but she'd unwittingly supplied a glowing character reference for Mia. He sat back, resisting the urge to rub his eyes. He wanted everything associated with this wedding to be a joy for Carla. He meant to ensure it went without a hitch.

If only he could be certain the damn wedding should go ahead!

The walls of the glassed-in meeting room pressed in on him. He wanted to be outside and in the fresh air. *Now!* He wanted to be away from the fresh juniper berry scent of the woman opposite. It had his mind turning to black ski runs in St Moritz, with the wind tearing at his hair and the cold making him feel alive. Which was ridiculous. While he might be on leave, this was no holiday. Besides, if there'd been less frivolity in his life recently Carla might never have become embroiled with a man like Thierry.

Carla's happiness—that was what he had to focus on. 'Is the lily pond far? Can you show it to me?'

'You want to see the lily pond *now*?'

'Yes.'

'What about your sister?'

'She's on the phone to her intended. She could be hours. I'll text her so she'll know where to find us.'

Dutifully he pulled out his phone.

Mia taking me to lily pond. Meet there.

He held it out for her to see and then hit 'send'.

Without another word Mia led him out into the warm summer sunshine and he filled his lungs with eucalypt-scented air. The small office block sat on the edge of a rectangle of lush lawn that had to be at least two football fields long. Covered picnic tables marched down each of its sides, shaded by a variety of gum trees, plum pines and bottle-brush trees. The red blossoms of the bottlebrushes had attracted a flock of rainbow lorikeets which descended in a noisy colourful rush.

A peacock strutted through the nearest picnic shelter, checking for crumbs and leftovers, while a bush turkey raked through a nearby pile of leaves. All around the air was filled with birdcalls and the scent of warmed native grasses. Groups of people had gathered around the picnic tables and on blankets on the grass. He could hear children's laughter from the playground he glimpsed through the trees.

'This place is popular.'

She gestured that they should take a path to the left. 'It is.'

Her dark brown hair, pulled back into a severe ponytail, gleamed rich and russet in the bright light. She didn't wear a scrap of make-up. Not that she needed to. She had a perfect peaches and cream complexion that he hadn't appreciated under the strip lighting of the office.

He pulled his mind back to the matter at hand. 'Can we book the entire reserve for the wedding?'

'I'm afraid not. Plum Pines is a public park. What we *can* do, though, is rope off the area where your event is being held to keep the general public out.'

'Hmm…' He'd have to rethink the security firm he'd initially considered hiring. The wedding security would be a bigger job than he'd originally thought.

She glanced up, her gaze sharp. 'Is that going to be a problem?'

'Not if I hire a good security firm.'

'Let me know if you'd like any recommendations.' She led him across a bridge spanning a large pond. 'Officially the park is open from seven a.m. to seven p.m.'

He stared out at the expanse of water, noting several black swans sitting on the edge of the far bank. 'Is this the lily pond?'

'No, it's the duck pond.'

He glanced down into the water and blinked when a tortoise poked its small head out of the water. 'That…' He halted to point. 'That was…'

She glanced over the railing. 'A Common Longneck Tortoise. The pond is full of them.'

Hands on hips, he completed a full circle, taking in the surroundings. Plum Pines was undeniably pretty, and the native forest rising up all around them undeniably grand. He'd visited some of the most exotic places the world had to offer and yet he'd somehow missed experiencing what was in his own backyard.

'I can't believe we're in the middle of the second largest city in New South Wales. It feels as if we're in the middle of the bush.'

'Yes, we're very privileged.'

That was a rote reply if he'd ever heard one—trotted out for the benefit of visitors. What did Mia really think of the place? Did she love it or loathe it? Her lips were pursed into a prim line that had him itching to make her smile again.

'You'll need to apply to the council for an event licence that'll allow the wedding to extend beyond those hours. There shouldn't be any issue with that, though.'

She moved off again, with her no-nonsense stride, and

after another glance at where the tortoise had disappeared he set off after her.

'Have you had any weddings that *haven't* extended beyond seven p.m.?' All of the weddings he'd ever attended had kicked on into the wee small hours.

'There's been a trend for morning weddings with lunchtime receptions. So, yes.'

She was so serious. And literal. He found himself starting to laugh.

She glanced at him, a frown crinkling her forehead. 'What's so funny?'

'You're not so good at small talk, are you?'

Her face fell and she stuttered to a halt. 'You want small talk?'

That made him laugh again. 'How do you enforce the seven p.m. closing time?'

'We close the gates to the car parks. There's a hefty fine involved to have the gates opened. Our people, along with your security firm, will have a list of your guests' number plates so they can come and go as they please.'

'Right.'

'And, as Plum Pines is in the middle of suburbia, we don't get much foot traffic or many homeless people looking for a place to put up for the night.'

That was something, he supposed.

She consulted her notepad. 'Do you know how many guests the bride and groom are planning to invite?'

'Carla informs me that she wants "a small and intimate affair".'

That frown crinkled her brow again. 'Do you happen to know what your sister's idea of "small" might be?'

'I wouldn't have a clue.' He had no idea if Thierry came from a large family or not. The other man had closed up like a clam when Dylan had asked him about them. 'I can't say that I know what she means by "intimate" either.'

Mia nodded. 'I think we can guess that fairly accurately—it probably includes fairy lights strung all around the marquee and surrounding trees, white linen tablecloths with centrepieces involving ivy and candles, vintage china and a string quartet.'

'You don't sound like you approve.'

She swung to face him. 'Mr Fair— Dylan. It's not for me to approve or disapprove. It's Plum Pines' job to help Carla plan the wedding she wants.'

'But—' He broke off.

'What were you going to say?'

He read the thought that flashed through her eyes—*Gordon Coulter promised nothing would be too much trouble.*

'Dylan, I'll do my best to deliver whatever is needed.'

Her moss-green eyes stared back at him, earnest and steady, and he found himself needing to pull a breath of air into cramped lungs. 'I need you to be as committed to this wedding as Carla.'

'I'm committed—I can promise you that.' Her teeth worried at her bottom lip. 'But that's not what you meant, is it? You want me to be exuberant and…and bouncy.'

He winced, realising how absurd that sounded when uttered out loud. He just wanted to see her smile again. *That* was what this was all about—and it was pure nonsense on his part.

He rubbed his hand across his nape. 'I think of weddings and I think of joy and excitement and…and *joy*.'

He wanted Carla's life filled with joy—not just her wedding. A fist tightened about his chest. If Thierry hurt her he'd—

Mia moved into his field of vision, making him blink. 'There's a lot of behind-the-scenes work that needs doing to make a wedding successful.' She pointed her pen at him. 'Joy and excitement are all well and good, but I figure my job is to keep a level head.'

A level head? That was exactly what he needed.

'Don't you believe someone can be quietly enthusiastic?' she asked.

'Of course they can. I'm sorry.' He grimaced. 'It's the bride who's supposed to go loopy, right? Not her brother.'

One of those rare smiles peeped out, making his heart thump.

'You're excited for her.' Too soon she sobered again. 'I'm naturally quiet. It doesn't mean I'm not invested.'

'Whereas I'm naturally gregarious.' It was what made him so good at his job. 'I sometimes forget that not everyone else is.'

'Do you still want to see the lily pond?'

'Yes, please.' He spoke as gravely as she did. 'My seeing the lily pond is not dependent on you being exuberant.'

He could have sworn that her lips twitched—for the briefest of moments. It sent a rush of something warm and sweet surging through his veins. He was glad he'd had a chance to meet her on his own. Carla had spoken of her often enough to make his ears prick up. It had been a long time since Carla had made a new female friend.

The question he needed to answer now, though—was Carla more than just a job to Mia? He'd give his right arm for Carla to have a girlfriend with whom to plan her wedding. And whatever the two of them dreamed up—schemed up—he'd make happen.

When he glanced back he found Mia staring at a point beyond him. He swung around to see an emu enclosure… and an emu sitting on the ground in the dirt. He glanced back to find her chewing her lip. 'Is that emu okay?' They *did* sit down, right?

She hesitated. 'Do you mind…?' She gestured towards the fence.

'Not at all.'

'Hey, Charlie—come on, boy!' Mia rattled the fence and the emu turned to stare, but when he didn't otherwise move she pulled out her phone. 'Janis? It's Mia. Charlie is looking decidedly under the weather. Can you send someone out to check on him?' Her lips pressed together as she listened to the person at the other end. 'He's sitting down and not responding to my calls.' She listened some more. 'But—'

She huffed out a breath and he could see her mentally counting to five.

'Right. If that's the best you can do.' She snapped the phone shut and shoved it back into her pocket.

'You're worried about him?'

One slim shoulder lifted. 'Charlie's been hand-raised. He's a social bird. Normally he'd be over here, begging for a treat. Everyone who works here is fond of him.'

Dylan glanced across at the emu. 'You want to go and give him the once over?'

She glanced around, as if to check that no one had overheard him. 'Would you mind?'

'Not at all.'

'It should only take me a moment. I just want to make sure he doesn't have something caught around his legs. Discarded plastic bags are the bane of our existence—they seem to blow in from everywhere.'

'I don't mind at all.'

Besides, he wanted her full attention once Carla arrived. He wanted her focussed on wedding preparations—not worrying about Charlie the Emu.

She moved towards a gate in the fence and unlocked it with a key she fished out from one of the many pockets of her khaki cargo pants.

She glanced back at him apologetically. 'I have to ask you to remain on this side of the fence. It's actually against the law for me to take you in with me.'

'Believe me, I'm happy to stay on this side of the fence, but…' he glanced across at Charlie '…that emu is huge. What if he attacks you?'

He couldn't in all conscious just stand here and do nothing.

'He won't hurt me. I promise.'

'In that case I promise to stay on this side of the fence.'

Nevertheless, he found his heart pounding a little too hard as she slipped into the enclosure and made her way towards the giant bird. She ran a soothing hand down its neck, not in the least intimidated by its size. He reminded himself that she was trained to deal with these animals, but he didn't take his eyes from her.

Slipping her arms beneath the bird, she lifted it to its knees, and Dylan could see something wrapped tight around its ankles. The poor bird was completely tangled! He watched in admiration as she deftly unwound it, shoving the remnants into her pocket. The entire time she crooned soothingly to the emu, telling him what a good boy he was and how pretty he was. Charlie leaned into her as much as he could, trusting her completely.

Finally she placed her arms beneath him with a cheery, 'Up we come, Charlie.'

The emu gave a kind of strangled *beep* before a stream of something green and vicious-looking shot out of the back of him, splattering all over the front of Mia's shirt. Only then did the bird struggle fully to its feet and race off towards a water trough. Mia stumbled backwards, a comical look of surprise on her face. She turned towards Dylan, utterly crestfallen and...and covered in bird poop.

Dylan clapped a hand over his mouth to hold back a shout of laughter. *Don't laugh!* An awful lot of women he knew would have simply burst into tears. If he laughed and then she cried he'd have to comfort her...and then he'd end up with bird poop all over *him* too.

Mia didn't cry. She pushed her shoulders back and squelched back over to the gate in the fence with as much dignity as she could muster. Still, even *she* had to find it difficult to maintain a sense of dignity when she was covered in bird poop.

She lifted her chin, as if reading that thought in his face. 'As you can see, Charlie left me a little present for my pains.'

He swallowed, schooling his features. 'You did a very good deed, Mia.'

'The thing is, when an emu gets stressed, the stress can result in…' she glanced down at herself, her nose wrinkling '…diarrhoea.'

'God, I'm *so* glad those birds can't fly!'

The heartfelt words shot out of him, and Mia's lips started to twitch as if the funny side of the situation had finally hit her.

Dylan couldn't hold back his laughter any longer. 'I'm sorry, Mia. You deserve better, but the look on your face when it happened… It was priceless!'

She grinned, tentatively touching the front of her shirt. 'That rotten bird! Here I am, supposedly trying to impress you and your sister with our marvellous facilities…and now you're going to live in fear of projectile diarrhoea from the native animals!'

The sudden image that came to his mind made him roar until he was doubled over. Mia threw her head back and laughed right alongside him. She laughed with an uninhibited gusto that transformed her completely. He'd glimpsed the mischievous imp earlier, but now she seemed to come alive—as if her mirth had broken some dam wall—as if she were a desert suddenly blooming with wildflowers.

Dylan's heart surged against his ribs and for a moment all he could do was stare. 'You should do that more often, you know. Laugh. You're beautiful when you laugh.'

She glanced up at him, the laughter dying on her lips. Something in the air shimmered between them, making them both blink. Her gaze lowered momentarily to his lips, before she turned beetroot-red. Swinging away, she stumbled across to the tap that stood by the gate in the fence.

Heat pulsed through him. So…the serious Mia wasn't immune to his charms after all?

The next moment he silently swore. *Damn!* He deserved a giant kick to the seat of his pants. She'd accused him of flirting earlier—but he hadn't meant to give her the wrong impression. He didn't want her thinking anything could happen between them. All flirtation and teasing on his part was entirely without intent.

She knelt at the tap and scrubbed at her shirt with a piece of rag. She must keep a veritable tool shed of handiness in those cargo pants of hers.

He watched in silence as she washed the worst of the mess from her shirt. 'I have a handkerchief if you need it.'

'Thank you, but I think this is the best I'm going to manage until I can change my shirt. Shall we continue on to the lily pond?'

'Yes, please.'

She gestured towards the path. 'Do you mind if I ring the office to give them an update on Charlie?'

'Not at all.'

And just like that they withdrew back into reserved professionalism. But something new pounded through Dylan—a curiosity that hadn't been there before. What an intriguing paradox Mia was proving to be...a fascinating enigma.

*Which you don't have time for.*

With a sigh, he pushed thoughts of Mia from his mind and forced his attention back to the impending wedding. He had to focus on what really mattered. He couldn't let Carla down—not when she needed him.

# CHAPTER TWO

THEY REACHED THE lily pond two minutes later. The moment Dylan clapped eyes on the enchanting glade he understood why Carla had fallen in love with it. True to its name, large green lily pads decorated a small but picturesque body of oval water. Native trees and shrubs curved around three of its sides. The fourth side opened out to a large circle of green lawn.

Mia pointed to that now. 'This area is large enough for our medium-sized marquee, which holds sixty guests comfortably. That leaves the area behind for the caterers to set up their tents and vans for the food.'

Carla chose that moment to come rushing up—which was just as well, as Dylan had found himself suddenly in danger of getting caught up on the way Mia's wet shirt clung to her chest.

Carla grinned at Mia—'Surprise!'—before taking Dylan's arm and jumping from one foot to the other. 'Isn't this just the most perfect spot?'

He glanced down at her—at her smile made radiant with her newfound happiness. 'It's lovely,' he agreed, resolve solidifying in his gut. This wedding had come out of left field, taking him completely by surprise. But if this was what Carla truly wanted, he meant to create the perfect wedding for her. 'Where's Thierry?'

A cloud passed across her face. 'Something's come up. He can't make it.'

*That* was the problem. Thierry. Dylan didn't like the man.

His sister had suffered enough misery in her life, and Dylan had every intention of protecting her from further heartache.

Carla moved towards Mia. 'Please tell me you're not cross with me.'

'So...you're not really Carly Smith, frequent visitor and keen student of environmentalism?'

Carla shook her head.

Mia glanced down at her notepad. 'With your background, I imagine you need to be careful with your privacy.'

Carla winced. 'Please tell me you don't hate me. You've been so kind. I love shadowing you when you're on duty for the wildlife displays. You never talk down to me or treat me like I'm stupid. Oh!' she added in a rush. 'And just so you know, I really *do* have a keen interest in the environment and conservation.'

Mia smiled. 'Of course I don't hate you.'

That smile made Dylan's skin tighten. When she smiled she wasn't plain. And when she laughed she was beautiful.

He pushed those thoughts away. They had no bearing on anything. Her smile told him what he needed to know—Mia genuinely liked his sister. *That* was what mattered.

'Right.' Mia consulted her notepad. 'I want to hear every tiny detail you have planned for this wedding.'

'Hasn't Dylan told you *anything*?'

Mia glanced at him. 'We didn't want to start without you.'

That was unexpectedly diplomatic.

He stood back while the pair started discussing wedding preparations, jumping from one topic to the next as if it made utterly logical sense to do so. He watched them and then shook his head. Had he really thought Carla needed exuberance from Mia? Thank heaven Mia had seen the wisdom in not trying to fake it. He silently blessed her tact in not asking where Mia's maid of honour or bridesmaids or any female relative might be too.

Carla didn't have anyone but him.

And now Thierry.

And Mia in the short term.

He crossed his fingers and prayed that Thierry would finally give Carla all that she needed…and all that she deserved.

Mia spent two hours with Carla and Dylan, though Dylan rarely spoke now Carla was there. She told herself she was glad. She told herself that she didn't miss his teasing.

Except she did. A little.

Which told her that the way she'd chosen to live her life had a few flaws in it.

Still, even if he had wanted to speak it would have been difficult for him to get a word in, with Carla jumping from topic to topic in a fever of enthusiasm.

She was so different from Carly Smith, the wide-eyed visitor to the park that Mia had taken under her wing. She took in the heightened colour in Carla's cheeks, the way her eyes glittered, how she could barely keep still, and nodded. Love was *exactly* like that and Mia wanted no part of it *ever again*.

Carla spoke at a hundred miles an hour. She cooed about the colour scheme she wanted—pink, of course—and the table decorations she'd seen in a magazine, as well as the cake she'd fallen in love with. She rattled off guest numbers and seating arrangements in one breath and told her about the world-class photographer she was hoping to book in the next. Oh, and then there was the string quartet that was apparently *'divine'*.

She bounced from favours and bouquets to napkins and place settings along with a million other things that Mia hastily jotted down, but the one thing she didn't mention was the bridal party. At one point Mia opened her mouth to ask, but behind his sister's back Dylan surreptitiously shook his head and Mia closed it again.

Maybe Carla hadn't decided on her attendants yet. Mia suspected that the politics surrounding bridesmaid hierarchy could be fraught. Especially for a big society wedding.

Only it wasn't going to be big. It was going to be a very select and exclusive group of fifty guests. Which might mean that Carla didn't want a large bridal party.

Every now and again, though, Carla would falter. She'd glance at her brother and without fail Dylan would step in and smooth whatever wrinkle had brought Carla up short, and then off she would go again.

Beneath Carla's manic excitement Mia sensed a lurking vulnerability, and she couldn't prevent a sense of protectiveness from welling through her. She'd warmed to Carly—Carla—the moment she'd met her. For all her natural warmth and enthusiasm she had seemed a little lost, and it had soothed something inside Mia to chat to her about the programmes Plum Pines ran, to talk to her about the animals and their daily routines.

As a rule, Mia did her best *not* to warm towards people. She did her best not to let them warm towards her either. But to remain coolly professional and aloof with Carla—the way she'd tried to be with Dylan—somehow seemed akin to kicking a puppy.

While many of her work colleagues thought her a cold and unfeeling witch, Mia *didn't* kick puppies. She didn't kick anyone. Except herself—mentally—on a regular basis.

'Can I come back with Thierry tomorrow and go over all this again?'

Why hadn't the groom-to-be been here *today*?

'Yes, of course.'

Hopefully tomorrow Nora would be back to take over and Mia would be safely ensconced on the reserve's eastern boundary, communing with weeds.

Carla glanced at her watch. 'I promised Thierry I'd meet

him for lunch. I have to run.' She turned to her brother. 'Dylan…?' Her voice held a note of warning.

He raised his hands, palms outwards. 'I'll sort everything—I promise. Mia and I will go back to the office and thrash it all out.'

Mia's chest clenched. Thrash what out? She didn't have the authority to thrash *anything* out.

She must have looked crestfallen, because Dylan laughed. 'Buck up, Mia. It'll be fun.' He waggled his eyebrows.

Mia rolled her eyes, but she couldn't crush the anticipation that flitted through her.

'I'll buy you a cup of coffee and a blueberry muffin.'

His grin could melt an ice queen.

Lucky, then, that she was made of sterner stuff than ice.

'You'll do no such thing.' She stowed her notepad in her back pocket as they headed back towards the main concourse. 'Gordon Coulter would be scandalised. All refreshments will be courtesy of Plum Pines.'

During the last two hours they'd moved from the lily pond back to the office, to pore over brochures, and then outside again to a vacant picnic table, where Carla had declared she wanted to drink in the serenity. Now, with many grateful thanks, Carla moved towards the car park while Mia led Dylan to the Pine Plum's café.

He grinned at the cashier, and Mia didn't blame the woman for blinking as if she'd been temporarily blinded.

'We'll have two large cappuccinos and two of those.' He pointed at the cupcakes sitting beneath a large glass dome before Mia had a chance to speak.

'You mean to eat two cupcakes and drink two mugs of coffee?' She tried to keep the acerbity out of her voice.

'No.' He spoke slowly as if to a child. 'One coffee and one cake are yours.'

Mia glanced at the cashier. 'Make that one large cappuccino, one pot of tea and *one* cupcake, thank you. It's to go on Nora's events account.'

Without further ado she led him to a table with an out-look over the duck pond.

'You're not hungry?' he asked.

She was ravenous, but she'd brought her lunch to work, expecting to be stranded on the eastern boundary, and she hated waste. 'I'm not hungry,' she said. It was easier than explaining that in Gordon Coulter's eyes the events account didn't extend to buying her any food. 'Besides, I don't have much of a sweet tooth.'

She frowned, unsure why she'd added that last bit.

For a moment he looked as if he were waging an inter-nal battle with himself, but then he folded his arms on the table and leaned towards her, his eyes dancing. 'Are you telling me, Mia…?'

She swallowed at the way he crooned her name, as if it were the sweetest of sweet things.

'…that you don't like cake?'

He said it with wide eyes, as if the very idea was scan-dalous. He was teasing her again. She resisted the almost alien urge to tease him back.

'I didn't say I didn't like it. It's just not something I ever find myself craving.'

His mouth kinked at one corner. Mia did her best to look away.

'Now I have to discover what it is you *do* crave.'

How could he make that sound so suggestive?

'Cheesecake? Ice cream?'

She narrowed her eyes. 'Why do I get the feeling you're trying to find something to use as a bribe?'

'Chocolate?'

Oh. He had her there. 'Chocolate is in a class of its own.'

He laughed, and something inside her shifted. *No shift-ing!* She had to remain on her guard around this man. He'd called her beautiful and something in her world had tilted. She had no intention of letting that happen again.

'You made my sister very happy today. From the bottom of my heart, thank you.'

It was the last thing she'd expected him to say. 'I… I was just doing my job.'

'It was more than that, and we both know it.'

She didn't want it to be more. This was just a job like any other. 'Naturally Carla is excited. I enjoyed discussing her plans with her.'

To her surprise, she realised she was speaking nothing less than the truth.

Their order was set in front of them. When the waitress left Dylan broke off a piece of cupcake, generously topped with frosting, and held it out to her. 'Would you like a taste?'

Unbidden, hunger roared through her. For the briefest of moments she was tempted to open her mouth and let him feed her the morsel. Her throat dried and her stomach churned. On the table, her hands clenched to fists.

She choked out a, 'No, thank you,' before busying herself with her tea.

*Why now*? Why should a man have such an effect on her *now*? In the last ten months she'd been asked out on dates… the occasional volunteer had tried to flirt with her…but nothing had pierced her armour.

*None of them looked like Dylan Fairweather.*

True. But was she really so shallow that someone's looks could have such an impact?

When she glanced back up she saw Gordon Coulter, glaring at her from the café's doorway. Had he seen Dylan offer her the bite of cake? *Great. Just great.*

She shuffled her mantel of professionalism back around her. 'Now, you better tell me what it is you promised Carla you'd sort out. It sounded ominous.'

He popped the piece of cake into his mouth and closed his eyes in bliss as he chewed. 'You have no idea what you're missing.'

And she needed to keep it that way.

She tried to stop her gaze lingering on his mouth.

His eyes sprang open, alive with mischief. 'I bet you love honey sandwiches made with the softest of fresh white bread.'

She had to bite her inner lip to stop herself from laughing. 'Honey makes my teeth ache.'

The man was irrepressible, and it occurred to her that it wasn't his startling looks that spoke to her but his childish sense of fun.

'Ha! But I nearly succeeded in making you laugh again.'

She didn't laugh, but she did smile. It was impossible not to.

Mia didn't do fun. Maybe that was a mistake too. Maybe she needed to let a little fun into her life and then someone like Dylan wouldn't rock her foundations so roundly.

He made as if to punch the air in victory. 'You should do that more often. It's not good for you to be so serious all the time.'

His words made her pull back. She knew he was only teasing, but he had no idea what was good for her.

She pulled her notepad from her pocket and flipped it open to a new page. 'Will you *please* tell me what it is you promised Carla you'd take care of?'

He surveyed her as he took a huge bite of cake. She tried not to fidget under that oddly penetrating gaze.

'Don't you ever let your hair down just a little?'

'This is my job. And this—' she gestured around '—is my place of employment. I have a responsibility to my employer to not "let my hair down" on the job.' She tapped her pen against the notepad. 'I think it's probably worth mentioning that you aren't my employer's only wedding account either.'

She spoke gently, but hoped he sensed the thread of steel beneath her words. There also were cages that needed cleaning, animals that needed feeding and logbooks to fill out. They weren't all going to get magically done while Dylan lingered over coffee and cake.

And it didn't matter how much he might temporarily fill her with an insane desire to kick back and take the rest of the day off—that wasn't going to happen.

'Ouch.' He said it with a good-natured grin. 'But you're right. Carla and I have taken up enough of your time for one day. Especially as we'll be back tomorrow.'

He was coming too? She tried to ignore the way her heart hitched.

'Mia, do you know what line of work I'm in?'

Even she, who'd spent most of her adult life living under a rock, knew what Dylan Fairweather did for a living. 'You created and run Fairweather Event Enterprises.' More widely known as Fairweather Events or FWE. Dylan had made his name bringing some of the world's most famous, not to mention *notorious*, rock acts to Australia.

Under his direction, Dylan's company had produced concerts of such spectacular proportions they'd gone down in rock history. His concerts had become a yardstick for all those following.

FWE had been in charge of last year's sensationally successful charity benefit held in Madison Square Garden in New York. He was regularly hired by royalty to oversee national anniversary celebrations, and by celebrities for their private birthday parties and gala events. Dylan Fairweather was a name with a capital N.

'The thing is…' He shuffled towards her, his expression intent now rather than teasing. 'I know that Plum Pines has its own events team, but *I* want to be the person running this particular show.'

Very slowly, she swallowed. 'By *"this particular show"*, I take it you're referring to Carla's wedding?'

He nodded.

Her heart thumped. Nora would be disappointed.

'I want to do this for Carla,' he continued, fully in earnest now. 'The only thing I can give her that's of any worth is my time. You have to understand it's not that I don't trust the Plum Pines staff, it's that I want to give my sister some-thing that'll actually *mean* something to her—something she can cherish forever.'

Mia almost melted on the spot. To have someone who cared about you so much that they'd go to such lengths... That was—

'Mia?'

She started. 'I'm afraid I don't have the kind of clout to authorise an arrangement like that. But I'll present your case to Nora and Mr Coulter. Please be assured they'll do every-thing they can to accommodate your and Carla's wishes.' She bit her lip. 'They may have some additional questions that they'd like to ask you.' Questions *she* lacked the exper-tise and foresight to ask.

He immediately slid his business card across the table to her. 'They can contact me at any time.'

She picked it up. It was a simple card on good-quality bond, with embossed lettering in dark blue—a deeper and less interesting shade than his eyes.

He slid another card across the table to her. 'Would you write down your number for me, Mia?'

She dutifully wrote down the Plum Pines office number, along with Nora's work number.

He glanced at it and his lips pursed. 'I was hoping for *your* number.'

Her hand shook as she reached for her tea. 'Why?'

'Because I think you could be an ally. You, I believe, ap-prove of my plan to be Carla's wedding co-ordinator.'

She hesitated. 'I think it's a lovely idea.' Surely it couldn't hurt to admit that much? 'But I think you ought to know that I have very little influence here.'

'I think you're selling yourself short.'

'If you want to speak to me directly, ring the office and ask them to page me.' She couldn't believe she'd told him to do that, but she couldn't find it in herself to regret the offer either.

For a moment she thought he'd press the matter. Instead he stood and held out his hand. 'Until tomorrow, then, Mia.'

She stood too and shook it, eager to be away from him. 'Goodbye, Dylan.'

She didn't tell him that in all likelihood she wouldn't see him tomorrow. Funny how suddenly the eastern boundary didn't seem as exciting a prospect as it had earlier in the day.

She'd barely settled down in the meeting room with the office laptop, to type up her copious notes for Nora, when the receptionist tapped on the glass door.

'Mr Coulter wants to see you, Mia.'

To grill her about how things had gone with the Fairweathers, no doubt. She'd have rather discussed it all with Nora first, but she couldn't very well refuse to speak to him.

Taking a deep breath, she knocked on his door, only entering when he bellowed, 'Come in.'

She left the door ajar. She didn't fully trust Gordon Coulter. 'You wanted to see me?'

'Yes.'

He didn't invite her to sit. The smile he sent her chased ice down her spine.

'It's my very great pleasure to inform you, Ms Maydew, that you're fired. Effective immediately.'

The room spun. Mia's chest cramped. She couldn't lose this job. It was all that she had. Her fingers went cold. She *needed* this job!

'You're terminating my contract? But...*why?*'

Dylan stood on the threshold of Gordon Coulter's office, his head rocking back at the words he heard emerging from the other side of the door.

Gordon Coulter was *firing* Mia?

'Your behaviour with Dylan Fairweather today was scandalous and utterly inappropriate. You're not here to make sexual advances towards our clients. You're here to perform

your duties as efficiently and as capably as possible—a duty
that's obviously beyond you and your bitch-on-heat morals.'

Darkness threatened the edges of Dylan's vision. Mia
hadn't made one inappropriate advance towards him—not
one! His hands curled into fists. A pity the same couldn't
be said for him towards her. He hadn't been able to resist
flirting with her in the café—just a little bit. He hadn't been
able to resist making her laugh again.

This was *his* fault. How could he have been so careless
as to put her in this position?

Gordon continued to wax lyrical on a list of Mia's imag-
inary faults and Dylan's insides coiled up, tight and lethal.
Gordon Coulter was a pompous ass!

'But even if I was prepared to overlook all that,' Gordon
continued, his tone clearly saying that he had no intention
of doing so, 'I refuse to disregard the fact that when you entered the emu enclosure you put the safety of a member of
the public at risk.'

*No way, buddy*!

Dylan backed up two steps and then propelled himself
forward with a cheery, 'Knock-knock!' before bursting into
the office.

Two sets of eyes swung to him. Mia's face was ashen.
Guilt plunged through him like a serrated-edge knife.

*You're nothing but a trust fund baby without substance
or significance.*

As true as that might be, it meant that he knew how to
act entitled and high-handed. He used that to his advantage
now, striding into the room as if he owned it and everything inside it.

'You moved very quickly to bring my proposal to the attention of your superiors, Mia. I can't tell you how much I
appreciate it.'

He took a seat across from Gordon, making himself completely at home.

'I hope you realise what a gem you have here, Gordon.'

He pulled Mia down to the seat beside him. How *dared* Gordon leave her standing like some recalcitrant child deserving of punishment and castigation? 'Have you finished telling Gordon about my proposal, Mia?'

'Um…no, not yet.'

She swallowed and he saw how valiantly she hauled her composure back into place. *Atta girl*!

'I'm afraid I haven't had a chance.'

'Oh, before I forget—' Dylan turned back to Gordon '—my sister and I will be returning tomorrow with Thierry. If he approves our plans, and if you accept my proposal, then we'll be booking Plum Pines as Carla and Thierry's wedding venue.'

Dollar signs all but flashed in Gordon's eyes. 'That's splendid news!'

'Carla has requested that Mia be available for tomorrow's meeting. I'm sure that won't be a problem.'

'Well, I—'

'Now to my proposal…' he continued, making it obvious that he took Gordon's agreement for granted. He saw Mia bite her lip, as if to hold back a laugh. The tightness in his chest eased a fraction.

'While I understand that Plum Pines has a talented and capable events team, I want to be completely in charge of Carla's wedding preparations—bringing in my own people, et cetera. I understand this isn't how Plum Pines normally operates, but if I promise to acquire all the necessary licenses and, as a show of gratitude, donate…say…a hundred thousand dollars to the Plum Pines Nature Fund, I was hoping you might make an exception.'

Gordon's fleshy mouth dropped open. He hauled it back into place. 'I'm sure we can find a way to accommodate such a reasonable request from such a generous benefactor.'

Dylan rubbed his hands together. 'Excellent.'

Gordon Coulter was ridiculously transparent. Rumour had it he was planning to run for mayor next year. A donation as sizable as Dylan's would be a real feather in his cap. Dylan just hoped the good people of Newcastle were smart enough not to elect such a small-minded bully to office.

He made a note to donate a large sum to Gordon's opponent's campaign.

'If there's any further way we can assist you, don't hesitate to ask. We're here to provide you with the very best service we can.'

'Well, now that you mention it... Carla would like Mia as her official liaison between FWE and Plum Pines.'

Gordon's face darkened. 'Mia doesn't have the necessary training. We can provide you with a far better level of service than that, and—'

'It's non-negotiable, I'm afraid.' He spoke calmly. 'If there's no Mia there'll be no Fairweather wedding at Plum Pines—and, sadly, no hundred-thousand-dollar donation.'

It was as simple as that, and Gordon could take it or leave it. If he refused to let Mia act as liaison then Dylan would whisk her away from Plum Pines and find a position for her in his own organisation. He was always on the lookout for good people.

In fact, poaching her was a damn fine plan.

Gordon wouldn't pass on it, though. Dylan knew his type too well.

'If you're happy with Mia's limited experience...' he began, in that pompous fashion.

'Supremely so.'

'I'll have to insist that she consult with Nora closely,' he blustered, in an attempt to save face.

'Absolutely.'

Gordon swallowed a few times, his jowls quivering. 'In that case I'll raise no objections.'

Dylan leant back in his chair. 'Excellent.'

Mia leaned forward in hers, her dark gaze skewering Gordon to the spot. 'And our earlier conversation...?'

His mouth opened and closed before he shuffled upright

in his seat. 'In the light of these…new developments, any further action will be suspended—pending your on-the-job performance from here on in.'

Very slowly she leaned back. Dylan silently took in the way her fingers opened and closed around each other. Eventually she nodded. 'Very well.'

Dylan stood. 'I understand you're a busy man, Gordon, so I won't take up any more of your valuable time. Mia…' He turned to her and she shot to her feet. 'I forgot to give you Carla's mobile number. You're going to need it. I'm afraid she'll be leaving you messages day and night.'

'That won't be an issue,' Gordon inserted. 'Mia understands that here at Plum Pines our clients are our priority. She'll be at your sister's beck and call twenty-four-seven.'

Dylan barely restrained himself from reciting the 'Maximum Ordinary Hours of Employment' section of the *New South Wales Industrial Relations Act*. Instead he gestured for Mia to precede him out through the door.

'Lead me to your trusty notepad.'

He closed the door behind them and Mia didn't speak until they were safely ensconced in the meeting room.

She swung to him. 'You did that on purpose, didn't you? You overheard him trying to fire me so you jumped in and saved my job.'

His chest expanded at the way she looked at him—as if he'd ridden in and saved the day.

She pressed a hand to her chest. 'I think I just fell a little bit in love with you.'

She was the strangest mix of seriousness and generosity he'd ever come across. And totally adorable to boot.

He leaned towards her, but she took a step backwards.

'Sorry, I shouldn't have said that. It was a stupid thing to say. I only meant I was grateful—*very* grateful—for you coming to my defence like you did.'

'You're welcome. Gordon is a pompous ass.'

'A pompous ass who has the power to terminate my train-eeship whenever he sees fit.'

'He'd need to show good cause in the Industrial Relations Court. Don't you forget that. In fact—' he widened his stance '—why don't you forget Gordon and Plum Pines and come and work for *me*?'

The beginnings of a smile touched her lips. It made his pulse beat that little bit harder.

'I don't believe I have enough...*exuberance* for your line of work, Dylan.'

'I was wrong about that. You're perfect.'

'No, I'm not!' Her voice came out tart. Too tart.

He frowned. 'I meant that your work ethic is perfect. Your customer service skills are impeccable.' That was *all* he'd meant.

She swallowed before gesturing for him to take a seat. 'If you want me working so closely with you and Carla then there's something you need to know about me.'

He sat in the chair at the head of the table. 'I know all I need to know.'

She fixed him with that compelling gaze of hers, but for the life of him he couldn't read her expression. She took the chair immediately to his left, gripping her hands together until her knuckles turned white.

'I'd rather be the one to tell you than for you to hear it from other sources.'

He straightened. What on earth...? 'I'm listening.'

He watched the compulsive bob of her throat as she swallowed. Her hands gripped each other so tightly he was sure she'd cut off the blood supply to her fingers if she weren't careful.

'Ten months ago I was released from jail after serving a three-year prison sentence for committing fraud. I think it's only fair that you know I'm an ex-convict.'

# CHAPTER THREE

MIA WAITED WITH a growing sense of dread for Dylan's face to close and for him to turn away.

His open-mouthed shock rang through her like a blow, but his face didn't close. He didn't turn away.

His frown did deepen, though, and she could read the thoughts racing behind the vivid blue of his eyes.

'No,' she said, holding his gaze. 'I wasn't wrongfully convicted, there were no mitigating circumstances.' She swallowed. 'Unless you want to count the fact that I was young and stupid.'

And utterly in thrall to Johnnie Peters. So in love she'd have done anything he'd asked of her. So in love she *had* done anything he'd asked of her.

'You're not going to tell me any more than that?'

Curiosity sharpened his gaze, but it wasn't the kind of avid, voyeuristic curiosity that made her want to crawl under a rock. It held a warmth and sympathy that almost undid her.

Swallowing again, she shook her head. 'It's sordid and unpleasant and it's in the past. According to the justice system, I've paid my debt to society. I won't ever steal again. I'll never break the law again. But I understand that in light of these circumstances my word isn't worth much. I'll completely understand if you'd prefer to deal with Nora rather than with me.'

He didn't say anything.

'You don't need to worry about my job. You've done enough to ensure I won't be fired…at least, not this week.' She'd aimed for levity, but it fell flat.

He lifted his chin. 'I meant what I said—come and work for me.'

She realised now what she'd known on a subconscious level after only ten minutes in his company—Dylan Fairweather was a good man.

'I appreciate the offer, I really do, but besides the fact that you don't know me—'

'I know you have a good work ethic. If the way you've treated Carla is anything to go by, where clients are concerned nothing is too much trouble for you. They're valuable assets in an employee.'

'According to Gordon I have a problem with authority.'

He grinned, and leaned in so close she could smell the nutmeg warmth of his skin. 'That's something we have in common, then.'

How was it possible for him to make her laugh when they were having such a serious conversation? She sobered, recalling her earlier impulsive, *I think I just fell a little bit in love with you.* She should never have said it. Instinct warned her that Dylan could wreak havoc on her heart if she let him.

She couldn't let him. She wasn't giving *any* man that kind of power over her again.

She pulled in a breath. 'I was fortunate to be awarded this traineeship. The opportunity was given to me in good faith and I feel honour-bound to make the most of it.'

'Admirable.'

It wasn't admirable at all. She needed a job—a way to earn a living. For the two-year tenure of her traineeship she'd be in paid employment. Maybe at the end of that time she'd have proved herself worthy and someone would take a chance on employing her. She needed a way to support herself. After what she'd done she couldn't ask the welfare system to support her.

'Do you have a passion for conservation?'

'Conservation is an important issue.'

'That's not the same thing,' he pointed out.

Passion was dangerous. She'd done all she could to excise it from her life. Besides, busying herself with weed extermination programmes, soil erosion projects, and koala breeding strategies—plants, dirt and animals—meant she had minimal contact with people.

And as far as she was concerned that was a *very* good thing.

'Here.' He pulled a chocolate bar from his pocket. 'This is the real reason I came back to the office.'

Frowning, she took it, careful not to touch him as she did so.

'You said chocolate belonged in a class of its own and…'

He shrugged, looking a little bit embarrassed, and something inside her started to melt.

*No melting!*

'I wanted to thank you for your patience with both Carla and me today.'

'It's—'

'I know—it's your job, Mia.'

*Dear Lord, the way he said her name…*

'But good work should always be acknowledged. And…' An irrepressible smile gathered at the corner of his mouth. 'I fear more of the same will be asked of you tomorrow.'

It took a moment for his words to sink in. 'You mean…?'

'I mean we want *you*, Mia. Not Nora. I want everything associated with this wedding to be a joy for Carla. She likes you. And that's rarer than you might think.' He suddenly frowned. 'How much will taking charge of this affect your traineeship? Will I be creating a problem for you there?'

He was giving her an out. If she wanted one. *If…*

She pulled in a breath. 'The wedding is nine months away, right?'

He nodded.

Being Carla's liaison wouldn't be a full-time job. Very slowly she nodded too. 'That leaves me plenty of time to continue with my fieldwork and studies.'

If it weren't for Dylan she wouldn't have a job right now *or* a chance to finish her traineeship. She owed him. *Big-time.* She made a resolution then and there to do all she could to make Carla's wedding a spectacular success.

Her gaze rested on the chocolate bar he'd handed to her earlier. She suddenly realised how she could tacitly thank him right now. Without giving herself time to think, she ripped off the wrapper and bit into it.

'I'm ravenous. And this is *so* good.'

As she'd known he would, he grinned in delight that his gift had given her pleasure. She closed her eyes to savour the soft milky creaminess, and when she opened them again she found his gaze fastened on her lips, the blue of his eyes deepening and darkening, and her stomach pitched.

She set the chocolate to the table and wiped damp palms down her trousers. 'I… This is probably a stupid thing to raise…'

He folded his arms. 'Out with it.'

'I don't believe you have any interest in me beyond that of any employer, but after what Gordon just accused me of…'

She couldn't meet his eyes. The thing was, Gordon had recognised what she'd so desperately wanted to keep hidden—that she found Dylan attractive. *Very* attractive. He'd woken something inside her that she desperately wanted to put back to sleep.

'I just want to make it clear that I'm not in the market for a relationship. *Any* kind of relationship—hot and heavy or fun and flirty.'

She read derision in his eyes. But before she could dissolve into a puddle of embarrassment at his feet she realised the derision was aimed at himself—not at her.

'No relationships? Noted.' He rolled his shoulders. 'Mia, I have a tendency to flirt—it's a result of the circles I move in—but it doesn't mean anything. It's just supposed to be a bit of harmless fun. My clients like to feel important and, as *they* are important to me, I like to make them feel valued. I plan celebrations, parties, and it's my job to make the entire process as enjoyable as possible. So charm and a sense of fun have become second nature to me. If I've given you the wrong impression...'

'Oh, no, you haven't!'

'For what it's worth, I'm not in the market for a relationship at the moment either.'

She glanced up.

*Why not?*

*That's no concern of yours.*

Humour flitted through his eyes. 'But what about friendship? Do you have anything against that?'

That made her smile. People like Dylan didn't become friends with people like her. Once the wedding was over she'd never see him again.

'I have nothing whatsoever against friendship.' She'd sworn never again to steal or cheat. A little white lie, though, didn't count. Did it...?

Thierry Geroux, Carla's fiancé, was as dark and scowling as Carla and Dylan were golden and gregarious. Mia couldn't help but wonder what on earth Carla saw in him.

She pushed that thought away. It was none of her business.

As if he sensed the direction of her thoughts, Thierry turned his scowl on her. She wanted to tell him not to bother—that his scowls didn't frighten *her*...she'd been scowled at by professionals. She didn't, of course. She just sent him one of the bland smiles she'd become so adept at.

'Do you have any questions, Mr Geroux?' He'd barely spoken two words in the last hour.

'No.'

'None?' Dylan double-checked, a frown creasing his brow.

'Stop bouncing,' Thierry said in irritation to Carla, who

clung to his arm, shifting her weight from one leg to the other.

'But, Thierry, it's so *exciting*!'

Nevertheless she stopped bouncing.

Thierry turned to Dylan. 'Carla is to have the wedding she wants. As you're the events expert, I'm sure you have that under control.'

He ignored Mia completely. Which suited Mia just fine.

Dylan turned back to Mia. 'There could be quite a gap between the end of the wedding ceremony and the start of the reception, while Carla and Thierry have photographs taken.'

Mia nodded. 'It;s often the case. With it being late spring there'll still be plenty of light left. I can organise a tour of the wildlife exhibits for those who are interested.'

'Oh!' Carla jumped up and down. 'Could we do that now?'

'Absolutely.'

The exhibits—a system of aviaries and enclosures—were sympathetically set into the natural landscape. A wooden walkway meandered through the arrangement at mid-tree height. This meant visitors could view many of the birds at eye level, practically commune with the rock wallabies sunning themselves on their craggy hillside, and look down on the wombats, echidnas and goannas in their pens.

At the heart of the wildlife walk—and the jewel in its crown—was the koala house. Set up like an enormous tree house, the wooden structure was covered on three sides to weatherproof it for visitors, with an arena opening out below full of native flora and an artfully designed pond.

The entire complex was enclosed in a huge aviary. A visitor could glance up into the trees to view the variety of colourful parrots, or along the rafters of the tree house to see the napping tawny frogmouths. Below were a myriad of walking birds, along with the occasional wallaby and echidna. But at eye-level were the koalas on their specially designed poles, where fresh eucalyptus leaves were placed daily. No wire or special glass separated man from beast—only a wooden railing and a ten-foot drop into the enclosure below.

'I *love* this place,' Carla breathed as they entered.

'This is really something,' Dylan murmured in Mia's ear.

His breath fanned the hair at her temples and awareness skidded up her spine. 'It's a special place,' she agreed, moving away—needing to put some distance between them.

When they'd looked their fill, she led them back outside to a series of small nocturnal houses—the first of which was the snake house.

Carla gave a shudder. 'No matter how much I try, I don't like snakes.'

They didn't bother Mia, but she nodded. 'We don't have to linger. We can move straight on to the amphibian house and then the possum house.'

'C'mon, Thierry.'

Carla tugged on his arm, evidently eager to leave, but he disengaged her hand. 'You go ahead. I find snakes fascinating.'

Finally the man showed some interest—*hallelujah!*

Thierry glanced at her. 'Mia might be kind enough to stay behind with me and answer some questions?'

The snakes might not bother her, but Mia loathed the caged darkness of the nocturnal houses, hating the way they made her feel trapped. She didn't betray any of that by so much of a flicker of her eyelids, though.

'I'd be happy to answer any questions.'

Dylan caught her eye and gestured that he and Carla would move on, and she nodded to let him know that she and Thierry would catch up.

She moved to stand beside Thierry, nodding at the slender green snake with the bright yellow throat that he currently surveyed. 'That's a tree snake. It's—'

'I can read.'

She sucked in a breath. Was he being deliberately rude?

She lifted her chin. He might be hard work, but she was used to hard work.

'They're very common,' she continued, 'but rarely seen as they're so shy. They seldom bite. Their main form of defence is to give off a rather dreadful odour when threatened.'

Mia was convinced there was a metaphor for life trapped in there somewhere.

'*You* give off a bad smell too.'

Thierry moved so quickly that before she knew what he was doing he had her trapped between the wall and a glass display unit—the olive python on the other side didn't stir.

'Dylan told us about your background—that you're nothing but a common little thief with a criminal record.'

The sudden sense of confinement had her heart leaping into her throat before surging back into her chest to thump off the walls of her ribs.

'When I was in jail—' with a supreme effort she kept her voice utterly devoid of emotion '—I learned a lot about self-defence and how to hurt someone. If you don't take two steps back within the next three seconds you're going to find yourself on your back in a screaming mess of pain.'

He waited the full three seconds, but he did move away. Mia tried to stop her shoulders from sagging as she dragged a grateful breath into her lungs.

He stabbed a finger at her. 'I don't like you.'

*And that should matter to me because...?* She bit the words back. She'd had a lot of practice at swallowing sarcastic rejoinders. She'd made it a policy long ago not to inflame a situation if she could help it.

'Carla and Dylan are too trusting by half—but you won't find *me* so gullible.'

Giving a person the benefit of the doubt did *not* make Dylan gullible.

'You're not a fit person for Carla to know. You stay away from her, you hear? If you don't I'll cause trouble for you... and that's a promise.'

'Is everything okay here?'

A strip of sunlight slashed through the darkness as Dylan came back through the doors. The doors were merely thick flaps of overlapping black rubber that kept the sun out. A few threads of light backlit him, haloing his head and shading his face. Mia didn't need to see his face to sense the tension rippling through him.

Without another word Thierry snapped away and moved through the rubber panels, his footsteps loud on the wooden walkway as he strode off.

'Are you okay?'

Dylan's concern, absurdly, made her want to cry in a way that Thierry's threats hadn't.

'Yes, of course.' She turned and gestured to the snakes. 'Just so you know: a reptile encounter can be arranged for the wedding guests too, if anyone's interested. Though it has to be said it's not to everyone's taste.'

Dylan took Mia's arm and led her back out into the sunshine, wincing at her pallor.

Her colour started to return after a few deep breaths and he found the rapid beat of his heart slowed in direct proportion.

'I heard the last part of what Thierry said to you.'

He hadn't liked the way Thierry had asked Mia to stay behind. It was why he'd doubled back—to make sure everything was okay.

'It's not the first time someone has taken exception to my past, Dylan, and I expect it won't be the last.'

Her revelation yesterday had shocked him—*prison!*—but he'd have had to be blind not to see how much she regretted that part of her life. He'd sensed her sincerity in wanting to create a new, honest life for herself. She'd paid dearly for whatever mistakes lay in her past. As far as he was concerned she should be allowed to get on with things in peace.

Thierry's threat, the utter contempt in his voice…

Dylan's hands clenched. It had been a long time since he'd wanted to knock someone to the ground. He'd wanted to deck Thierry, though. He'd wanted to beat the man black and blue.

He dragged a hand down his face. It had only been the thought of who'd pay for his actions—Mia—that had stopped him.

*You didn't even think of Carla!*

Mia stared up at him, her gaze steady. 'Don't blame Thierry. He only has Carla's welfare in mind.'

'It doesn't excuse his behaviour.' A scowl scuffed through him. 'The man's a bully and a jerk. What the hell does Carla see in him?'

She gestured that they should continue along the path towards the amphibian house. 'Don't you know?'

He didn't have a single clue.

'Haven't the two of you talked about him?'

*Not really.* But to say as much would only reveal what a poor excuse for a brother he'd been to Carla these last twelve months.

He glanced across at Mia and found that she'd paled again, but before he could ask her if she was okay she'd plunged into the darkness of the amphibian house. Was she worried about running into Thierry again?

He plunged right in after her.

'Do you want to linger?'

He couldn't have said how he knew, but he sensed the tension coiling through her. 'No.'

She led them back outside and gulped in a couple of breaths. She stilled when she realised how closely he watched her.

He reached out to stop her from moving on. 'What's wrong?'

She glanced away. 'What makes you think anything's wrong?'

When she turned back, he just shrugged.

Her shoulders sagged. 'I'd rather nobody else knew this.'

Silently, he crossed his heart.

She looked away again. 'I don't like the nocturnal houses. They make me feel claustrophobic and closed in.

*They were like being in jail!*

He had to stiffen his legs to stop himself from pitching over.

'I'm fine out here on the walkways, where we're above or beside the enclosures and aviaries, but the nocturnal houses are necessarily dark...and warm. The air feels too close.'

She finished with a deprecating little shrug that broke his heart a little bit.

In the next moment he was gripped with an avid need to know everything about her—were her parents still alive? How had they treated her when she was a child? What made her happy? What did she really want from life? What frightened her right down to her bones? What did she do in her spare time? What made her purr?

That last thought snapped him back. He had no right to ask such questions. He shouldn't even be considering them. What he should be doing was working out if Carla was about to make the biggest mistake of her life. *That* was what he should be focussed on.

'What about when you're down below?' he found himself asking anyway. 'When you have to go into the cages to clean them out...to feed the animals?'

He saw the answer in her eyes before she drew that damn veil down over them again.

'It's okay. It's just another part of the job.'

*Liar.* He didn't call her on it. It was none of his business. But it begged the question—why was Mia working in a place like this when enclosed spaces all but made her hyperventilate?

They found Carla and Thierry waiting for them beside the kangaroo enclosure.

The moment she saw Mia, Carla grabbed her arm. 'I want to become a volunteer!'

Mia smiled as if she couldn't help it 'Volunteers are always welcome at Plum Pines.'

Her tone held no awkwardness and Dylan's shoulders unhitched a couple of notches. Thierry's strictures hadn't constrained the warmth she showed to Carla, and he gave silent thanks for it.

Thierry pulled Mia back to his side, gently but inexorably. 'Stop manhandling the staff, Carla.'

Dylan lifted himself up to his full height. 'That's an insufferably snobbish thing to say, Thierry.'

Carla's face fell and he immediately regretted uttering the words within her earshot.

Thierry glared back at him. '*You* might be happy consorting with criminals, Dylan, but you'll have to excuse me for being less enthused.'

'Ex.' Mia's voice cut through the tension, forcing all eyes to turn to her. 'I'm an *ex*-criminal, Mr Geroux. Naturally, I don't expect you to trust me, but you can rest assured that if my employers have no qualms about either my conduct or my ability to perform the tasks required of me, then you need have no worries on that head either.'

'We *don't* have qualms!' Carla jumped in, staring at Thierry as if a simple glare would force him to agree with her.

Thierry merely shrugged. 'Is volunteering such a good idea? You could catch something…get bitten…and didn't you notice the frightful stench coming from the possums?'

'Oh, I hadn't thought about the practicalities…'

She glanced at Mia uncertainly and Dylan wanted to throw his head back and howl.

'You'd need to be up to date with your tetanus shots. All the information is on the Plum Pines website, and I can give you some brochures if you like. You can think about it for a bit, and call the volunteer co-ordinator if you have any questions.'

Thierry scowled at her, but she met his gaze calmly. 'Maybe it's something the two of you could do together.'

Carla clapped her hands, evidently delighted with the idea.

Thierry glanced at his watch with an abrupt, 'We have to go.' He said goodbye to Dylan, ignoring Mia completely, before leading Carla away.

'An absolute charmer,' Dylan muttered under his breath.

Mia had to have heard him, but she didn't say anything, turning instead to a kangaroo waiting on the other side of the fence and feeding it some titbit she'd fished from her pocket. He glanced back at Carla and a sickening cramp stretched through his stomach—along with a growing sense of foreboding.

Mia nudged him, and then held out a handful of what looked like puffed wheat. 'Would you like to feed the kangaroo?'

With a sense of wonder, he took it and fed the kangaroo. He even managed to run his fingers through the fur of the kangaroo's neck. The tightness in him eased.

'Do you have anything pressing you need to attend to in the next couple of hours?'

She shook her head. 'Nora has instructed me to give you all the time and assistance you need. Later this afternoon, if I'm free, she's going to run through some things that I probably need to know—help me create a checklist.'

'Will you meet me at the lily pond in fifteen minutes?'

She blinked, but nodded without hesitation. 'Yes, of course.'

Mia was sitting at the picnic table waiting for him—her notepad at the ready—when he arrived with his bag of goodies.

If he hadn't been so worried about Carla's situation he'd

have laughed at the look on her face when he pulled forth sandwiches, chocolate bars and sodas.

'This is a working lunch, Mia, not some dastardly plot to seduce you.'

Pink flushed her cheeks. 'I never considered anything else for a moment.'

To be fair, she probably hadn't. She'd made it clear where she stood yesterday. When he'd gone back over her words it had struck him that she really *hadn't* thought him interested in her. She'd just been setting boundaries. And if that boundary-setting hadn't been for his benefit, then it had to have been for hers. Which was interesting.

He took the seat beside her rather than the one opposite.

Why was Mia so determined to remain aloof?

He didn't want her aloof.

He wanted her help.

He took her notepad and pen and put them in his pocket. 'You won't need those.' He pushed the stack of sandwiches, a can of soda and a couple of chocolate bars towards her. 'Eat up while I talk.'

She fixed him with those moss-green eyes, but after a moment gave a shrug and reached for the topmost sandwich. She didn't even check to see what it was.

He gestured to the stack. 'I didn't know what you'd like so I got a variety.' He'd grabbed enough to feed a small army, but he'd wanted to make sure he bought something she liked.

She shrugged again. 'I'm not fussy. I'll eat pretty much anything.'

He had a sudden vision of her in prison, eating prison food, and promptly lost his appetite.'

'Dylan?'

He snapped his attention back. 'Sorry, I'm a bit distracted.'

She bit into her sandwich and chewed, simply waiting for him to speak. It occurred to him that if he wanted her help he was going to have to be honest with her.

A weight pressed down on him. Yesterday afternoon she'd looked at him with such gratitude and admiration—as if he were a superhero. Nobody had ever looked at him like that. He didn't want to lose it so quickly.

*Not even for Carla's sake?*

He straightened. He'd do anything for Carla.

He opened his can of soft drink and took a long swallow before setting it back down. 'I'm ashamed to admit this, but over the last twelve months I've neglected Carla shamefully. She and Thierry have only been dating six months, and the news of their engagement came as a shock. This will probably sound ridiculously big brotherly, but… I'm worried she's making a mistake.'

Mia stared at him for a moment. 'You and Carla seem very close.'

'We are.'

'So why haven't you spent much time together recently?'

How much of the truth did he have to tell her?

He scrubbed a hand through his hair. 'There's an older family member who I have…difficulties with. It's impossible to avoid him when I'm in Australia, and I've wanted to avoid a falling out, so…'

'So you've spent a lot of time overseas instead?'

'Rather than putting up with said family member, I flitted off to organise parties. There was a Turkish sultan's sixtieth birthday party, and then a twenty-fifth wedding anniversary celebration for a couple of members of the British aristocracy. I did some corporate work on the Italian Grand Prix. Oh, and there was a red carpet film premiere that I did just for fun.'

She blinked, as if he'd just spoken in a foreign language. In some ways he supposed he had.

'So there you have it—I'm a coward.'

He lifted his arms and let them drop, waiting for her eyes to darken with scorn. She just stared back at him and waited for him to continue, her gaze not wavering.

He swallowed. 'I came home for Carla's birthday…and for two days over Christmas.' It hadn't been enough! 'That's when she announced her engagement. That's when I realised I'd spent too long away.'

But Carla had finally seemed so settled…so happy. She'd refused to come and work for FWE, preferring to focus on her charity work. Nothing had rung alarm bells for him… until he'd met Thierry.

Mia didn't say anything, but he could tell from her eyes how intently she listened.

'When I heard what he said to you in the reptile house I wanted to knock him to the ground.'

She halted mid-chew, before swallowing. 'I'm very glad you didn't.'

It had only been the thought that Gordon would somehow bring the blame back to her and she'd lose her job that had stilled his hand.

'What he said to you…' His hand clenched and unclenched convulsively around his can of drink. 'I'm sorry you were put into a position where you were forced to listen to that.'

'It's not your responsibility to apologise on behalf of other people, Dylan.'

Maybe not, but it *felt* like his fault. If he'd taken the time to get to know Thierry better before now…

She reached out and placed a sandwich in front of him. 'And you need to remember that just because he dislikes *me*, and my background, it doesn't necessarily make him a bad person.'

Dylan was far from sure about that.

'Even if I didn't have a criminal record, there's no law that says Thierry has to *like* me.'

'Mia, it's not the fact that he doesn't like you or even that he was rude to you that worries me. What disturbs me is the fact that he threatened you.'

'I can take care of myself.'

She said the words quietly and he didn't doubt her. He wished she didn't *have* to take care of herself. He wished she was surrounded by an army of people who'd take care of her. He sensed that wasn't the case, and suddenly he wanted to buy her a hundred chocolate bars… But what good would that do?

*No substance, Dylan Fairweather. You don't have an ounce of substance.*

The words roared through him. He pulled air in through his nose and let it out through his mouth—once, twice.

'I have less confidence,' he said finally, 'in Carla's ability to take care of herself.' He met Mia's dark-eyed gaze. 'What if he talks to *her* the way he spoke to you? What if he threatens *her* in the same way he threatened you?'

# CHAPTER FOUR

DYLAN COULDN'T KNOW it, but each word raised a welt on Mia's soul. The thought of a woman as lovely as Carla, as open and kind as she was, being controlled and manipulated, possibly even abused, by a man claiming to love her...

It made her stomach burn acid.

It made her want to run away at a hundred miles an hour in the other direction.

She recalled how Thierry had trapped her against the wall in the reptile house and her temples started to throb.

She set her sandwich down before she mangled it. 'Have you seen anything to give you cause for concern before now?'

Those laughing lips of his, his shoulders, and even the laughter lines fanning out from his eyes—all drooped. Her heart burned for him. She wanted to reach out and cover his hand, to offer him whatever comfort she could.

*Don't be an idiot.*

Dylan might be all golden flirtatious charm, but it didn't mean he'd want someone like *her* touching him. She chafed her left forearm, digging her fingers into the muscle to try and loosen the tension that coiled her tight. She wasn't qualified to offer advice about family or relationships, but even *she* could see what he needed to do.

'Can't...?' She swallowed to counter a suddenly dry throat. 'Can't you talk to Carla and share your concerns?'

'And say what? *Carla, I think the man you're about to marry is a complete and utter jerk*?' He gave a harsh laugh. 'She'd translate that as me forcing her to choose between her brother and her fiancé.'

From the look on his face, it was evident he didn't think she'd choose him. She thought back to the way Carla had clung to Thierry's arm and realised Dylan might have a point.

'How about something a little less confrontational?' She reached for a can of soda, needing something to do with her hands. 'Something like… *Carla, Thierry strikes me as a bit moody. Are you sure he treats you well?*'

He gave a frustrated shake of his head. 'She'd still read it as me criticising her choice. I'd have to go to great lengths to make it as clear as possible that I'm not making her choose between me and Thierry, but the fact of the matter is—regardless of what I discover—I have no power to stop this wedding unless it's what Carla wants. And if she *does* marry him and he *is* cruel to her… I want her to feel she's able to turn to me without feeling constrained because I warned her off him.'

His logic made sense, in a roundabout way, but it still left her feeling uneasy. 'You know, you don't have a lot to go on, here. One incident isn't necessarily indicative of the man. Perhaps you need to make a concerted effort to get to know him better.'

'I mean to. I'm already on it.' Her surprise must have shown, because he added. 'It doesn't take fifteen minutes to buy a few sandwiches, Mia. I made a couple of phone calls before meeting you here.'

She frowned, not really knowing what that meant. 'Did you find out anything?'

'Not yet.'

And then she realised exactly what he'd done. 'You hired a private investigator?'

'Yep.'

'Don't you think that's a little extreme?'

'Not when my sister's happiness and perhaps her physical well-being is at stake.'

She recalled Thierry's latent physical threat to her and thought Dylan might have a point. Still…

'I want to ask for your assistance, Mia.'

'Mine?' she squeaked. What on earth did he think *she* could do?

'I want you to befriend Carla. She might confide in you— especially as Thierry has made it clear that he doesn't like you.'

Had he gone mad? 'Dylan, I can be as friendly towards Carla as it's possible to be.' She'd already resolved to do so. 'But when we get right down to it I'm just one of the many people helping to organise her wedding. We don't exactly move in the same social circles.'

'I've thought about that too. And I've come up with a solution.'

She had a premonition that she wasn't going to like what came next.

He leaned towards her. 'If Carla thought that we were dating—'

'*No!*' She shot so far away from him she was in danger of falling off the bench.

He continued to survey her, seeming not put off in the least by her vehemence. He unwrapped a chocolate bar and bit into it. 'Why not?'

She wanted to tell him to eat a sandwich first—put something proper into his stomach—but it wasn't her place…and it was utterly beside the point.

'Because I don't date!'

'It wouldn't be *real* dating,' he said patiently. 'It'd be pretend dating.'

She slapped a hand to her chest. 'I work hard to keep a low profile. I don't need my past coming back and biting me more often than it already does. I have a plan for my life,

Dylan—to finish my field officer training and find work in a national park. Somewhere rural—' *remote* '—and quiet, where I can train towards becoming a ranger. All I want is a quiet life so I can live peacefully and stay out of trouble. Dating you *won't* help me achieve that. You live your life up among the stars. You're high-profile.' She pointed to herself. 'Low-profile. Can you see how that's not going to work?'

He tapped a finger against his mouth. 'It's a valid point.'

He leaned towards her, his lips pressed into a firm, persuasive line. It took an effort not to let her attention become distracted by those lips.

'What if I promise to keep your name out of the papers?'

'How? Australia's golden-boy bachelor slumming it with an ex-jailbird? *That* story's too juicy to keep under wraps.'

Heaven only knew what Gordon Coulter would do with a headline like that.

'I've learned over the years how to be *very* discreet. I swear to you that nobody will suspect a thing.'

'Will Thierry be discreet too?' she asked, unable to hide the scorn threading her voice as she recalled his threat to make trouble for her.

'You leave Thierry to me.'

*With pleasure.*

Dylan pushed his shoulders back, a steely light gleaming in his eyes, and she had to swallow. The golden charmer had gone—had been replaced by someone bigger, harder…and far more intimidating. Beneath his laughing, charismatic allure, she sensed that Dylan had a warrior's heart.

His nostrils flared. 'I'll make sure he doesn't touch you.'

She couldn't have said why, but she believed him—implicitly. Her heart started to thud too hard, too fast. 'Dylan, surely you'd be better off concocting this kind of scheme with one of Carla's friends? They'd—'

'She doesn't have any. Not close. Not any more.'

*Why ever not?*

His face turned to stone, but his eyes flashed fire. 'Two years ago Carla's boyfriend ran off with her best friend.'

Mia closed her eyes.

'Carla went into a deep depression and pushed all her friends away. She's never been the sort of person to have a lot of close friends—a large social circle, perhaps, but only one or two people she'd consider close—and…'

'And it was all a mess after such a betrayal,' she finished for him, reading it in his face and wanting to spare him the necessity of having to say it out loud. 'Loyalties were divided and some fences never mended.'

He nodded.

She leapt up, needing to work off the agitation coursing through her. 'Dylan, I…'

'What?'

She swung back to him. 'I don't know how we can pull off something like that—pretending to date—convincingly.'

She sat again, feeling like a goose for striding around and revealing her agitation. When she glanced across at him the expression in his eyes made her stomach flip-flop. In one smooth motion he slid across until they were almost touching. He smelt fresh and clean, like sun-warmed cotton sheets, and her every sense went on high alert.

He touched the backs of his fingers to her cheek and she sucked in a breath, shocked at her need to lean into the contact. Oh, this was madness!

'Dylan, I—'

His thumb pressed against her mouth, halting her words. Then he traced the line of her bottom lip and a pulse thumped to life inside her. She couldn't stop her lip from softening beneath his touch, or her mouth from parting ever so slightly so she could draw the scent of him into her lungs.

'I don't think you realise how lovely you are.'

Somewhere nearby a peacock honked. Something splashed in the lily pond. But all Mia could focus on was the man in front of her, staring down at her as if…as if she were a cream bun he'd like to devour…slowly and deliciously.

It shocked her to realise that in that moment she wanted nothing more than to *be* a cream bun.

*Dangerous.*

The word whispered through her. Some part of her mind registered it, but she was utterly incapable of moving away and breaking the spell Dylan had woven around them.

'Sweet and lovely Mia.'

The low, warm promise in his voice made her breath catch.

'I think we're going to have exactly the opposite problem. I think if we're not careful we could be in danger of being *too* convincing…we could be in danger of convincing ourselves that a lie should become the truth.'

A fire fanned through her. Yesterday, when he'd flirted with her, hadn't it just been out of habit? Had he meant it? He found her attractive?

'Dylan…' His name whispered from her. She didn't mean it to.

His eyes darkened at whatever he saw in her face. 'I dreamed of you last night.'

*Dangerous.*

The word whispered through her again.

But it didn't feel dangerous. It felt *right* to be whispering secrets to each other.

His thumb swept along the fullness of her bottom lip again, pulling against it to explore the damp moistness inside, sensitising it almost beyond bearing. Unable to help herself, she flicked out her tongue to taste him.

'Mia…' He groaned out her name as if it came from some deep, hidden place.

His head moved towards her, his lips aiming to replace his thumb, and her soul suddenly soared.

*Dangerous.*

Dangerous and glorious. This man had mesmerised her from the moment she'd first laid eyes on him and—

*Mesmerised...?*

*Dangerous!*

With a half-sob Mia fisted her hands in his shirt, but didn't have the strength to push him away. She dropped her chin, ensuring that his kiss landed on her brow instead of her lips.

She felt rather than heard him sigh.

After three hard beats of her heart she let him go. In another two he slid back along the bench away from her.

'As I said, I don't think being convincing will be a problem. However much you might deny it, something burns between us—something that could be so much more than a spark if we'd let it.'

It would be foolish to deny it now.

'Why do you have a no-dating rule?' he asked.

His words pulled her back. With an effort, she found her voice. 'It keeps me out of trouble.'

He remained silent, as if waiting for more, but Mia refused to add anything else.

'Maybe one day you'll share your reasoning with me, but until then I fully mean to respect your rules, Mia.'

He did? She finally glanced up at him.

The faintest of smiles touched his lips. 'And, unlike you, I'm more than happy to share my reasons. One—' he held up a finger '—if I don't respect your no-dating rule I suspect I have no hope of winning your co-operation where Carla's concerned.'

Self-interest? At least that was honest.

He held up a second finger. 'And, two, it seems to me you already have enough people in your life who don't respect your wishes. I don't mean to become one of their number.'

Despite her best efforts, some of the ice around her heart cracked.

He stared at her for a long moment, his mouth turning

grim. 'I fancied myself in love once, but when things got tough the girl in question couldn't hack it. She left. Next time I fall in love it'll be with a woman who can cope with the rough as well as the smooth.'

His nostrils flared, his eyes darkening, and Mia wondered if he'd gone back to that time when the girl in question had broken his heart. She wanted to reach out and touch his hand, pull him back to the present.

She dragged her hands into her lap. 'I'm sorry, Dylan.'

He shook himself. 'It's true that I'm attracted to you, but you've just pointed out how very differently we want to live our lives—high-profile, low-profile. In the real world, that continual push and pull would make us miserable.'

Mia had to look away, but she nodded to let him know that she agreed. It didn't stop her heart from shrivelling to the size of a gum nut.

'Your no-dating rule obviously rules out a fling?'

'It does.' Anything else would be a disaster.

'So these are our ground rules. With those firmly in place we shouldn't have any misunderstandings or false hopes, right? We just need to remember the reasons why we're not dating at the moment, why we're not looking for a relationship, and that'll keep us safe.'

She guessed so.

He drummed his fingers on the picnic table. 'It occurs to me that I haven't given you much incentive to help me out. I'm a selfish brute.'

His consideration for Carla proved that was a lie.

'I've no intention of taking advantage of you. I'm fully prepared to pay you for your time.'

She flinched at his words, throwing an arm up to ward them off. 'I don't want your *money*, Dylan.'

What kind of person did he think she was?

*A thief!*

She dragged in a breath. 'I went to jail for fraud. Do you think I'd accept money under dubious circumstances again?'

He swore at whatever he saw in her face. 'I'm sorry—
that was incredibly insensitive. I didn't mean I thought you
could be bought. I just meant it's perfectly reasonable for
you to be financially compensated for your time.'

'No.'

'It doesn't have to be dubious. I'd have a contract drawn
up so there wasn't a hint of illegality about it.'

His earnestness made the earlier sting fade, but... 'Tell
that to the judge.'

He looked stricken for a moment—until he realised she
was joking.

'No money changes hands between us,' she said.

He looked as if he wanted to keep arguing with her, but
finally he nodded. 'Okay.'

She let out a pent-up breath.

'So, Mia, what I need to know is...what do *you* want?
You help me. I help you.'

He'd already saved her job. She hated to admit it, but that
made her beholden to him. She rubbed her forehead. Besides,
if Carla was in danger of being controlled, dominated, bullied... She swallowed, remembering Johnnie Peters and all
he'd convinced her to do. She remembered how she'd sold
her soul to a man who'd used her for his own ends and then
thrown her away. If Carla were in danger, this would be a
way for Mia to start making amends—finding redemption—
for the mistakes of the past.

The thought made her stomach churn. She didn't want
to do this.

*What? You think redemption is easy? You think it's sup-
posed to be a picnic? It should be hard. You should suffer.*

She brushed a hand across her eyes, utterly weary with
herself.

'What do you want, Mia.'

She wanted to keep her job. Yesterday she'd have trusted
him with that piece of information. Today— She glanced

across at him. Today she wasn't convinced that he wouldn't use it against her as a weapon to force her co-operation.

*Who are you kidding? You already know you're going to help him. No force necessary.*

But it would be unwise of her to forget that beneath the smiling charm Dylan had a warrior's heart. And warriors could be utterly ruthless.

She forced her mind off Dylan and to her own situation. He'd ensured her job was safe for the moment...and for the next nine months until Carla's wedding took place. She'd have less than six months left on her traineeship then. Surely she could avoid Gordon's notice in that time? Hopefully he'd be busy with council elections.

*If Carla's wedding takes place.*

'There has to be something you want,' Dylan persisted, pushing a chocolate bar across to her.

What *did* she want? One thing came immediately to mind.

She picked up the bar of chocolate and twirled it around. 'Carla's wedding is going to be a big deal, right?'

'A huge deal. If it goes ahead.'

She glanced at him. 'If Thierry does turn out to be your worst nightmare, but Carla still insists on marrying him, will you still go ahead and give her the wedding she's always dreamed of?'

A muscle worked in his jaw. 'Yes.'

She couldn't explain why, but that eased some of the tightness in her shoulders. She stared down at the chocolate bar. 'So—considering this low profile of mine—when you and your people start distributing press releases and giving media interviews about the wedding, I'd like you to give the credit to Plum Pines and Nora and FWE without mentioning my name at all.'

His brows drew down over his eyes. 'But that's unfair! Credit should go where it's due. Being associated with Carla's wedding could open doors for you.'

Or it could bring her past and the scandal to the front pages of the gossip rags. 'You asked me what I wanted. I'm simply telling you.'

He swung back to scowl at the lily pond. 'I don't like it. It goes against the grain. But if it's what you really want, then consider it done.'

She closed her eyes. 'Thank you.'

'But now you have to tell me something else that you want, because I *truly* feel as if I'm taking utter advantage of you.'

She glanced up to find him glaring at her. For some reason his outrage made her want to smile.

'What do I want?' she shrugged. 'I want to be out on the eastern boundary, helping with the weed eradication programme.'

Dylan stared at Mia and his heart thumped at the wistful expression that flitted across her face. He had a feeling that she didn't have a whole lot of fun in her life. Not if weed extermination topped the list of her wants.

If she agreed to his fake dating plan he resolved to make sure she had fun too. It would be the least he could do. There might be a lot of things he wasn't good at, but when it came to fun he was a grandmaster.

He rose. 'Okay, let's go and do that, then.'

'We?' She choked on her surprise.

He sat again, suddenly unsure. 'You'd prefer to go on your own?'

'Oh, it's not that. I… It's just…'

He could almost see the thoughts racing across her face. *It's hard work, dirty work, menial work.* 'You don't think I'm up to it, do you?'

'It's not that either—although it *is* hard work.' She leaned towards him, a frown in her eyes. 'Dylan, you run a world-class entertainment company. I'm quite sure you have better things to do with your time. I expect you're a very busy man.'

He shook his head. 'I'm on leave.' He'd taken it the moment Carla had announced her engagement. 'I have capable staff.'

And he couldn't think of anything he'd rather do at the moment than lighten Mia's load.

Inspiration hit him. 'Listen to this for a plan. If I become a volunteer here that might encourage Carla to become a volunteer too. If you get to work with her and build up a friendship then the fake dating stuff will be easier.'

Her frown cleared. 'There might even be no need for fake dating stuff.'

Maybe. Maybe not. He couldn't explain it, but the thought of fake dating Mia fired him to life in a way nothing else had in a long time. He'd relish the chance to find out what really make her tick.

'We need a cover story.' He rubbed his hands together. 'I can tell Carla that you piqued my interest—hence the reason I became a volunteer—and then we worked together, discovered we liked each other…and things have gone on from there.'

She screwed up her nose. 'I guess that *could* work…'

He grinned at her. 'Of course it'll work.'

She suddenly thrust out her jaw. 'I'm not going to spy on Carla for you.'

'I'm not asking you to. I'm asking you to become her friend.'

'If this works—if Carla decides she wants to be friends—then I mean to be a proper friend to her. And if that clashes with your agenda—'

He reached over and seized her hand, brought her wrist to his lips. Her eyes widened and her pulse jumped beneath his touch. A growing hunger roared through him. He wanted to put his tongue against that pulse point and kiss his way along her arm until he reached her mouth.

As if she'd read that thought in his face she reclaimed

her hand. He forced himself to focus on the conversation, rather than her intriguing scent.

'I'm asking nothing more than that you be Carla's friend.'

The way her gaze darted away betrayed her assumed composure. 'That's okay, then. As long as we're on the same page.'

'The same page' meant no fling, no relationship...no kissing. He had to keep things simple between them. There was too much at stake.

'Definitely on the same page,' he assured her.

Starting something with Mia was out of the question. She wouldn't last the distance any more than Caitlin had. His whole way of life was anathema to her.

A fist reached inside his gut and squeezed. Caitlin had left him at the absolute lowest point in his life. The devastation of losing his parents *and* her had... It had almost annihilated him. The shock of it still rebounded in his soul. The only thing that had kept him going was Carla, and the knowledge that she'd needed him. He'd found his feet. Eventually. He wasn't going to have them cut out from under him again by repeating the same mistakes.

He turned to find Mia halfway through a sentence.

'... I mean, we can give you overalls, but that's not going to really help, is it?'

She was worried he'd ruin his *clothes*? 'I have my workout gear in the car.'

She folded her arms. 'Along with a four-hundred-dollar pair of trainers, no doubt? I don't want to be held responsible for wrecking *those*.'

He had no idea how much his trainers had cost. But she was probably right. 'Couldn't you rustle me up a pair of boots?'

She gave a reluctant shrug. 'Maybe. Are you sure you want to do this?'

'Absolutely.'

'We'll need to register you as a volunteer. There'll be

forms to fill out and signatures required to ensure you're covered by the Plum Pines insurance.'

The more she tried to put him off, the more determined he became.

He rose with a decisive clap of his hands. 'Then let's get to it.'

She rose too, shaking her head. 'Don't say you weren't warned.

'What's going on here?' Gordon boomed, coming into the office just as Dylan emerged from the change room wearing the overalls and boots that Mia had found for him.

She sat nearby, already dressed for an afternoon of hard work.

She shot to her feet. 'Dylan—'

*'Mr Fairweather,'* Gordon corrected with a pointed glare.

'Dylan,' Dylan confirmed, deciding it would be just as satisfying to punch Gordon on the end of his bulbous nose as it would Thierry. He glanced at Mia and wondered when he'd become so bloodthirsty. 'I've decided to register as a volunteer.' He shoved his shoulders back. 'I want to see first-hand what my hundred-thousand-dollar donation will be subsidising.'

Gordon's jowls worked for a moment. 'It's very generous of you to give both your money *and* your time to Plum Pines…'

Behind Gordon's back, Mia gestured that they should leave. Dylan shrugged himself into full supercilious mode and deigned to nod in the other man's direction.

'Good afternoon, Gordon.'

'Good afternoon, Mr Fairweather.'

Dylan didn't invite Gordon to call him by his Christian name—just strode out through the door that Mia held open for him.

Behind him he heard Gordon mutter to the receptionist, 'Bloody trust fund babies,' before the door closed behind them.

Mia grinned as she strode along beside him. 'I think he likes you.'

He glanced at her grin and then threw his head back and roared.

'What on earth…?'

The moment Dylan rounded the side of their family home—affectionately dubbed 'The Palace'—Carla shot to her feet. Behind her a vista of blue sea and blue sky stretched to the horizon. It was a view he never tired of.

'Dylan, what on *earth* have you been doing? You're so… dirty! Filthy dirty. *Obscenely* dirty.'

He grinned. 'I signed up as a volunteer at Plum Pines. That was an inspired idea of yours, by the way. The place is amazing.'

She started to laugh, settling back into the plump cushions of the outdoor sofa. 'I have a feeling it's a certain Plum Pines employee rather than a newfound enthusiasm for conservation that has you *truly* inspired.'

He sobered. *What on earth…?* That was supposed to come as a surprise.

He managed a shrug. 'I like her.'

'I can tell.'

*How* could she tell?

*She couldn't tell!*

Romance had addled Carla's brain, that was all. She wanted everyone travelling on the same delirious cloud as she. It made her see romance where none existed. But he could work that to his advantage.

'I'm not sure she likes me.'

'And you think by becoming a volunteer it'll make her look upon you with a friendlier eye?'

'Along with my newfound enthusiasm for weed eradication.'

Carla laughed—a delightful sound that gladdened his heart. There'd been a time when he'd wondered if he'd ever hear her laugh again.

'She won't take any of your nonsense, you know.'

He eyed his sister carefully. 'Would it bug you if I asked her out?'

'Not at all.' She studied her fingernails. 'If you'll promise me one thing.'

'Name it.'

'That you won't judge Thierry too harshly based on today's events. He wasn't at his best. He's very different from us, Dylan, but I love him.' She turned a pleading gaze on him. 'Please?'

He bit back a sigh. 'Okay.'

'Thank you!'

He widened his stance. 'But I want to get to know him better before you two tie the knot.'

'That can be arranged.' Her smile widened. 'We can double date!'

*Perfect.*

'Perhaps,' he said, not wanting to appear too eager to share Mia with anyone else. 'Are you going to let him talk you out of volunteering?'

'Not a chance.' She laughed. 'I'm signing up first thing tomorrow.'

# CHAPTER FIVE

MIA STARED INTO the mirror and rubbed a hand across her chest in an effort to soothe her racing heart.

*You look fine.*

Dylan had assured her that tonight's date—*fake*date— was casual, not dressy. They were meeting Carla and Thierry at some trendy burger joint for dinner and then going on to a movie.

She really needed to go shopping for some new clothes. She'd not bothered much with her appearance since getting out of jail. She'd avoided pretty things, bright colours, shunning anything that might draw attention.

She glanced back at the mirror. Her jeans and pale blue linen shirt were appropriately casual, if somewhat bland. The outfit wouldn't embarrass her. More to the point, it wouldn't embarrass Dylan. On impulse she threaded a pair of silver hoops through her ears.

For the last five days Dylan had spent every morning at Plum Pines, helping her dig out weeds. And for the entire time he'd remained unfailingly cheerful and good-natured. He'd never once made her feel as if he was counting down the hours until he'd met his side of the bargain.

He continued to flirt outrageously—not just with her but with all the other female volunteers too. It made her feel safe.

She shook her head at that thought. She had to remain vigilant, make sure she didn't become too comfortable around him.

She swung away from the mirror, tired of her reflection. The fact remained that she had limited wardrobe options and this was the best that she could muster. Brooding about it was pointless. Besides, she had more important things to worry about.

Like what on earth was she going to add to the conversation tonight?

She strode into her tiny living room and dropped to the sofa. She needed to come up with five topics of conversation. She glanced at the clock. *Fast!* Dylan would be here to collect her in fifteen minutes. She chewed on her bottom lip. No matter how much she might want to, she couldn't sit through dinner without saying anything. That wouldn't be keeping her end of the deal.

Dear God! What to talk about, though? *Think!*

A knock sounded on the door.

Her gaze flew to the clock. He was early. And she hadn't come up with even one topic of conversation!

Dylan hated to admit it, but he couldn't wait to catch a glimpse of Mia out of uniform. Not that he had anything against her uniform, but there was only so much khaki cotton twill a man could take.

In some deep hidden part of himself lurked a male fantasy he should no doubt be ashamed of, but… He'd love for Mia to answer the door in a short skirt and sky-high heels. *So predictable!* He had a feeling, though, that Mia probably didn't own either.

Still, he'd make do with jeans and a nice pair of ballet flats. That would be nice. Normal. And maybe away from work she'd start to relax some of that fierce guard of hers.

He knocked again and the door flew open. He smiled. *Bingo!* She wore jeans and ballet flats. With the added bonus of surprisingly jaunty earrings that drew attention to the dark glossiness of her hair. He'd not seen her with her hair down before. He had an insane urge to reach out and run his hand through it, to see if it were as soft and silky as it promised.

He curved his hand into a fist and kept it by his side. He'd meant to greet her with his typical over-the-top gallantry—kiss her hand, twirl her around and tell her she looked good enough to eat—except the expression in her eyes stopped him.

He made no move to open the screen door, just met her gaze through its mesh. 'What's wrong?'

Puffing out a sigh, she pushed the door open and gestured him in. 'You're early.'

'If you haven't finished getting ready I'm happy to wait. You look great, by the way.' He didn't want her thinking that he thought she didn't *look* ready. He didn't want her stressing about her appearance at all.

'No, I'm ready. I just… I don't do this, you know?'

'Date? Yes, so you said. It's not a date, Mia.'

Her living room was small. In fact the whole cottage was tiny. She'd told him earlier in the week that she rented one of the Plum Pines workers' cottages. There was a row of three of them on the south side of the reserve. From what he could tell, she ate, breathed and slept Plum Pines. He glanced around. Which seemed odd when she'd clearly taken few pains to make her cottage cosy and comfortable.

'Are you sure about this plan, Dylan?'

He turned back, frowning at her unease. 'What are you worried about?'

One slim shoulder lifted. 'That I'll embarrass you.' She gestured for him to take a seat on the sofa. She planted herself on a hard wooden chair at the little dining table pressed hard up against one wall.

She moistened her lips and he realised she wore a pale mocha-coloured lipstick. Desire arrowed straight to his groin. Gritting his teeth, he did his best to ignore it. For pity's sake, he'd warned himself off her—that should have been that!

He gritted his teeth harder. Apparently not. But, while he might find her attractive, he didn't have to act like a teenager. He needed to put her at her ease—not crank up the tension further.

'I can't imagine how you think you'll embarrass me.'

'I'm… I'm not much of a talker, but I know I need to keep up my share of the conversation tonight.'

His heart stilled before surging against the walls of his ribs.

She lifted her hands, only to let them drop back to her lap. 'I've been trying to come up with five fool-proof topics of conversation so that…' She shrugged again. 'So that I'm pulling my weight.'

In that moment he wanted nothing more than to tug her into his arms and hug her. He had a feeling that would be the last thing she'd want. He contented himself with leaning towards her instead. She wore a soft floral scent and he pulled it as far into his lungs as he could.

'I don't expect you to become a sudden chatterbox. It's not who you are. I don't want you to change. I like you just the way you are. So does Carla.'

Was she worried that the better they got to know her the less they'd like her? The thought disturbed him.

'It's just…you and Carla are so bubbly and fun. I should hate to put a dampener on that.'

She thought he was *fun*? A smile tugged through him. 'You mean Carla and I are noisy chatterboxes who dominate the conversation and won't let anyone else get a word in edgewise.'

Her eyes widened. 'I did *not* say that!'

He burst out laughing. After a moment she rolled her eyes, resting back in her seat.

'You must've worked out by now that Carla and I love an audience.'

She gave a non-committal, 'Hmm…'

'And you have to remember Thierry will be there, and no one could accuse call *him* of liveliness.'

'I'm not sure I want to be compared to Thierry.'

He tried a different tack. 'How did the school group go this afternoon?'

Her face lit up. 'They had a great time. It's so funny to watch them the first time they touch a snake or a lizard.'

He picked up the book sitting on her coffee table—a recent autobiography of a famous comedian. 'Good?'

'Yes, very. She's as funny on the page as she is on the television.'

He set the book back down. 'Did you hear about that prank the engineering students at the university pulled with the garden gnomes?'

She sent him an odd look. 'I saw the photos in the paper. It was rather cheeky...but funny.'

'What's a dish you've always meant to cook but never have?'

Her frown deepened. 'Um...veal scaloppini.'

'I couldn't help noticing that these cottages don't have any off-street parking.'

Her eyes narrowed. 'And...?'

'And I didn't see a car parked out the front, which leads me to conclude that you don't have a car.'

She folded her arms. 'That's correct.'

'Are you planning to get one?'

'Maybe.'

'When?'

Her forehead creased. 'What is this, Dylan? Twenty Questions?'

'There you go. There's your five topics of conversation, should you need them—a funny incident at work, a book recommendation, a local news story, does anyone have a recipe for veal scaloppini they'd recommend, and I'm thinking of getting a small to medium-sized hatchback—what should I get?'

She pushed her hair back behind her ears, all but glaring at him, before folding her arms again. 'How do you know I want a hatchback?'

'You're young and you don't have kids, which means you don't have to settle for a station wagon yet.'

She unfolded her arms, but then didn't seem to know what to do with them. She settled on clasping them in her lap. And then she smiled—*really* smiled—and it lit her up from the inside out. Her dark eyes danced and he felt a kick inside that should have felled him.

'Five topics of conversation—just like that.' She snapped her fingers. 'You managed it effortlessly. How can you make it so easy?'

'Probably the same way you can identify the difference between a bush orchid and a noxious weed.' He grinned, referencing an incident earlier in the week when he'd set about eradicating the wrong plant.

She continued to stare at him as if he were amazing, and he had the disconcerting feeling that he could bask in that admiration forever. He shrugged. 'Practice. In my line of work I have to talk to a lot of people. Though, if the truth be told, the sad fact is that I have a talent for frivolity and nonsense.'

'Good conversation is neither frivolous nor nonsensical.'

He waggled his eyebrows. 'It should be if you're doing it right.'

She didn't laugh. She met his gaze, her face sober. 'It's not nonsense to put someone at ease.'

His gut clenched up all over again. If he continued to put her at her ease would she eventually let him kiss her?

He stiffened. He and Mia were *not* going to kiss. They weren't going to do anything except find out if Thierry deserved Carla. Full stop.

This was nothing more than a case of opposites attracting. He and Mia were too different—too mismatched—to make

things work in the long term. And he refused to do anything
to hurt her in the short term. She'd been through enough.

By the end of dinner Dylan could cheerfully have strangled
Thierry. The only contributions he'd made to the conversation had been negative, except when Carla had won a grudg-
ing concession that his gourmet burger was *'okay'*.

Mia, for all her worry, had been a delightful dinner com-
panion. And nobody had needed to ask her if *her* burger was
good. The expression on her face after she'd taken her first
bite had made him grin.

Thierry had scowled.

From what Dylan could tell, scowling was Thierry's de-
fault setting.

When a lull had occurred in the conversation Mia had
mentioned the book she was reading and asked if anyone
else had read it.

Thierry had ignored the question.

Carla had invited Mia to join her book group.

Mia had kept her expression interested, but in her lap her
fingernails had dug into her palms, creating half-moons in
her flesh that he'd wanted to massage away.

She'd swallowed. 'Are you sure I'd be welcome?'

'All are welcome! We meet at the library on the first
Wednesday of the month.'

'Well…thank you. It sounds like fun.' And she'd promised to read the following month's book.

Dylan had wanted to hug her. He hadn't known that asking her to befriend Carla, and the specific details involved,
would be so difficult for her. The thing was, friendship didn't
seem to be an issue at all. He sensed that both women genuinely liked each other. But going out and mixing with people
was obviously a challenge for Mia.

He couldn't help thinking, though, that locking herself
away and hiding from the world wasn't the right thing to do.

He'd taken his cue from her, however, and gone out of

his way to invite Thierry for a game of golf. Thierry had declined, saying he didn't play the game. Dylan had then tried inviting him out on his yacht, but Thierry had declined that too, saying he was too busy with work at the moment.

His heart had sunk when Carla had avoided his gaze. What on earth did she *see* in the man?

Now dinner was over, and they were finally seated in the cinema—Mia on one side of him and Carla and then Thierry on the other—Dylan let out a sigh of relief, no longer obligated to attempt small talk with his sister's fiancé.

It wasn't until the cinema darkened, though, that he suddenly remembered Mia's thin-lipped, pale-faced reaction to the nocturnal houses. *Damn it!* Did the cinema have the same effect?

He touched her arm and she started.

'Is being here uncomfortable for you? Is it like the nocturnal houses?' He kept his voice low so no one could overhear.

'No, it's fine. High ceiling…and it's cool. Those things make a difference.' Her eyes gleamed in the dim light. 'Actually, I'm really looking forward to the film.'

It made him wonder when had been the last time *he'd* relished an outing as simple as this one. Reaching over, he took her hand. When she stiffened, he leaned closer to whisper, 'It's just for show.'

It wasn't, though. He held her hand because he wanted to. He leaned in closer because he wanted to breathe in that subtle floral scent she wore.

When the movie started her hand finally relaxed in his as if she'd forgotten it was there. For the next ninety minutes Dylan experienced the romantic comedy tactilely—entirely through Mia's reactions. They weren't reactions visible in her face, but evident only via her hand in his—in the twitches, squeezes, sudden letting go, in her hand's tension and relief. He sat there spellbound as Mia worried for and cheered on the romantic leads. All of it rendered for him through her fingers.

What miracle allowed him to read the language of her hand so fluently? His heart surged against his ribs. He had to be careful not to let his fascination with this woman grow. *Very* careful. Nothing good could come of it.

When Dylan pulled up outside the front of Mia's cottage at the end of the evening she didn't invite him in.

She shook her head when he reached for his door handle. 'You don't need to walk me to my door.'

But what if he wanted to?

*This isn't a real date.*

He nodded. 'Right.'

She undid her seat belt. 'I just wanted to say…' She swung back, and even in the dark he could see the wariness in her eyes. 'I did have a nice time tonight, Dylan. Thank you.'

'I'm not after thanks. I want to apologise. For Thierry. Again.'

She shook her head. 'Not your place.'

He clocked the exact moment when she gave in to her curiosity.

'But why in particular this time?'

There'd been an excruciatingly awkward moment at dinner. Carla had asked Mia what the last film she'd been to see had been, and Mia had paled. Thierry had pounced with a narrow-eyed sneer.

'It might be more pertinent to ask, *When was the last time you went to the movies?*'

Dylan's gut had churned and an ugly heat had flushed through him.

Mia had answered with a quiet, 'It'll be over four years since I've been to see a movie.'

And the reason why—the fact she'd been in jail—had pulsed in all the spaces between them.

Dylan couldn't imagine Mia in prison—he couldn't make it make sense. But then he recalled her Spartan cottage and wondered if she'd actually left prison at all.

He rubbed a hand across his chest, trying to dislodge the hard ball that had settled there. 'Thierry went out of his way to make sure everyone remembered *why* you'd not been to see a film in so long.'

She glanced down at her hands. 'Dylan—'

'It wasn't only rude, it was unkind.' How could Carla marry someone like that?

Mia rubbed her hands down the front of her jeans. Finally she glanced at him. 'No matter how much you try to ignore it or justify it, the fact I've been in prison is not a small issue.'

He reached out to cup her face. 'Mia, you're more than your past. You're more than the mistakes that landed you in jail.'

Her bottom lip trembled. The pain that flashed through her eyes speared straight into his gut.

She reached up and with a squeeze removed his hand. 'It's kind of you to say that, but it's not what it feels like. It feels huge. It was a defining moment in my life. I completely understand why other people take issue with it.'

With that she slipped out of the car and strode up to her front door.

Dylan waited until she was safely ensconced inside and the veranda light was switched off with an unambiguous 'the night is over' conviction. With a sigh he didn't understand, he turned the car towards home.

Mia set her sandwich down and unclipped her ringing phone. 'Mia Maydew.'

'Mia, it's Dylan and I have brilliant news.'

The sound of his voice made her pulse gallop. She swallowed and did her best to sound cool and professional. 'Which is…?'

'I have an appointment with Felipe Fellini—the photographer Carla's been so hot for.'

That made her brows lift. She hadn't thought the guy did

weddings or celebrity functions any more. Still, the Fair-weathers had a lot of clout.

'She must be over the moon.'

'I haven't mentioned it to her yet. He's agreed to a meeting—nothing more. I don't want to get her hopes up until it's official.'

Dylan was certainly going above and beyond where Carla's wedding was concerned. Especially when he wasn't even convinced that it would go ahead.

Correction—he wasn't convinced that the groom was worthy of the bride. That was an entirely different matter.

'Mia, are you still there?"

'Yes. I... That's great news.' She tried to gush, but she wasn't much of a one for gushing. 'I'm very impressed.'

'Liar.' He laughed. 'You couldn't care less.'

'I want Carla's wedding to be perfect.' And she didn't care how surly, bad-tempered or humourless Thierry happened to be. With her whole heart she hoped he treated Carla with respect, that he made her happy...that he did indeed deserve her.

'That I *do* believe. The thing is, Felipe wants to meet at Plum Pines this afternoon—two o'clock, if possible. He's only in Newcastle for a couple of days, and his decision on whether or not to take the job apparently depends on the potential locations Plum Pines offers for wedding shots. He wants to start with the lily pond.'

In other words he wanted *her* to be available at two this afternoon to take Felipe around.

'That won't be a problem.'

She'd finished supervising the weed eradication programme last week. She was in the process of helping Veronica create an action plan for a particularly inaccessible area on the northern boundary. That, along with path maintenance, was what her week consisted of.

'Are you on your lunchbreak?'

She traced a finger along the wooden edge of the picnic table. 'I am.'

'Excellent! That means we can chat.'

She stared up into the eucalypt canopy above and shook her head. Dylan *always* wanted to chat. The sooner he got back to FWE and his usual work the better. He wasn't the kind of guy who liked sitting around and twiddling his thumbs, and she had a feeling Carla's wedding wouldn't have his full attention until he'd passed judgement on Thierry.

She suspected he rang her just to 'chat' in an effort to remove the sting of Thierry's incivility. Which was totally unnecessary. Only she didn't know how to say so without sounding ungracious.

'What are you having for lunch?'

She was having what she always had. 'A sandwich.'

'What's in it?'

She lifted the top slice of bread. 'Egg and lettuce. Why is this important?' Nevertheless, she found herself suppressing a smile.

'Are you having chocolate once you finish your *delicious* sandwich?'

She choked back a laugh. 'I refuse to have chocolate with *every* meal. I have a banana.'

'But you're missing a food group! You have carbohydrate, protein, a fruit and a vegetable, but no dairy. Chocolate is dairy. It makes for a rounded meal, Mia.'

She couldn't help but laugh. 'I'll see you at two, Dylan.'

She hung her phone back on her belt, a frown building through her. In the last fortnight Dylan had developed the habit of calling her a couple of times a week—always during her lunchbreak. Some days he didn't mention the wedding at all. She sometimes thought his sole reason for calling was simply to make her laugh. But why would he do that?

Was it really all for Carla's benefit?

*Do you think he's doing it for your benefit? Do you really think he could be interested in you?*

It was a ludicrous notion—utter wishful thinking. They'd set their ground rules. Dylan wasn't any more interested in a relationship than she was, and a fling was out of the question. But the wisdom of that reasoning didn't dissipate the heat building between them. It didn't quash the thrill that raced through her whenever she heard his voice. It didn't stop her from looking forward to seeing him this afternoon.

She bit into her sandwich. Since when had the prospect of a meeting become more attractive than tromping along solitary paths with loppers and a pair of secateurs?

She had to be careful around Dylan. *Very* careful. She couldn't go falling for his charm. Never again would she be a man's sap, his puppet. Not even one as alluring and attractive as Dylan. She'd sworn never to travel that particular path again.

*Couldn't you just kiss him once anyway? Just to see?*

The illicit thought came out of left field. She stiffened. No, she could not!

No *way* was she kissing Dylan. Any kissing was absolutely and utterly out of the question. That way led to the slippery slope of lost good intentions and foolish, deceitful dreams. She wasn't descending that slope again. She had no intention of falling into the pit that crouched at its bottom.

*So…that's a no, then?*

*A definite no!*

She wrapped up what was left of her sandwich and tossed it into a nearby bin. A glance at her watch told her she could manage an hour's worth of path maintenance before she had to get back to meet with Dylan and his photographer. Wrestling with overgrown native flora sounded exactly what she needed.

Neither the exercise nor Mia's resolution to resist Dylan's appeal stopped her every sense from firing to life the moment she clapped eyes on him that afternoon. It made her want to groan in despair.

*No despair*! She'd only need despair if she gave in to her attraction—if she handed her heart to him on a platter and became his willing slave. The attraction part of the equation was utterly normal. She'd defy *any* woman to look at Dylan and not appreciate him as the handsomest beast she'd ever laid eyes on.

Not that he *was* a beast. Not when he moved towards her, hand outstretched, a smile of delight on his face at seeing her. Then he was an utter sweetheart.

She couldn't stop herself from smiling back.

*It's polite to smile.*

Polite or not, she couldn't help it.

He kissed her cheek, his warm male scent raising gooseflesh on her arms.

'Mia…' He ushered her towards the other man. 'I'd like you to meet Felipe Fellini.'

She shook the photographer's hand. 'I've heard a lot about you, Mr Fellini.'

'Yes, yes, it is inevitable. Now *this*…' He gestured to encompass the lily pond and its surrounds. 'You must tell me that you have something better, something more original for me to work with than this.'

He strutted through the area in a coat embroidered with wild, colourful poppies, flinging his arms out in exaggerated disappointment while speaking in an affected American-Italian accent.

Mia stared at him, utterly flummoxed. Never, in all of her twenty-five years, had she ever come across someone like Felipe Fellini!

She moistened her lips. 'I…uh…you don't like it?'

'Ugh, darling! You *do*? I mean, *look* at it!' He pointed at the pond, the grass, a tree.

Behind Felipe's back, Dylan started to laugh silently. Mia had to choke back her answering mirth. 'I… I can't say as I've ever really thought about it.'

He swatted a hand in her direction. 'That's because you're

not an *artiste*. My sensitivities are honed to within an inch of their lives, darling.'

It should have been dismissive, but the words held a friendly edge and she suddenly realised he was having the time of his life.

She planted her hands on her hips. 'What's wrong with it?'

'It's a cliché. An utter cliché.'

'But isn't that what a wedding is all about?'

The question slipped out before she could censor it. She wished it back the moment both men spun to face her—Felipe with his hands up to cover his mouth as if utterly scandalised, Dylan contemplating her with those deep blue eyes, his delectable lips pursed.

'Dylan, *darling*, it appears I've met a creature I never thought existed—a truly unromantic woman.'

Dylan folded his arms, nudging the other man with his shoulder. 'I saw her first.'

Felipe spluttered with laughter. 'Darling, I'm not a ladies' man—but if I were…you'd be in trouble. I'd have her eating out of my hand in no time.'

Mia started to laugh. She couldn't help it. Felipe, it appeared, enjoyed flirting and games every bit as much as Dylan.

'Come along, you unromantic girl.' Felipe draped an arm across her shoulders with a smirk in Dylan's direction. 'Show me something worthy of my talents.'

Dylan fell in behind them with a good-natured grin. Mia led them to the utility she'd parked further down the track. One hundred and eighty hectares was a lot of ground to cover. They wouldn't manage it all on foot before dark.

Felipe discounted the first two spots Mia showed him—a forest glade of wattle, with low overhanging branches, and a pocket of rainforest complete with a tiny trickling stream.

'Clichéd?' she asked.

'Totally.'

'You don't know what you want, but you'll know it when you see it, right?'

Dylan's chuckle from the back seat filled the interior of the car, warming Mia's fingers and toes.

'I'll have none of your cheek, thank you, Dylan Fairweather. You, sir, are an uncultured and coarse Philistine.' He sniffed. 'I understand you have a *Gilmore* on your wall.'

For a moment Dylan's eyes met Mia's in the rear-vision mirror. 'You're welcome to come and admire it any time you like, Felipe.'

'*Pah!*'

At Mia's raised eyebrow, Dylan added, 'Jason Gilmore—like Felipe, here—is a world-class photographer.'

Felipe gave a disbelieving snort and Mia found herself grinning, Dylan and Felipe's high spirits momentarily rubbing off onto her.

'I've never heard of Jason Gilmore, but I've heard of Felipe. So I'm not sure this Mr Gilmore can be all that good. He certainly can't be in the same class as Felipe.'

Felipe reached out and clasped the hand she had on the steering wheel, pressing his other to his heart. 'I *love* this girl.'

In the next instant he almost gave her a heart attack.

'Stop!' he screeched.

She slammed on the brakes, and even though they weren't going fast gravel still kicked up around them from the unsealed road. Before she could ask Felipe what was wrong, he was out of the car and moving with remarkable agility through the neighbouring strip of bush.

She glanced at Dylan in wordless enquiry.

He shook his head. 'I have no idea. But I suspect we should follow him.'

'This!' Felipe declared when they reached him.

Mia stared. 'It's a fallen tree.'

He seized her by the shoulders and propelled her to the tree, ordered her to straddle it. Next he forced Dylan to straddle it as well, facing her. Mia straightened and folded her arms, frowning at the photographer.

'Why do you frown at me?' He glared at Dylan. 'Why does she frown at me? Make her stop.'

'Uh… Mia…?'

'I can see that *you*—' she pointed a finger at Felipe '—will have no regard for Carla's dress.'

'*Pah!* This is art. If Carla wants art then she will need to make sacrifices. Now, do as I say and lean in towards each other.'

Whipping out his camera, he motioned with his hands for them to move closer together.

He heaved an exaggerated sigh. 'As if you're about to kiss. Mia, darling, I know you don't have a romantic bone in your delightful body, but you have a pulse, and you have to admit that your fellow model is very pretty. I need to capture the light and the landscape. Art is *work*.'

She glanced at Dylan to see if he'd taken Felipe's 'pretty' remark as a slight on his masculinity. She found him grinning.

He winked at her. 'You heard what the man said.' And then he puckered up in such an exaggerated way that any threat inherent in the situation was immediately removed. She puckered up too.

With the odd, 'Tsk!' as if in disapproval of their antics, Felipe set about taking photographs.

The flash made Mia wince.

'Headache?' Dylan asked.

'I just don't like having my photo taken.' The last time a flash had gone off in her face had been when she'd been led from the courthouse…in handcuffs. It wasn't a memory she relished.

As if he could sense her ambivalence, Dylan leapt to his feet.

'Darling!' Felipe spluttered. 'I—'

'You'll have to make do with just me as a model, Master Fellini. Run!' he muttered out of the corner of his mouth to Mia.

So she did. She shot to her feet and all but sprinted away, to stand behind and to one side of Felipe, in amongst the bracken fern.

She watched the two men's antics with growing enjoyment. Felipe barked out orders and Dylan promptly, if somewhat exaggeratedly, carried them out. He flirted with the camera without a scrap of self-consciousness. Felipe, in turn, flirted outrageously back.

*Double entendres* flew through the air until Mia found herself doubled up with laughter. It was just so much *fun* watching Dylan!

Without warning, Felipe turned and snapped a shot of her.

She blinked, sobering in an instant.

Dylan was immediately puffed up, all protective.

Felipe beamed as he stared down at his camera. 'Perfect!'

# CHAPTER SIX

MIA SWALLOWED. 'WHAT do you mean, *perfect*?'

He gestured her over. 'Come and see.'

She didn't want to see. She wanted to run away to hack and slash hiking trails, to fill in potholes and be away from people with their unspoken questions and flashing cameras.

*Dylan's not like that.*

Dylan was the worst of the lot!

She forced reluctant feet over to where Felipe stood with his camera held out to her. Dylan moved across too, and she sensed the tension in his shoulders, in the set of his spine.

'You said you just wanted to test the light—to get a sense of scale and a feel for the locations, figure out how to make them work for you.'

'Darling, I'm an *artiste*. My mind, my eyes, my brain… they're always searching for the perfect shot.'

She went to take the camera from him, but he shook his head.

'Just look.'

She leaned in to look at the display on the screen. Her gut clenched up tight at what she saw.

Dylan leaned over her right shoulder. 'Holy cow…'

In the photograph, Mia stood knee-high in bracken fern, bent at the waist with her head thrown back, her mouth wide with laughter and her eyes crinkled and dancing. The entire picture rippled with laughter. She didn't know how Felipe had managed it, but when she stared at the photo she could feel delight wrap around her and lift her up.

He'd made her look beautiful.

She swallowed and straightened, bumping into Dylan. She moved away with a murmured apology.

'You see what I mean?' Felipe demanded. 'The picture is perfect.'

Her temples started to throb. 'It's a lie.'

'Art doesn't lie, darling.'

She was aware of how closely Dylan watched her, of how darkly his eyes throbbed as they moved between the image of her on the camera and the flesh and blood her. She found him just as disturbing as Felipe's photograph.

'Will you sign a release form, darling, allowing me to use that photograph in my next exhibition? This is *precisely* what I need.'

Her mouth dried. She had a plan. That plan was to remain in the background. *This* wasn't remaining in the background.

Her hands curled into fists. 'No.'

Felipe switched the camera off with a sniff. 'That photograph could be the centrepiece of my next exhibition. And, darling, I don't actually *need* your permission. I was only being polite. This is a public place. As such, I'm free to take photographs of anything I please.'

Instinct told her that pleading with him would do no good. Her stomach started to churn.

'How much would a photograph like that sell for?'

She'd been aware of Dylan growing taller and sterner beside her. She glanced up and realised he'd transformed into full warrior mode. A pulse started up in her throat, and a vicarious thrill took hold of her veins even as she bit back a groan.

Felipe waved him away. 'It's impossible to put a price on a photograph like that. I have no intention of selling it.'

'Sell it to me *now*.'

Dylan named a sum that had her stomach lurching.

'No!' She swung round to him and shook her head. 'Don't even think about it. That's a ludicrous amount of money for a stupid photograph.'

He planted his hands on his hips. 'It's obvious you don't want it shown in a public exhibition. Let me buy it.'

She folded her arms to hide how much her hands shook. 'I don't want it hanging on your wall either.'

Why would he pay such a huge sum for a photograph of her anyway?

*Because he cares?*

She pushed that thought away. She didn't want him to care. She hadn't asked him to care!

As if he'd read that thought in her face, Dylan thrust out his jaw, his eyes glittering. 'Felipe, sell me the photo.'

She stabbed a finger at the photographer. 'You'll do nothing of the sort.'

Felipe turned to Dylan, hands raised. 'You heard what the lady said, darling.'

Dylan glowered—first at her and then at the photographer. 'Okay, let me make myself crystal-clear. If that photograph is ever displayed publicly I'll bring the biggest lawsuit you've ever seen crashing down on your head.'

Felipe merely smiled. 'The publicity will be delicious!'

Mia grabbed Dylan's arm and shook it, but her agitation barely seemed to register. It was as useless as rattling iron bars.

'You will do absolutely nothing of the sort!' she said.

His brows drew down low over his eyes, his entire mien darkening. 'Why not?'

'Because you don't own me. You don't get to make decisions for me.' She swung to Felipe. '*You* don't own me either. In a just world you wouldn't get to make such a decision either.'

Nobody said anything for a moment.

'Mia, darling…'

She didn't want to hear Felipe's excuses and justifications.

She turned towards the car. 'I thought art was supposed to make the world a better place, not a worse one. I think it's time we headed back.'

'*Darling!*'

She turned to find Felipe removing the memory card from the camera. He took her hand and closed her fingers over it. 'It's yours. I'm sorry.'

Relief almost made her stagger. 'Thank you,' she whispered, slipping it into her top pocket and fastening the button. She tried to lighten the mood. 'I expect for an *artiste* like yourself great photos are a dime a dozen.'

'No, darling, they're not,' he said, climbing into the car.

All the while she was aware of the brooding way Dylan watched her, of the stiff movements of his body, betraying…*anger*? It made her heart drum hard against her ribs.

'That photograph is truly unique, but I could not exhibit it without your blessing. I do not wish anyone to feel diminished by my art.'

She nodded. Felipe was a good man. So was Dylan. She was surrounded by people she didn't deserve.

'But if you should have a change of heart…ever change your mind…' He slipped a business card into her hand.

She nodded. 'You'll be the first to know.'

She didn't add that a change of heart was highly unlikely. She had a feeling he already knew that.

She glanced in the rear-vision mirror to find Dylan staring at her, his gaze dark and brooding. She had no idea what he was thinking…or what he must think of *her*. Her pulse sped up again. Did he hate her after what she'd said?

She didn't want him to hate her.

She had a feeling, though, that it would be better for both of them if he did.

Dylan showed up at her cottage that night.

Without a word she ushered him in, wondering at her own lack of surprise at seeing him.

'I wanted to discuss what happened this afternoon,' he said without preamble.

'I don't see that there's much to discuss.' She turned towards the kitchen. 'Can I get you something to drink—tea or coffee? I have some light beer if you'd rather.'

'No, thank you.'

*Good.* They could keep this quick, then. She grabbed some water for herself and motioned him to the sofa, taking a seat at the table.

Dylan didn't sit. He stood in the middle of the room, arms folded, and glared at her.

She heaved a sigh. 'I'm sorry, Dylan, but I'm not a mind-reader. What exactly did you want to discuss?'

'I didn't appreciate your implication this afternoon that I was trying to own you. I simply felt responsible for putting you in a situation that had obviously made you uncomfortable. I set about fixing the situation. I don't see how that can be seen as trying to control you.'

She stared into her glass of water. 'I appreciate your intentions were good, but it doesn't change the fact that you didn't ask me my opinion first.'

'There wasn't time!' He flung an arm out. 'Where people like Felipe are concerned it's best to come at them hard and fast.'

'And what if I told you that your solutions were more horrifying to me than the initial problem?'

'Were they?'

'Yes.'

He widened his stance. 'Why?'

She stood then too, pressing her hands to her stomach. 'Ever since I got out of jail I've had one objective—to keep a low profile, to keep out of trouble. A lawsuit would create a hundred times more furore than an anonymous photograph in some exhibition.'

He straightened, his height almost intimidating. Not that

it frightened her. She sensed that frightening her was the last thing he wanted.

'Are you concerned that someone from your past will track you down?'

'No.' And she wasn't. That was all done with.

His hands went to his hips. 'Look, I understand your dismay at the thought of publicity, but what on earth was wrong with *me* buying the photograph?'

'I'm already beholden enough to you!'

'It's my money. I can do as I please with it.'

'Not on my watch, you can't. Not when you're spending that money solely for my benefit.'

He stared at her with unflinching eyes. 'You'd rather have let that picture go public then be beholden to me?'

She met his gaze. 'Yes.'

He wheeled away from her. When he swung back his eyes were blazing.

Before he could rail at her about ingratitude and stubbornness, she fired a question back at him. 'If Felipe had sold you that photograph, would you have given it to me?'

He stilled. His chin lowered several notches. 'I'd have promised to keep it safe.'

They both knew it wasn't the same thing. She could feel her lips twist. 'So, in the end, it was Felipe who did what I truly wanted after all.'

A tic started up in his jaw. 'This is the thanks I get for trying to help you?'

She refused to wither under his glare. 'You weren't trying to help me. What you're angry about is missing your chance to buy that picture.'

He moved in closer. 'And that scares the pants off of you, doesn't it?'

*Bullseye.*

She refused to let her fear show. 'I've told you where I stand on relationships and romance. I don't know how I can make it any plainer, but offering such a ludicrous sum for a photo of me leads me to suspect that you haven't heard me.'

'Some women would've found the gesture romantic.'

*Exactly.*

'Not me.'

He shoved his hands in his pockets and strode around the room. Mia did her absolute best not to notice the way the muscles of his shoulders rippled beneath the thin cotton of his business shirt, or how his powerful strides ate up the space in her tiny living room. He quivered like a big cat, agitated and undecided whether to pounce or not.

She knew exactly how to soothe him. If she went to him, put her arms around his neck and pressed her length against his, he'd gather her in his arms and they'd lose themselves to the pleasure they could bring each other.

The pulse at her throat pounded. She gripped her hands together. It wouldn't help. It might be possible to do 'uncomplicated' when it came to a fling, but refused to risk it.

If only that knowledge could cool the stampede of her blood!

He swung around. 'You might have your heart under lock and key, Mia, but you have no right to command mine.'

*He wasn't promising her his heart.* Heat gathered behind her eyes. He wasn't promising anything more than a quick roll in the hay, and they both knew it.

'You're forgetting the ground rules. We promised!'

'Just because I wanted that photo it doesn't mean I want *you.*'

But they both knew he desired her in the most primitive way a man could want a woman. And they both knew she desired him back. They were balancing too narrowly on a knife-edge here, and she couldn't let them fall.

She clamped her hands to her elbows. Wrapped up in his attraction for her were feelings of pity, a desire to make things better, and perhaps a little anger. It was an explosive combination in a man like Dylan—a nurturer with the heart of a warrior. He knew as well as she did that they could never fit into each other's lives. But hard experience had taught her that the heart didn't always choose what was good for it.

He leaned in so close his breath fanned her cheek. 'Did you destroy the photo?'

She wanted to say that she had.

*No lying. No stealing.*

She pulled in a ragged breath. 'No.'

'You *will* give it to me, you know.'

She shook her head. 'I have no need of your money.'

He ran the backs of his fingers down her cheek, making her shiver. 'I didn't say anything about buying it from you, Mia. I meant that eventually you'll give it to me as a gift.'

She wanted to tell him to go to hell, but his hand snaked behind her head and he pulled her mouth close to his own and the words dried in her throat.

Dear Lord, he was going to kiss her!

'The girl in that photograph is the woman you're meant to be. I know it and you know it.'

He was wrong! She didn't deserve to be that girl. She deserved nothing more than the chance to live her life in peace.

His breath fanned across her lips, addling her brain. She should step away, but she remained, quivering beneath his touch, hardly knowing what she wished for.

He pressed a kiss to the corner of her mouth. Her eyes fluttered closed as she turned towards him…

And then she found herself released.

'You want me as much as I want you.'

Her heart thudded in her ears. She had to reach out and steady herself against a chair.

'I don't know why the thought of being happy scares you.'

Disappointment and confusion battled with relief and her common sense, and it took a moment for his words to sink in. She pushed her shoulders back, but didn't lift her chin in challenge. She didn't want him to take chin-lifting as an invitation to kiss her.

'I am happy.'

Easing back from him, she seized her glass of water and took several steps away.

'Liar.'

He said the word softly, almost like a caress. He had a point. The thing was, she didn't need happiness. She just needed to stay on track.

She kept her back to him. 'I don't mean this to sound harsh, Dylan, but my happiness is not dependent on my sleeping with you.'

'I'm not talking about myself, here, Mia, or my ability to make you happy. I'm removing myself from the equation.'

'How convenient.'

'I think you're just as imprisoned now as you were when you were in jail.'

She spun around at that, water sloshing over the side of her glass. 'If you believe that, then it just goes to show how naïve you are.'

He blinked and then nodded. 'I'm sorry, I didn't mean that to sound glib.'

She didn't say anything. She just wanted him gone.

'Was it really so awful?'

She closed her eyes at the soft question. 'Yes.' She forced her eyes open again. 'I am *never* going back. And happiness is a small price to pay.'

His eyes throbbed at her words.

'I think it's time you left, Dylan.'

He stared at her for a long moment, but finally he nodded. 'Are you still okay for Saturday?'

For reasons known only to himself, Dylan had booked her and Carla in for a day of beauty treatments at a local spa. In the evening Mia, and presumably Thierry, were to dine with the Fairweathers at their coastal mansion.

Despite her curiosity about Dylan's home, she wasn't looking forward to either event. But she'd promised.

'Yes, of course.'

'Carla and I will collect you at ten.'

'I'll be ready.'

She'd need to go shopping before then. She had a feeling that she owned nothing appropriate for dinner at the Fair-weather estate.

'You're very tense.'

Mia did her best to relax beneath the masseuse's hands, but found it almost impossible. She'd been poked and prod-ded, scrubbed and wrapped, and waxed and tweezed to within an inch of her life.

People did this for *fun*?

What she'd really like was to ask the masseuse to hand her a bathrobe, find her a cup of tea and leave her alone to soak up the glorious view on the other side of the picture window.

The spa was located on the sixth floor of an upmarket beachside hotel that boasted a sweeping view of Newcastle beach. It would be a relief and a joy to spend half an hour contemplating gold sands and blue seas.

'It's probably because of all the hard physical work she does,' Carla said from the massage table beside Mia's, her voice sounding like nothing more than a blissed-out sigh. 'Isn't this a gorgeous treat, Mia?'

'Gorgeous,' she murmured back. She might have made a no-lying promise, but in this instance the lie was lily-white. She had no intention of dampening Carla's enjoyment. That had been the one good thing about all this—spending time with Carla.

So Mia didn't ask for a bathrobe and a cup of tea. She gritted her teeth instead and endured a further forty minutes of kneading, pummelling and rubbing down.

'Change of plan,' Carla announced, waving her phone in the air as she and Mia moved towards Dylan in the hotel bar.

Mia swallowed and nodded in his direction, not able to meet his eye, glad to have Carla there as a buffer.

He turned on his bar stool. 'Change of plan?'

Mia glance up to find him staring straight at her. All she could do was shrug. She had no idea what Carla's change of plan entailed.

Meeting his gaze made her mouth go dry. Looking at him had the oddest effect on her. She should look away. If she could, perhaps she would. Instead, she gazed at him hungrily. He wore a pair of sand-coloured cargo shorts and... and a Hawaiian shirt that should have made him look silly, but didn't.

It made him look... She swallowed again. He looked like a Hollywood heartthrob, and as he raised the beer he nursed to his lips, a searing hunger burned a trail through her.

'Yes.' Carla finished texting before popping her phone into her handbag. 'Thierry's coming to collect me.'

He was? Carla was leaving her alone with Dylan?

Ooh...*horrible* plan!

'I've talked Mia into spending not just the evening with us, but the rest of the afternoon as well. So you'll need to take her home to collect her things. Thierry and I will meet you by the pool at four.'

With a perfumed air-kiss, Carla dashed out. Mia didn't know where to look. She glanced at her feet, at the window, at the bar.

'Would you like a drink?'

She glanced at his glass, still three-quarters full, and with a sigh slid onto the bar stool beside his. 'Do you think they'd make me a cup of tea?'

'I'm sure of it. English Breakfast, Earl Grey or Chamomile?'

'Earl Grey, please.'

He ordered the tea and without further ado asked, 'What's wrong?'

Straight to the heart of the matter. It shouldn't surprise her.

'Are you feeling awkward after the words we exchanged on Tuesday evening?'

She wished she could say no, but that lie *wouldn't* be lily-white.

'Aren't you?'

She doubted she'd ever have the power to hurt him, but she *had* disappointed him. She suspected women rarely turned Dylan down.

*For heaven's sake, why would they? You must be crazy!*

'Mia, you've every right to speak your mind. I might not like what you have to say, but there's no law that says you have to say things with the sole purpose of pleasing me. The only person you need to please is yourself.'

Did he mean that?

'I came on unnecessarily strong. I was upset…and I was prepared to throw our agreed ground rules out of the window.' He dragged a hand down his face. 'I'm sorry. You were right to hold firm.'

Her heart had no right to grow so heavy at his words.

'I know a relationship between us wouldn't work. And you've made it clear that a fling is out of the question.' He wrapped both hands around his beer. 'The thing is, I like you. It's as simple and as complicated as that.'

Her eyes burned.

'I'm sorry.' He grimaced. 'Can we be friends again?'

She managed a nod.

They were quiet while the barmen slid her tea in front of her. When she glanced back to him he sent her a half-grin. 'How did you enjoy the treatments?'

'Oh, I…' She hesitated too long. 'It was lovely.' She scrambled. 'Thank you.'

'You're lying!'

She debated with herself for a moment and then nodded. 'I hated it.'

His brows drew down low over his eyes, fire sparking in their depths. 'Was anybody rude or unpleasant…or worse?'

'No!' Before she could stop herself she reached out and touched his arm, wanting to dispel his dark suspicions. 'Everyone was attentive and professional. I couldn't fault any-one. It was me—not them. I just… I just don't like being touched by people I don't know.'

She closed her eyes and pulled in a breath. He must think her a freak.

When she opened them she found him staring down at her, his lips rueful. 'I'm sorry. It seems I'm constantly forc-ing you to do things you hate.'

She waved that away. 'It's not important. It's all in a good cause.'

'It does matter.'

'Let's talk about Carla and—'

'No.'

Mia blinked.

'Let me apologise. I'm sorry I took it for granted that you'd enjoy a spa day.'

'The majority of women would.'

'You're not the majority of women.'

That was true, but if she dwelled on that fact for too long she might throw up.

'Apology accepted.'

He sat back and she found she could breathe again. He had the oddest effect on her—she simultaneously wanted to push him away and pull him closer.

*Maybe this time it wouldn't be like it was with Johnnie.*

Maybe. Maybe not. But even if Dylan were willing she had no intention of finding out. She couldn't risk it.

She pushed those thoughts firmly out of her mind. 'Now, can we talk about Carla?'

He grinned. 'Absolutely.'

Despite her confusion she found herself smiling back. 'That was the one good thing about today. I enjoy spending time with her. She's good company.'

'Did she confide anything in you?'

Mia poured herself some tea and stared down into the dark liquid. 'She's totally in love with Thierry. Even if he *is* all your worst fears rolled into one, I can't see how you'll be able to stop this wedding.'

He dragged a hand down his face and her heart went out to him.

'But on the plus side…'

He glanced up, his eyes keen. 'Yes?'

How to put this delicately…? 'I've had some close experience with women who've been in emotionally and physically abusive relationships.'

His eyes went dark. 'How close?'

She knew what he wanted to know—if *she'd* ever been in an abusive relationship. She sidestepped the unspoken question. 'My father was abusive to my mother.'

'Physically?'

'Not quite.' Though that latent threat had hung over every fraught confrontation. 'But he was emotionally abusive until I don't think she had any sense of self left.'

'I'm sorry.'

'I'm not telling you this so you'll feel sorry for me. I'm telling you because I don't see any of the same signs in Carla that I saw in my mother. Carla is neither meek nor diffident. She's kind and easy-going, and I suspect she's peace-loving, but I wouldn't describe her as submissive or compliant. I don't think she's afraid of Thierry's displeasure.'

'Changes like the ones you describe in your mother— they don't happen overnight. They're the result of years of abuse.'

He had a point.

'There are men out there who prey on emotionally vulnerable women.'

He didn't need to tell *her* that. 'You think Carla is emotionally vulnerable because of what happened between her boyfriend and her best friend?'

He ran a finger through the condensation on his glass of beer. 'It's one of the reasons. She was only sixteen when our parents died. It was a very difficult time for her.'

'I expect it was a difficult time for you too. How old were *you*?'

'Twenty-one.'

Twenty-one and alone with a sixteen-year-old sister. Mia swallowed. 'It must've been devastating for you both. I'm sorry.'

He looked haggard for a moment. 'It was tough for a while.'

*Understatement, much?*

'And then there's the Fairweather name...'

She shook her head, not knowing what he meant.

'It's hard to know if the people we meet like us for ourselves or whether what they see is the money, the tradition, and the power behind the name.'

'But... That's awful!' To have to go through life like that... 'So that's why Carla didn't tell me who she really was when we first met.'

He nodded. 'I've not been sure of any woman since Caitlin.'

Her mouth went dry. 'The girl who broke your heart?'

'The very one.' He lifted his beer and drank deeply.

*Leave it alone!*

'You said she couldn't handle it when things got rough. Did she...?' She frowned. 'Did she dump you when you were in the middle of your grief for your parents?'

Pain briefly flashed in his eyes, and she went cold all over when he gave one curt nod.

She had to swallow before she could speak. 'I'm sorry.'

He sent her a self-deprecating half-smile that made her want to cry. 'I was head over heels for her. We'd been dating for two years. I had our lives all mapped out—finish uni, get married, see the world. I thought she was my rock. I wanted to be hers. I thought we were...not perfect—never that—but special.' He shrugged. 'I was a fool.'

The grief in his eyes caught at her. 'You were so young,

Dylan. You couldn't possibly have known she wouldn't last the distance. She probably didn't know either.'

He turned his head, his gaze sharpening. 'The thing is, I know you haven't the slightest interest in my money or my name. Funny, isn't it?'

'Hilarious.' She swallowed, understanding now, in a way she hadn't earlier, how serious he was about not pursuing a relationship. The realisation should have been comforting. 'But we both know we wouldn't fit.'

He stared into his glass. 'Building something worthwhile with someone is more than just being attracted to them.'

'Very true.' She wished her voice would emerge with more strength. 'You need to have shared values…to want the same things from life.'

That wasn't them.

He drained his beer. 'Luckily for us we have our ground rules to keep us on the straight and narrow.'

Her heart thudded hard. 'Amen.'

'Are you ready to go?'

She started to nod and then broke off to fiddle with the collar of her shirt. 'I have a problem.'

'Tell me,' he ordered. 'Fixing problems is my specialty.'

'Carla mentioned swimming and lounging by the pool. But the thing is… I don't have a swimsuit.'

He stared at her, and then he smiled—really smiled. 'That's a problem that's easily remedied.'

# CHAPTER SEVEN

WHEN DYLAN PARKED the car at the shopping centre Mia removed her seat belt and turned fully to face him. 'We're not going to do the *Pretty Woman* thing in here, Dylan.'

He knew exactly what she meant and a secret fantasy—or not so secret, in this case—died a quick death.

He didn't argue with her. He'd already forced her into too many situations that she hadn't wanted this week.

He wanted to make her smile. Not frown.

He wanted to make her life a little bit easier. Not harder. And he had been making it harder. He couldn't deny that.

*Then walk away now. Leave her be.*

The look on her face when Felipe had snapped that photograph of her... It burned through his soul now. He'd wanted to make it up to her. He'd wanted to make things right. Nothing before had ever stung him the way her rejection of his aid had done.

She heaved out a sigh. 'Are we going to have to argue about this?'

He shook his head. 'Tell me exactly what you want to have happen in there.' He nodded towards the shops.

'I want to walk into a budget chain store, select a pair of board shorts and a swim-shirt, and pay for them with my own money. I then want to leave.'

Precise and exact.

'Can I make one small suggestion?'

She stared at him as if she didn't trust him and it occurred to him that he didn't blame her. His heavy-handed attempts to come to her defence last Tuesday hadn't been entirely un-selfish. He'd wanted that photo.

He'd taken one look at it and he'd wanted it for himself.

He couldn't even explain why!

It was pointless denying his attraction to her, but he had no intention of falling for Mia. It would be a replay of his relationship with Caitlin all over again, and he'd learned his lesson the first time around.

It was just... Mia had got under his skin. He hated the way Thierry treated her. He hated the way Gordon treated her. He chafed at how hard her life was—at the unfairness of it. He wanted her to feel free to laugh the way she had in Felipe's photograph.

*It's not your job to make her laugh.*

Maybe not, but what harm would it do?

He shook himself, realising the pause in their conversa-tion was in danger of becoming too charged.

'It's just a small suggestion.'

She pursed her lips. He did his best not to focus on their lushness, or the need that surged into his blood, clenching hard and tight about his groin. If he stared at them too long she'd know exactly where his thoughts had strayed, and that would be a disaster. For whatever reason, she was de-termined to ignore the attraction between them. Today he didn't want to force her to face anything she didn't want to face or do anything she didn't want to do.

'Okay.' She hitched up her chin. 'What's this *small* sug-gestion?'

Her tone told him it had better be small. Or else. Her *'or else'* might be interesting, but he resisted the temptation. Today was about making things easier for her.

'I have it on pretty good authority that swim-shirts can chafe.'

She folded her arms, her lips twisting as if she thought he was spinning her a story.

'So you might want to buy a one-piece suit to wear underneath. And, while shirts are great for avoiding sunburn, they don't protect your face, arms and legs, so you might consider adding sunscreen to your shopping list too. And a hat.'

She smiled, and the noose that had started to tighten about his neck eased. 'I have sunscreen at home. I use it for work. But a new hat might be nice.'

He stared at that smile and then fumbled for the door handle. He needed to get out of the car now or he'd be in danger of kissing her.

'Let's go shopping.'

Mia looked cute in her board shorts and swim-shirt—a combination of blue and pink that set off the warmth of her skin and provided a perfect foil for the dark lustre of her hair. She'd look cute in the modest one-piece that he knew she wore beneath too, and while he'd be lying if he said he didn't care about seeing her in a bikini, a large part of him simply didn't care what she wore. That large part of him just wanted her to relax and be happy.

He glanced across. She reclined on a banana lounger, staring at her toes and smiling.

He moved to the lounger beside hers. 'What are you smiling at?'

Her cheeks went a delicious pink. 'Oh, I...'

He leaned closer, intrigued. ''Fess up.'

Her eyes danced. Not long ago they'd all enjoyed a rousing game of water volleyball in the pool, and it had improved everyone's mood—even Thierry's.

'This is going to sound utterly frivolous, but... I'm admiring my toes.'

He glanced at her toes and she wiggled them at him.

'I haven't had painted toenails since I was fifteen or sixteen...and the pedicurist has made them look so pretty.'

They were a shiny fairy-floss pink…and totally kissable.

'I think I'll sit here and admire them too. They're too cute for words.'

She laughed, and something inside him soared.

'I've had a really nice afternoon, Dylan. I just wanted to say thank you.'

'You're welcome. I'm hoping the fun continues well into the evening.'

She glanced across at Carla and Thierry, sitting at a table on the other side of the pool, a giant umbrella casting them in shade. 'Thierry seems a bit more relaxed today. Maybe pool volleyball is the secret to his soul.'

He found himself strangely reluctant to focus on the other couple's real or imagined issues at the moment. 'Would you like to see the Jason Gilmore?' At her frown he added, 'You remember. The photographer Felipe scoffed at?'

She hesitated, and then gestured out in front of her. 'Can it compete with this?'

He stared out at the view spread before them and then rested his hands back behind his head. 'Nothing can compete with this view.'

And it was all the better too for having Mia's toes in the foreground.

'You have a pool that looks like it belongs in a resort.'

The pool was long enough for laps, curving at one end to form a lagoon, with an island in the middle—a handy spot for resting drinks and nibbles. There was an infinity edge that had utterly bewitched Mia when she'd first seen it.

He nodded. The pool *was* amazing. 'But even better is the view beyond it.'

The Fairweather mansion sat on a headland, and the forest leading down the cliff obscured the beach below, but the Pacific Ocean was spread out before them in all its sapphire glory. Waves crashed against rocky outcrops and the spray lifted up into the air in a spectacular display of the ocean's power. It was elemental, primal and magnificent.

'We're incredibly lucky to live here.'

'You are,' she said, but her voice lacked any resentment. She glanced across at him. 'I suspect you work very hard for your luck.'

He gestured to the pool and the house. 'We inherited this from our parents.'

She gazed at him, her eyes moss-dark. 'And yet I bet you'd give it all up to spend just one more day with them.'

Her words hit him squarely in the secret, private part of himself that he let no one but Carla see. If only he could see his father again and ask his advice about how best to deal with his uncle. If only he could sit down with his mother and ask her how he could best support Carla. To have the chance to simply hug them one more time…share a meal with them…laugh with them. His chest burned with the ache of their absence.

'I'm sorry. I didn't mean to make you sad.'

He pushed himself out of his grief. 'Not sad.'

She shot him a tiny smile. 'You're a dreadful liar, Dylan.'

For some reason that made him laugh. 'I miss them. I don't know what else to say.'

'You don't have to say anything.'

With Mia he felt that might indeed be true.

'Is this photograph of yours in your bedroom?'

He stared at her, and a grin built through him. 'Did you think I was trying to whisk you away under false pretences?'

She pointed a finger at him, her lips twitching. 'I'm on to your tricks. You are *not* to be trusted.'

'Ah, but do you *want* me to be trustworthy?' He seized her finger and kissed it.

She sucked in a breath, her eyes widening, and it was all he could do not to lean across and kiss her for real.

If he kissed her now, she'd run.

And he was starting to realise that he'd do just about anything to make her stay. He had no idea what that meant.

'However, in this instance, madam, I'm being eminently trustworthy. The photo hangs in the formal lounge.'

She glanced at her toes, the view, and then at him. 'In that case I should like to see it.'

He rose, holding out his hand to her. She hesitated for a beat before putting her hand in his and letting him help her to her feet. He laced his fingers through hers, intent on holding on for as long as she'd let him.

'Why do you keep it in the formal lounge rather than the living area?'

'You'll understand when you see it.'

She left her hand in his and it felt like a victory.

The moment Mia clapped eyes on the photograph she understood why Dylan didn't keep it in the more informal living areas. Even distracted as she was by Dylan's touch, his fingers laced casually through hers as if he was used to holding hands with a woman, the power of the photograph beat at her.

In her entire life she'd only ever held hands with three men—her father, when she'd been very small, Johnnie, when she'd been very stupid, and now Dylan.

*You're no longer either very young or very stupid.*

She wasn't convinced about the latter.

She tugged her hand from his to take a step closer to the picture and he let her go—easily and smoothly.

'It's…awe-inspiring.'

She wasn't sure she'd be able to live with it every day. It was so powerful. She wasn't even sure where the power came from…

On the surface it seemed a simple landscape—a preternaturally still ocean with not a single wave ruffling its surface. In the foreground crouched a grassy headland, with every blade of grass as still as the water—unruffled by even the tiniest of breezes. But storm clouds hung low over the ocean, turning the water a menacing monochrome. Behind the photographer, though, the sun shone fierce, piercing the picture with a powerful light, making each blade of grass stand out in brilliant green relief. The contrast—so odd and so true—held her captive.

'What do you think?'

She had to swallow before she could speak. 'Your Mr Gilmore has caught that exact moment before a storm hits— before the wind rushes through and the clouds cover the sun. It's…it's the deep breath. It's like a duel between light and dark, good and evil.'

He moved to stand beside her. 'I feel that too.'

'And you know that in this instance the dark is going to win…'

'But?'

'But I can't help feeling it's not going to prevail—the dark is only temporary. Once the storm has worn itself out the sun will reign supreme again.'

They stood in silence and stared at it. Mia stiffened.

'It's about grief and hope,' she blurted out, unable to stop herself. 'It makes me feel sad and hopeful, and happy…and incredibly grateful, all at the same time.'

She turned to him and found all her emotions reflected in his face.

He nodded. 'I know.'

'It's the most amazing picture I've ever seen.'

'It's the second most amazing one *I've* seen.'

She'd started to turn towards the photo again, but at his words she turned back with a raised eyebrow. 'You've seen something to top this?'

'That photo Felipe took of you—it made me feel all of that and more.'

It was as if a hand reached out to squeeze her chest, making breathing all but impossible. 'Oh, I…'

She didn't know what to say, and the spell was broken when Carla burst into the room.

'Oh, Dylan!'

It seemed to her that he turned reluctantly. 'What's wrong?'

Carla wrung her hands, making odd noises in her throat, and Dylan's gaze sharpened.

Mia stepped forward to take her hand. 'What is it, Carla?'

Carla grasped her hand in a death grip. 'Oh, Mia, there aren't enough apologies in the world.' Turning to Dylan, she said, 'Uncle Andrew has just arrived.'

Her words seemed to age Dylan by ten years. It didn't take a rocket scientist to work out that there was no love lost between them and their uncle. He must be an utter ogre if his arrival could cause such an expression to darken Carla's eyes. As if…as if she might be *afraid* of the man.

Mia glanced at the photograph that dominated the wall and then pushed her shoulders back, aching to see Carla and Dylan smiling and laughing again.

'So…your uncle is a storm?'

Dylan's gaze speared hers. She sent him a small smile.

'I have a relative like that. I guess we'll just have to weather him.' She winked at Carla. 'Who knows? Maybe Thierry will charm him.'

Carla choked back a laugh.

Dylan glanced at the photo and something in his shoulders unhitched. He reached out and gave Mia a one-armed hug, pressing his lips to her hair. It was friendly and affectionate, not seductive, but it heated her blood all the same.

'Come on, then,' he said. 'Let's go and face the dragon.'

Over dinner Mia discovered that the elder Fairweather was everything she most feared—an intimidating authoritarian with views that were as narrow as they were strong. He was the kind of man who took his privilege for granted, but considered it his God-given duty to ensure that no one else in his family did.

Add to that the fact that Andrew Robert Fairweather was a Federal Court judge—he sent people to jail for a living—and Mia could feel her legs start to shake.

*This* was the person who'd replaced Carla and Dylan's

parents as role model and guardian? Her stomach rolled in a slow, sickening somersault. For all their trust fund money and fancy education, Mia didn't envy Dylan and Carla one jot. She found her heart going out to them in sympathy.

'It's past time I was introduced to this man you mean to marry, Carla. As you won't bring him to meet me, I've had to resort to descending on you unannounced.'

'You're welcome here any time, Uncle Andrew.' Dylan's smile didn't reach his eyes. 'Your room is always kept ready for you.'

'Humph!' He fixed his gaze on Mia. 'Who are *you*?' he barked.

Three years in prison had taught Mia to hide all visual evidence of fear. It had also taught her to fly beneath the radar. 'I'm Mia. Just a friend of Carla and Dylan's.'

He immediately passed over her to start grilling Thierry.

Thierry, it appeared, ticked every box on the elder Fair-weather's list of what was desirable. As a self-made man in the world of finance, Thierry had power, position, and money of his own. They even knew some of the same people.

If Andrew Fairweather had expected Thierry to fawn he'd be sadly disappointed, but for the moment at least he didn't seem to hold that against the younger man.

Their exchange took the heat off the rest of them for a good fifteen minutes. Three sets of shoulders lowered a fraction. Dylan, Carla and Mia even dared to nibble at their thin slices of smoked salmon.

It wasn't until the entrée had been cleared away and a delicious risotto served that Fairweather Senior turned his attention back to his niece and nephew.

'Pray tell, Carla Ann, what are *you* doing with the education you've been so fortunate to have had? Frittering it away like your brother, no doubt?'

Carla glanced at Dylan. The older man had to be joking, right?

'Carla has no need to work for a living,' Thierry inserted

smoothly. 'She's in the fortunate position of being able to help others—a role she takes seriously and one I'm happy to support. Recently she's been busy working on charitable projects, including some important conservation work. I couldn't be more proud of her.'

*Wow! Go, Thierry.* Mia didn't blame Carla in the least for the look of unabashed adoration that she sent him.

Dylan glanced at Mia and raised an eyebrow. She could only shrug in answer.

'Well, what about *you*?'

His uncle fixed Dylan with a glare that made Mia quail internally. Silence stretched and she searched for something that would help ease the tension that had wrapped around the table.

She forced a forkful of food to her mouth and made an appreciative noise. 'This meal is really lovely. I'd... I'd like to become a better cook.'

Everyone stared at her. Her stomach curdled. She loathed being the centre of attention. She grasped the lifeline Dylan had given her on a previous occasion.

'I've always wanted to make veal scaloppini. I don't suppose anyone has a good recipe for that particular dish, do they?'

It was Thierry, of all people, who answered. 'I have a fool-proof recipe.'

Thierry *cooked*? She shook off her surprise. 'Would you be willing to share it?'

'Yes.'

Andrew Fairweather's face darkened. 'Dylan, I—'

'Maybe I could make it and you could all come to dinner at my place to try it?'

Carla finally got with the programme. 'What a lovely idea, Mia.'

From the corner of her eye Mia could see Mr Fairweather opening his mouth again, his hard gaze burning in Dylan's direction. She set her fork down.

'Maybe we should set a date?'

She couldn't seem to help herself, but she had a feeling she'd say anything to halt the malice she could see sitting on the end of the older man's tongue.

'What about Saturday two weeks from now?' Carla suggested.

'I'm free.' She had no social plans slotted into her calendar at all.

When she glanced at Dylan she found him smiling at her.

'Sounds great. If you're sure?'

Her stomach started to churn. She was very far from sure, but she couldn't back out now. 'If it's a disaster we'll just call out for pizza.'

She'd aimed for light, but even though both Dylan and Carla laughed it occurred to Mia then that nothing could lighten the mood around the table.

'Back to business!' Mr Fairweather boomed. 'Dylan, I want to know what you're working on at the moment.'

All her offer of dinner had done was delay the inevitable. His uncle fired question after question at Dylan—all of them designed to put him on the defensive, all of them designed to make him look small.

A frown built through her. But...*why*?

She glanced from Dylan to his uncle, trying to understand the animosity that crackled between them. Carla said nothing, just stared down at her plate of untouched food. Thierry met her gaze, but there was no help to be had there. His curled lip was directed at *her*, not at Fairweather Senior.

'You were given all of the tools to make something of yourself and you've wasted them,' Andrew Fairweather was saying.

*No, he hadn't!*

'I'm sorry I've disappointed you, sir.'

*No! A hundred times no!* Dylan shouldn't apologise to this man. In whose world could Dylan ever be construed as a failure? How could anyone conceivably interpret Dylan's achievements as worthless or lacking in value?

Would *no one* stick up for him?

Fairweather Senior slammed his knife and fork down. 'You could've done something *important*! Instead you've wasted the opportunities presented to you on trivial nonsense. You should be ashamed of yourself. You lack backbone and brains and you're—'

'You are *so* wrong!' Mia shot to her feet, quailing inside but unable to sit and listen to Dylan being run down like that any longer. 'What Dylan does is neither shallow nor trivial. He brings people's dreams to life. Don't you realise how important that is?'

'Important? He throws *parties* for a living. It's disgraceful!'

'You really mean to tell me you can't see the merit in what Dylan does?' Her daring and defiance made her stomach churn, but she couldn't stop herself. She turned to Dylan. 'How long have you had to put up with this?'

'Mia, I—'

She swung back to his uncle. 'Your nephew provides people with memories they can treasure for a lifetime. Dylan doesn't just "throw parties"—he doesn't just light sparklers and eat cake. He creates events that mark milestones in people's lives. He creates events that honour their accomplishments. He provides an opportunity for people to celebrate their achievements with their families, their friends and their peers. That's what life is about. It's not trivial or shallow. It's *important*!'

'*Duty* is what's important!'

Mia swallowed and reminded herself that she wasn't on trial here. Regardless of how much she displeased him, Fairweather Senior couldn't send her to jail simply for disagreeing with him.

'I agree that working hard and being a useful member of society is important—it's what we should all strive for.

And Dylan does both those things.' She lifted her hands sky-wards. 'Can't you *see* how hard he works? Can't you *see* how talented he is? He has a gift—he's a creator of dreams. And if you can't see the value in that then I pity you.'

She dropped her crisp linen napkin to the table. 'If you'll all excuse me for a moment…?'

She turned and walked out of the dining room. Every-thing started to shake—her hands, her knees…her breath. Letting herself out of a side door, she stumbled down a se-ries of steps and collapsed onto a low retaining wall that stood just beyond the light of the house. Dropping her head to her knees, she felt her shoulders shaking with the sobs she couldn't hold back.

'Shh…'

She found herself lifted and planted in Dylan's lap. His arms moved about her, holding her securely against him. His warm scent surrounded her.

'Why are you crying, Mia? You were magnificent.'

'I scared myself.' She hiccuped through her sobs. 'I… Men like your uncle scare me.'

'Men like that scare everyone. But at the moment I think he's more afraid of you.'

He said it to make her laugh, but she was still too shaken. She lifted her head and scrubbed her fists across her face. Dylan slapped her hands away and dried her face gently with the softest of cotton handkerchiefs.

'Look at me,' he urged gently.

'No.' She stared instead at her hands, but she couldn't prevent herself from leaning into him and taking comfort from his strength and his warmth.

'Why not?'

She pulled in a shaky breath. 'Because I know what I'll see in your face, Dylan, and I don't deserve it.'

'You don't think you deserve admiration and gratitude?'

'I don't.'

'Mia, you—'

'It was a man like your uncle who sentenced me to three years in jail. And he was right to do so. I'd broken the law. I'd taken money that didn't belong to me.'

She hadn't kept it, but that was neither here nor there.

'That's why my uncle scares you?'

She met his gaze then. 'I meant everything I said at the table. Every single word.'

His eyes throbbed into hers. 'I know.'

'But, Dylan, don't you see? All it would've taken was for Thierry to tell your uncle that I'm an ex-convict and that would've instantly negated everything I'd said.'

'Not in my eyes.'

No, not in Dylan's eyes. She reached up and touched his cheek. 'But it would in your uncle's…and most other people's too.'

He turned his head to press a kiss to her hand. She went to pull it away but he pressed his hand on top of it, trapping it between the heat of his hand and the warmth of his face.

'Does it matter what people like my uncle think?'

'Yes.'

'Why?'

'Because it means that whenever I stand up against some injustice, as soon as my background is known my protests have no effect, no impact. In fact it usually makes things worse—as if their association with me taints them. I might as well have kept my mouth shut.'

'You're wrong.'

The intensity of his gaze held her trapped. She couldn't look away.

'After you left just then, Carla announced to the table at large that she was proud of me. It's the very first time she's ever stood up to him.'

Her heart pounded against the walls of her chest. 'Have *you* ever stood up to him?'

'On Carla's account—but never my own.'

She couldn't stop herself from brushing his cheek with her thumb. It turned his eyes dark and slumberous.

*Dangerous.*

The word whispered through her, but she didn't move away. She liked being this close to Dylan.

'You shouldn't let him treat you the way he does.'

'I realised that tonight for the first time. I've made a lot of excuses for him over the years. He lost his brother, and he and my aunt provided a home for Carla when our parents died.' He shrugged. 'The family tradition of law and politics is important to him, but I had no intention of ever following that path. Letting him rant and rave at me seemed a small price to pay, but...'

'But?' she urged, wanting him to break free from all the belittling and bullying.

'But I hadn't realised until tonight how much I'd let his voice get inside my head. Somewhere over the years I'd unknowingly started to agree with him—started to define myself by his standards. But tonight you stood up and reminded me of why I do what I do. And I felt proud of it.'

She smiled. It came from way down deep inside her.

Dylan stared at her. His gaze lowered to her lips and the colour of his eyes darkened to a deep sapphire. A pulse started up in the centre of her.

'I want to kiss you, Mia.'

Her heart fluttered up into her throat. 'Oh, that would be a very, *very* bad idea.'

'Why?'

A part of her wished he'd just seize her lips with his and be done with talking.

*Crazy thought!*

'Because...' It was hard to talk with her heart hammering in her throat. 'Because I've made it clear where I stand in relation to romance and relationships.'

'And you think I want more?'

They'd set their ground rules, but...

'Do you?'

'Things change.' He spoke slowly, frowning.

His reply frightened her, and yet she didn't move away.

'I haven't changed.' She'd meant the declaration to sound defiant, but it came out whisper-soft and full of yearning. She couldn't drag her gaze from the firm promise of his lips.

'If you really don't want me to kiss you, I won't.' He trailed his fingers down her throat and along her collarbone. 'I meant to say earlier that I love your dress.'

The change of topic should have thrown her, but she grasped it like a lifeline. 'It's new. I bought it especially.' She hadn't been able to resist the raspberry-coloured linen dress once she'd tried it on.

'For tonight? For me?'

Her eyes met his.

*No lying.*

'Yes.'

His fingers continued to trail delicious paths of sensation across her skin. 'Are you sure your stance on romance hasn't changed?'

She couldn't look away. 'Positive.'

*Liar.*

'I still want to kiss you.'

She should move away, put an end to this insanity.

'And I think you want that too.'

Her heart beat so loud she thought he must hear it.

'Would you like me to kiss you, Mia?'

Her pulse thumped. 'I'll own to some curiosity,' she managed.

'Is that a yes?'

She met his gaze and nodded. 'Yes.'

# CHAPTER EIGHT

MIA REALISED HER mistake the moment Dylan's mouth claimed hers.

She'd thought his first touch would be gentle, but it wasn't. It was sure and firm and a complete assault on her senses.

Dylan wanted to overwhelm her with sensation—perhaps in punishment for her 'my stance on romance hasn't changed' comment. He wanted to thank her for sticking up for him at the dinner table… And somehow both of those impulses cancelled out the underlying threat in the other and dragged Mia under as if she'd been picked up by a giant wave.

She wound her arms around his neck and held on, waiting for the crash to come as the wave barrelled her along… But it didn't slam her down as she'd feared. Dylan's arms cradled her, holding her safe, and in the end all Mia could do was sink into them.

He nibbled her bottom lip, coaxing her to open to him. And she did. She wanted to hesitate, to hold back, but she couldn't. His tongue laved her inner lips and something inside her unfurled. His tongue coaxed hers to dance and something inside her sparked to life, filling her veins with heat and her soul with joy.

Dylan deepened the kiss, kissing her so thoroughly and with such intensity that his name was wrenched from her throat.

He lifted his head for a moment, his eyes glittering, and she suddenly realised that the flirtatious charmer had been stripped away to reveal the warrior beneath. And every potent ruthless sinew of his being was focussed wholly on *her*.

It should have made her afraid.

But she wasn't afraid of him. All she had to do was tell him to stop. And she knew that he would.

One corner of his mouth lifted, as if he'd read that thought in her face. 'You think I'm going to give you a chance to *think*, Mia?'

Her heart thumped. 'Dylan, sex won't make a scrap of difference. I—'

The force of his kiss pushed her head back. One of his hands traced the length of her—slowly, lazily—and Mia couldn't help but kiss him back with just as much force, hunger ravaging her body.

She wanted this man.

If she couldn't have him she thought she might die.

And then his hand was beneath the skirt of her dress… and her hands were where they shouldn't be…

And somewhere nearby a door slammed.

Mia stiffened and pulled her hands to her lap. Dylan tugged her skirt down and put his arms around her, holding her close, just as Carla came around the side of the house.

She pulled up short when she saw them. 'I hope I'm not interrupting anything.'

Dylan laughed, the rumble vibrating through Mia's body in a delicious wave of sensation. 'Of course you're interrupting something.'

Carla waved that away. 'I wanted to let you know that Uncle Andrew has left. He's decided to stay at his club in town before heading back to Sydney tomorrow.'

Mia gripped her hands together. 'I'm sorry. I had no right to cause such a scene—'

'You were wonderful! I wish…' Carla hauled in a breath.

'I wish I'd had the gumption to say something like that to him years ago.'

'Carla,' Dylan began, 'you—'

'No.' She fixed him with a glare. 'You've always stuck up for me. I should've done the same for you.'

She turned to Mia. Mia tried to remove herself from Dylan's lap, but he held her there fast.

'The thing is,' Carla said, thankfully unaware of Mia's agitation, 'I've always been so terribly afraid of him. But tonight when you said you pitied him I realised you were right. And…' she shrugged '…now I find I'm not as afraid.'

Dylan frowned. Mia had to fight the urge to smooth his brow.

'I don't want you to be afraid of anyone,' he said.

Mia knew he meant Thierry.

Carla waved that away. 'I just wanted to make sure the two of you were okay. And to let you know the coast is clear.'

'We're fine.'

'And you, Mia?' Carla checked despite her brother's assurance.

'I'm fine too.'

'Carmen—' she was the Fairweathers' housekeeper '—is making ice cream sundaes.'

'We'll be along in five minutes.'

'Don't let him sweet-talk you into anything you're not ready for, Mia.'

'Cross my heart,' Mia promised, but that reminded her that Carla knew her brother's reputation. It reminded her that Dylan had a lot of experience with women while she had very little experience with men.'

Carla sent them a cheeky grin. 'But I *will* say the two of you do look cute together.'

Mia had to fight the urge to drop her face to her hands and weep. How could she have let things go this far?

Carla disappeared and Mia tried once again to rise from Dylan's lap, but his arms tightened about her.

'Do you really mean to ignore that kiss?'

His hand splayed against her hip, as if to urge her to feel what he was feeling.

'That kiss was amazing...intense.' His face darkened. 'It was a whole lot more than just a kiss and you know it.'

Her heart thumped. If she let them, his words could weave a spell about her. She couldn't let that happen.

'Yes,' she said. And then, so he knew what she was referring to, she added, 'Yes, I *do* mean to ignore that kiss.'

Her words made him flinch. Heat gathered behind her eyes and her throat started to ache.

'To punish yourself?' The question was scratched out of him—a raw rasp.

'No.' She refused to let the tears building behind her eyes to fall. 'To save myself.'

'I don't understand.'

The throb in his voice had her closing her eyes. 'And I hope to God you never do.'

This time when she tried to get up he let her.

Dylan watched Mia walk away and his heart pounded against the walls of his ribs. He wanted her with a savagery that frightened him.

He couldn't recall wanting Caitlin like this.

He couldn't recall wanting any woman with this kind of hunger!

He wanted to shred their ground rules to pieces—tear them up and burn them. He wanted Mia in his bed.

*But do you want her in your heart?*

The roaring inside him screeched to a halt. He swallowed. *No.*

*But you're prepared to seduce her? To make things harder for her.*

He shot to his feet. He wouldn't make them harder! He'd make sure she enjoyed every moment of their time together.

He'd make her laugh and he'd lavish her with gifts. He'd give her anything she wanted.

*Except the quiet life she craves.*

He whirled around, hands fisted. She was wrong about that. She should be living life to the full—not hiding herself in the shadows. She should be living her life like the woman in Felipe's photograph—full of joy and laughter. If only he could get her to see that.

If only…

He stilled. If he managed that, then maybe she'd rip up those ground rules herself and welcome some fun—some pleasure—into her life. It was worth a shot.

Thrusting out his jaw, he moved towards the house.

Mia sat at a picnic table, listlessly feeding a peacock what looked to be part of her usual lunchtime sandwich, and something in Dylan's chest tightened. It was four days since their kiss and she looked pale and tired. She looked the way he felt. It didn't give him the slightest sense of satisfaction or triumph.

He wanted her. His lips tightened. And she wanted him.

She had another think coming if she thought he'd give up. He wanted to know what she'd meant by saving herself, and he had every intention of finding out. Once he knew, he'd be able to develop a game plan for knocking down those walls of hers.

She half turned, as if she'd sensed his presence, dropping her sandwich when their gazes collided. The peacock immediately pounced on it.

Dylan forced his legs forward. 'It's just as well I brought these or you'd go hungry.' He dropped a couple of chocolate bars to the table before taking the seat opposite. 'How are you, Mia?'

'I'm okay.' She reached for one of the chocolate bars but didn't unwrap it, worry lurking in the depths of her eyes. 'How are *you*?'

He'd meant to tell her that he couldn't sleep at night for thinking of her. Instead he shot her a grin and winked. 'I'll be a whole lot better once I've eaten this.'

He seized the second chocolate bar and was rewarded when her shoulders unhitched a fraction.

'I'm glad you dropped by today,' she said.

He stared at her. For a moment he felt like punching the air. He didn't push her, though. He'd let her tell him why in her own time.

'Carla asked me to give you this.' He pulled a piece of paper from his pocket. 'It's Thierry's veal scaloppini recipe.'

'Why didn't she give it to me herself?'

He shrugged, hoping he hadn't given himself away. 'She said she was busy.' And he'd latched on to any excuse to see Mia. 'Maybe she thought I'd see you first.'

'Are you busy? There's something I'd like you to see.'

'I'm free as a bird.' Even if he hadn't been he'd have cancelled any appointment for her.

'Good. Come with me.'

She led him along a narrow track through dense native forest. Everything was hushed and serene. He marvelled anew that such a place existed in the middle of the city. Mia didn't talk and he was content to follow behind, admiring the dark lustre of her hair and the innate grace of her hips.

After ten minutes she slowed. Turning to him, she put a finger to her lips and then held down the branch of a Bottle-brush tree, gesturing for him to look.

He glanced at her, wondering what on earth she'd brought him here to see. He turned to survey the view and sucked in a breath. Moving closer, he held the branch for himself while Mia moved off to one side.

She'd brought him via a circuitous route to the far side of the lily pond. Just in front of him—no more than twenty yards away—stretched out on a picnic blanket, were Carla and Thierry. Carla's head was in Thierry's lap and he was idly combing his fingers through her hair. She laughed up at him at something he'd said.

Dylan's heart started to thump. He stared from his sister's face to her fiancé's face and back again. Eventually Mia's fingers wrapped about the top of his arm and she pulled him away. Pressing her finger to her lips again, she led him along a different path until they emerged into a rocky clearing. She sat on a boulder and stared at him with pursed lips.

He fell down onto a neighbouring rock, his mind racing. Finally he glanced across at her. 'I have *never* seen Carla that happy.'

She nodded, as if the sight of that much happiness had awed her.

'How did you know they were there?'

'I accidentally stumbled across them on Monday. I noticed Thierry's car in the car park a little while ago and figured they'd be there again today.'

'She's totally in love with him…and…and completely *happy*.'

'Did you notice the way he looked at her?'

He had. An ache stretched behind his eyes. 'He looked at her as if she were the most precious person on earth.' His shot to his feet and paced up and down for a bit before swinging back to Mia. 'A man who looks at a woman like that is never going to hurt her. He's going to do everything in his power to protect her, to cherish her…to make her happy.'

Mia nodded.

He started to pace again. Seeing Carla and Thierry together like that, so unguarded, it should put his mind at rest…

He collapsed back on his rock and Mia reached out to clasp his hand briefly. 'Dylan, you're not losing Carla. You're gaining a brother-in-law.'

'But he's such an unpleasant man!'

She sat back. 'I suspect the more you get to know him, the better you'll come to like him.'

Could she be right?

'I also think...'

He glanced up, suddenly on guard. There was something too tight in her voice, which was at odds with the casual way she ran her fingers along a tall spike of native grass.

'You also think...?' he prompted.

She rubbed her hand across her throat, not looking at him. 'I think our dating pretence is no longer necessary.'

*She told you kissing her would be a bad idea.*

He hadn't known it would have her bringing their relationship to such an abrupt halt!

*There is no relationship.*

But he wanted there to be. Not a relationship, *exactly*, but a relationship of sorts.

He was careful to keep his thoughts hidden. He didn't want to scare her off more than he already had—didn't want her retreating further. He hadn't got where he was today by revealing his hand too soon.

'You're probably right,' he said instead.

She seemed to tense up and then relax in equal measure. He ducked his head to hide his smile. Mia Maydew was one conflicted lady. If she'd just let him help solve that conflict...

'Please tell me you're not going to dump Carla as abruptly?'

Her head shot up. 'Of course I'm not going to dump Carla. Carla and I will be friends for as long as she wants us to be friends.' She folded her arms and glared at him. 'And, Dylan, I hate to point this out, but I'm not dumping *you* either. We were never going out to begin with. We were only pretending.'

'I wasn't pretending when I kissed you. And I don't care how good an actress you are, Mia, I don't think you were pretending either.'

She moistened her lips and swallowed. The pulse at the base of her throat fluttered like a caged thing. A ravaging hunger swept through him. If he kissed her now, here in this quiet, private place where they wouldn't be interrupted…

'Don't even think about it!'

Her eyes flashed fire. So much for not showing his hand. He stared at the ground and pulled in a breath, nodding. 'Sorry, I lost my head for a moment—let it drift to where it shouldn't have gone.'

He shoved his shoulders back and lifted his chin.

'Though if I'm ever fortunate enough to make love with you, Mia, it'll be in place where I'll have the opportunity to show you in every way I know how just how beautiful and desirable I find you. There'll be no rush. And your comfort will be paramount.'

Her eyes grew round.

He leaned in close. 'I've no inclination for a quick roll on spiky grass, where we'd be half eaten by ants and mosquitos or happened upon by unsuspecting hikers. When I make love to you, Mia, I mean for you to be fully focussed on me.'

She swallowed.

He brushed his lips across her ear. 'And when it happens I promise that you will be.'

She leapt away from him, glancing at her watch. 'My lunchbreak is almost up. I have to get back to work.'

He followed her to the main picnic area. It was awash with people enjoying the afternoon sun.

A question pressed against the back of his throat, but he held it in until they were fully surrounded by people. 'Will you give me one more fake date?'

Her hands went to her hips. 'Why?'

It would give him something to work towards. It would give him time to come up with a plan to overcome her objections to an affair.

'I want a chance to grill Thierry in a non-confrontational way, in a place that's not intimidating…and you *did* invite us all to dinner.'

Her shoulders suddenly sagged. 'I did, didn't I?'

She'd only done it to try and keep the peace, to try and head off his uncle's vitriol.

'You can cry off if you want. I can make your excuses easily enough. Nobody will mind.' He didn't want her looking so careworn—not on his account. 'Cooking for guests can be stressful if you haven't done it in a while.' He gave an exaggerated eye-roll. 'And I suspect I've stressed you out enough already.'

Her lips twitched. 'The cooking doesn't worry me. It's only for four—not fourteen.'

'What *does* worry you, then?'

She hesitated. 'My house.'

He couldn't gauge what she meant, but the way her hands twisted together caught at him. 'What's wrong with your house? I know it's small, but none of us are going to care about that.'

'It looks like a prison cell.'

He winced at her bluntness.

'It's bare and uninviting and…and I'm ashamed of it.'

'You've no reason to be ashamed of it. It's clean and functional. Neither Carla nor I care about things like that. And if Thierry does then he's an idiot.'

One slim shoulder lifted. 'I know it shouldn't matter. It's just… I have no talent for making things look nice.' She stared at a copse of trees. 'Maybe I could get a magazine or two, for tips on how to make it look a bit better.'

'I can help you with that.'

She raised an eyebrow, but he waved her scepticism away. 'You don't want a complete makeover. You just want it to look a little cheerier…a bit warmer, right?'

She nodded, but the wariness didn't leave her eyes.

'Look, I'm not an interior designer, but I've had to consult on set designs for concerts and themes for parties. Seriously, we could spruce up your little cottage with nothing more than a few accessories. I swear you'll be amazed at how easy it is.'

She didn't say anything.

'What's your budget?' he asked, so she'd know he wasn't offering to pay for anything, that he wasn't trying to bribe her.

She named a sum that, while small, would easily cover what she needed.

He rubbed his hands together. 'We can work with that.'

Her eyes narrowed. She folded her arms, her fingers drumming against her upper arms. 'What on earth do *you* know about budgets?'

It was a fair question. 'I had a crash course when I started up my company. And I'm given a budget from my clients for every event I take on. If I want to make money I have to stick to it.'

She glanced down at her hands. 'I'm sorry—that was ungracious. Of course you—'

'I'm a trust fund baby, Mia. If I chose I could live in the lap of luxury for the rest of my life without having to lift a finger. You're not the first person to question my credentials.'

She stared up at him, a frown in her eyes. 'You *haven't* chosen to live that way, though.'

He shrugged. 'I wanted something more. I wanted to create something of my own. Besides, the family tradition is not to sit idly back and rest on one's laurels. And as neither law nor politics interested me...'

'You decided to forge your own path?'

'And—as you so succinctly reminded me last Saturday night—I should be proud of that. And I am.'

She nodded.

'So, in return, will you let me help you decorate your cottage? We might not be dating for real, but there's no rule that says we can't be friends, is there?'

She chewed her lip.

Dylan's heart dipped. '*Is* there?'

'I...'

She moistened her lips and a sudden thirst welled inside him.

'I've largely kept to myself since…over the last eleven months.'

Would she *ever* confide the hows and the whys that had landed her in prison? He could search out police reports, court records—and he had no doubt that Thierry had done exactly that—but he didn't want to. He wanted Mia to tell him herself. It was obvious she regretted her crime. And she'd paid her debt to society. But her past still haunted her.

His heart surged against his ribs. 'Do you resent my and Carla's intrusion into your life?'

'No. I… I'd forgotten how nice it is to have friends.'

As those words sank in his mouth dried. 'I'm honoured to be your friend, Mia.' He swallowed. 'Carla would say the same if she were here. Neither of us take our friends for granted.'

'I know. It seems strange, when we're from such different backgrounds, that we can have so much in common.'

He rolled his shoulders in an effort to loosen the tension in them. 'Shall we go shopping, then? On Saturday? To spruce up your cottage?'

'I'm working till midday.'

'I'll call for you at one.'

'Um…'

She hesitated, and he knew it was a big step for her.

'Okay.'

He gave in to the temptation of kissing her cheek. 'I'll see you on Saturday.'

When he reached the end of the path he looked back to find her still watching him. He lifted his hand in farewell. With a visible start she waved back, before disappearing along a path between the office and a picnic table.

His hands clenched. Had anyone ever put her first? Fought for her? Put everything on the line for her?

He knew the answer in his bones—no, they hadn't.

*Do you want to be the next person to let her down?*

He *wasn't* going to let her down! He was going to show her how to live. When they parted company, she'd be glad they'd met. *That* was his objective.

Mia gazed around her tiny living room and could barely credit the difference a few knick-knacks made. She'd never had a chance to try her hand at decorating before. Her father had maintained a rigid view on what was and wasn't respectable—a line her mother had never crossed—and Mia hadn't even been allowed to put up posters in her room. She'd learned early on that it was easier to submit and keep the peace than to rebel.

When she'd met Johnnie his home had already been beautifully furnished. She'd been in awe of his taste. And in the two years between leaving home and moving in with Johnnie she'd lived such a hand-to-mouth existence there'd been no money left over for decorating the mean little rooms she'd rented.

And then there'd been prison. She'd learned to make do with as little as possible there. She'd left the place with the same attitude, but for the first time she questioned that wisdom. It was true that she didn't want to get too attached to material things—like Johnnie had. But it wasn't a crime to make her living space comfortable. It wasn't a crime to make it welcoming for visitors.

'Earth to Mia?'

She snapped back when a hand was waved in front of her face.

'You were miles away,' Dylan teased. He gestured to the room. 'Do you like it?'

'I love it.'

Shopping with Dylan today had been…*fun*. It had also been a revelation. She'd thought he'd walk through the shops and select the things she needed—like her father and Johnnie would have done. He hadn't, though. He'd asked her opinion every step of the way.

'I love the colour scheme you've chosen.' He planted his hands on his hips and glanced around. 'It makes everything so much lighter in here.'

'The colour scheme was a joint effort. I'd never have known where to start.'

He'd taken her shopping and asked her what colours she liked. She'd eventually settled on a china-blue and a sandy taupe. She now had scatter cushions and throw rugs in those colours on the couch, as well as a tablecloth on the table. New jars in a jaunty blue lined the kitchen counter, a vase and some knick-knacks sat on the mantel, and two beach prints in funky faded frames hung on the walls. A jute rug with a chocolate-coloured border rested beneath the coffee table and a welcome mat sat at the door.

Mia turned a full circle. 'It's made such a difference.' She clasped her hands beneath her chin and let out a long pent-up breath. A breath she felt she'd been holding ever since she'd proffered the dinner invitation. 'I no longer need to feel embarrassed.'

'A vase of fresh flowers here.' Dylan touched a spot on the kitchen counter. 'Maybe a plant on the coffee table or the hall table there, and the room will be perfect.'

Yellow-headed daisies in the kitchen and an African violet on the coffee table. 'I'll get them through the week.'

He grinned at her. 'Even better—it all came in under-budget!'

His delight with himself made her laugh. She watched his face light up with pleasure as he studied the room he'd helped her to transform and her heart started to thud against her ribs.

Friends? She didn't believe in promises and words, but Dylan's actions today had spoken volumes. He'd given her his friendship willingly and generously. He'd treated her like a friend.

Now it was her turn.

# CHAPTER NINE

'WITH US COMING in under-budget and all…' Mia's mouth started to dry. 'Well, I was thinking…how about I buy you dinner as a thank-you?'

Dylan swung to her, his eyes alert and watchful…hopeful.

'As a friend,' she added. She didn't want him getting the wrong impression.

'When?'

She strove for a shrug. 'This evening, if you're free.'

'I'm free.' He glanced down at himself. He wore a pair of cargo shorts and a button-down cotton shirt. So did she. 'Can we go somewhere casual?'

'Casual sounds good.' Casual sounded perfect!

'I know—gorgeous evening…end of summer and all that… There's this great pizza place down near the beach. It does takeaway.'

His face lit up and all she could do was stare. When—how?—had he learned to milk enjoyment from every moment?

'When was the last time you had pizza on the beach?'

'I… Never.'

'C'mon, then.' He took her hand and led her to the front door. 'That's an oversight that should be corrected immediately.'

* * *

'See? Didn't I tell you this was an inspired idea?' Dylan claimed a patch of pristine white sand and grinned at her.

Mia bit back a laugh and spread out a towel so he could place the pizza boxes onto it. 'I'll reserve judgement until I've tried the pizza.' She dropped two bottles of water to the towel too, and then turned to survey the view spread out in front of them.

They had another half an hour of light—possibly longer. The water reflected the last of the sun's brilliance in tones of pink, gold and mauve. Barely a breath of breeze ruffled her hair, and the only sounds were the whoosh of the waves rushing up onshore, the cries of the seagulls wheeling overhead and the laughter of a family group picnicking further along the sand. To her left, Newcastle's famous Nobby's Lighthouse sat atop the headland. Straight out in front of her was the Pacific Ocean.

So much space. So much room to breathe.

She pulled in a deep breath before turning to find Dylan watching her. With a self-conscious shrug she sat beside him. But not too close. She kept the pizza boxes between them. 'You couldn't have chosen a better spot. It's wonderful down here.'

'A perfect night for a picnic. Now, try a piece of this pizza.'

She took a piece from the proffered box and bit into it. The flavours melted on her tongue and it was all she could do not to groan in appreciation. 'Good…' she murmured. 'Seriously good.'

They munched pizza in silence for a bit. The longer they sat there, the lighter Mia started to feel. Dylan reminded her of all the pleasures—big and small—that the world held. Even after almost eleven months she was still afraid of giving herself over to enjoyment.

'A penny for them.'

His voice broke into her thoughts.

'One moment you were enjoying all of this and the next moment you weren't.'

'Oh!' She swung to him. 'I'm having a lovely time. Truly.'

Her stomach clenched. She'd come here to tell him the truth.

*So tell him the truth.*

She finished off her piece of pizza and reached for a paper napkin. 'If you want to know the truth, I'm afraid of enjoying it too much.'

'Why?'

She couldn't look at him. 'In case I do something stupid and it's taken away from me again.'

He was silent for a couple of beats. 'You're talking about prison?'

She nodded.

'Is there any reason to believe you'll end up back there?'

Not if she remained vigilant.

'I find it hard to take my liberty for granted.' She grimaced. 'You don't understand how much you take it for granted until it's taken away. Prison is a punishment—it's supposed to be unpleasant. The thought of messing up and ending up back in there...' She shivered. 'So sometimes I find myself lost in a moment of enjoyment and then I remember jail and I wonder... I wonder how I could cope if I found myself back there again.'

He leaned towards her, drenching the air with a hint of smoky nutmeg. It mingled with the scents of ocean and pizza and she couldn't recall relishing anything more in her life. She wanted to close her eyes and memorise that scent, so she could pull it out and appreciate it whenever she needed to.

'Mia, you're a different person now. You won't make the same mistakes again.'

She wasn't convinced—especially on that last point. 'I think you need to know my story.'

'I'd like to know it very much.'

'It's sordid,' she warned.

She couldn't make this pretty for him, no matter how much she might want to. He just shrugged, his eyes not leaving her face. It made her mouth dry.

'Have you really not looked me up?' There'd be newspaper articles and court reports he could access.

'I wanted to hear the story from you—not from some so-called factual report that leaves out the truly relevant facts.'

She had a feeling that should have surprised her, but it didn't. She glanced down at her hands. 'I think I mentioned that my father was a…a difficult man.'

'Emotionally abusive to your mother?'

She nodded, fighting the weariness that wanted to claim her. 'When I was sixteen I finally stood up to him.'

'What happened?'

'He gave me a black eye and kicked me out.'

Dylan's hands fisted.

'I found temporary shelter in a homeless refuge and got work waitressing.'

'School?'

'I couldn't manage school *and* work.' She blew out a breath. 'That's something prison *did* give me—the opportunity to finish my high school education. It's my high school diploma that made me eligible for the traineeship at Plum Pines.'

'Right.'

She couldn't tell what he was thinking so she simply pushed on. 'When I was eighteen I met a man—Johnnie Peters. He was twenty-five and I thought him so worldly. I'd had a couple of boyfriends, you understand, but nothing serious.'

'Until Johnnie?'

'Until Johnnie…' She swallowed the lump that threatened her throat. It settled in her chest to ache with a dull throb. 'He swept me off my feet. I fell hopelessly in love with him.'

A muscle in Dylan's jaw worked. 'Would I be right in suspecting he didn't deserve you?'

She could feel her lips twist. It took all her strength to maintain eye contact with Dylan. 'The key word in my previous sentence was *hopelessly.*' She stared back out to sea. 'I had a lot of counselling when I was in jail. I understand now that there are men out there who target foolish, naïve girls. Which is exactly what I was.'

He reached out to squeeze her hand. 'You were young.'

She pulled her hand from his. 'When something looks too good to be true, it usually is. I knew that then, but I ignored it. He made me feel special, and I wanted to be special.' She gripped her hands together. 'He organised a new job for me—nine to five—where I was trained in office administration. It seemed like a step up. I was ridiculously grateful not to be on my feet all day, like I had been when waitressing.'

When she'd been in prison she'd longed for that waitressing job—aching legs and all. She should have been grateful for what she'd had. Content.

'He moved me into his lovely house and bought me beautiful clothes. He was a stockbroker, and I thought he could have his pick of women. I felt I was the luckiest girl alive.'

'He cut you off from your family and friends...controlled your finances?'

'My family had already cut me off, but...yes.' That was something she'd come to realise during sessions with her counsellor. 'Things seemed perfect for a couple of years. What I didn't realise was that he had a gambling problem.'

'What happened?' he prompted when she remained silent.

'He started asking me to deposit cheques into accounts that weren't in my name and then to withdraw the funds.'

'You gave all the money to him?'

'I gave him everything.' She'd been an idiot. 'Of course it was only a matter of time before I was traced on CCTV.'

'And Johnnie?'

'He was cleverer than I. He was never seen in the vicinity of any of the banks at the time, and he denied all knowledge.'

His mouth grew taut. 'The scumbag fed you to the wolves.'

She turned to him, the ache in her chest growing fierce. 'He was even smarter than that, Dylan. He convinced me to feed *myself* to the wolves. I told the police he was innocent.'

Anger flared in his eyes. 'How long did it take you to realise what he was?'

Her stomach churned. She'd told herself it would be better for Dylan to despise her than it would be for him to love her. A part of her died inside anyway.

'About four months into my sentence…when he hadn't been to see me…when he stopped answering my letters.'

'Then you turned him in to the authorities?'

She shook her head.

'You continued to let him walk all over you?'

She stiffened at the censure in his voice. 'Three things, Dylan. One—I had no proof. Especially not after the testimony I'd given in his favour. Any testimony to the contrary would've simply been written off as the ravings of a disaffected lover. Two—I needed to draw a line under that part of my life and move forward. And three—I deserved my punishment. Nothing was ever going to change that.'

'He *manipulated* you!'

'And I let him. I *knew* what I was doing was wrong. The first time I cashed a cheque he told me it was for his elderly aunt. The second time he said it was a favour for a work colleague. The third time he just asked me to do it for him, said that he was in trouble. I knew then that I was breaking the law, but I did it anyway. He never physically threatened me. I just did it.'

'But I bet the emotional threat of him breaking up with you hung over every request?'

It had. And she hadn't been able to face the thought of losing him. Talk about pathetic! 'I told you it was sordid.'

'Three years seems a long sentence for a first offender.'

She moistened her lips. 'I stole a *lot* of money.'

He stared out to sea and her heart burned at the conflict

reflected in his face. 'You made a bad choice and you've paid for it.' He turned, spearing her with his gaze. 'Would you make the same decision again, given what you know now?'

'Of course not. But we don't get the chance to live our lives over. We just have to find ways to live with our mistakes.'

'Shunning the simple pleasures in life won't help you do that.'

He had a point.

His brows drew down low over his eyes. 'Don't you worry about other young women he might have targeted?'

Her heart started to thump. Trust Dylan to worry about vulnerable women he didn't even know. She glanced down at her hands. 'Fourteen months into my sentence Johnnie attempted an armed hold-up on a security van. He wasn't successful. He was sentenced to fifteen years. I think the foolish young women of the world are safe from him for the moment.'

'Good.'

Neither one of them went back to eating pizza.

'Is that why you let men walk all over you?'

She stiffened. 'I don't let *you* walk all over me.'

His lips twisted, though his eyes remained hard. 'There's hope for me yet, then.'

'No, there's not! I—'

'You've let Gordon, Thierry and Felipe all treat you like you're worthless. Your father and Johnnie both treated you badly. Do you *really* hold yourself so cheaply?'

Her heart surged against her ribs. 'Neither my father nor Johnnie are in my life any more. Thierry doesn't matter to me one jot! Felipe *didn't* take advantage of me. And as for Gordon…'

Dylan folded his arms and raised his eyebrows.

'He has the power to fire me. Keeping my head beneath the parapet where he's concerned is the smartest course of action. It won't be forever.'

'There'll always be Gordons in your life in one form or another. Are you going to turn yourself into a doormat for all of them?'

'If I do it'll be none of your business!'

'Why tell me all of this, then?'

'Because if we're going to be *friends*—' she ground the word out '—eventually the press will find out who I am and my story will come out. And it wouldn't be fair to have the press spring something like that on you without preparing you first.'

He dragged a hand down his face.

'And…'

He stilled. 'And…?'

She didn't want to continue, but she had to. It was the reason she'd started this conversation. 'And I wanted you to understand why I have no intention of ever pursuing another romantic relationship.'

He stared at her, but she couldn't read the expression in his eyes.

'Because you were burned once?'

'Because I don't like who I am when I'm in love. I refuse to become that person again.'

He shot to his feet. 'Are you likening me to this Johnnie Peters?'

She shot to her feet too. 'Of course not!'

He stabbed a finger at her. 'That's *exactly* what you're doing. You're saying that if you let yourself be vulnerable to me, I'll take advantage of you.'

She could feel herself start to shake. 'This is about me, not you!'

'Garbage. I—'

He broke off when a bright flash momentarily blinded both of them. Mia realised two things then—night had fallen…and someone had just snapped their photo.

Without another word, Dylan charged off into the darkness.

Biting back a groan, Mia set off after him.

\* \* \*

Dylan hurled himself at the shape that had emerged in the darkness, bringing the anonymous photographer down.

He tried to clamp down on the rage that had him wanting to tear things apart with his bare hands. He wanted to tear apart the men who'd let Mia down—her father, the despicable Johnnie Peters. He wanted to tear apart her mistaken view of herself as some kind of spineless push-over. He wanted to tear apart her view of *him*! Most of all he wanted to tear himself apart, and he didn't know why.

*Don't tear the photographer apart. He's just doing his job.*

'Fair go, Fairweather!'

Dylan pushed himself upright as Mia came running up. She shone the torch on her phone on the photographer, confirming Dylan's suspicions. A hard ball lodged in his belly.

'Percy Struthers. What the hell do you think you're doing, sneaking up on me again *now*?'

Percy had created a PR firestorm last year, when Dylan had been in charge of a Turkish sultan's sixtieth birthday celebrations. Percy had released a photo of Dylan and the Sultan's very beautiful youngest daughter, linking them romantically. It had been a lie, of course, but try telling *that* to an enraged Turkish sultan...

Percy Struthers was the grubbiest of the gutter press, and trouble with a capital T.

Mia had broken the law—she'd done wrong and she'd paid the price—but the world was full of immoral, unethical people who lied and cheated. Were *they* sent to jail? Hardly! Some of them were applauded and clapped on the back for it—like tabloid journalists and politicians.

'It's news whenever a new woman turns up in your life—you know that.'

'Give me the camera.'

With a sigh, Percy handed it over.

Dylan stood and indicated for Mia to shine her torch

on the camera. With a flick of his fingers he removed the memory stick.

Percy clambered to his feet, caught the camera when Dylan tossed it back to him. 'It won't stop the story, you know.'

'Without a photograph the story won't gain traction.'

They both knew that.

The photographer gave an ugly laugh. 'But one of us will eventually get a photo—you can't remain on your guard twenty-four-seven.'

Beside him, Mia stiffened. Dylan wanted to throw his head back and howl. This was her worst nightmare, and it was he who'd dragged her into it.

'I know who she is,' Percy continued. 'And I know what she's done.'

Her *absolute* worst nightmare.

'Aren't you afraid she's on the make? That you're simply her latest target?'

He felt rather than saw Mia flinch. A ball of fury lodged in his gut.

*Don't rise to the bait. Don't give the pond scum anything. Don't feed the frenzy.*

It hit him suddenly how much his name, his position, were black marks against him in Mia's book.

Percy gave another of those ugly laughs. 'An ex-con? *Really*, Dylan? What are you trying to prove? Or have you developed a taste for a bit of rough?'

Dylan reached out and took Mia's hand. 'I think we're done here.'

'Run along, darlin'.' The photographer smirked. 'We all know what you're after.'

And then he called her a name that no man should ever call a woman.

Dylan whirled around, his right hand fisted, and smashed him square on the nose. Blood burst from it as the man reeled backwards to sprawl on the ground. Pain shot up Dylan's arm.

Mia sucked in a breath, and even in the darkness he could see the way her eyes flashed.

Percy cursed. 'You'll pay for that, Fairweather.'

Mia tried to tug her hand from Dylan's but he refused to relinquish it. He towed her in the direction of the car instead. He had to get out of here before he did something truly despicable—like beat Percy Struthers to a pulp.

Mia sat in tight-lipped silence all the way home, only unfolding her arms to push herself out of the car once he'd pulled up at the front of her cottage. She slammed it with a force that made him wince.

He had to jog to catch up with her. She didn't hold the front door open for him, letting it fall behind her, meaning he had to catch it. But at least she hadn't slammed it in his face. He told himself that was something.

'You're…uh…cross with me?'

She turned on him, and her eyes flashed with so much anger the hair at her temples seemed to shake with it.

She seized his right hand and glanced down at it. 'Does it hurt?'

'Yes.'

'Good.'

She dropped it as if it burned her. Moving to the freezer, she took out a packet of frozen peas. Grabbing his hand, she slammed it on top of his grazed knuckles. It didn't really hurt any more, but he winced anyway, hoping it would give her more bloodthirsty impulses a measure of satisfaction. And he submitted when she pushed him towards one of her hard wooden chairs—not so hard now they sported pale blue chair pads.

She lifted his left hand and dropped it on top of the peas to hold them in place, then retreated to sit on the sofa and glower at him.

The silence started to saw on his nerves. 'You think I'm an idiot?'

'Totally.'

'He had no right to call you what he did.'

'You are *utterly* infuriating!' Her hands balled into fists. 'What he called me was despicable, but the best thing you could've done was walk away without giving him the satisfaction of reacting.' She shot to her feet and started to pace. 'Oh, but, *no*—you couldn't manage that, could you? No! Your honour demanded reparation for the lady—regardless of how much more difficult you'd be making it for said lady!'

He shifted on the chair. 'I…uh…'

'The story will break in the tabloids, the ugliest accusations will be made, and I'll be hounded by reporters and photographers at work. *Hell!*' She flung her arms out. 'Just wait until Gordon catches wind of this. I'll be out on my ear.' She swung to him, thumping a hand to her chest. 'I *need* to finish this traineeship. I need a decent qualification so I can get a job.'

'I've already told you—come and work for me.'

'I don't *want* to work for you!'

Her rejection stung. He shot to his feet then too. 'That's right—you'd rather bury yourself in some godforsaken place where you can sentence yourself to a life of solitary confinement.'

'That's *my* decision to make.'

He wanted to hurl the peas across the room. Except he didn't want to ruin the pretty new furnishings. He had to settle for dropping them in the sink instead.

He moved back into the middle of the room. 'I have no intention of making light of your experiences with the criminal justice system, but you're letting one experience colour your entire life.' That hard lump of anger in his chest rose up into his throat. 'And I am *not* Johnnie Peters.'

Her entire frame shook. 'I told you—this is about *me*. Not you.' She didn't yell, but her words speared through him as if they'd come at him at great volume. 'You *punched* a man tonight, Dylan. That photographer can have you charged with assault. He'd be within his rights.'

It was true. It had been foolish to react. He couldn't find it in himself to regret it, though.

'And you made *me* an eye witness to the event.'

He swung back to meet her gaze. What he saw there made his heart burn.

'If I were in love with you, and you asked me to lie to the police about what had happened tonight...'

She didn't finish the sentence, but her pallor made his stomach churn.

'You're afraid you'd perjure yourself for me?'

'If I fell in love with you, Dylan, I'm afraid I'd risk everything again.'

He reached out to curl his fingers around her shoulders. 'I would *never* ask that of you.'

She moved away until his hands dropped back to his sides. 'The best way for me to avoid that kind of temptation is to avoid romantic attachments altogether. All I want is a quiet life. It doesn't seem too much to ask. It doesn't seem like such a big sacrifice to make.'

Ice sped through his veins. 'You're mistaken if you think living a half-life isn't a sacrifice. It'll keep you out of jail, it'll keep you out of trouble, but there are worse things than jail.'

She blinked, as if that wasn't a thought that had ever occurred to her.

'Living a life without love is one of them. And here's another thing for you to think about. If I fell in love with *you*—' he pointed a finger at her '—who's to say you wouldn't have the same power over me that Johnnie had over you? Who's to say you wouldn't force me to turn my back on my principles?'

The words spilled from him with an uncanny truth that left him reeling.

Her mouth dropped open.

He forged on, not understanding what was happening to him. 'Do you think I'd lie, steal or perjure myself for you?'

Her hands twisted together. 'You might lie for me…if it wasn't a big lie.'

He widened his stance. 'But the rest?'

She bit her lip and finally shook her head. 'No.'

'What makes you think *you* would, then?'

'My past tells me I'm weak.'

'Do you really think three years in prison—with all the education and counselling you received—hasn't made you stronger?'

She still labelled herself as weak-willed and easy to manipulate. He understood her fear of prison, and her determination never to find herself back behind bars, but she was wrong. She might let people like Gordon push her around, but she was as strong as one of the Plum Pines the reserve was named after.

Behind the dark moss of her eyes he could see her mind racing. He mightn't have convinced her. *Yet.* But he'd given her something to think about.

He snaked his hand behind her head and drew her face close to his.

'What are you doing?' she squeaked.

'I'm giving you something else to think about. Do you *really* want to live without this, Mia?'

He wanted to slam his lips to hers and kiss her with all the pent-up frustration tearing at his soul. He didn't. She'd tensed, ready to resist such an assault. And he didn't want to hurt her. If she'd let him he'd do everything he could to make her happy.

He touched his lips to hers gently, slowly exploring the lush lines of her mouth—savouring her. He poured all of himself into the kiss, wanting to give her as much pleasure as he could.

With a shiver and a sigh she sank against him, her hands fisting in his shirt. At his gentle demand she opened up to him and he felt as if he was home. Murmuring her name, he moved to gather her close—only to find a hand planted on his chest, pushing him away.

'Stop.'

He released her immediately.

Her chest rose and fell as if she'd been running. 'You shouldn't be kissing me.'

He couldn't think of anything he'd rather do.

'What you should be doing is readying yourself for the PR disaster that's about to hit.'

He remained silent until she lifted her gaze to his. 'I promise you won't lose your job.'

She snorted her disbelief. 'Will you please warn Carla too? I think it'd be a good idea if you told her all that I told you tonight.'

'You want Carla to know?'

'It seems only fair.'

'No.' He refused to be a party to her shutting herself off from people. 'If you're truly her friend, Mia, then *you* tell her.'

With that, he spun on his heel and left.

Dylan stumbled down Mia's front steps, feeling as if he'd descended a drop of a thousand feet. He put out a hand to steady himself, but there was nothing to grab on to. He stood there swaying, praying he'd find his balance soon.

What had just happened?

*Idiot!*

The word screamed over and over in his mind, but he didn't know why.

What was so idiotic about anything he'd done tonight? Mia might think him an idiot for punching Percy Struthers, but the man had deserved it. Given the chance, he'd do it again! And he wasn't an idiot for refusing to be labelled as another Johnnie Peters either.

Pain shot into his jaw from clenching his teeth too hard. He was *nothing* like Johnnie Peters!

He lurched over to his car and flung the door open, but he didn't get in.

He wasn't an idiot for fighting against Mia's mistaken view of herself. She wasn't weak! She was one of the strongest women he knew.

Stronger than Caitlin.

He froze. Where had *that* come from?

But… Mia *was* stronger than Caitlin.

His mouth dried, and his heart was pounding so hard it sent nausea swirling through him. Mia was *exactly* the kind of woman who'd go the distance with a man—who'd take the good times with the bad, who'd weather the storms. Mia wouldn't turn tail and run at the first sign of trouble. If things got tough she'd dig her heels in and wait it out.

*Idiot!*

It finally hit him why that word kept going round and round in his mind. He collapsed on to the car seat. He'd been telling himself all this time that what he wanted with Mia was an affair, but that was a lie.

He wanted it all. *He loved her.* He wanted a chance to build a life with her.

His vision darkened. He raked his hands through his hair. All this time he'd thought he'd been keeping his heart safe… and yet the whole time he'd been falling in love with her.

His hands clenched about the steering wheel. He would *not* give up! Mia had told his uncle that he, Dylan, made dreams come true. Was there the slightest chance on earth that he could make *her* dreams come true?

If he wanted to win her heart he had to find out.

# CHAPTER TEN

THE STORY DIDN'T break on Monday or Tuesday. It didn't break on Wednesday or Thursday either. There wasn't a single item in the newspapers about Dylan, let alone any shady ex-convict women he might be dating.

Not that they *were* dating.

Even if he'd made it clear that he'd like to be.

Mia's wilful heart leapt at the thought, avoiding all her attempts to squash its exuberance.

She'd finally gathered up the courage to ring Carla on Tuesday night. Carla had claimed she didn't care about Mia's history—that she only cared about the kind of person Mia was now. Mia had even believed her.

She hadn't seen Dylan all week. He hadn't dropped by Plum Pines during her lunchbreak. He hadn't rung her for no reason at all other than to talk nonsense until she started to laugh in spite of herself. He hadn't even rung to talk about the wedding.

Despite her best intentions, she missed him.

She didn't just miss him—she *ached* for him.

On Friday morning, when it was barely light, she rushed the one and a half kilometres to the nearest newsagent's to buy a newspaper. Again, nothing.

Saturday dawned—the day of her dinner party—and still no scandal broke. She could hardly imagine what strings

Dylan had pulled to hush up the story. Could she start to breathe more easily?

It didn't make the memory of their encounter with the photographer fade, though. She physically flinched whenever she recalled the moment Dylan had punched the other man. Was he *crazy*? He could have been hauled off in a paddy wagon and thrown in a cell overnight! All because someone had called her a bad name.

Couldn't he see that for the rest of her life there'd be people who'd be happy to call her bad names? What would he do—punch them *all* on the nose?

Dylan deserved better than that.

*So do you.*

The thought whispered through her and she had to sink down into the nearest chair. Her heart thumped, the pulse in her throat pounded and her temples throbbed.

*There are worse things than prison.*

Dylan was right.

Shame, sharp and hot, engulfed her. She'd stolen money from people—people who hadn't deserved it. Knowing she was capable of that—living with that knowledge—was the worst thing of all. She'd willingly spend another three years in prison if it would rid her of the taint. But it wouldn't. Nothing would. Saying sorry to the people she'd hurt, doing her jail time, being a model prisoner, having the counselling—none of that had helped.

The only way she could ensure she never did something like that again was to stay away from people as much as she could.

Heat burned the backs of her eyes. She pressed a fist to her mouth. She wanted to believe Dylan—believe that she'd changed, become stronger, that no one could manipulate her now. His face rose up in her mind…a beautiful dream she'd kept telling herself was out of reach. Her every atom yearned towards him.

With a half-sob, she closed her eyes. She couldn't reach for that dream until she was certain she'd changed.

But how could she ever be certain of that?

Mia glanced at the plate of nibbles she'd set on the coffee table—some nice cheese and fancy crackers, along with some fat feta-stuffed olives. Should she add some grapes to the platter?

She clasped and unclasped her hands. She wasn't serving an entrée—just a main and a dessert...and these pre-dinner nibbles.

She peered into the refrigerator to check on the individual crème-brûlées she'd prepared earlier. What if they'd spoiled?

They hadn't.

She glanced at the wine. What if she'd chosen the wrong sort? She knew nothing about wine. The man at the liquor store had been helpful, but still…

What if nobody wanted wine? What if they wanted something she didn't have? She'd stocked up on mineral water and cola. She'd filled umpteen ice cube trays, so there'd be plenty of ice, but… She hadn't thought to buy port. What if someone wanted an after-dinner port? Or sherry!

She twisted her hands together. What if she ruined the veal scaloppini?

*We'll call out for pizza.*

What if she spilled a whole bottle of wine?

*We'll mop it up.*

What if—?

*Relax.*

The voice in her head sounded suspiciously like Dylan's. Funnily enough, it *did* help calm her panic.

*It's just a dinner for friends. Nothing to get het up about.*

A knock sounded at the front door and her heart immediately leapt into her throat.

They were twenty minutes early!

*Does it matter?*

Yes. No. She didn't know.

She wiped her palms down her pretty pink summer dress—another extravagant spur-of-the-moment purchase. She'd been making a few of those since she'd met Dylan— not that she could find it in herself to regret them.

Pulling in a breath, she went to answer it. Dylan stared at her from behind the screen. He held a bottle of wine and a bunch of flowers, but she barely noticed them against the intensity of his burning blue eyes.

Swallowing, she unlatched the screen and pushed it open. 'Come in.'

He kissed her cheek—all formality—and handed her the wine and flowers. 'Gifts for the hostess.'

She swallowed again, her senses drenched with the nutmeg scent of him. 'Thank you.'

While he might be physically close, his reserve made him seem a million miles away. Her fingers tightened around the stems of the flowers. She had no idea how to breach that distance. She wasn't even sure she should attempt it.

'I didn't know if you'd come.' She moved behind the kitchen counter to find a vase for the flowers—yellow-headed daisies.

'I'd have let you know if I couldn't make it.'

Of course he would. He had impeccable manners.

She glanced up to find him scrutinising her living room, a frown—small but unmistakable—settling over his features.

She set the vase of flowers on the kitchen bench and walked across. 'What's wrong?' Maybe he hated cheese and olives. She could have sworn he'd eaten them the night she'd dined at the Fairweather mansion.

He gestured to the room. 'Do you mind if I make a few adjustments?'

'Knock yourself out.'

He immediately shifted the cushions out of their perfect alignment and shook out her throw rug before casually draping it across the sofa. He took a decorative rock from the mantel and placed it on the coffee table, pushed the platter of cheese and olives from the centre further towards one end. He moved the vase of fresh flowers she'd bought that morning to the end of the mantel, rather than dead centre, and then pulled a magazine and a book from the magazine rack, all but hidden by the sofa, and placed them on the little table by the door.

'There!' He dusted off his hands. 'Now the place looks lived in.'

Mia blinked. His few simple changes had made a big difference. The room now radiated warmth rather than stiff awkwardness.

Her hands went to her hips. 'How do you even know how to do that?'

He shrugged. 'You just need to relax a bit more, Mia.'

Relaxing around Dylan... Was that even possible?

She swallowed. 'I spoke to Carla through the week.'

'I know. She's talked of little else.'

Mia couldn't work out whether he was pleased about that or not.

'Carla's the reason I'm early. She seemed to think you might need a hand, and that I should be the one to offer it.'

He didn't smile.

She gestured to the room, trying to lighten the mood. 'Obviously she was right.'

He just stared at her, his eyes blue and brooding.

She pressed a hand to her stomach. 'I...uh... I think I have everything under control.' She kicked into hostess mode. 'Can I get you a drink? Beer, wine...soft drink?'

He chose wine. She poured wine for both of them and invited him to help himself to the cheese and olives. They sat there barely talking, barely looking at each other. Mia excused herself and pretended to do something in the kitchen.

They were rescued from their excruciating awkwardness when Carla and Thierry arrived fifteen minutes later.

'Oh, look at your cottage!' Carla gushed, hugging her. 'It's so quaint and pretty.'

Carla's kindness eased some of the burning in Mia's soul, and she could only give thanks that his sister's presence made Dylan a little more sociable. Thierry neither hugged her nor kissed her cheek. Not that she'd expected him to do either. He barely said hello.

The veal scaloppini was a melt-in-the-mouth success. The dinner, however, wasn't. Dylan complimented her on the food, made small talk about nothing of note, and every time Mia glanced at him a knife twisted into her heart. His despondency—his *unhappiness*—was her fault.

She hated it that she'd hurt him. And she didn't know how to make it right. More to the point, she didn't know if she *should* make it right.

Carla's eyes grew increasingly narrow as she glanced from Mia to Dylan. Thierry just continued to survey Mia with his usual and by now familiar suspicion.

She told a funny story about a wombat at Plum Pines but only Carla laughed.

She mentioned that she was considering getting a car and asked if they had any opinions on what she should buy. Thierry said he wasn't interested in cars.

Carla gaped at him. 'Liar!'

'I'm interested in *sports* cars. Mia can't afford one of those.'

'Don't be so rude!'

'No, Thierry's right,' Mia jumped in. 'I'm just after something reliable and economical.'

Dylan then subjected them all to a long, monotonous monologue about the pros and cons of a particular model of hatchback that had their eyes glazing over and Mia wishing she'd never asked the question in the first place.

'What is *wrong* with you two?' Carla finally burst out at the two men. 'I think it's brave of Mia to tell us the full story of her past. I don't care what the two of you think—it doesn't change the way *I* feel about her. She's been a lovely friend to me.'

'Carla, that's really nice of you.' Mia's heart hammered up into her throat. 'But I think you ought to know that Dylan doesn't have an issue with my past either.'

Carla folded her arms, her eyes flashing. 'Then what's the problem? What's wrong with the pair of you?'

'That's none of your business,' Thierry bit out.

'Dylan is my brother. Mia is my friend. Of *course* it's my business.' She turned to Mia. 'Is it because of that incident with the photographer?'

Dylan's hands clenched about his knife and fork. 'Why the hell did you have to tell Carla about that anyway?' he shot at Mia.

An answering anger snapped through her. 'I didn't know it was a state secret. Besides, I thought it only fair that Carla be prepared for the story to break.'

'I told you I'd take care of it!'

'You'll have to excuse my scepticism. I didn't know your reach was both long and powerful enough to stop a story that juicy from making the headlines.'

'There's a lot you don't know about me!'

He glared at her.

She glared back.

'Why did you wait until Tuesday night to tell Carla?'

The question ground out of Thierry, cutting through everything else.

Mia moistened her lips. 'Because I was afraid that once she knew the whole truth she'd despise me.'

Thierry leaned towards her. On her other side she felt Dylan tense.

'She *should* despise you.'

'Thierry!'

Carla's pallor caught at Mia's heart.

'Ignore him. He has a giant chip on his shoulder because his father was in and out of prison all through his childhood.'

Mia's jaw dropped as Thierry's animosity made sudden and perfect sense.

Thierry shot to his feet. 'I told you that in the strictest confidence!'

They all stared after him as he slammed out of the house.

Carla leapt up too, grabbing her handbag. 'I'll call you tomorrow,' she said to Mia, before racing after him.

Mia glanced at Dylan. Did *he* mean to slam out of her cottage as well?

He stared back, his mouth a hard straight line, and she realised he meant to do no such thing.

She swallowed. 'Dessert?'

'Please.'

Before Mia could retrieve the crème-brûlées the cottage phone rang. That phone hardly ever rang.

She lifted the receiver. 'Hello?'

'This is Andrew Fairweather, Ms Maydew—Dylan and Carla's uncle. Perhaps you remember me?'

His tone of voice said, *Of course you remember me.*

'Yes, sir, I do.'

'A disturbing report has reached me claiming that you and my nephew are romantically involved. Well?'

His tone reminded her of her father. Her hands trembled. *You stood up to your father.*

She pushed her shoulders back. 'No comment.'

'I know about your background, young lady!'

Her fingers tightened about the receiver. 'I can't say as I'm surprised.' She glanced at Dylan to find him watching her closely.

'I'm giving you a friendly warning.'

*Oh, yes—very friendly.*

'Stay away from my nephew and niece or you *will* be sorry.'

'I'll keep that in mind.'

The line went dead. She dropped the receiver to the cradle and made for the kitchen.

'Was that the press?' Dylan demanded.

She set a crème-brûlée in front of him and slid into her seat. 'Have a taste.'

He looked as if he wanted to argue, but he spooned some of the dessert into his mouth and an expression of bliss spread across his face. He swore—just a little swear word—in an expression of wonder, not of alarm or anger. 'This is *amazing*.'

She stared at him, her chest clenching and unclenching, her skin going hot and cold, and something inside her melted so fast she wanted to cry out loud at the shock of it.

*She loved him.*

She loved him utterly, but she couldn't see how things between them could ever work out.

'Mia?'

She straightened. 'It wasn't the press on the phone, Dylan. It was your uncle.'

Dylan swore—one of the rudest words he knew.

Mia flinched. For all that she'd been to jail, she was no hardened criminal.

'I'm sorry. I shouldn't have said that.

She waved his apology away. 'It doesn't matter.'

It *did* matter. She deserved better. 'He warned you off?'

'Yes.'

He set his spoon down. 'What did he threaten you with?'

Her lips lifted a fraction. 'It wasn't a threat, but a "friendly warning".'

As if that were somehow different! He wished to God he could smile with her, but his sense of humour had deserted him. It had abandoned him when he'd walked away from her last week.

Fear had taken its place. Fear that he would never find a way to win her love.

'And it wasn't specific—just a general warning to stay away from you and Carla or I'd be sorry.'

'Are you going to heed him?'

She picked up her spoon and pressed it gently to the crust of her crème-brûlée until it cracked. 'Surely you and Carla have some say in the matter?'

He stilled. That felt like progress. 'You're not going to buckle under to his bullying?'

'Your uncle reminds me of my father. I stood up to my father and the world didn't come crashing down. Mind you—' her sigh arrowed into his chest '—it didn't do me any good either.'

The smile she sent him made his eyes burn.

'I suspect that if he chooses, your uncle could cause trouble for me.'

'And all you want is a quiet life?'

She lifted her eyes heavenward. 'I *crave* a quiet life.'

*Life with him would never be quiet.*

She brought her spoon down on top of her dessert again, shattering the toffee crust further. 'But me standing up to your uncle isn't going to be enough for you, Dylan, is it?' She met his gaze, her eyes troubled. 'You want more from me, and I don't know if I can give it to you.'

He straightened *I don't know* was a monumental improvement on *No chance at all*.

'You want our relationship to become physical, and you assure me you can keep that news under wraps from the press. I'm even starting to believe you. But can you promise me—?'

He leaned across and pressed a finger to her lips. 'First things first.' He needed to remove a significant problem before focusing on the reasons behind her softening. 'You think my uncle can cause problems for you at work with Gordon?'

'The thought has crossed my mind.' She stabbed the spoon into her dessert. 'I liked my plan—gain a useful qualification that'll keep me in employment—but I think it's time to say goodbye to it.'

He removed the crème-brûlée from her grasp and placed

it out of reach before she totally mangled it. 'You have a new plan?' Even though he knew it was a long shot, he couldn't help hoping he featured in this Plan B of hers.

'I think I'd better start looking for unskilled work—factory work or waitressing. At a pinch I suppose I could join the fruit-picking circuit.'

A hand reached out and wrung his heart. *'No!'*

Her raised eyebrow told him he had no say in the matter.

'I *won't* leave you worse off than I found you. I *won't* be responsible for that.'

*Too late.*

The words whispered through him, leaving a bitter aftertaste. 'I promise to do everything in my power to ensure you keep your job at Plum Pines.'

He could see that while she believed the sincerity of his intention she didn't think he'd be able to achieve the desired outcome. She had a point. His uncle held a lot of sway.

He drummed his fingers on the table. 'Right. If that doesn't work… Look, I know you don't want to work for FWE, but you could still do a traineeship with the company.' He drummed his fingers harder as his mind raced. 'I'd put you under one of my managers. You'd hardly see me. Our paths would barely cross.' He'd make sure they didn't if it would help her accept his offer. 'After two years of working for FWE, you could get a job anywhere in the industry. Job security would never be an issue for you again.'

'Dylan, I—'

He held up his hand. 'This is only a fall-back plan, in case you're fired from Plum Pines. I don't want to be responsible for you losing your job. Ever since I've met you, all I've done is cause you trouble.' He started to tick off the list on his fingers. 'Gordon tried to fire you for flirting with me, when I was the one doing the flirting. I introduced you to Thierry, who tried to play the heavy with you. Felipe put you in an untenable position when he snapped that photograph. The press have tried to go to town on you. And now my uncle has threatened you. It's not a list to be proud of.'

She glanced away. When she turned back, her eyes were dark and troubled. 'I fear you're paying for it too, though,' she said.

She was worth any price he had to pay. Which would be fine if he were the one paying the piper and not her. When he looked at the facts baldly, he'd done nothing but cause her trouble.

'That really is quite a list.' For the briefest of moments her eyes twinkled. 'It hasn't been all bad. You've bought me chocolate, and I've had my toenails painted. And I got the opportunity to see some amazing art.'

It was a paltry list in comparison.

She pressed her hands together. 'Most importantly, though, we now know Thierry isn't mistreating Carla.'

That *was* something. He'd never have found that out if it weren't for Mia.

'I've also learned some decorating tips and had the opportunity to cook veal scaloppini. What more could a girl want?'

A whole lot more!

He dragged a hand back through his hair. 'Dinner tonight was truly awful. Not the food,' he added quickly. 'The atmosphere.' And that had mostly been his fault too.

Mia pleated the tablecloth. 'I thought you were sulking.'

He couldn't seem to find any middle ground where she was concerned. 'I've been trying to give you some space, but the effort is killing me.'

As soon as he said it he knew the admission was too much. Mia sat further back in her seat. Further away from him. He had to swallow a groan at the pain that cramped his chest.

Pulling in a breath, he forced himself to focus on the important topic of their conversation. 'Please tell me that if you do lose your job you'll allow FWE to employ you. I can't stand the thought of bringing that much trouble to your door.

I know it means working in events management, rather than in conservation, but once you've gained the qualification you can arrange your working hours so you can study at night for a different qualification if you want. If I'm reading you correctly, it's job security that's really important to you.'

She was silent for several long moments, but eventually something in her shoulders unhitched. 'Okay.'

He stared at her. 'You mean it?'

'I'm really, *really* hoping I don't lose my position at Plum Pines.'

'We'll call that Plan A.'

'But if I do lose it, then, yes... I'd like to accept your offer of a position at FWE. We can call that Plan B'

'You'll trust that I won't try and take advantage of the situation?'

She nodded, and he found that he could smile. If she trusted him that far...

He rubbed his hands together. 'I feel we're making progress.'

'Progress?' The word squeaked out of her. 'How?'

He leaned towards her. 'I want to throw our ground rules out the window, Mia. I thought I only wanted an affair with you—fun, pleasure, satisfaction.'

At each word her eyes widened.

'But I was wrong. I want a whole lot more than that. I want—'

She pressed her fingers to his lips before he could tell her he loved her. Her throat bobbed convulsively. 'You're moving too fast for me.'

He pressed a kiss to her fingers before wrapping her hand in his. 'I'll slow down.'

'Do you even know how to do that?'

'I'll learn.'

Her brow creased. 'Dylan, I can't promise you anything.'

'I know. I might have hope, but I don't have any expectations. I have no right to expect anything from you.'

Dark eyes stared into his. 'You have so much faith in me, and I have so little in myself.'

She had to find that faith or there'd be no chance for them. They both knew that.

Her gaze drifted down to his mouth. Her eyes darkened and her lips parted, as if she couldn't get enough air into her lungs.

'And yet your beauty continues to addle my brain,' she murmured, almost to herself. 'That can't be good.'

An answering desire took hold of him, his stomach muscles tightening and his skin tingling. 'I think it's excellent.'

She moistened her lips, her chest rising and falling. 'Would you like to stay the night?'

For a moment he couldn't breathe. His free hand clenched and then unclenched, before clenching again. 'I would *love* to stay the night, but you told me sex wouldn't make a difference.'

Her mouth opened, but no sound came out.

'Can you promise me that it *will* make a difference, Mia?'

Her gaze slid away and she shook her head.

He pulled in a breath and held strong. 'I want more than crumbs from you. I want everything.'

She looked as if she wanted to run away. 'I'm sorry. That was stupid of me. Especially when I just asked you to slow down.' She rubbed her brow. 'We should bring this evening to a close and you should say goodnight.'

He rose, forcing her to rise too. If he didn't leave soon he'd be in danger of settling for anything, however small. 'It's a hostess's duty to escort her guests to the door.'

She bit back a smile as he pulled her along in his wake. 'You're just angling for a kiss.'

He backed her up against the wall. 'It excites me to know you're burning for me.'

Her breath hitched. 'You promised slow.'

'It's just a kiss, Mia.'

'Nothing is *just* anything with you, Dylan. We both know that.'

'Then tell me to stop.'

Her gaze moved from his eyes to his mouth. 'Just a kiss?'

He grinned down at her and shook his head. 'I mean to leave you *really* burning, Mia.'

Her eyes widened. 'I—'

He covered her mouth with his own, keeping the caress gentle until she relaxed beneath his touch, her lips moving against his, her mouth opening to him... And then, without warning, he deepened the kiss, intensifying it using his lips, tongue, teeth. His hands pressed into the small of her back until her full length was against his. He used every weapon in his armoury to assault her senses.

*'Dylan...'*

His name was a groan of need on her lips, and it nearly drove him mad. She tangled her hands in his hair, drawing him closer as she tried to crawl into his skin, inflaming him beyond endurance. He pressed her back against the wall, his hands sliding down over her backside, his fingers digging into her buttocks, pulling her up and into him, his need for her a fire in his blood.

She wanted him too. They could have each other and...

He eased away from her. Their eyes locked. He wanted so much more than this from her, but he knew that if she asked him to stay now, he would.

She pulled in a breath, as if reading that thought in his face. With something that sounded like a sob, she planted a hand to his chest and gently pushed him away.

'Go.'

# CHAPTER ELEVEN

MIA BARELY SLEPT that night. She gave up trying just before dawn. So when Carla pulled up at the front of the cottage just after six a.m. Mia happened to be sitting on her front step, nursing a mug of coffee.

She stood and opened the front gate, ushered Carla through. Carla trudged up the path and collapsed on to the step, and Mia's heart clenched at the sight of her friend's red-rimmed eyes.

Then she noted the faint blue bruise on Carla's right cheekbone and a hot pit of anger burned in her belly.

She brushed her fingers beneath it, unable to stop her eyes from filling. 'Not Thierry?'

Carla's eyes filled too. 'No. He's a jerk, but not that much of a jerk.'

'Not Dylan.'

It was a statement rather than a question. Dylan would never strike a woman.

Carla gave a short laugh. 'I think he'd rather throw himself off a cliff than hurt a woman.' She glanced at Mia and rolled her eyes. 'I mean *physically* hurt a woman. From what I can tell he's broken his fair share of hearts. The fact you're up so early leads me to believe he's given *you* a sleepless night.'

Mia felt her lips twist. 'In this instance I believe it's safe to say I've returned the favour.'

Carla's attempt at a smile almost broke Mia's heart. She sat down and put her arm around Carla's shoulders. 'Your uncle?'

Carla rested her head against Mia's. 'Yes…' she whispered.

*The swine!*

They sat like that for a while, letting the early-morning peace seep into their souls.

A sigh eventually shuddered out of Mia. 'He hit you because of me, didn't he? Because you refused to end our friendship. I'm sorry I've caused trouble for you, Carla. You don't deserve it.'

Carla lifted her head. 'He hit me because I refused to obey him—because I'm choosing to live my life the way I see fit. And it's not the first time it's happened.'

Mia called him one of the worst names she could think of.

A giggle shot out of Carla, but she nodded in agreement.

'C'mon.' Mia hauled her to her feet. 'Have you had an *ounce* of sleep?'

Carla shook her head.

She led her inside and pushed her in the direction of the bathroom. 'Go wash your face.' She pulled a soft cotton nightie from a drawer and ordered her to put it on, then pulled the covers back from her bed. 'In.'

'Oh, but…'

'We'll make a game plan after you've had some sleep.'

Carla glanced at the bed. 'A couple of hours *would* be good.' She glanced back at Mia, biting her lip. 'I really, *really* don't want to see either Thierry or Dylan at the moment. I know it's asking a lot of you, Mia, but I just…'

'You want to sort through things at your own pace. That's understandable.'

'I'm tired of men thinking they know what's best for me, telling me what to do.'

'I'll take care of Thierry and Dylan if they show up.'

Carla climbed into the bed.

Mia pulled the covers up to her chin, squeezed her hand briefly. 'Sleep well.'

She fortified herself with more coffee and went to sit back out on the front step to keep guard.

Dylan showed up at nine o'clock.

He looked tired and haggard and her heart went out to him. She forgave him—a little—for her own sleepless night.

He collapsed onto the step beside her. 'I've been looking for her for a couple of hours.' He gestured to Carla's car. 'Thierry rang at seven. I thought she was with him. That's when I realised she was missing. I'm glad she's here.'

Thierry chose that moment to pull up behind Dylan's car.

'She's a grown woman, Dylan. If she chooses to spend the night elsewhere, surely that's her business? Not to mention her prerogative. I'm sure *you* wouldn't appreciate it if she sent out a search party whenever *you* didn't come home.'

He thrust out his jaw. 'She's not answering her phone.'

'Likewise.'

She said it as gently as she could, but Dylan's eyes narrowed, the irises going a deep sapphire.

Thierry charged up the path. 'I want to see her!'

'I'm sure you do.' She kept her voice calm. 'But the fact of the matter is she doesn't want to see either of you at the moment.'

'Me?' Dylan shot to his feet. 'Why doesn't she want to see *me*?'

'I believe the phrase was, "I'm tired of men thinking they know what's best for me."'

Both men's jaws dropped.

Dylan paced.

Thierry just stood there with his hands clenched. He glanced at the door.

'It's locked,' Mia said. 'And if either one of you has the slightest interest in her well-being you won't start banging on the door. She's asleep.'

Dylan halted his pacing. 'You put her to *bed*?'

'I did.'

Thierry rested his hands on his knees, his face grey. 'I don't know what to do. I've been such an idiot.'

Dylan leapt forward and grabbed him by his shirtfront and shook him. 'What the *hell* have you done to her?'

'If I have to get the hose out to cool the pair of you off, I will.'

Those blue eyes swung to her. She read the anger in them—and the indecision.

'Let him go, Dylan. Carla is perfectly aware that the two of you have her best interests at heart, but she's entitled to a time out whenever she needs one. She doesn't have to consult with either of you beforehand.'

Dylan stared into her eyes so intently it felt as if he was scouring her soul. Finally, with a nod, he released Thierry. 'Sorry.'

Thierry straightened his shirt. 'No problem.'

She glanced back at Thierry. 'I don't know what your argument was about last night, but if you're truly sorry—'

'I am!'

'Then I suggest you come up with an honest explanation for why you behaved the way you did, promise to do better in the future, and have a heartfelt and grovelling apology ready.'

His fists opened and closed several times. He nodded hard. 'Right.'

His earnestness almost made her smile. 'Flowers might help too.'

His chin lifted. 'I can come back?'

She knew she wouldn't be able to keep him away indefinitely.

'You can come back at four. I'm not making any promises. It's up to Carla to decide if she wants to see you or not.'

'Right.' He swung away and made for the gate. He halted when he reached it and turned back. 'Thanks.'

With a nod, he was gone.

Had Thierry just *thanked* her? Wow!

Both she and Dylan watched him drive away—Mia from her spot on the step, Dylan from where he stood in wide-legged masculine magnificence on her pocket of front lawn.

As soon as Thierry's car had disappeared, he swung back to face her. 'Okay, you can let me see her now.'

'I'm sorry, Dylan, but the same holds true for you too.'

'You have to be joking!' He stalked across to loom over her. 'You *know* I only have Carla's best interests at heart.'

She stood, using the step to give her a height advantage. 'Has it never occurred to you that all your big brotherly protectiveness—some might call it *over*-protectiveness—could be a *little* stifling?' She uttered 'little' in such a way that he couldn't miss the fact that she meant *a lot*.

He gaped at her. 'It's my job to look out for her.'

'She's an adult. She can look out for herself.'

'Just because your family let you down, it doesn't mean that's the way every family works.'

He spoke the words in a voice so low and controlled it sent ice tiptoeing down her spine.

He held out his hand, palm flat, eyes glittering. 'Give me the key.'

Her heart quailed, because she suddenly realised what a betrayal he would see this as—her keeping him from his sister. She wanted to weep. She'd finally found the one sure way to distance him, and now that she had she didn't want to use it.

*Give him the key.*

She lifted her chin and forced steel to her spine. 'No.' Planting her hands on her hips, she leaned towards him. 'Carla doesn't want to see you at the moment. Go home, Dylan. Stop being a bully.'

His hands fisted and his entire body started to shake. 'I could take it from you by force.'

She folded her arms and raised an eyebrow. They both knew he wouldn't.

He swore and she flinched. He didn't apologise, but she didn't expect him to.

'A *bully*?' The word ground out of him. 'I can't believe you're lumping me in the same class as Thierry.'

The pain in his words cut at her. 'I *do* put you in the same class as Thierry. Thierry loves Carla—adores her. He'd lay his life down for her. I know you would too. It doesn't change the fact that Carla doesn't want to see either of you for the time being.'

His eyes blazed, but his face turned to stone. He turned and stormed down the path, leaving as she'd ordered him to.

The backs of her eyes burned and her vision blurred. A lump lodged in her throat. Whatever fragile link had bound them together had been severed, and she felt the pain of it deep down inside her. It tore at something she thought might never be fixed.

At the gate, he halted. His shoulders sagged. She hated it that she'd hurt him, but she readied herself for a different form of attack.

He came back, his face sombre, his eyes throbbing. 'I owe you an apology. I just acted like a two-year-old throwing a tantrum because he's been denied what he wants. But I'm worried about Carla.'

'I know.'

He clasped her shoulders. 'Is she okay?'

He stared into her eyes and she realised he meant to trust whatever she told him. Her mouth went dry.

'Mia?'

Her heart thudded, though she couldn't explain why. 'She's upset.'

'With Thierry?'

'I suspect so. But mostly with your uncle.'

Dylan's lips pressed together in a tight line. 'His car was at the house when I got back last night. It was late, so he was already in bed. He left after breakfast. We shared a few home truths. I don't think he'll be back. I told him that if he caused trouble for you at your place of employment you'd come and work for FWE. I don't think your job will be in jeopardy from *that* region, Mia.'

'I... Thank you.'

'I didn't know he'd spoken to Carla.'

It wasn't her place to tell him about his uncle's violence. 'I think that after some sleep, and some lunch and some talking, Carla will be fine. She just needs time to clear her head.'

He squeezed her shoulders and then released her. 'Okay.'

He really meant to trust her?

'Thank you for looking after her.'

'She's my friend. Of course I'm going to look out for her.'

His eyes throbbed into her. 'I don't mean to be a bully.'

It took all the strength she had not to reach out and touch his face. 'I know that too.' And he wasn't—not really. 'If you were really a bully you'd have taken the key from me by force.'

'You don't see it, do you?' he said.

A desolation that made her heart catch stretched through his eyes. Her mouth went dry. 'What don't I see?'

'I just harangued you, bullied you, all but emotionally blackmailed you, but you held firm. You chose to do what you thought was right rather than submit to my will. Do you still believe you're weak and easy to manipulate?'

She froze. 'I...'

The yard spun.

'I can't keep doing this, Mia.'

Her gaze speared back to his. 'What do you mean?'

'I love you.'

Her heart stuttered in her chest.

'You *know* I love you. With everything that's inside me. I'd do anything to win your love. But it's not enough, is it? You're still so far away. I lose myself and I get so frustrated... I start to yell and then I turn into a bully.'

'Dylan, I—'

He pressed his fingers to her lips. 'I love you, Mia. I want to have a life with you. But I won't bully you into that. If you ever come to me, I want it to be because you love me too.'

She did love him, but...

Confusion swirled through her and she couldn't make sense of the riot raging through her. The smile he sent her made her want to cry.

He leaned forward and pressed a kiss to her brow. 'Tell Carla if she needs anything to call me.'

She nodded.

He held her gaze for a moment. 'I mean to give you all the space you want, Mia. If you change your mind, you know where to find me.'

Fear clutched at her heart.

With a nod, he turned and strode away. This time he didn't stop at the gate.

Every step that he took away from her increased the ache in her chest tenfold.

Carla slept until noon.

'Did Thierry show up?'

'He did. So did Dylan.'

'What did he say?'

'Dylan said you're to call him if you need anything.'

'What did *Thierry* say?'

*Oh.* 'The man is half out of his wits with worry for you... and fear that you're going to dump him.'

'Good!'

'I told him to come back at four. I didn't guarantee that you'd see him. But if you really don't want to see him again he'll need to hear it from you.'

Carla bit her lip.

'Can things not be fixed?' Mia asked.

Carla folded her arms. 'I guess that depends on him. He wants to be all strong and solitary and untouchable—but that's *not* how relationships work. It's not how *marriage* works.'

Each and every one of those darts found their mark, although they hadn't been aimed at her.

Mia rubbed a hand across her chest, trying to ease the ache there. 'I believe he's sincere in wanting to make amends.'

'You think I should see him?'

She recalled the absolute happiness on Carla's face when she and Thierry had picnicked. 'I think you should give him a hearing. I think things can be patched up.'

The other woman tried to hide it, but she brightened at Mia's words. 'What about Dylan?'

'I think you should call him.'

'I meant what about *you* and Dylan?'

*Oh.* She glanced down at her hands. 'I don't know. I need to go somewhere quiet and think.'

'So there's hope?'

She met Carla's gaze. 'I *hope* there's hope.'

After a moment Carla said, 'I'm going to ring Dylan. I want Uncle Andrew charged with assault.'

Mia's head shot up, a fierce gladness gripping her. 'Good for you. Women shouldn't have to put up with violence at the hands of men.'

Carla twisted her hands together. 'It'll create a media circus, though.' She eyed Mia uncertainly. 'And the reason for our argument will come out—which means you'll be spotlighted in the media too.'

'Me?'

Carla reached out and took Mia's hand. 'I know how much you've dreaded the media getting hold of the story that you and Dylan are dating. If the thought of publicity freaks you out that much, I won't go ahead with it.'

Her heart thumped. She waited for dread and fear to fill her, but they didn't. *Why* wasn't she crippled with fear?

The answer came to her in an instant. Ever since she'd

been released from jail she'd thought that scandal and losing her job, losing the chance of the quiet life she craved, were the worst things that could happen to her. She'd been wrong. Watching Dylan walk away this morning—that had been the worst thing.

Very slowly she shook her head. 'It doesn't freak me out. At least, not much.' She met her friend's gaze. 'You have every right to slay your dragons. I'll help in any way I can.'

Carla wrapped her in a hug. 'Thank you.'

At four o'clock Mia let herself into the Plum Pines office. Sunday was one of the busiest days as far as the general public were concerned—lots of barbecues, picnics and viewing of the exhibits. It was a busy day for the volunteers who helped to run the wildlife displays too, but the administration of the reserve was a strictly Monday-to-Friday enterprise. Which meant she'd have the office to herself.

With a heart that pounded too fast, she switched on one of the computers and then pulled Felipe's memory card from her pocket. Swallowing hard, she retrieved the image he'd snapped of her.

It filled the screen. She flinched and had to look away.

*It's only a photograph!*

She glanced back and tried to study the picture objectively, but after only a few seconds she had to look away again.

Muttering something rude under her breath, she pushed out of her chair and paced across to the far wall. Hauling in a breath, she turned back to the image once more.

Her heart squeezed tight and her eyes filled. Felipe had captured something that attracted and repelled her at the same time. He'd captured something that both soothed and frightened her.

*What was it?*

In that photo her expression was so unguarded it made her head spin. Was it hope?

She moved back towards the computer monitor to study the image more minutely, biting down on her thumbnail.

Hope was part of it, but…

She reached out and touched the face on the screen.

That smile…

The emotion pulsing through the photograph was *joy*. It was so present she could almost feel the laughter wrap around her.

Joy? She'd spent so long feeling ashamed of herself, so determined not to repeat her mistakes, she'd forgotten. She'd forgotten she had a lot of good inside her too.

Her hands clenched and unclenched. She'd told herself that she couldn't have fun and hope and joy in her life because she didn't deserve them—not after the things she'd done.

But…

She'd made a mistake—a big one—but that mistake didn't have to define the rest of her life unless she let it. Her heart hammered against her ribs. She didn't need to shut herself away. She just needed to choose the right path… the right life.

She fell back into the chair, her cheeks wet. There wasn't a tissue in sight, so she dried her cheeks on the sleeves of her shirt and sniffed rather inelegantly.

'Right, then.'

She might as well start living that life right away.

She seized the phone and punched in a number.

'Felipe Fellini.'

'Felipe, it's Mia.'

'Mia, darling—what can I do for you?'

She told him.

After she'd hung up she pulled in a breath and rang Dylan.

He answered immediately. 'Mia! Is everything okay?'

His caller ID must have given her away.

The sound of his voice made her throat dry and she had to clear it before she could speak. 'Yes.'

'I've spoken to Carla. Are you sure you're all right with the publicity that a suit against Andrew will involve?'

She nodded, and then realised he couldn't see her. 'I'm sure.'

There was a pause. 'That's a surprise.'

She nodded again, more to herself this time. 'Yes.'

'What can I do for you?'

'I was wondering…' She wiped a damp palm down her jeans. 'I was wondering if I could invite you on a date next Saturday night. There's something I want you to see.'

'Has this anything to do with Carla and Thierry?'

'No. It's to do with me.'

'What time would you like me to pick you up?'

Dylan's heart thumped when he knocked on Mia's door. All week he'd alternated between hope and despair. Hope that this was the new beginning with Mia that he craved. Despair that this would be her way of bringing things between them to an end once and for all.

She opened the door. For a moment all he could do was stare. 'You look stunning!'

She wore a scarlet dress with a shimmering satin bodice, fitted beneath her breasts. The skirt fell to her knees in a cloud of chiffon that moved as she walked.

She pushed a strand of hair behind her ear. 'You look very nice yourself.'

He was glad he'd worn a dinner jacket. Especially when her hand fluttered up to her throat, as if the sight of him made it hard for her to breathe. The smile she sent him, though, held a hint of shyness—like a girl on her first date.

This probably *was* her first real date in nearly four years. Tenderness washed over him.

After she'd locked the front door he held out his arm, ridiculously pleased when she placed her hand in the crook of his elbow. 'Your chariot awaits.'

For good or for ill, he had a feeling he'd remember tonight for the rest of his life.

'Where are we going?'

She gave him an inner-city address. He had no idea what was there, but he didn't ask any further questions. He'd let the evening unfold at the pace she chose for it.

Dylan glanced out of the car window. Light spilled from the industrial-sized windows of a warehouse. He opened his mouth to ask Mia if she was sure she had the address right, but closed it again when she lowered her window and waved a card at an attendant standing on the footpath. The attendant directed them to a parking spot in front of the warehouse's huge double doors—the doors were closed except for a smaller door inset into one of them.

He switched off the ignition and turned to her. 'What *is* this?'

'I—' She broke off and hauled in a breath.

That wave of tenderness washed over him again, threatening to crush him. He reached for her hand. 'Are you nervous?'

'A little.'

'Of me?'

'Yes.'

The word whispered out of her and something blossomed in his chest. *Hope.* And it took firm root. 'You don't need to be nervous about me, Mia.'

He was hers. All hers. He didn't tell her out loud that he loved her, but he pressed a kiss to her palm, knowing that if she wanted to see it his love for her would be written all over his face.

Her gaze travelled over him and her breath snagged, her gaze catching on his mouth. Hunger and need chased themselves across her face. An answering hunger roared through him.

'Oh!' Her hand tightened in his. 'You can distract me *so* easily!'

The grin inside him built. 'Excellent.'

'Before you distract me further, I want to show you something. And then I want to talk.'

'And *then* can I distract you?' He waggled his eyebrows.

She gurgled back a laugh. 'Perhaps. If you still want to.'

He'd definitely still want to.

Without another word, he pushed himself out of the car and went around to open her door. She took his arm.

'This—' she gestured to the building in front of them '—is something of a first. Felipe has been prevailed upon to give the people of Newcastle a preview of his up-and-coming Sydney show.'

Dylan's stared at her. 'Who prevailed upon him?'

She moistened her lips. 'Me.'

*She* had?

Before he could ask what that meant, Felipe came towards them, arms outstretched.

'Darlings!' He kissed them on both cheeks in flamboyant greeting. 'I'm honoured to have you as my guests. Come!'

Dylan's head whirled as Felipe gave them a personal tour of some of the most amazing photographs Dylan had ever seen—his commentary both entertaining and revelatory.

Dylan glanced at Mia. She'd contrived this for *him*? Because she knew he appreciated art and photography? His heart gave a giant kick. Nobody had ever arranged anything so perfect for him in all his life. It had to mean *something*.

'And this, darlings, is the *pièce de résistance*! The jewel in my crown.'

Felipe led them around a screen to an enormous photograph positioned on one of the warehouse's end walls.

*Mia*!

He took a step towards it and Mia's hand slipped from his arm. It was the photograph of Mia! Her joy, her laughter and her love greeted him from the wall and he almost stopped breathing.

His every muscle tightened. He swung back to her, hands fisted at his sides. He'd lost the ability to be charming. Everything had been stripped away except raw need. 'What does this mean?'

Mia glanced at Felipe, who put a key into her hand.

'Lock up when you're done.'

She nodded her thanks.

It was only then that Dylan realised they were alone in this magnificent space. The show had been for him alone.

Mia didn't speak until the clang of a door informed them that Felipe had left. She moistened her lips. 'Are you cross that I gave Felipe permission to use the photograph in his exhibition?'

'Cross? No.' He glanced at the photo again and searched himself. He didn't feel disappointment either. Only wonder. 'I just want to know what all this means.'

'It means I've finally realised you were right.'

She moved to stand beside him and gestured up at the picture, though he could only look at *her*—the flesh and blood woman.

'That *is* the person I should become. It's…' She met his gaze. 'It's the real me.'

Her admission stunned him.

'I've realised that I deserve to be happy. More to the point, I've realised I *want* to be happy. And I've realised that being a field officer and leading a quiet life *won't* make me happy.'

She glanced at the photo and then at him.

'*You* make me happy, Dylan.'

He stared at her, humbled by the vulnerability in her eyes.

'I… I couldn't be happy until I forgave myself for my past.' Her hands twisted together. 'I know I've hurt you, and I'm so sorry for that. Truly. I'm hoping I haven't hurt you so badly that you can't forgive me. I'm hoping—'

He didn't let her finish. He kissed her instead.

The shock of his assault made her wobble on her heels, but he wrapped an arm about her waist and pulled her close, steadying her. She wrapped her arms around his neck and kissed him back.

When he lifted his head her eyes glittered and her chest rose and fell. And then she smiled, and it was just like the smile in the frame behind her—full of joy and love.

'That felt an awful lot like a you-still-love-me-too kiss.'

He stroked his fingers down her face. 'I will *always* love you.'

She took his face in her hands. 'I promise I will look after your heart and be the best person I can for you.'

He stared into her eyes, humbled all over again. 'Nobody has ever made a more meaningful vow to me. I'll cherish it forever.'

A cheeky smile peeped out. 'Good, because I'm also going to ask you to give me a job. I quit Plum Pines yesterday.'

He gaped. She just grinned back at him, so delighted with herself that he had to laugh.

'I don't want to be a field officer, and I don't want to be an events manager either. I just want you to give me a regular office job so I can put myself through a psychology major at university. I want to be a counsellor.' She lifted her chin. 'I think I have something of value I could offer to people.'

He ran his hands up and down her back, revelling in the way it made her shiver. 'How about I gift you the opportunity for full-time study as a wedding present?'

She went very still and Dylan held his breath.

'You want to *marry* me?' she whispered.

Very gently he took his arms from around her and, gripping both her hands, went down on one knee. 'Beautiful Mia, will you do me the very great honour of becoming my wife?'

Tears shone in her eyes. When she nodded, they spilled onto her cheeks.

He rose and she threw her arms around his neck. 'I can't

think of anything I want more than to spend the rest of my life with you, Dylan.'

He laughed for the sheer joy of it, swinging her around. 'How does November sound? We have a wedding going begging. We might as well use it.'

She eased back. 'What on earth are you talking about? Carla and Thierry have made up and—'

'They flew out to Vegas yesterday.'

She gaped. 'No!'

'So… November is ours if we want it.'

An enormous smile spread across her face. 'It's…perfect!'

He glanced at the photo on the wall and then down at her. 'No, Mia, *you're* perfect.'

She touched his face, her smile radiant. '*We're* perfect. Together.'

He couldn't top that, so he kissed her instead.

# EPILOGUE

CARLA AND THIERRY bundled Mia out of the limousine and whisked her straight inside the small marquee that had been set up especially for her benefit—to shield her from the press and allow her a chance to freshen up.

As they'd only driven from her suite at an inner-city hotel with glorious views of the harbour to Plum Pines Reserve— a drive of less than fifteen minutes—she didn't really see what kind of freshening up was required. Unless she was supposed to try and quieten the excited dervishes whirling in her stomach. She had no chance of stilling *those*. She wasn't sure she wanted to.

Perhaps she should try and tame the grin that made her face ache? But she had no hope—nor desire—to do that either.

Carla, stunning in her hot-pink bridesmaid's dress, crouched down to adjust Mia's skirts.

Mia laughed ruefully. 'I went overboard, didn't I? I look like an oversized meringue.'

'You look *gorgeous*.' Carla continued to fluff up the skirts. 'Your dress is *beautiful*.'

The moment Mia had clapped eyes on the confection of raw silk and pearl beading she'd fallen in love with it. Apparently when she had said that she meant to live life to the full rather than hide in the shadows she'd meant it.

She hugged herself. 'It *is* beautiful.'

'I can't wait to see Dylan's face when he sees you.'

Today, nobody could mistake Mia for anything other than what she was—the bride, the centre of attention, the belle of the ball marrying her prince.

Those dervishes whirled faster and faster. Her cheeks ached from smiling. She lifted her chin. She wasn't ashamed of her joy. She wanted to share it with everyone.

She turned to find Thierry surveying her with his now familiar unsmiling gaze.

He nodded. 'You look stunning.'

She wriggled with excitement. 'I *feel* stunning. I'm so happy I think I could float off into the atmosphere.'

For the briefest of moments Thierry smiled, and it tempered the severe lines of his face. When he smiled, she could see why Carla had fallen for him.

She touched his arm. 'Thank you for agreeing to give me away.' He hadn't hesitated when she'd asked. He'd agreed immediately.

'I'm honoured.' One shoulder lifted. 'I'm starting to think I'd do anything you asked of me.'

From behind him, Carla sent her a wink.

Thierry frowned. 'You're sure we're okay?'

She rolled her eyes. 'I swear to God, Thierry, if you apologise to me one more time we're going to fall out.'

He shuffled his feet. 'It's just… I'm really sorry I misjudged you.'

Given his background, and the hardships his father's choices had forced on his family, Mia couldn't blame him for his reservations where she'd been concerned.

'As I misjudged myself, I can hardly blame you for doing the same. But it's all in the past now, and that's where it'll remain. It's time to move on.'

That was her new motto and she'd embraced it with gusto.

She reached out to take Carla and Thierry's hands. 'You're my family now—my sister and brother. I can't tell you how fortunate that makes me feel.'

Carla's eyes filled. Thierry cleared his throat a couple of times.

Mia blinked hard. She would *not* ruin her eye make-up. She wanted to look perfect for Dylan. 'So that's a yes—we're *very* okay.'

On impulse, they all hugged—before Carla tut-tutted and said something about crushing Mia's dress.

Mia laughed at her fussing, but a wave of excitement somersaulted through her. 'Oh, is it time yet? I can't wait—'

The flap of the marquee flew open and Felipe appeared. He clasped his hands beneath his chin when he saw her.

'Radiant!' he pronounced, before whisking a compact from somewhere and touching a powder puff lightly to her nose. He kissed the air above her cheeks. 'Perfect!'

He pulled out his camera and snapped a couple of pictures.

She waggled a finger at him. 'Don't forget—those photos are mine and Dylan's. None are to mysteriously appear in an exhibition.'

'Cross my heart, darling. Besides, your dishy intended is paying me enough to make it worth my while.' He pouted. 'Also, he made me sign some awful form full of lawyer-speak.'

Mia laughed.

'I've been sent to tell you everything is ready.'

'Oh!' She clasped her hands together.

'Nervous, darling?'

'Excited.'

He squeezed her hands. 'I wouldn't have missed this for the world.'

And then he was gone.

Carla handed her a bouquet of pink and white peonies. 'Ready?'

A lump lodged in her throat. All she could do was nod.

Thierry held the flap of the marquee open to reveal the red carpet that would lead her to Dylan. Carla set off down the carpet first. Thierry made Mia wait until Carla was half-way down the makeshift aisle before stepping after her.

Mia was vaguely aware of the beautiful music playing, of the murmurs of appreciation from their wedding guests, but her focus was wholly centred on the man standing at the other end.

His blond hair gleamed golden in the sunlight. His broad shoulders and strong thighs were outlined to perfection in his tuxedo. His heart was in his eyes. He didn't try to hide it from anyone, and she wasn't sure she'd ever seen anything more beautiful in her life.

Awe rose up through her…and more happiness than her body could contain. It spilled from her eyes and onto her cheeks.

He took her hand. His throat bobbed with emotion as he swallowed.

'You're so beautiful you make my eyes water,' she whispered, not caring about her make-up.

He smiled down at her. 'You're so beautiful you make my heart sing.'

The celebrant cleared her throat. 'Ready?'

Mia smiled up at Dylan. 'Yes.'

The service was simple but heartfelt. The reception was the epitome of joy and elegance. Mia felt like a fairytale princess.

After the meal had been eaten, toasts made, the cake cut and the bridal waltz completed, Dylan took her hand and they sneaked outside to stand at the wooden railing overlooking the lily pond. Lights twinkled in the trees, glimmering across the water's surface.

Dylan took her face in his hands and kissed her. A sweet, gentle kiss that promised a lifetime of kisses.

'Happy?' he murmured, easing back.

'More than I ever thought possible.' She smiled up at him before glancing back towards the marquee. 'Has anyone ever told you that you know how to throw a fabulous party?'

'What can I say? I'm gifted.'

She gurgled back a laugh. 'Look.' She pointed to Carla and Thierry dancing. 'They look gorgeous together.'

Dylan snorted. 'Carla should've had a wedding like this! *Elopement?*' He snorted again.

Mia leaned back against him. 'You just love any excuse to throw a party.'

'What's wrong with a party?'

'Absolutely nothing. I adore parties. I'm especially loving this one.'

She bit her lip then, and glanced up at him again.

'Are you sorry your Uncle Andrew isn't here?' The man might be a miserable excuse for a human being but he was still Dylan's uncle.

'Not a bit. I'll be happy if I never clap eyes on him again.'

There hadn't been enough evidence to charge Andrew with assault against Carla, but the scandal hadn't done the older man any favours. Especially since a young intern who worked in his office had made similar allegations against him. He'd been suspended pending an internal inquiry. If found guilty he'd lose his job. His political ambitions would be nothing more than dust.

Mia glanced up into her new husband's face and knew Andrew wouldn't be making trouble for any of them ever again.

Dylan smiled down at her. 'The day I won your heart was the luckiest day of my life.'

She turned in his arms, resting her hands against the warm hard contours of his chest. 'I'm the real winner, Dylan. You made me believe in love again. You showed me the power it had to do good. Whatever happens in the future, I'll never forget that lesson.' She touched her fingers to his face. 'I love you. I'm going to spend the rest of my life making you very, *very* happy.'

She wondered if her face reflected as much love as his did. She hoped so.

'Want to know what would make me happy right now?' he murmured, a wicked light flitting through his eyes. 'A kiss.'

Laughing, she reached up on tiptoe and pressed her lips to his, telling him in a language that needed no words how much she loved him.

\* \* \* \* \*

# HIRED BY
# THE BROODING
# BILLIONAIRE

## KANDY SHEPHERD

To my daughter Lucy for her invaluable
help in 'casting' my characters.

# CHAPTER ONE

SHELLEY FAIRHILL HAD walked by the grand old mansion on Bellevue Street at least twenty times before she finally screwed up enough courage to press the old-fashioned buzzer embedded in the sandstone gatepost. Even then, with her hand on the ornate wrought-iron gate, she quailed before pushing it open.

The early twentieth-century house was handsome with peaked roofs and an ornate turret but it was almost overwhelmed by the voracious growth of a once beautiful garden gone wild. It distressed her horticulturalist's heart to see the out-of-control roses, plants stunted and starved of light by rampant vines, and unpruned shrubs grown unchecked into trees.

This was Sydney on a bright winter's afternoon with shafts of sunlight slanting through the undergrowth but there was an element of eeriness to the house, of secrets undisturbed.

In spite of the sunlight, Shelley shivered. *But she had to do this.*

It wasn't just that she was looking for extra work—somehow she had felt compelled by this garden since the day she'd first become aware of it when she'd got lost on her way to the railway station.

The buzzer sounded and the gate clicked a release. She pushed it open with a less than steady hand. Over the last weeks, as she'd walked past the house in the posh inner-eastern suburb of Darling Point, she'd wondered about who lived there. Her imagination had gifted her visions of a broken-hearted old woman who had locked herself away from the world when her fiancé had been killed at war. Or a crabby, Scrooge-like old man cut off from all who loved him.

The reality of the person who opened the door to her was so different her throat tightened and the professional words of greeting she had rehearsed froze unsaid.

Her reaction wasn't just because the man who filled the doorframe with his impressive height and broad shoulders was young—around thirty, she guessed. Not much older than her, in fact. It was because he was so heart-stoppingly good-looking.

A guy this hot, this movie-star handsome, with his black hair, chiselled face and deep blue eyes, hadn't entered into her imaginings for a single second. Yes, he seemed dark and forbidding—but not in the haunted-house way she had expected.

His hair lacked recent acquaintance with a comb, his jaw was two days shy of a razor and his black roll-neck sweater and sweatpants looked as though he'd slept in them. The effect was extraordinarily attractive in a don't-give-a-damn kind of way. His dark scowl was what made him seem intimidating.

She cleared her throat to free her voice but he spoke before she got a chance to open her mouth.

'Where's the parcel?' His voice was deep, his tone abrupt.

'Wh-what parcel?' she stuttered.

He frowned. 'The motherboard.'

She stared blankly at him.

He shook his head impatiently, gestured with his hands. 'Computer parts. The delivery I was expecting.'

Shelley was so shocked at his abrupt tone, she glanced down at her empty hands as if expecting a parcel to materialise. Which was crazy insane.

'You...you think I'm a courier?' she stuttered.

'Obviously,' he said. She didn't like the edge of sarcasm to the word.

But she supposed her uniform of khaki trousers, industrial boots and a shirt embroidered with the logo of the garden design company she worked for could be misconstrued as courier garb.

'I'm not a courier. I—'

'I wouldn't have let you in the gate if I'd known that,' he said. 'Whatever you're selling, I'm not buying.'

Shelley was taken aback by his rudeness. But she refused to let herself get flustered. A cranky old man or eccentric old woman might have given her worse.

'I'm not selling anything. Well, except myself.' *That didn't sound right.* 'I'm a horticulturalist.' She indicated the garden with a wave of her hand. 'You obviously need a gardener. I'm offering my services.'

He frowned again. 'I don't need a gardener. I like the place exactly as it is.'

'But it's a mess. Such a shame. There's a beautiful garden under there somewhere. It's choking itself to death.' She couldn't keep the note of indignation from her voice. To her, plants were living things that deserved love and care.

His dark brows rose. 'And what business is that of yours?'

'It's none of my business. But it...it upsets me to see the garden like that when it could look so different. I... I thought I could help restore it to what it should be. My rates are very reasonable.'

For a long moment her gaze met his and she saw something in his eyes that might have been regret before the shutters went down. He raked both hands through his hair in what seemed to be a well-worn path.

'I don't need help,' he said. 'You've wasted your time.' His tone was dismissive and he turned to go back inside.

Curious, she peered over his shoulder but the room behind him was in darkness. No wonder with all those out-of-control plants blocking out the light.

Her bravado was just about used up. But she pulled out the business card she had tucked into her shirt pocket so it would be easy to retrieve. 'My card. In case you change your mind,' she said. It was her personal card, not for the company she worked for. If she was to achieve her dream of visiting the great gardens of the world, she needed the extra income moonlighting bought her.

He looked at her card without seeming to read it. For a moment she thought he might hand it back to her or tear it up. But he kept it in his hand. The man was rude, but perhaps not rude enough to do that. Most likely he would bin it when he got inside.

*Nothing ventured, nothing gained.* Her grandmother's words came back to her. At least she'd tried.

'Close the gate behind you when you leave,' the man said, in a voice so cool it was as if he'd thrown a bucket of icy water over her enthusiasm for the garden.

'Sure,' she said through gritted teeth, knowing she would have to fight an impulse to slam it.

As she walked back down the path she snatched the opportunity to look around her to see more of the garden than she'd been able to see over the fence. Up closer it was even more choked by weeds and overgrowth than she'd thought. But it was all she'd ever see of it now.

*Strange, strange man,* she mused.

Strange, but also strangely attractive. The dark hair, the dark clothes, those brooding blue eyes. He was as compelling as the garden itself. And as mysterious. Maybe he didn't own the house. Maybe he was a movie star or someone who wanted to be incognito. Maybe he was a criminal. Or someone under a witness protection plan. She hadn't lived long enough in Sydney to hear any local gossip about him. But why did it matter? She wouldn't be seeing him again.

*She looked like a female warrior.* Declan watched the gardener stride down the pathway towards the gate. Her long, thick plait of honey-coloured hair fell to her waist and swayed with barely repressed indignation. She was tall, five ten easily, even in those heavy-duty, elastic-sided work boots. The rolled-up sleeves of the khaki shirt revealed tanned, toned arms; the man-style trousers concealed but hinted at shapely curves and long legs. She looked strong, vigorous, all woman—in spite of the way she dressed. Not what he thought of as a gardener. He glanced down at her card—*Shelley Fairhill*.

The old-fashioned name seemed appropriate for a lover of flowers, all soft focus and spring sunbeams. But the woman behind the name seemed more like the fantasy warrior heroine in the video games that had brought him his first million when he was just eighteen—the assassin Princess Alana, all kick-butt strength, glistening angel wings and exaggerated curves born of his adolescent yearnings. With her deadly bow and arrow Alana had fought many hard-won battles in the fantasy world he had created as a refuge from a miserable childhood.

He could see in this gardener something of the action woman who had kept on making him millions. Billions when he'd sold Alana out. Right now Shelley Fairhill was all tense muscles and compressed angst—seething, he imagined, with unspoken retorts. He could tell by the set of her shoulders the effort she made not to slam the gate off its hinges—he had no doubt with her muscles she could do that with ease. Instead she closed it with exaggerated care. And not for a second did she turn that golden head back to him.

Who would blame her? He'd rejected her pitch for employment in a manner that had stopped just short of rudeness. But Shelley Fairhill should never have breached that gate. He'd only buzzed it open in a moment of distraction. He'd been working for thirty-six hours straight. The gate was kept locked for a reason. He did not want intruders, especially a tall, lithe warrior woman like her, crossing the boundaries of his property. And he liked the garden the way it was—one day the plants might grow over completely and bury the house in darkness like a fortress. *He wanted to be left alone.*

Still, she was undeniably striking—not just in physique but in colouring with her blond hair and warm brown eyes. He couldn't help a moment of regret torn painfully from the barricades he had built up against feeling—barricades like thorn-studded vines that twined ever tighter around his heart stifling all emotion, all hope.

Because when he'd first seen her on his front doorstep for a single, heart-stopping moment he'd forgotten those barriers and the painful reasons they were there. All he'd been aware of was that he was a man and she was a beautiful woman. *He could not allow that boy-meets-girl feeling to exist even for seconds.*

For a long moment he looked at the closed gate, the out-of-control tendrils of some climbing plant waving long, predatory fingers from the arch on top of it, before he turned to slouch back inside.

# CHAPTER TWO

DECLAN GRANT. SHELLEY puzzled over the signature on the text that had just pinged into her smartphone.

Contact me immediately re work on garden.

She couldn't place the name. But the abrupt, peremptory tone of the text gave her a clue to his identity.

For two weeks, she had pushed the neglected garden and its bad-mannered—though disturbingly good-looking—owner to the back of her mind. His reaction to her straightforward offer of help had taken the sheen off her delight in imagining how the garden could blossom if restored.

The more she'd thought about him, the more she'd seethed. He hadn't given her even half a chance to explain what she could do. She'd stopped walking that way to the railway station at Edgecliff from the apartment in nearby Double Bay she shared with her sister. And drove the long way around to avoid it when she was in the car. All because of the man she suspected was Declan Grant.

Her immediate thought was to delete the text. She wanted nothing to do with Mr Tall, Dark and Gloomy; couldn't imagine working with him in any kind of harmony. Her finger hovered over the keypad, ready to dispatch his message into the cyber wilderness.

And yet.

*She would kill to work on that garden.*

Shelley stared at the phone for a long moment. She was at work, planting a hedge to exact specifications in a new apartment complex on the north shore. By the time she crossed the Sydney Harbour Bridge to get back to the east side it would be dark. Ideally she didn't want to meet that man in the shadowy gloom of a July winter nightfall. But she was intrigued. And she didn't want him to change his mind.

She texted back.

This evening, Friday, six p.m.

Then to be sure Declan Grant really was the black-haired guy with the black scowl:

Please confirm address.

The return text confirmed the address on Bellevue Street.

I'll be there, she texted back.

With the winter evening closing in, Shelley walked confidently up the pathway to the house, even though it was shrouded in shadow from the overgrown trees. The first thing she would do if she got this gig would be to recommend a series of solar-powered LED lights that would come on automatically to light a visitor's path to the front door. *Maybe he wanted to discourage visitors by keeping them in the dark.*

She braced herself to deal with Declan Grant. To be polite. Even if he wasn't. *She wanted to work on this garden.* She had to sell herself as the best person for the job, undercut other gardeners' quotes if need be. She practised the words in her head.

But when Declan opened the door, all her rehearsed words froze at the sight of his outstretched hand—and the shock of his unexpected smile.

Okay, so it wasn't a warm, welcoming smile. It was more a polite smile. A professional, employer-greeting-a-candidate smile that didn't quite reach his eyes. Even so, it lifted his face from grouch to gorgeous. *Heavens, the man was handsome.* If his lean face with the high cheekbones and cleft in his chin didn't turn a woman's head his broad shoulders and impressive height surely would.

She stared for a moment too long before she took his proffered hand, his hard warm grip—and was suddenly self-consciously aware of her own work-callused hands. And her inappropriate clothes.

He was attractive—but that didn't mean she was attracted to him. Apart from the fact he was a total stranger and a potential employer, she liked to think she was immune to the appeal of very good-looking men. Her heart-crushing experience with Steve had ensured that. Too-handsome men had it too easy with women—and then found it too easy to destroy their hearts.

No. It was not attraction, just a surge of innate feminine feeling that made her wish she'd taken more care with her appearance for this meeting with Declan Grant.

After work, on a whirlwind visit back to the tiny apartment in Double Bay, she'd quickly showered and changed. Then swapped one set of gardening gear for another—khaki trousers, boots and a plain shirt without any place of employment logo on the pockets. When she'd told her sister she was going to see the potential client in the mysterious overgrown garden in Darling Point, Lynne had been horrified.

'You're not going out to a job interview looking like *that*,' Lynne had said. 'What will any potential employer think of you?'

'I'm a gardener, not a business person,' Shelley had retorted. 'I'm hardly going to dress in a suit and high heels or pile on scads of make-up. These clothes are clean and they're what I wear to work. I hope I look like a serious gardener.'

Now she regretted it. Not the lack of suit and high heels. But jeans and a jacket with smart boots might have been more suitable than the khaki trousers and shirt. This was a very wealthy part of Sydney where appearances were likely to count. Even for a gardener.

She'd got in the habit of dressing down in her male-dominated work world. Gardening was strong, physical work. She'd had to prove herself as good as—better than—her male co-workers. Especially when she had long blond hair and a very female shape that she did not want to draw attention to.

But Declan looked so sophisticated in his fine-knit black sweater and black jeans, clean-shaven, hair brushed back from his forehead, she could only gawk and feel self-conscious. Yes, her clean but old khaki work clothes put her at a definite disadvantage. Not that *he* seemed to notice. In fact she got the impression he was purposely not looking at her.

'Let's discuss the garden,' he said, turning to lead her into the hallway that had seemed so dark behind him in daylight.

She tried to keep her cool, not to gasp at the splendour of the entrance hall. The ornate staircase. The huge chandelier that came down from the floors above to light up the marble-tiled floor. Somehow she'd expected the inside of the house to be as run-down and derelict as the garden.

Not so. It had obviously been restored and with a lot of money thrown at it.

She followed him to a small sitting room that led off the hallway. It was furnished simply and elegantly and she got the impression it was rarely used. Heavy, embroidered curtains were drawn across the windows so she couldn't glimpse the garden through them.

He indicated for her to take a seat on one of the over-stuffed sofas. She perched on its edge, conscious of her gardening trousers on the pristine fabric. He sat opposite, a coffee table between them. The polished surface was just asking for a bowl of fresh flowers from the garden to sit in the centre. That was, if anything was blooming in that jungle outside.

'I apologise for mistaking you for a courier the last time we met,' he said stiffly. 'I work from home and still had my head in my workspace.'

Shelley wondered what he did for work but it was not her place to ask. To live in a place like this, in one of Sydney's most expensive streets, it must be something that earned tons of money. She put aside her fanciful thoughts of him being in witness protection or a criminal on the run. That was when he'd said 'no' to the garden. Now it looked likely he was saying 'yes'.

'That's okay,' she said with a dismissive wave of her hand. 'It was just a misunderstanding.' She wanted to get off on the right foot with him, make polite conversation. 'Did your computer part arrive?'

'Eventually, yes.'

He wasn't a talkative man, that was for sure. There was an awkward pause that she rushed to fill. 'So it seems you've changed your mind about the garden,' she said.

His face contracted into that already familiar scowl. Shelley was glad. She'd been disconcerted by the forced smile. This was the Declan Grant she had been expecting to encounter—that she'd psyched herself up to deal with.

'The damn neighbours and their non-stop complaints. They think my untended garden lowers the tone of the street and therefore their property values. Now I've got the council on my back to clear it. That's why I contacted you.'

Shelley sat forward on the sofa. 'You want the garden cleared? Everything cut down and replaced with minimalist paving and some outsize pots?'

He drew dark brows together. 'No. I want the garden tidied up. Not annihilated.'

She heaved a sigh of relief. 'Good. Because if you want minimalist, I'm not the person for the job. There's a beautiful, traditional garden under all that growth and I want to free it.'

'That…that's what someone else said about it,' he said, tight-lipped, not meeting her eyes.

'I agree with that person one hundred per cent,' she said, not sure what else to say. *Who shared her views on the garden restoration?*

Her first thought was Declan had talked to another gardener. Which, of course, he had every right to do. But the flash of pain that momentarily tightened his face led her to think it might be more personal. Whatever it might be, it was none of her business. She just wanted to work in that garden.

He leaned back in his sofa, though he looked anything but relaxed. He crossed one long, black-jeans-clad leg over the other, then uncrossed it. 'Tell me about your qualifications for the job,' he said.

'I have a degree in horticultural science from Melbourne University. More importantly, I have loads of experience working in both public and private gardens. When I lived in Victoria I was also lucky enough to work with some of the big commercial nurseries. I ran my own one-woman business for a while, too.'

'You're from Melbourne?'

She shook her head. 'No. I lived most of my life in the Blue Mountains area.' Her grandmother had given refuge to her, her sister and her mother in the mountain village of Blackheath, some two hours west of Sydney, when her father had destroyed their family. 'I went down south to Melbourne for university. Then I stayed. They don't call Victoria "The Garden State" for nothing. I loved working there.'

'What brought you back?' He didn't sound as though he was actually interested in her replies. Just going through the motions expected of a prospective employer. *Maybe she already had the job.*

'Family,' she said. It was only half a lie. No need to elaborate on the humiliation dished out to her by Steve that had sent her fleeing to Sydney to live with her sister.

'Do you have references?'

'Glowing references,' she was unable to resist boasting.

'I'll expect to see them.'

'Of course.'

'What's your quote for the work on the garden?'

'A lot depends on what I find in there.'

She'd been peering over the fence for weeks and knew exactly what she'd do in the front of the garden. The back was unknown, but she guessed it was in the same overgrown state. 'I can give you a rough estimate now, but I have to include a twenty per cent variation to cover surprises. As well as include an allowance for services like plumbing and stonemasonry.'

'So?'

She quoted him a figure that erred on the low side—but she desperately wanted to work on this garden.

'Sounds reasonable. When can you start?'

'I have a full-time job. But I can work all weekend and—'

The scowl returned, darkening his features and those intense indigo eyes. 'That's not good enough. I want this done quickly so I can get these people off my back.'

'Well, I—'

'Quit your job,' he said. 'I'll double the amount you quoted.'

Shelley was too stunned to speak. That kind of money would make an immense difference to her plans for her future. And the job could be over in around two months.

He must have taken her silence as hesitation. 'I'll triple it,' he said.

She swallowed hard in disbelief. 'I... I didn't mean...' she stuttered.

'That's my final offer. It should more than make up for you leaving your employer.'

'It should. It does. Okay. I accept.' She couldn't stop the excitement from bubbling into her voice.

She wasn't happy with the job at the garden design company. And she was bored. The company seemed to put in variants of the same, ultra-fashionable garden no matter the site. Which was what the clients seemed to want but she found deathly dull. 'I'm on contract but I have to give a week's notice.'

*Aren't you being rash?* She could hear her sister's voice in her head. *You know nothing about this guy.*

'If you can start earlier, that would be good,' he said. 'Once I've made my mind up to do something I want it done immediately.'

*Tell him you'll consider it.*

Shelley took a deep, steadying breath. 'I would love to get started on your garden as soon as I can. I'll work seven days a week if needed to get it ready for spring.'

'Good.' He held up his hand. 'Just one thing. I don't want anyone but you working on the garden.'

'I'm not sure what you mean?'

'I value my privacy. I don't want teams of workmen tramping around my place. Just you.'

She nodded. 'I understand.' Though she didn't really. 'I'm strong—'

'I can see that,' he said with narrowed eyes.

Some men made 'strong' into an insult, felt threatened by her physical strength. Was she imagining a note of admiration in Declan's voice? A compliment even?

'But I might need help with some of the bigger jobs,' she said. 'If I have to take out one of those trees, it's not a one-person task. I have to consider my safety. That…that will be an extra cost, too. But I know reliable contractors who won't rip us off.'

*Us.* She'd said *us.* How stupid. She normally worked in close consultation with a client. Back in Victoria, where she'd worked up until she'd arrived back in New South Wales three months ago, she actually numbered satisfied clients among her friends. But she had a feeling that might not be the case with this particular client.

There would be no *us* in this working relationship. She sensed it would be a strict matter of employer and employee. Him in the house, her outside in the garden.

He paused. 'Point taken. But I want any extra people to be in and out of here as quickly as possible. And never inside the house.'

'Of course.'

Declan got up from the sofa and towered above her. He was at least six foot three, she figured. When she rose to her feet she still had to look up to him, a novel experience for her.

'We're done here,' he said. 'You let me know when you can start. Text me your details, I'll confirm our arrangement. And set up a payment transfer for your bank.' Again came that not-quite-there smile that lifted just one corner of his mouth. Was he out of practice? Or was he just naturally grumpy?

But it did much to soothe her underlying qualms about giving up her job with a reputable company to work for this man. She hadn't even asked about a payment schedule. For him to suggest it was a good sign. A gardener often had to work on trust. After all, she could hardly take back the work she'd done in a garden if the client didn't pay. Though there were methods involving quick-acting herbicides that could be employed for purposes of pay back—not that she had ever gone there.

'Before I go,' she said, 'is there anyone else I need to talk to about the work in the garden? I... I mean, might your...your wife want input into the way things are done?' *Where was Mrs Grant?* She'd learned to assume that a man was married, even if he never admitted to it.

His eyes were bleak, his voice contained when he finally replied. 'I don't have a wife. You will answer only to me.'

She stifled a swear word under her breath. Wished she could breathe back the question. It wasn't bitterness she sensed in his voice. Or evasion. It was grief.

What had she got herself into?

Her grandmother had always told her to think before she spoke. It was advice she didn't always take. With a mumbled thank you as she exited the house, she decided to keep any further conversation with Declan Grant strictly related to gardening.

\* \* \*

Declan hoped he'd made the right decision in hiring the beautiful Shelley to work in his garden. The fact that he found her so beautiful being the number one reason for doubt.

There must be any number of hefty male gardeners readily available. She looked as capable as any of them. But he'd sensed a sensitivity to her, a passion for her work, that had made him hang onto her business card despite that dangerous attraction. If he had to see anyone working in Lisa's garden he wanted it to be her.

Four years ago he and Lisa had moved into this house, her heart full of dreams for the perfect house and the perfect garden, he happy to indulge her. 'House first,' she'd said of the house, untouched for many years. 'Then we'll tackle that garden. I'm sure there's something wonderful under all that growth.'

Instead their dreams had withered and died. Only the garden had flourished; without check it had grown even wilder in the sub-tropical climate of Sydney.

He would have been happy to leave it like that. It was only the neighbours' interference that had forced him to take action. Shelley Fairhill could have a free rein with the garden—so long as it honoured what Lisa would have wanted. And it seemed that was the path Shelley was determined to take.

Not that he would see much of the gorgeous gardener. She had told him she liked to start very early. As an indie producer of computer games, he often worked through the night—in touch with colleagues on different world time zones. They'd rarely be awake at the same time. It would make it easy to avoid face-to-face meetings. That was how he wanted it.

Or so he tried to convince himself. Something about

this blonde warrior woman had awakened in him an instinct that had lain dormant for a long time. Not sexual attraction. He would not *allow* himself to be attracted to her, in spite of that dangerous spark of interest he knew could be fanned into something more if he didn't stomp down hard on it. *He had vowed to have no other woman in his life.* But what he *would* give into was a stirring of creative interest.

He had lost Princess Alana when he'd sold her out for all those millions to a big gaming company. He didn't like the way they'd since changed her—sexualised her. Okay, he'd been guilty of sexualising his teenage creation too. She'd been a fantasy woman in every way—which was why she'd appealed so much to the legions of young men who had bought her games. But he hadn't given Alana what looked like a bad boob job. Or had her fight major battles bare-breasted. Or made her so predatory—sleazy even.

But he hadn't been inspired to replace her. Until now. In the days since he'd met Shelley he'd been imagining a new heroine. Someone strong and fearless, her long golden hair streaming behind her. In a metal breastplate and leather skirt perhaps. No. That had been done before. Wielding a laser sword? That wasn't right either. Princess Alana's wings had been her thing. Warrior Woman Shelley needed something as unique, as identifying. And a different name. Something more powerful, more call to action than the soft and flowery Shelley.

He headed back to his study that took up most of the top floor. Put stylus to electronic pad and started to sketch strong, feminine curves and wild honey-coloured hair.

# CHAPTER THREE

DECLAN PACED THE marble floor of his entrance hall. Back
and forth, back and forth, feverish for Shelley to arrive for
her first day of working on his garden. He'd actually set
an alarm to make sure he wouldn't miss her early start—
something he hadn't done for a long time. He raked his
hands through his hair, looked down at his watch. *Where
was she?*

In the ten days since he'd met with Shelley at the house,
he had lived with the fantasy warrior-woman character
who was slowly evolving in his imagination. Now he was
counting down the minutes to when he got to see his inspiration again in the flesh. Not in the actual flesh. Of course
not. His musings hadn't got him *that* far.

At eight a.m. on the dot, she buzzed from the street and
he released the gate to let her in. Then opened the front
door, stepped out onto the porch and watched through
narrowed eyes as she strode up the pathway towards him.

He took a deep breath to steady the instant reaction that
pulsed through him. She didn't disappoint. Still the same
strength, vigour and a fresh kind of beauty that appealed
to him. Appealed strictly in a creative way, that was. He
had to keep telling himself that; refuse to acknowledge
the feelings she aroused that had nothing to do with her as
merely a muse. As a woman, the gardener was off-limits.
*Any woman was off-limits.* He hadn't consciously made

any commitment to celibacy—but after what had happened to Lisa he could not allow himself to get close to another woman. That meant no sex, no relationships, *no love*.

Shelley wore the same ugly khaki clothes—her uniform, it seemed—with a battered, broad-brimmed canvas hat jammed on her head. She swung a large leather tool bag as if it were weightless. It struck him that if the gardener wanted to disguise the fact she was an attractive woman she was going the right way about it. Her attire made him give a thought to her sexual preference. Not that her personal life was any of his concern. Perhaps he could make his prototype warrior of ambivalent sexuality. It could work. He was open to all ideas at this stage.

'Good morning, Mr Grant,' she carolled in a cheerful voice edged with an excitement she couldn't disguise. She looked around her with eager anticipation. 'What a beautiful sunny morning to start on the garden.'

*She really wanted to do this—he could have got away with paying her half.* Not that he would have haggled on the price. He was scrupulous about paying people fairly—despised people who didn't.

Her words were accompanied by a wide, generous smile that revealed perfect teeth. The smile lingered in her eyes. Eyes that were the colour of nutmeg—in harmony with the honey-gold of her hair. Not that he could see more than a few wisps of that as it was jammed up under her hat. He wished he could see her hair out and flowing around her shoulders. And not just for inspiration.

'Call me Declan,' he said. 'Not Mr Grant. He's my father.' Though these days his father went by the title His Honour as a judge in the Supreme Court of New South Wales.

Besides, Declan didn't do people calling him 'Mister'. Especially a girl who at twenty-eight was only two years younger than himself. Her age had been on the résumé she'd emailed him. Along with an impressive list of references that had checked out as she'd said they would. She appeared to be exactly what she said she was, which was refreshing in itself.

'Sure, Declan,' she said. 'Call me Shelley. But never Michelle. That's my full name and I hate it.'

'Shelley it is,' he said.

She buzzed with barely harnessed energy. 'I'll start clearing some of the overgrowth today—show your nosy neighbours you mean business. But first I really want to have a good look at what we've got here. Can you show me around?' She put down her leather tool bag.

His first thought was to tell her to find her own way around the garden. But that would sound rude. And he wanted to correct the bad first impression he'd made on her. Not only because he was her employer. But also because if he was going to base a character on her, he wanted her to stick around. He had to stomp down again on the feeling that he would enjoy seeing her here simply because she was so lovely. *She was out of bounds.*

'There's not a lot I can tell you about the garden,' he said. 'It was overgrown when I bought it.'

'You can leave the plants to me. But it'll save time if you give me the guided tour rather than have me try to figure out the lay of the garden by myself.'

He shrugged. 'Okay.'

'Is there a shed? Tools? Motor mower?'

'I can show you where the shed is—from memory there are some old tools in there.'

'Good,' she said. 'Let's hope they're in working order, though I do have equipment of my own, of course.'

'I bought this house as a deceased estate,' he said. 'An old lady lived here for many years—'

'So I was half right,' Shelley said, her mouth tilting in amusement.

'What do you mean by that?'

'I imagined an eccentric old lady living here—a Miss Havisham type. You know, from *Great Expectations* by Charles Dickens.'

'I am aware of the book,' he said dryly. He hadn't expected to be discussing literature with the gardener.

'Or a cranky old man.' Her eyes widened and she slapped her hand to her mouth. 'Oh. I didn't mean—'

'So you encountered a cranky younger man instead.'

She flushed, her smooth, lightly tanned skin reddening on her cheekbones.

'I'm sorry, that's not what I—'

'Don't apologise. I do get cranky. Bad mannered. Rude. Whatever you'd like to call it. Usually after I haven't had any sleep. Be forewarned.'

She frowned. 'I'm not sure what you mean.'

'I work from my home office and I'm online until the early hours, sometimes through the night.'

'No wonder you get cranky if you don't get enough sleep.'

He would bet she was an early-to-bed-and-early-to-rise type. *Wholesome.* That was the word for her—and he didn't mean it as an insult.

'I catch up on sleep during the day,' he said.

'Like a vampire,' she said—and clapped her hand over her mouth again. 'I'm sorry, I didn't mean to say that.'

'You don't have to apologise for that either. I actually find the idea amusing.'

'I'm sorry— There I go apologising again. What I meant to say is that I sometimes speak before I think. Not just sometimes, lots of times. I've been told I need to be more…considered in what I say.'

'So far you haven't offended me in any way.' She was so earnest he was finding it difficult not to smile at how flustered she'd become.

'I'll stay out of your way as much as possible, then.'

'That might be an idea,' he said. Then wondered why he didn't like the thought of her avoiding him. He'd been living on his own for a long time and he liked it that way.

*Reclusive. Aloof. Intimidating.* The labels had been hurled at him often enough. By people who had no idea of the intensity of the pain that had made him lock himself away. People who expected him to get over something he'd never be able to get over. Never be able to stop blaming himself for.

'What do you do that makes you work such unsociable hours?' Shelley asked.

*Unsociable.* That was the other label.

'I'm an independent producer of computer games.' Then there was his other work he preferred to keep secret.

'Really?' She dismissed his life work with a wave of her hand. 'I don't have time for computer games. I'd rather be outside in the fresh air and sunlight than hunched in front of a computer or glued to a phone.'

He glared at her. More out of habit than intent.

She bit her lower lip and screwed up her face in repentance. 'Oh, dear. I've done it again. Now I've really insulted you.'

'I didn't take it as an insult,' he said through gritted teeth.

'Do you invent games? That could be fun.' Her attempt to feign interest in gaming was transparent and somehow endearing.

'I have done,' he said. 'Have you heard of the Alana series?'

She shook her head and strands of her hair escaped her

hat. They glinted gold in the morning sunlight. 'I played some game with a little purple dragon when I was younger but, as I said, I'd rather be outside.'

'Yet you read?'

'Yes. And these days I listen to audio books if I'm working on a job on my own. I spend a lot of time by myself in this line of work. If I'm in a team it's different, of course.'

'Seems like a good idea,' he said.

'Oh, don't think I don't give one hundred per cent to the job. I do. And your garden is so interesting to me I'll be fully engaged. I dare say I won't get to finish another book until I complete my work here.'

'I wasn't criticising you,' he said. 'If you want to listen to books or music that's fine by me. As long as you get the work done and don't disturb me.'

'Thank you,' she said. She glanced at her watch. 'I'm aching to see the rest of the garden. Tell me, is there a fountain there? I so want there to be a fountain.'

He smiled. Her enthusiasm was contagious. 'There is a fountain. But it doesn't work.'

She fell into step beside him as he headed around the side of the house. Her long strides just about matched his. 'The pump for the fountain is probably broken. Or clogged. Or there could be a leak in the basin,' she said.

'All possibilities just waiting there for you to discover,' he said.

She completely missed the irony of his words. 'Yes. I'm so excited to get it working again. I love water features. They add movement to a garden, for one thing. And attract birds.'

He nodded thoughtfully. 'I hadn't realised that. About water adding movement. But when you think about it, it makes sense.'

'A garden isn't just about plants. There are so many

elements to consider. Of course, being a horticulturalist, plants are my primary interest. But a garden should be an all-round sensory experience, not just visual.'

She stopped, tilted her head back and sniffed. 'Scent is important too. There's a daphne somewhere in this garden. I can smell it. It's a small shrub with a tiny pink flower but the most glorious scent. It blooms in winter.' She closed her eyes and breathed in. 'Oh, yes, that's daphne, all right.' She sighed a sigh of utter bliss. 'Can you smell it?'

Declan was disconcerted by the look of sensual pleasure on Shelley's face, her lips parted as if in anticipation of a kiss, her flawless skin flushed, long dark lashes fanned, a pulse throbbing at the base of her slender neck. *She was beautiful.*

He had to clear his throat before he replied. 'Yes, I can smell it. It's very sweet.'

She opened her eyes and smiled up at him. How had he not noticed her lovely, lush mouth?

'They're notoriously temperamental,' she said. 'Daphne can bloom for years and then just turn up its toes for no reason at all.'

'Is that so?' Ten minutes in Shelley's company and he was learning more about gardening than he ever wanted to know. 'The name of the old lady who owned this house before me was Daphne.'

He thought Shelley was going to clap her hands in delight. 'How wonderful. No wonder there's daphne planted here. It's great to have a plant to echo someone's name. I often give friends a rose that's got the same name as them for a present. A 'Carla' rose for a Carla. A 'Queen Elizabeth' for an Elizabeth.' She paused. 'I don't know if there's a rose called Declan, though. I'll have to check.'

He put up his hand in a halt sign. 'No. Please. I don't want a Declan plant in this garden.'

'Okay. Fair enough. I don't know that Declan is a great name for a rose anyway. Fine for a man. Excellent for a man, in fact…' Her voice dwindled. She looked up at him, pulled a self-deprecating face. 'I'm doing it again, aren't I?'

'Declan is not a good name for a rose, I agree.' She should be annoying him; instead she was amusing him.

'I… I'm nervous around you,' she said. 'Th…that's why I'm putting foot in mouth even more than usual.' She scuffed the weed-lined path with her boot. It was a big boot; there was nothing dainty about this warrior woman.

'Nervous?'

'I… I find you…forbidding.'

*Forbidding.* Another label to add to the list.

He shifted from one foot to another, uncomfortable with the turn the conversation was taking. 'I can see how you could think that,' he said. What he *wanted* to say was he'd put a force-field around himself and it was difficult to let it down—even to brief a gardener. Especially when the gardener looked as she did—made him react as she did.

She looked up at him, tilted her hat further back off her face. Her brown eyes seemed to search his face. For what? A chink in his forbiddingness?

'You see, I so want to do this job right,' she said. 'There's something about the garden that's had me detouring on my walks to and from the station just to see it. I'm so grateful to your neighbours for forcing you to do something about it and employ me.' She slapped her thigh with a little cry of annoyance. 'No! That's not what I meant. I meant I'm so grateful to you for giving me this chance to spend the next few months working here. I… I don't want to blow it.'

'You haven't blown it,' he said. 'Already you've shown me I made the right decision in hiring you for this job.'

Relief crumpled her features. 'Seriously?'

'Seriously,' he said. If he was the man he used to be, the man for whom 'forbidding' would never have been a label, he might have drawn her into a comforting hug. Instead he started to walk again, heading to the back of the property where the garden stretched to encompass land of a size that had warranted the multimillions he'd paid for it.

She fell in step beside him. 'So tell me about Daphne— the old lady who owned the house before you. I wonder if she planted the garden.'

'I have no idea. It was my...my wife who was...was interested in the garden.'

How he hated having to use the past tense when he talked about Lisa. He would never get used to it.

'Oh,' Shelley said.

He gritted his teeth. 'My wife, Lisa, died two years ago.' Best that Shelley didn't assume he was divorced, which was often the first assumption about a man who no longer lived with his wife.

The stunned silence coming from the voluble Ms Fairhill was almost palpable. He was aware of rustlings in the trees, a car motor starting up out in the street, his own ragged breath. He had stopped without even realising it.

'I... I'm so sorry,' she finally murmured.

Thank God she didn't ask how his wife had died. He hated it when total strangers asked that. As if he wanted to talk about it to them. As if he *ever* wanted to talk about it. But Shelley was going to be here in this garden five days a week. If he told her up front, then she wouldn't be probing at his still-raw wounds. Innocently asking the wrong questions. Wanting to know the details.

'She... Lisa...she died in childbirth,' he choked out.

No matter how many times he said the words, they never got easier. *Died in childbirth.* No one expected that to happen in the twenty-first century. Not in a country with an advanced health-care system. Not to a healthy young couple who could afford the very best medical treatment.

'And…and the baby?' Shelley asked in a voice so low it was nearly a whisper.

'My…my daughter, Alice, died too.'

'I'm so, so sorry. I… I don't know what to say…'

'Say nothing,' he said, his jaw clenched so tightly it hurt. 'Now you know what happened. I won't discuss it further.'

'But…how can you live here after…after that?'

'It was our home. I stay to keep her memory alive.'

*And to punish himself.*

# CHAPTER FOUR

SHELLEY DIDN'T KNOW where to look, what to say. *How could she have got him so wrong?* Declan was a heart-broken widower who had hidden himself away to mourn behind the high walls of his house and the wild growth of his garden. And she had called him Mr Tall, Dark and Grumpy to her sister. She and Lynne had had a good old laugh over that. Now she cringed at the memory of their laughter. Not *grumpy* but *grieving.*

She couldn't begin to imagine the agony of loss the man had endured. Not just his wife but his baby too. No won-der he carried such an aura of darkness when he bore such pain in his soul. And she had told him he was *forbidding.* Why hadn't she recognised the shadow behind his eyes as grief and not bad temper? There'd been a hint of it the night of her interview with him but she'd chosen to ignore it.

Truth was, although she was very good at understand-ing plants—could diagnose in seconds what was wrong with ailing leaves or flowers—she didn't read people very well. Somehow she didn't seem to pick up cues, both ver-bal and non-verbal, that other more intuitive folk noticed. No wonder she had believed in and fallen in love with a man as dishonest and deceptive as Steve had been. She just hadn't seen the signs.

*'Shelley excels at rushing in where angels fear to tread.'* Her grandmother used to say that quite often.

She was going to have to tread very lightly here.

'So it…it was your wife who realised this garden needed to be set free?'

He didn't meet her eyes but looked into the distance and nodded.

'Only she…she wasn't given the time to do it,' she said.

Mentally, Shelley slammed her fist against her forehead. How much more foot in mouth could she get?

Declan went very still and a shadow seemed to pass across his lean, handsome face and dull the deep blue of his eyes. After a moment too long of silence he replied. 'The reason I hired you was because you said much the same as she did about the garden.'

*Think before you speak.*

'I… I'm glad.' She shifted from foot to foot. 'I'll do my best to…to do what she would have wanted done to the… to her garden.'

'Good,' he said. 'She would have hated to have it all dug up and replaced with something stark and modern.' He took a deep, shuddering breath. 'No need to talk about it again.'

Shelley nodded, not daring to say anything in case it came out wrongly. If she stuck to talk of gardening she surely couldn't go wrong.

He started to walk again and she followed in his wake. She wouldn't let herself admire his broad-shouldered back view. *He was a heartbroken widower.*

Even if he weren't—even if he were the most eligible bachelor in Australia—he was her employer and therefore off-limits.

Then there was the fact she had no desire for a man in her life. Not now, not yet. *Maybe never.*

After the disastrous relationship with Steve that had made her turn tail and run back to Sydney from Melbourne, she'd decided she didn't want the inevitable painful disruption a man brought with him.

She'd learned hard lessons—starting with the father who had abandoned her when she was aged thirteen— that men weren't to be trusted. And that she fell to pieces when it all went wrong. She'd taken it so badly when it had ended with Steve—beaten herself up with recrimination and pain—she'd had to resign from her job, unable to function properly. No way would she be such a trusting fool again.

As she followed her new boss around the side of the house, she kept her eyes down to the cracked pathway where tiny flowers known as erigeron or seaside daisies grew in the gaps. She liked the effect, although some would dismiss them as weeds. Nature sometimes had its own planting schemes that she had learned to accommodate. If there was such a thing as a soft-hearted horticulturalist that was her—others were more ruthless.

She was so busy concentrating on not looking at Declan, that when he paused for her to catch up she almost collided with his broad chest. 'S-sorry,' she spluttered, taking a step back.

How many times had she apologised already today? She had to be more collected, not let his presence fluster her so much—difficult when he was so tall, so self-contained, *so darn handsome.*

'Here it is,' he said with an expansive wave of his hand. Even his hands were attractive: large, well-shaped, with long fingers. 'The garden that is causing my neighbours so much consternation.' He gave the scowl that was already becoming familiar. 'The garden I like because it completely blocks them from my sight.'

'That…that it does.'

There must be neighbours' houses on either side and

maybe at the back but even the tops of their roofs were barely visible through the rampant growth. But, overgrown as it was, the garden was still a splendid sight. The front gave only a hint of the extent of the size of land that lay behind the house.

She stared around her for a long moment before she was able to speak again. 'It's magnificent. Or was magnificent. It could be magnificent again. And…and so much bigger than I thought.'

Declan's dark brows drew together. 'Does that daunt you?'

He must be more competent than she at reading people—because she thought she had hidden that immediate tremor of trepidation.

'A little,' she admitted. 'But I'm more exhilarated by the challenge than worried I might have bitten off more than I can chew.'

'Good. I'm confident you can do it. I wouldn't have hired you if I wasn't,' he said.

Shelley appreciated the unexpected reassurance. She took a deep breath. 'Truly, this is a grand old garden, the kind that rarely gets planted today. A treasure in its own way.'

'And the first thing you see is the fountain,' he said.

'Yes,' she said. 'It's very grand.'

'And very dry,' he said.

The fountain she'd so hoped to see was classical in style, three tiers set in a large, completely dried-out rectangular pond edged by a low sandstone wall. It took quite a stretch of the imagination but she could see water glinting with sunlight flowing into a pond planted with lotus and water iris interspersed by the occasional flash of a surfacing goldfish. *She could hardly wait to start work on it.*

And, beyond her professional pride in her job, she wanted Declan's approval.

Behind the fountain, paved pathways wound their way through a series of planted 'rooms' delineated by old-fashioned stonework walls and littered with piles of leaves that had fallen in autumn. Graceful old-style planters punctuated the corners of the walls. Some of them had been knocked over and lay on their sides, cracked, soil spilling out. The forlorn, broken pots gave the garden a melancholy air. *It was crying out for love.*

And she would be the one to give this beautiful garden the attention it deserved. *It would be magnificent again.*

She turned to Declan. 'Whoever planted this garden knew what they were doing—and had fabulously good taste. Everything is either really overgrown or half choked to death but the design is there even at a quick glance. It will be a challenge, but one I'm definitely up for.'

He nodded his approval. 'It's like anything challenging—take it bit by bit rather than trying to digest it whole. In this case weed by weed.'

She was so surprised by his flash of humour she was momentarily lost for words. But she soon caught up. 'You've got that right. Man, there are some weeds. I've already identified potato vine—it's a hideous thing that strangles and is hard to get rid of. Morning glory is another really invasive vine, though it has beautiful flowers. It's amazing what a difference a lot of Aussie sunshine can do to an imported "garden invader". The morning glory vine is a declared noxious weed here, but they nurture it in greenhouses in England, I believe. And there's oxalis everywhere with its horrible tiny bulbs that make it so difficult to eradicate.'

'Who knew?' he said.

She couldn't tell whether he was being sarcastic or not. Was that a hint of a smile lifting the corners of his mouth and a warming of the glacial blue of his eyes?

Okay, maybe she'd gone on too much about the weeds.

'That's the nasty stuff out of the way.' It was her turn to smile. 'And now to the good stuff.'

'You can see good stuff under all the "garden invaders"?' he said, quirking one dark eyebrow.

'Oh, yes! There's so much happening in this garden— and this is winter. Imagine what it will be like in spring and summer.' She heaved a great sigh of joyous anticipation. *She was going to love this job.*

And it seemed as if Declan Grant might not be as difficult to work with as she had initially feared. That hint of humour was both unexpected and welcome.

She pointed towards the southern border of the garden. 'Look at the size of those camellia bushes shielding you from your neighbours. They must be at least sixty years old. More, perhaps. The flowers are exquisite and the glossy green leaves are beautiful all year round.'

He put up his hand in a halt sign. 'I don't want you getting rid of those. The woman who lives behind there is particularly obnoxious. I want to screen her right out.'

'No way would I get rid of them,' she said, horrified. Then remembered he was the client. 'Uh, unless you wanted me to,' she amended through gritted teeth. 'That particular white flowering camellia—*camellia japonica* "Alba Plena", if you want to be specific—is a classic and one of my favourites.'

'So you're going to baffle me with Latin?' Again that quirk of a dark eyebrow.

'Of course not. I keep to common names with clients who don't know the botanical names.' *Uh-oh.* 'Um, not that I'm talking down to you or anything.'

'Both my parents are lawyers—there was a bit of Latin flying around our house when I was a kid.'

'Oh? So you know Latin?' She understood the Latin-based naming system of plants, but that was as far as it went.

He shook his head. 'I was entirely uninterested in learning a dead language. I was way more interested in learning how computers talked to each other. Much to my parents' horror.'

'They were both lawyers? I guess they wanted you to be a lawyer too.' His mouth clamped into a tight line. 'Or... or not,' she stuttered.

There was another of those awkward silences she was going to have to learn to manage. He was a man of few words and she was a woman of too many. But now that she understood the dark place he was coming from, she didn't feel so uncomfortable around him.

She took a deep breath. 'Back to the camellias. I think we'll find there's a very fine collection here. Did you know Sydney is one of the best places to grow camellias outside of China, where they originate?'

His expression told her he did not.

'Okay. That's way more than you wanted to know and I'm probably boring you.' *When would she learn to edit her words*?

He shook his head. 'No. You're not. I know nothing about gardening so everything you tell me is new.' His eyes met hers for a long moment. 'I guess I'm going to learn whether I want to or not,' he said wryly.

'Good. I mean, I'm glad I'm not boring you. I love what I do so much but I realise not everyone else is the same. So just tell me to button up if I rabbit on too much.'

'I'll take that on board,' he said with another flash of the smile that so disconcerted her.

She looked around her, both to disconnect from that

smile and hungry to discover more of the garden's hidden treasures. 'I want to explore further and think about an action plan. But the first thing I'll do today is prune that rather sick-looking rose that's clambering all over the front of the house. Winter is the right time of year to prune but we're running out of time on that one. It's dropped most of its leaves but in spring it must be so dense it blocks all light from the windows on the second floor.'

'It does,' he said. 'I like it that way.' His jaw set and she realised he could be stubborn.

'Oh. So, do I have permission to prune it—and prune it hard?'

He shrugged. 'I've committed to getting rid of the jungle. I have to tell you to go ahead.'

'You won't regret it. It's a beautiful old rose called "Lamarque". If I prune it and feed it, bring it back to good health, come spring you'll have hundreds of white roses covering the side of the house.'

He went silent again. Then nodded slowly, which she took for assent. 'Lisa would have loved that.'

Shelley swallowed hard against a sudden lump in her throat at the pain that underscored his words. It must be agony for him to stand here talking to her about his late wife when he must long for his Lisa to be here with him. *Not her.*

She forced herself not to rush to fill the silence. No way could she risk a foot-in-mouth comment about his late wife. Instead she mustered up every bit of professional enthusiasm she could.

'When I've finished, the garden will enhance the house and the house the garden. It's going to be breathtaking. Your neighbours should be delighted—this garden will look so good it will be a selling point for them to be near it.'

'I'm sure it will—not that I give a damn about what they

think,' said Declan with a return of the fearsome scowl. He looked pointedly at his watch. 'But I have to go back inside.' He turned on his heel.

Shelley suspected she might have to get used to his abruptness. It was as if he could handle a certain amount of conversation and that was all. And her conversations were twice as long as anyone else's.

*Think before you speak.*

'Wait,' she said. 'Can you show me the shed first? You know, where there might be garden tools stored.'

He paused, turned to look back to her. A flicker of annoyance rippled over his face and she quailed. He seemed distracted, as if he were already back in his private world inside the house—maybe inside his head.

He was, she supposed, a creative person whereas she was get-her-hands-dirty practical. He made his living designing games. Creative people lived more in their heads. She was very much grounded on solid earth—although she sometimes indulged in crazy flights of the imagination. Like wondering if he was a criminal. Or an incognito movie star—he was certainly handsome enough for it. But she'd been half right about the Miss Havisham-like Daphne.

'The shed is over there at the north end of the garden,' he said.

Without another word he started to stride towards it. Even with her long legs, Shelley had to quicken her pace to keep up.

The substantial shed looked to be of a similar age to the house and was charmingly dilapidated. The door had once been painted blue but was peeling to reveal several different paint colours dating back to heaven knew how long. A rose—she couldn't identify which one immediately—had been trained to grow around the frame of the door.

If the shed were hers, she wouldn't paint that door. Just sand and varnish it and leave the motley colours exactly as they were. It would not only be beautiful but a testament to this place's history.

*As if.*

She was never likely to own her own house, garden or even a shed. Not with the exorbitant price of Sydney real estate. Worse, she had loaned Steve money that she had no hope of ever getting back. Foolish, yes, she could see that now—but back then she had anticipated them getting engaged.

One day, perhaps, she might aspire to a cottage way out of town somewhere with room for not just a shed but a stable too.

In the meantime, she was grateful to Lynne for letting her share her tiny apartment in return for a reasonable contribution to the rent. All her spare dollars and cents were being stashed away to finance that trip to Europe.

Come to think of it, this shed looked to be bigger than Lynne's entire apartment in nearby Double Bay. *'Double Pay,'* her sister joked.

The door to the shed was barred by a substantial bolt and a big old-fashioned lock. It was rusted over but still intact. Even the strength in Declan's muscled arms wasn't enough to shift it. He gave the door a kick with a black-booted foot but it didn't budge.

He ran his hand through his hair. 'Where the hell is the key? I'll have to go look inside for it.'

He was obviously annoyed she was keeping him from his work but she persevered.

'I'd appreciate that. I'd really like to see what's in there.'

She hoped there would be usable tools inside. While she had a basic collection, she was used to working with equipment supplied by her employer. She didn't want to have to take a hire payment from her fee.

He turned again to head towards the house.

'Sorry,' she said. *There went that darn sorry word again.* 'But one more thing before you go. Is there…well, access to a bathroom? I'll be working here all day and—'

'At the side of the house there's a small self-contained apartment,' he said. 'You can use the bathroom there. I'll get you that key too. A door leads into the house but that's kept locked.'

'Are you sure? I thought maybe there was an outside—'

'You can use the apartment,' he said, in a that's-the-end-of-it tone.

'Thank you,' she said.

'Take a walk around the garden while I go hunt for the keys,' he said. 'I might be a while.'

She watched him as he headed towards the back entrance of the house. Did he always wear black? Or was it his form of mourning? It suited him, with his dark hair and deep blue eyes. The black jeans and fine-knit sweater—cashmere by the look of it—moulded a body that was strong and muscular though not overly bulky. If he spent long hours at a computer, she wondered how he'd developed those impressive muscles.

She realised she'd been staring for a moment too long and turned away. It would be too embarrassing for words if her employer caught her ogling the set of his broad shoulders, the way he filled those butt-hugging jeans. *He was very ogle-worthy.*

She put her disconcerting thoughts about her bereaved boss behind her as—at last—she took the opportunity to explore the garden. Slowly scanning from side to side so she didn't miss any hidden treasures, she walked right around the perimeter of the garden and along the pathways that dissected it. *It was daunting but doable.*

Dew was still on the long grass and her trousers and boots got immediately damp but she didn't care. Sydney winter days were mild—not like the cold in other places she'd lived in inland Victoria and New South Wales where frost and even snow could make early starts problematical and chilblain-inducing. The cold didn't really bother her. Just as well, as she'd set her heart on finding a job in one of the great gardens of the stately homes in England, where winters would be so much more severe than here.

The scent of the daphne haunted each step but she didn't immediately find where it was growing. She would have to search for that particular gem under the undergrowth. There was no rush. She had time to get to know the idiosyncrasies this particular landscape would present to her.

Every garden was different. The same species of plant could vary in its growth from garden to garden depending on its access to sunlight, water and the presence of other vegetation. She suspected there would be surprises aplenty in a garden that had been left to its own devices and was now coming into her care.

A flash of purple caused her to stop and admire a lone pansy blooming at the base of a lichen-splashed stone wall. She marvelled at the sheer will to survive that had seen a tiny seed find its way from its parent plant to a mere thimbleful of hospitable soil and take root there. It didn't really belong there but no way would she move it.

Not only had she learned to expect the unexpected when it came to Mother Nature, she had also learned to embrace it.

*Declan Grant was unexpected, unexplained.* She batted the thought away from where it hovered around her mind like an insistent butterfly. He was her boss. He was a widower. *He wasn't her type.*

Her experience with men had been of the boring—she'd broken their hearts—and the bad boys—they'd broken hers. She suspected Declan was neither. He was a man who had obviously loved his wife, still revered her memory.

Her thoughts took a bitter twist. He was not the kind of man who cheated and betrayed his wife. Not like Steve, who had pursued her, wooed her, then not until she'd fallen deeply in love with him had she found out he was married.

Steve's wife had confronted her, warned her off, then looked at her with pity mingled with her anger when she had realised Shelley had had no idea that her lover was married.

Shelley still felt nausea rise in her throat when she re-membered that day when her life based on a handsome charmer's lies had collapsed around her. She'd felt bad for the wife, too, especially when the poor woman had wearily explained that Shelley hadn't been the first of Steve's infi-delities and would most likely not be the last. Even after all that, Steve had thought he could sweet-talk his way back into her affections, had been shocked when she'd both lit-erally and figuratively slammed the door in his face.

The only vaguely comforting thing she'd taken away from the whole sordid episode in her life was that she'd behaved like an honourable 'other woman' when she'd discovered she was a mistress not an about-to-be fiancée. Not like the other type of 'other woman' who had with-out conscience seduced her father away from his family.

Now she swallowed hard against the remembered pain, took off her hat and lifted her face to the early-morning sun. Then she closed her eyes to listen to the sounds of the garden, the breeze rustling the leaves, the almost im-perceptible noise of insects going about their business, the gentle twitter of tiny finches. From high up in the camellias came the raucous chatter of the rainbow lorikeets—the multicoloured parrots she thought of as living jewels.

Out here in the tranquillity of the garden she could forget all that had hurt her so deeply in the past. Banish thoughts of heartbreak and betrayal. Plan for a future far away from here. *'You might have more luck with the English guys.'* She hadn't known whether to laugh at Lynne's words or throw something at her sister.

But she didn't let herself feel down for long—she never did. Her spirits soared at the privilege of working in this wonderful garden—and being paid so generously to do it.

Getting used to working with a too-handsome-for-comfort boss was something she would have to deal with.

# CHAPTER FIVE

DECLAN LOCATED THE keys to both the shed and the apartment without too much difficulty. But the tags attached to them were labelled in Lisa's handwriting and it took him a long moment before he could bear to pick them up. He took some comfort that she would be pleased they were at last being put to use.

Before he took the keys out to Shelley, he first detoured by the front porch and grabbed her leather tool bag from where she had left it. He uttered a short, sharp curse it was so heavy. Yet she had carried it as effortlessly as if it were packed with cotton wool. No wonder her arms were so toned.

He lugged it around to the back garden.

No Shelley.

Had she been put off by the magnitude of the task that faced her and taken off? Her old 4x4 was parked on the driveway around the side of the house and he might not have heard it leave. He felt stabbed by a shard of unexpected disappointment at the thought he might not see her again. He would miss her presence in his garden, in his life.

Then he saw sense and realised there was no way she would leave her tool bag behind.

He soon caught sight of her—and exhaled a sigh of relief he hoped she didn't hear.

His warrior-woman gardener had hopped over the wall

and jumped down into the metre-deep empty pond that surrounded the out-of-commission fountain. There she was tramping around it, muttering under her breath, her expression critical and a tad disgusted as though she had encountered something very nasty. Her expression forced from him a reluctant smile. In her own mildly eccentric way, she was very entertaining.

For the first time, Declan felt a twinge of shame that he had let the garden get into such a mess. The previous owner had been ill for a long time but had stubbornly insisted on staying on in her house. Both money and enthusiasm for maintenance had dwindled by the time she had passed away. When he and Lisa had moved in, he had organised to get the lawns mowed regularly. But even he, a total horticultural ignoramus, had known that wasn't enough.

In fact he had mentioned to his wife a few times that maybe they should get cracking on the garden. Her reply had always been she wanted it to be perfect—compromise had never been the answer for Lisa—and she needed to concentrate on the house first.

Her shockingly unexpected death had thrown him into such grief and despair he hadn't cared if the garden had lived or died. *He hadn't cared if he had lived or died.* But now, even from the depths of his frozen heart, he knew that Lisa would not have been happy at how he had neglected the garden she had had such plans for.

Grudgingly he conceded that maybe it was a good thing the neighbours had intervened. And a happy chance that Shelley Fairhill had come knocking on his door.

Not that he would ever admit that to anyone.

She looked up as he approached, her face lit by the open sunny smile that seemed to be totally without agenda. Early on in his time as a wealthy widower he had encoun-

tered too many smiles of the other kind—greedy, calcu-
lating, seductive. It was one of the reasons he had locked
himself away in self-imposed exile. He did not want to
date, get involved, marry again—and no one could convince him otherwise no matter the enticement.

'Come on in, the water's fine,' Shelley called with her
softly chiming laugh.

Declan looked down to see the inch or so of dirty water
that had gathered in one corner of the stained and pitted
concrete pond. 'I wouldn't go so far as to say that,' he said
with a grimace he couldn't hide.

He intended to stand aloof and discuss the state of the
pond in a professional employer-employee manner. But,
bemused at his own action, he found himself jumping
down into the empty pond to join her.

'Watch your nice boots,' she warned. The concrete bottom of the pond was discoloured with black mould and the
dark green of long-ago-dried-out algae.

Declan took her advice and moved away from a particularly grungy area. The few steps brought him closer
to her. *Too close.* He became disconcertingly aware of
her scent—a soft, sweet floral at odds with the masculine way she dressed. He took a rapid step back. Too bad
about his designer boots. He would order another pair online from Italy.

If she noticed his retreat from her proximity Shelley
didn't show it. She didn't shift from her stance near the
sludgy puddle. 'How long has this water been here?' she
asked.

'There was rain yesterday,' he said, arms crossed.

Sometimes he would go for days without leaving the
temperature-controlled environment of his house, unaware
of what the weather might be outside. But yesterday he'd
heard rain drumming on the slate tiles of the roof as he'd

made his way to his bedroom in the turret some time during the early hours of the morning.

Shelley kicked the nearest corner of the pond with her boot. Her ugly, totally unfeminine boot. 'The reason I ask is I'm trying to gauge the rate of leakage,' she said. 'There are no visible cracks. But there could be other reasons the pond might not be holding water. Subsidence caused by year after year of alternate heating and cooling in the extremes of weather. Maybe even an earth tremor. Or just plain age.'

She looked up to him as if expecting a comment. How in hell would he know the answer?

'You seem to know your stuff,' he said.

'Guesswork really,' she admitted with a shrug of her shoulders, broad for a woman but slender and graceful.

'So what's the verdict?' he asked.

'Bad—but maybe not as bad as it could be if it's still holding water from yesterday. Expensive to fix.'

'How expensive?'

He thought about what she'd said about a fountain bringing movement to a garden. The concept as presented by Shelley appealed to him, when first pleas and then demands from the neighbours to do something about the garden never had.

'I'm not sure,' she said. 'We might have to call in a pool expert. Seems to me it's very old. How old is the house?'

'It was built in 1917.'

Thoughtfully, she nodded her head. 'The fountain is old, but I don't think it's *that* old. I was poking around the garden while you were inside. It has the hallmarks of one designed around the 1930s or 40s. I'd say it was inspired by the designs of Enid Wilson.'

'Never heard of her.'

Gardening had never been on his agenda. Until now. Until this warrior had stormed into his life.

'Enid Wilson is probably Australia's most famous landscape designer. She designed gardens mainly in Victoria starting in the 1920s and worked right up until she died in the1970s. I got to know about her in Melbourne, although she did design gardens in New South Wales, too.'

'Really,' he drawled.

She'd asked him to tell her to button up if she rabbited on. Truth was, he kind of liked her mini lectures. There was something irresistible about her passion for her subject, the way her nutmeg eyes lit with enthusiasm. *She was so vibrant.*

She pulled a self-deprecating face. 'Sorry. That was probably more than you ever wanted to know. About Enid Wilson, I mean. I did a dissertation on her at uni. This garden is definitely based on her style—she had many imitators. Maybe the concrete in the pond dates back to the time it was fashionable to have that style of garden.'

'So what are your thoughts about the pond? Detonate?' he said.

'No way!' she said, alarmed. Then looked into his face. 'You're kidding me, right?'

'I'm kidding you,' he said. His attempts at humour were probably rusty with disuse.

'Don't scare me like that,' she admonished. 'I'm sure the fountain can be restored. It will need a new pump and plumbing. I don't know how to fix the concrete though. Plaster? Resin? A pond liner? Whatever is done, we'd want to preserve the sandstone wall around it.'

He looked at the fountain and its surrounds through narrowed eyes. 'Is it worth repairing?' Could anything so damaged ever come back to life to be as good as new? *Anything as damaged as a heart?*

'I think so,' she said.

'Would it be more cost-effective to replace it with something new?' he asked.

She frowned. 'You mean a reproduction? Maybe. Maybe not. But the fountain is the focal point of the garden. The sandstone edging is the same as the walls in the rest of the garden.'

'So it becomes a visual link,' he said. He was used to thinking in images. He could connect with her on that.

She looked at the faded splendour of the fountain with such longing it moved him. 'It would be such a shame not to try and fix it. I hate to see something old and beautiful go to waste,' she said. 'Something that could still bring pleasure to the eye, to the soul.'

He would not like to be the person who extinguished that light in her eyes. Yet he did not want to get too involved, either. He scuffed his boot on the gravel that surrounded the pond. 'Okay. So we'll aim for restoration.'

'Thank you!' Those nutmeg eyes lit up. For a terrifying moment he thought she would hug him. He kept his arms rigidly by his sides. Took a few steps so the backs of his thighs pressed against the concrete of the pond wall.

He hadn't touched another woman near his own age since that nightmare day he'd lost Lisa. Numb with pain and a raging disbelief, he'd accepted the hugs of the kind nursing staff at the hospital. He'd stood stiffly while his mother had attempted to give comfort—way, way too late in his life for him to accept. The only person he'd willingly hugged was Jeannie—his former nanny, who had been more parent to him than the mother and father he'd been born to. Jeannie had held him while he had sobbed great, racking sobs that had expelled all hope in his life as he'd realised he had lost Lisa and the child he had wanted so much and his life ever after would be irretrievably bleak.

He wasn't about to start hugging now. Especially with this woman who had kick-started his creative fantasies awake from deep dormancy. Whom he found so endearing in spite of his best efforts to stay aloof.

'Don't expect me to be involved. It's up to you,' he said. 'I trust you to get it right.'

'I understand,' she said, her eyes still warm.

Did she? Could she? Declan had spent the last two years in virtual seclusion. He did not welcome the idea of tradespeople intruding on his privacy. *Only her.* And yet if he started something he liked to see it finished. When it was in his control, that was. Not like the deaths he'd been powerless to prevent that had changed his life irrevocably.

'Call in the pool people,' he said gruffly. 'But it's your responsibility to keep them out of my hair. I don't want people tramping all over the place.'

'I'll do my best,' she said. 'Though harnesses and whips might not be welcomed by pool guys. Or other maintenance workers we might have to call in.'

He released another reluctant smile in response to hers. 'I'm sure you'll find a way to charm them into submission.'

As she'd charmed her way into what his mother called Fortress Declan. He realised he had smiled more since he'd met her than he had in a long, long time.

She laughed. 'I'll certainly let them know who's boss,' she said. 'Don't worry, I've had to fight to be taken seriously in this business. If anyone dares crack a blonde joke, they'll be out of here so fast they won't know what hit them.'

He would believe that. A warrior woman. In charge.

He clambered out of the empty pond. Thought about offering Shelley a hand. Thought again. *He did not trust himself to touch her.*

Turned out he wasn't needed. He'd scarcely completed

the thought before agile Shelley effortlessly swung herself out of the pond with all the strength of an athlete. He suspected she wasn't the type of woman who would ever need to lean on a man. Yet at the same time she aroused his protective instincts.

'Are we sorted?' he said brusquely. 'You deal with the pond. I've got work to do.'

He actually didn't have anything that couldn't be put off until the evening. But he didn't want to spend too much time with this woman. Didn't want to find himself looking forward to her visits here. He'd set an alarm clock this morning so he wouldn't miss her. That couldn't happen again.

He pulled out the keys from his pocket. 'I'll open the shed for you. Then I'm disappearing inside.'

To stay locked away from that sweet flowery scent and the laughter in her eyes.

Like much of this property outside the house, the shed was threatening to fall down. Declan found the lock was rusty from disuse and it took a few attempts with the key before he was able to ease the bolt back from the door of the shed.

Unsurprisingly, the shed was a mess. It was lined with benches and shelves and stacked with tools of varying sizes and in various states of repair. Stained old tins and bottles and garden pots that should have been disposed of long ago cluttered the floor. The corners and the edges of the windows were festooned in spider webs and he swore he heard things scuttling into corners as he and Shelley took tentative steps inside.

Typically, she saw beyond the mess. 'Oh, my gosh, it's a real old-fashioned gardener's shed with potting benches and everything,' she exclaimed. 'Who has room for one of these in a suburban garden these days? I love it!'

She took off her hat and squashed it into the pocket of her khaki trousers. That mass of honey-blond hair was twined into plaits and bunched up onto her head; stray wisps feathered down the back of her long, graceful neck. The morning sunlight shafting through the dusty windows made it shine like gold in the dark recesses of the shed.

An errant strand came loose from its constraints and fell across her forehead. Declan jammed both hands firmly in the pockets of his jeans lest he gave into the urge to gently push it back into place.

He ached to see how her hair would look falling to her waist. Would it be considered sexual harassment of an employee if he asked her to let it down so he could sketch its glorious mass? He decided it would. And he did not want to scare her off. She stepped further into the shed, intent on exploration.

'Watch out for spiders,' he warned.

In his experience, most women squealed at even the thought of a spider. Sydney was home to both the deadly funnel web and the vicious redback—he would not be surprised if they had taken up abode in the shed.

Shelley turned to face him. 'I'm not bothered by spiders,' she said.

'Why does that not surprise me?' he muttered.

'I'd never be a gardener if I got freaked out by an itty-bitty spider,' she said in that calm way she had of explaining things.

'What about a great big spider?' There was something about her that made him unable to resist the impulse to tease her. But she didn't take it as teasing.

'I'm still a heck of a lot bigger than the biggest spider,' she said very seriously.

Was it bravado or genuine lack of fear?

'Point taken,' he said. He looked at her big boots that

could no doubt put an aggressive spider well and truly in its place.

'Snakes, now…' she said, her eyes widening, pupils huge in the gloom of the shed. 'They're a different matter. I grew up on a property out near Lithgow, west of the mountains. We'd often see them. I'd be out riding my horse and we'd jump over them.' She shuddered. 'Never got used to them, though.'

'Have you always been so brave and fearless?' he asked.

'Is that how I appear to you?' she asked. 'If so, I'm flattered. Maybe I do a good job of hiding my fears—and snakes are one of them.'

'Not too many snakes in Darling Point,' he said, wondering about her other fears.

'I hope not, it's so close to the city,' she said. 'Though I'll still approach the undergrowth outside with caution. I've been surprised by red-bellied black snakes in north shore gardens.'

Could the fantasy warrior woman forming in his imagination vanquish snakes under foot? Or evil-doers in the guise of snakes? Hordes of alien shape-shifter spiders? No. This new princess warrior would be more defender than attacker. Saving rather than destroying. But would that make the character interesting to the adolescent boys who were his main market?

He realised how much he'd changed since he'd created the assassin Alana with her deadly bow and arrow. Then he'd been angry at the world with all the angst of a boy who'd been told too often that he'd been unplanned, unwanted. His parents had been surprised by his mother's pregnancy. He'd been told so often he'd been 'an accident' but the sting of the words never diminished, never lessened the kick-in-the-gut feeling it gave him. Destruction, death even, had been part of the games he'd created with so much success.

Now he'd suffered the irreversible consequence of death in real life rather than in a fantasy online world where characters could pick themselves up to fight again. He could never again see death as a game.

Shelley reached into her tool bag and pulled out a pair of thick leather gauntlet gloves. 'I dare a spider to sink its fangs through these,' she challenged.

'I hope they don't get close enough for that to happen,' he said.

*Gloves.* There was something very sensual about gloves. Not the tough utilitarian gardening gloves Shelley was pulling onto her hands. No. Slinky, tight elbow-length gloves that showed off the sleek musculature of strong feminine arms, the elegance of long fingers. He itched to get back to his study and sketch her arms. Not Shelley's arms. Of course not. *He could not go there.* The arms of fictional warrior Princess As Yet Unnamed—he gave himself permission to sketch hers.

'There's a treasure trove in here,' Shelley exclaimed in delight as she poked through corners of the shed that had obviously been left undisturbed for years.

He had to smile at a woman who got excited at a collection of old garden implements. You'd think they were diamond-studded bracelets the way she was reacting. It was refreshing. Shelley was refreshing. He had never met anyone like her.

'Looks like a bunch of rusty old tools to me,' he said.

A motley collection of old garden implements was leaning against the wall. She knocked off the dust and cobwebs from a wooden-handled spade before she picked it up and held it out for him to examine.

'This is vintage,' she said. 'Hand forged and crafted

with skill. Made to last for generations. It's a magnificent piece of craftsmanship. Valuable too. You'd be surprised what you could sell this for. Not that you probably need the money.' She flushed pink on her high cheekbones. 'Sorry. That just slipped out.'

'You're right. I don't need the money.'

He had accumulated more money than he knew how to spend and yet it kept on rolling into his bank accounts. He didn't actually need to work ever again. Did his private work for little recompense. The odd hours his work entailed were something to keep the darkness at bay. Since Lisa and their baby had died he had suffered badly from insomnia. Sleep brought nightmares where he was powerless to save his wife and daughter. Where he tortured himself with endless 'if onlys' repeated on a never-breaking loop.

'What do you plan to do with these tools?' he said.

She brandished the shovel. 'Use them, of course. Though they'll need cleaning and polishing first.' She looked up. 'I'll do that on my own time,' she added.

He liked her honesty. Doubted that Shelley would charge him for five minutes that she wasn't working.

'No need for that,' he said. 'Count restoring these heirloom tools as part of your work here.'

*Heirloom?* Where did that word come from to describe decrepit garden implements? Was it an attempt to please her?

He so nearly added: *I'll come down and help you with them.* But he drew the words back into his mouth before there was a chance of them being uttered. There would be no cosy sessions down in this shed, cleaning up tools, chatting, getting to know each other.

Shelley was his gardener. And, unwittingly, his muse. That was all she could ever be to him. *No matter how he was beginning to wish otherwise.* That was all any woman, no matter how lovely or how endearing, could be.

Shelley cautiously let herself into the apartment attached to the back of the house with the key Declan had given her. Even though she had his permission, she felt like an intruder. She sucked in a breath of surprise when she got inside. The apartment was more generous in size than she had imagined. Heck, the *shed* here was bigger than the apartment where she lived. This appeared positively palatial by comparison.

The decoration seemed brand-new—stylish in neutral tones with polished wooden floorboards and simple, timeless furnishings in whitewashed timber and natural fabrics. It was posh for staff quarters—which was what she assumed the apartment was.

Had anyone ever lived here since it had been renovated?

She'd taken off her boots at the door. On feet encased in tough woollen work socks, she tiptoed through the rooms: a living room furnished with a stylish, comfortable-looking sofa and a big flat-screen television set; a dining area; a smart, compact kitchen; a bedroom with a large bed and an elegant quilt; a small, immaculate bathroom. It was the most upscale granny flat she'd seen—it wouldn't be out of place on the pages of a design magazine. There was a door at the end of the kitchen she thought might be a pantry. But it was locked and she realised it must be the door into the house. That made sense for staff quarters.

Shelley trailed her hand along the edge of the sofa and wondered about Lisa, Declan's late wife. She must have been a nice person to go to so much trouble to decorate this apartment for a housekeeper. She herself had been in too many grotty staff facilities to know the difference.

Her heart contracted inside her at the thought of the

tragedy that had played out in this house. Lisa had had her whole life ahead of her, everything to look forward to. And Declan. How could he ever get over it?

She herself had trust issues. Would find it difficult to ever trust a man enough to love again. But loss on this scale was unimaginable. Could Declan ever let himself trust in a future again?

Subdued by the thought, she once again reminded herself how lightly she would have to tread around this man. And that she must not—repeat not—let herself be attracted to him for even a second. She sensed giving into that would lead to heartbreak the like of which she had never even imagined.

# CHAPTER SIX

SHELLEY WAS BECOMING Declan's guilty pleasure. From the windows of his office that took up most of the top floor of the house, he could watch her unobserved as she worked in the garden below.

Her energy and output were formidable as she systematically went about getting his garden back into shape. Right now she was on her hands and knees weeding a garden bed in the mid-morning sunshine. They'd had a discussion about the use of herbicides and come to the mutual decision to use an organic-based poison only when needed for the toughest of the garden invaders.

*Garden invaders.* He was taken by the term, wondered if he could use it for Princess No-Name's game. Not that young male gamers were likely to be interested in gardens—but invaders, yes.

However the pros and cons of spraying weeds were not on his mind as he watched Shelley below in the garden. He admired the way she performed such mundane tasks as weeding or pruning with such strength, grace and rhythm. The play of her muscles, the way she stretched out her arms and long legs and massaged the small of her back after she'd been working in the one place for any length of time all appealed.

Now she was kneeling and he tried to ignore the way her

shapely backside wiggled into his view when she leaned forward to locate and pull weeds.

*Dammit—when had gardening ever been sexy?*

He pushed the answer to the question he had posed himself to the back of his mind. *Since Shelley had become his gardener.*

She'd been here two weeks and he was more and more impressed by her. Her professionalism. Her knowledge. Her unfailing good humour. And that was on top of her beauty. Was she too good to be true? He kept contact with her to a minimum but he was super aware of her all the time she was on the property.

*Too aware.*

He had to remind himself he had vowed not to let another woman into his thoughts. Guilt and constant regret dictated that.

Even though he'd been told over and over again he was not responsible for Lisa and his daughter's deaths, he blamed himself. He should have responded quicker when Lisa had told him she was getting rapidly increasing contractions. Not begged for ten minutes to finish the intricate piece of code he'd been writing. Ten minutes that could have made a difference.

His fault.

His own, obsessed workaholic fault.

*Selfish, self-centred and single-minded.* He and Lisa hadn't quarrelled much—they'd had a happy marriage—but when they had, those were the accusations she had hurled at him. The anger had never lasted more than minutes and she'd laughed and said she hadn't meant a word of it. But he knew there was some truth there.

Because Lisa had told him she wasn't ready to have children. Had wanted to spend a few more years establishing her career in marketing before they started a family.

He'd cajoled, wheedled, begged her to change her mind. Because he'd wanted at least three children to fill up the many empty bedrooms of this house. Children who would grow up knowing how loved and wanted they were.

And look what had happened.

Lisa's death cast a black shadow on his soul. And Alice…he could hardly bear to think about Alice, that tiny baby he'd held so briefly in his arms, whose life had scarcely started before it had ended.

Their deaths were his fault.

*He didn't deserve a second chance at happiness.*

Down in the garden, Shelley leaned back on her heels and reached into the pocket of her sturdy gardener's trousers and took out her mobile phone. He hadn't heard it ring from where he was but she was obviously taking a call. He was near enough to see her smile.

As she chatted she looked up at the house, the hand that wasn't holding her phone shading her eyes. She couldn't possibly see him from here. He didn't want her to think he was some kind of voyeur. Just in case, he stepped back from the light of the window into the shadows of his office.

The furnishings in his shades-of-grey workspace were dominated by a bank of computer monitors. This was where he lived, his bedroom in the turret above.

Separate from the computers was a large drawing board he had set up to catch the best light from the window. He'd done some preliminary work on Princess No-Name on the computer. Design software could only do so much.

Now he'd gone back to sketching her with charcoal on paper. The old techniques he'd learned from his artist grandmother. Pinned up on a corkboard above the drawing board were sketches of various angles of the princess warrior's head, her arms, the curve of her back. On the sketchpad was a work in progress of her—okay, of Shelley—looking over her shoulder with her hair flowing over her neck.

But the old ways had their limitations too. What fun he could have using motion-capture software to animate his princess warrior character. But to do that he would have to ask Shelley to model for him. To dress her in a tight black spandex suit that revealed every curve. To attach reflective sensors to her limbs and direct her to act out movements from the game.

In the anonymity of a big, professional studio—perhaps. In the intimacy of his office? *No way.* Much too dangerous.

Further back from the window, though still in the good light, was his easel, where he had started a preliminary painting of the character in acrylic paint. The painting formed the only splash of colour in the monotone room where he spent so much time alone.

The painting was pure indulgence; this kind of image would not be easily scanned for animation. He hadn't painted for years, not since before he was married. But his newly sparked creativity was enjoying the subtle nuances of colour and texture the medium was able to give Princess No-Name.

Shelley's warrior strength and warm blonde beauty had kick-started his imagination but her connection to nature was what was now inspiring him to create his new character. He'd found himself researching the mythical Greek, Roman and Celtic female spirits of nature and fertility. Gaia. Antheia. Flora. The Green Woman. Mother Nature.

He was painting his Shelley-inspired warrior heroine in a skin-tight semi-sheer body stocking patterned with vines and leaves. The gloves that hugged her arms to above her elbows were of the finest, palest green leather. She strode out in sexy, thigh-high suede boots the colour of damp moss. As contrast, he'd painted orange flower buds in various stages of unfurling along the vines.

It would be only too easy to imagine Shelley wearing the exact same outfit. He drew in his breath at the thought of it.

*But he could not go there.*

Better he reined in his imagination when it came to thinking too closely about Shelley's shape.

He had purposely used Princess Alana's body as a template for Princess No-Name. Shelley's slim, toned arms were there, yes. But he did not want to focus on her breasts, her hips, her thighs to the extent it would take to draw them. That could be misconstrued.

*She was his muse—that was all.*

His imagination filled in his princess warrior's glorious mane of hair with fine brushstrokes. *If only Shelley would let her hair down for him.*

He modelled his new creation's face on Shelley's strong, vibrant face—with her lovely lush mouth exaggerated into artistic anime proportions. Her eyes were the exact same nutmeg as Shelley's, with added glints of gold and framed by the kind of long, long lashes that owed more to artifice than nature.

His princess was inspired by Shelley, but she was not Shelley—he had to keep telling himself that. His new warrior was a distinct character in the unique style of his bestselling games. She would be a worthy successor to Princess Alana.

A name flashed into his head. *Estella.* He thought the name probably meant star—bright and shining and bold. Yes. It was perfect. Princess Alana. Princess Estella. It fitted. And gave a vague nod to 'Shelley'.

Maybe her weapons could be ninja throwing stars—

sharp and deadly. No. Too obvious, and far too vicious for his Princess Estella.

Wonder Woman had her golden lasso of truth. Maybe Estella could have a magical lariat to incapacitate and capture. *But not kill.* He didn't want Princess Estella taking lives. He kept on painting, working in a fluorescent green lariat looped around her shoulder.

He stepped back, looked at his work with critical, narrowed eyes. Estella was gorgeous; she would make an awesome warrior heroine. But there was something lacking; he needed to add a unique characteristic to make her stand out in the sea of gaming heroines. He hadn't got it right yet.

*He needed to spend more time with Shelley.*

Purely for inspiration, of course. There must be no doubt it was for any other reason. Other than to oversee the ongoing work in the garden.

So why did the thought of that flood him with excited anticipation that went far beyond the boundaries that restricted employer and employee? Or artist and muse?

Declan had been so engrossed in his work, several hours had gone by without him realising. He glanced down to the garden to see Shelley talking to a man—a tall, well-built man with blond hair. He pulled up abruptly, paintbrush in hand. *Who the hell was he?*

Then he realised the guy wore the same kind of khaki gardening gear as she wore. He must be the horticulturalist she'd asked could she call in to help with getting rid of some large trees she said had no place in the garden.

The man was standing near her. As Declan watched he brought his head close to Shelley and said something that made her laugh. Echoes of her laughter reached him high up in his room.

Declan's grip tightened on the paintbrush. He didn't like seeing her with another man. Was this guy a boyfriend? *A lover?* He realised how very little he knew about his beautiful gardener. *How much he wanted to know.*

He was shocked at the feeling that charged through him, like a car with a dead battery being jump-started after long disuse by a blast of electric current.

*Jealousy.*

Shelley sensed Declan in the garden before she saw him. The vibrations of his feet on the ground? The distant slam of the door as he'd left the house? Or was it her hyper awareness of him?

She loved working in this garden, in two weeks had achieved so much. But the day seemed…empty if she didn't see him. Even if he came only briefly into the garden to make some quip about her passion for old garden implements. Or to ask if she'd fought off any spiders today. She would update him on her progress and go back to work, not knowing when she'd next see him. *On edge until she did.*

The days he didn't come into the garden at all were days she felt oddly let down and went home feeling dispirited. No. Not just dispirited. Verging on depressed. Which was not like her at all.

Today she had even more cause for concern. Her gardening buddy Mark Brown had just called around to assess what equipment he'd need for the job he was helping her with the next day.

'You mean you don't know who Declan Grant is?' he'd asked.

'He told me he produced computer games,' she'd replied.

'You could say that,' Mark had said. 'The guy is a gaming god, Shelley, a tech wizard. Every guy in the world my age must have grown up with Princess Alana. And she's just one of his incredibly popular games.'

'He might be well known in the gaming world, but I'd never heard of him,' she said, on the defence.

Mark's words had made her feel ignorant until she'd reminded herself that when she was younger gaming had pretty much been a boy thing. *A boring boy thing.* She hadn't known who Declan Grant was. Declan had blanked at the mention of Enid Wilson. Each to his own.

'He used to go by the tag of ArrowLordX—I don't know that he plays with mere mortals these days. He was an indie but sold out to one of the huge companies.' Mark had looked around him and whistled. 'This place must be worth millions—pocket change to him, though, the guy's a billionaire.' He'd narrowed his eyes. 'I hope he's paying you fairly.'

'M-more than fairly,' she'd stuttered. 'He's a generous employer.'

'Yeah. The deal you've got me is good. I'll be back tomorrow to earn it.'

She would have liked to introduce Mark to Declan but she was scrupulous about not disturbing her employer, intruding on his privacy. If she needed a response from him she texted him. She from the garden, he in his house. The only time she saw him was when he chose to seek her out.

By the time she looked up to see Declan heading towards her, Mark had gone.

It was lunchtime and she was sitting near a bank of azaleas—already budding up for spring—to shelter from the light wind that had sprung up. As her employer approached she put her sandwich back into the chilled lunchbox she brought with her to work and schooled her face into a professional gardener-greeting-boss expression.

She couldn't let it show how happy she was to see him. How his visits had become the highlights of her day.

*Her boss. A grieving widower. Not for her.* She had

taken to repeating the phrases like a series of mantras. Now she had to add: *her* billionaire *boss—totally out of her league.*

But when she looked up to see him heading towards her she couldn't help the flutter of awareness deep inside her, the flush that warmed her cheeks. Her knees felt shaky and she stumbled as she got up to greet him.

She'd got used to his abrupt ways, his sly humour that she didn't always get, the way he challenged her to justify her decisions. But she would never get used to the impact of his tall, broad-shouldered body and his extraordinarily handsome face.

This was the first time she'd seen him dressed in anything but black. His jeans were the deepest indigo—only a step away from black really, but it was a step. His sweater was charcoal grey, open at the neck to reveal a hint of rock-solid pecs and pushed up to his elbows to bare strong, muscled forearms.

'Don't get up,' he said. 'I didn't realise I was interrupting your lunch.'

'I haven't actually started eating,' she said. She didn't want to be caught at a disadvantage munching on a cheese and salad sandwich. It would be just her luck to have a shred of lettuce on her tooth when she was trying to be serious and professional around him.

His brow furrowed. 'Do you usually eat outside? Why don't you make use of the kitchen in the apartment?'

'Oh, but I wouldn't... I couldn't. I just dash in there to use the bathroom.'

'Please feel free to use the kitchen too,' he said.

'Thank you,' she said, knowing she wouldn't. She still felt like an intruder every time she went in there.

Declan put his hands behind his back, rocked on his heels. 'You were talking to a man earlier,' he said.

She nodded. 'He's the gardener who's coming to help me tomorrow. His name is Mark Brown. I would have liked to introduce you to him but I didn't think it was worth interrupting you with a text.'

'Is he a friend of yours?'

His question surprised her. But she remembered how concerned Declan was about strangers intruding on his privacy. 'Yes, he is, actually. We were at uni together in Melbourne and both moved to Sydney at about the same time. He's a very good horticulturalist. I could have just hired a tree-removal guy but we need to be careful with some of the surrounding plants. Luckily Mark was available. I can vouch for him one hundred per cent.'

'Lucky indeed,' he said. His eyes were cool, appraising, unreadable. 'Is he your boyfriend?'

Shelley stared at Declan, too flabbergasted at first to speak. 'What? Mark? No!' She'd often got the feeling Mark would like to be more than friends but she didn't see him that way.

'Do you have a boyfriend?' Declan asked.

Those extraordinary blue eyes searched her face. There was something darkly sensual about him that went beyond handsome. Something she should not be registering.

*Boss. Widower. Not for her.* Frantically she repeated the mantra in her mind. At the same time her body was zinging with awareness.

'No. I don't have a boyfriend. And I… I don't *want* a boyfriend.'

'I see,' he said, nodding, as his speculative gaze took in her drab, serviceable gardening gear—a tad grubby after a morning spent weeding. She was also sporting protective pads made from foam and hard nylon strapped around her knees. *'Nothing could be more unattractive or unappeal-*

*ing to a man,'* her sister, Lynne, had chortled when she had first seen Shelley decked out in her knee pads.

'No. You don't understand,' she said to Declan. 'I don't want a girlfriend either. I mean, I don't want a girlfriend ever.' *Foot in mouth again.* 'I like men. I'm not gay. I'm happy being single.'

Was that relief that lightened his eyes? Relief she was single? That she wasn't gay? Both?

'No plans for marriage and family?' he asked, which surprised her.

She shook her head. 'Plenty of time for that yet. My career is too important to me right now.'

He didn't reply. Of course, she couldn't resist chattering on to fill the silence that fell between them. 'There… there was a boyfriend in Melbourne. It didn't work out. I'm planning to travel after I finish your job. No point in getting involved with anyone in Sydney if I'm leaving. Men… well, men are more trouble than they're worth.' *And she just said that to a man.* Again she mentally beat her fist against her forehead.

'I get it,' he said and she got the distinct impression he was trying not to smile. There was another long pause, which this time she refused to fill. 'So your *friend* Mark is coming tomorrow?' he said finally.

'Yes,' she said, jumping on the change of subject. 'Let me show you what we'll be doing.'

Declan glanced at his watch. Shelley gritted her teeth. He always seemed to want to be anywhere but in his garden with her. At first she had found it insulting. Now she was beginning to realise it was just his way.

She'd learned now not to ask if she was boring him. Her policy was to take him as she found him. Fact was, though, she liked him way more than she should. She would be very disappointed if he cut short this time with him and headed back indoors.

Not that she would ever let him know that.

'Come let me show you what happens when people misguidedly plant indoor plants out in the garden,' she said.

He frowned. 'I don't get what you mean,' he said.

'You'll see,' she said, thankful that he started to follow her and not to stride off back to the house.

She led him to the area of garden near the eastern border with the house next door. 'These two trees are probably the main points of contention for your neighbours,' she said. 'They're *ficus benjamina*.'

'More Latin,' he said with that quirk of his dark eyebrow she was beginning to find very appealing. 'Translate, please.'

'Otherwise known as weeping fig,' she explained. 'A very popular potted plant. But planted out in the garden in this climate they can grow to thirty metres in height. Their roots are invasive and damaging.' She pointed. 'They've already damaged the fence and probably your neighbour's paving and underground plumbing pipes too. They're a tree suited to a park, not a domestic garden.'

'So a *giant* garden invader?' he said.

'Exactly. They have to go.'

Declan indicated the neighbour's house. 'He's already invoiced me for repairs.'

'Really? A neighbour would do that? Did you pay him?'

He scowled. She would hate to ever see that formidable expression aimed at her. 'I told you, I want these people off my back. I paid him.'

She shrugged. Seemed as if whatever he had paid would be water off a billionaire's back. 'You shouldn't hear any more from them once Mark and I get these darn trees out—and all the potato vine twined around them. There's a big mulberry on the other border fence—we'll get rid of that too.'

'A mulberry tree? I never knew we had one. I like mulberries. My grandmother had a mulberry tree and I'd spend hours up its branches.'

She had a sudden flash of a little black-haired boy with purple mulberry stains all around his mouth and mischief in his blue eyes. He must have been an adorable child.

She diverted her thoughts to the adult Declan. 'The mulberry tree here I want to get rid of is too close to the fence. Don't worry, there's another one planted as a specimen tree in the middle of the lawn that we'll leave. I like mulberries too and it's not causing any trouble there. It's a pity I won't be around when the tree fruits or I'd bake you a mulberry pie.'

*Oh, dear heaven, had she actually said that to her boss?* She closed her eyes and wished herself far, far away from Declan's garden.

She opened her eyes and he was still there, tall, dark and formidable. He made a sound in response that sounded suspiciously like a strangled laugh. 'You bake pies as well as your other talents?'

'Little Miss Practical, that's me,' she said with a self-effacing laugh. 'My grandmother taught me to cook when we—my mum and my sister—went to live with her after my father booted us out of our home.'

She flushed. 'Sorry, too much information.' She looked around her, frantic to change the subject. 'Whoever designed this garden way back when really *was* paying homage to Enid Wilson. Fruit trees as part of the garden instead of in an orchard. Thyme everywhere as groundcover. Indigenous plants when they weren't really fashionable. I think—'

As she started her next sentence a teasing gust of wind

snatched off her hat. She clutched at her head in vain to see her hat tumbling along the ground.

She went to chase after it, but Declan beat her to it and picked it up. 'I've got it,' he said.

It was such an old, battered hat she felt embarrassed he was touching it. He turned it over in his hand and went to put it back on her head. The movement brought him very close.

*His mouth.* For the first time she noticed his mouth. His full lips, the top lip slightly narrower than the other. The dark growth of his beard already visible at lunchtime.

*Lots of testosterone.*

The thought came from nowhere and paralysed her. She stood dead still, wondering what might come next, scarcely able to breathe, her heart thudding too fast.

His eyes looked deep into hers and she couldn't read the expression in their deep blue depths. He tossed the hat aside. Then reached down and around to the back of her head.

She'd got ready in a hurry that morning and had piled her hair out of the way with only the aid of a single claw-grip clip to keep it in place. With one deft movement Declan had it undone. Her heavy mass of hair untwisted and fell around her shoulders and her back, all the way to her waist. *She felt as if he'd undressed her.*

With a hand that wasn't quite steady, she went to push away the long layers that fell across the front of her face but Declan slid it away with his. Slowly, sensuously he pushed his fingers through her hair then ran his hands over her shoulders to come to rest at the small of her back where her hair reached.

'Beautiful,' he murmured in a low, husky voice.

Shelley didn't know whether he meant her or her hair or something else entirely. Shivers of pleasure tingled through her at his touch. She felt dizzy, light-headed and realised she'd been holding her breath. As she let it out in a slow sigh, she swayed towards him, her mouth parting not just for air but for the kiss she felt was surely to follow. His head dipped towards her. She didn't know that she wanted this. Wasn't sure—

Abruptly he dropped his hands from her waist. His expression darkened like the build-up of black cloud before a storm.

'This shouldn't have happened,' he said in a voice that was more a growl torn from the depths of his being.

Shocked, she struggled to find her voice. 'I… I…'

'Don't say it,' he said, his voice brusque and low. 'There's nothing to be said.' He stepped back with savage speed. 'My…my apologies.'

With that he turned on his heel and strode away from her, leaving her grateful for the support of the sturdy trunk of the doomed fig tree.

Still trembling, she watched him, his broad shoulders set taut with some emotion—anger?—as he turned the bend in the sweep of lawn marked by the wall with the tumbledown urn and out of sight. He couldn't wait to get away from her.

What the heck had that been about? And what did it mean for her relationship with her secretive, billionaire boss?

# CHAPTER SEVEN

NOTHING, AS IT turned out. The episode meant nothing, she realised in the days that followed. Days where she saw very little of Declan and neither of them mentioned the incident. The longer it went unsaid, the less likely it would ever be aired.

The Rapunzel incident—as she had begun to call it in her mind. Fancifully, she thought of it as: 'Shelley, Shelley, let down your golden hair.' *Let down your hair—and then nothing.* She blushed as she remembered how she had *yearned* for him to take it further.

The moments Declan had spent releasing her hair from its restraint and caressing her had begun to take on the qualities of a distant dream. Making a joke of it—even if only to herself—somehow took the sting out of what had happened.

The way he had avoided her since both puzzled and hurt. But she couldn't—*wouldn't*—let it bother her. Because while she was hurt in one way, she felt relieved in another.

Nothing could come of the incident. He was the billionaire boss, she was the gardener who needed the generous salary he had agreed to pay her. She should be grateful he hadn't taken advantage of that. Be *glad* he hadn't kissed her. She'd worked for men who had made her feel distinctly uncomfortable to be alone with them when she'd been working on their properties. It was one reason she dressed the way she did for work.

Besides, she had another more pressing concern to occupy her thoughts.

Her sister's boyfriend, Keith, had proposed to Lynne. The newly engaged couple wanted to live together as they planned their wedding. And the apartment in Double Bay she shared with Lynne was way, way too small for her to live with them in any privacy.

She had to find somewhere else to live—pronto. Keith wouldn't move in until she moved out. She was happy for her sister; Keith was a really nice guy and just what Lynne needed. Neither of them was pressing her to go, but of course they wanted to start their new life together as soon as they could.

But it was a difficult rental market in Sydney. Apartment hunting meant showing up for an open day and hoping like heck she made a better impression on the letting agent than the other people lined up with her to inspect the same property. There was a one-room apartment open today in nearby Edgecliff and she needed to see it.

In the three weeks she'd been working for Declan she hadn't taken a lunch hour, just grabbed twenty minutes to down the sandwich and coffee in a flask she'd brought from home. She'd wanted to get as much work as possible done in the shorter daylight hours at this time of year.

It was now well into August and the garden was showing definite signs of the early southern hemisphere spring: jonquils scented the air and the nodding pink heads of hellebores gave delight in the cooler, shadier corners of the garden. She had found the elusive daphne, cleared the tough kikuyu grass that was smothering it and made sure it would survive.

But today, four days after the Rapunzel incident, she

needed to take an extended lunch hour. Technically, she should ask Declan's permission for extra time off, but it wasn't really that kind of working relationship. He seemed to take her on trust and she would never take advantage of that. She decided to keep him in the loop anyway.

After a morning's hard work, she was fortunate she had the bathroom in the housekeeper's apartment in which to shower and change. She needed to look smart and responsible, as though she could afford the rent, the deposit and all the other expenses that came with renting an apartment. Expenses that would take a substantial chunk out of her savings.

Lynne and Keith had sprung this on her. As she towelled herself dry she found herself wishing—unreasonably, she knew—that Keith had put off his proposal until she had finished this job and was taking off for Europe.

Six months would be the minimum lease she could sign. She could end up trapped in Sydney for longer than she would choose to be. She wanted to be in Europe by October to see the gardens in autumn. Maybe she should consider a short-term house-share or even house-sitting.

Twenty-eight and still without a home of her own—she couldn't help but be plagued by a sense of failure when she thought about her limited options.

She slipped into the clothes she'd brought with her to change into—the world's most flattering skinny-leg trousers in a deep shade of biscuit teamed with a businesslike crisp white shirt, and topped with a stylish short trench coat in ice-blue with contrasting dark buttons. She finished off with a blue-and-black leopard-print scarf around her neck and short camel boots with a medium stiletto heel.

Lucky for her, Lynne was a fashion buyer for a big retailer and could get her clothes at a sizeable discount. Lynne also had excellent taste in the choices she made for her, which made up for Shelley's own tendency to slide into whatever felt most comfortable.

As she pulled her hair into a high ponytail and slicked on some make-up she thought she scrubbed up rather well.

Still feeling like an intruder in the apartment, she perched on the edge of the sofa and texted Declan.

I need to take a long lunch hour today—will make up the time.

His text came back straight away.

Can I see you before you go? Come to the front door.

Puzzled, Shelley put down her phone. She hadn't been inside the house since the evening of her interview. She hoped she wasn't to be reprimanded for anything. She had a feeling Declan hadn't been too impressed with the way she'd brought Mark in—though arranging for extra help was quite within their terms of agreement.

She flung her fake designer tote bag—a present from a friend, who'd bought it in Thailand—over her shoulder and headed around to the front of the house.

Declan had lost count of the times he had berated himself for giving in to the temptation to free Shelley's glorious hair from its constraints. *For touching her.* It had been out of order. Unprofessional. *Wrong.*

Even if it had only been in the interests of research for Princess Estella.

*Or so he'd told himself.*

For a moment he had let that self-imposed force field slip—with disastrous consequences. Now she obviously felt uncomfortable around him. And he could not rid his mind of the memory of how it had felt to be so intimately close to her—and her trembling response to his touch.

He felt he owed Shelley an explanation. But he was more fluent in JavaScript than he was at talking about anything personal. How did he explain why he had to keep her at arm's length? That he was not free to pursue another woman?

Technically, yes, he was a widower and able to marry again. But the day Lisa had died he had shut down emotionally. He had imprisoned himself in chains of grief and guilt, shrouded himself in the darkness of self-blame.

Lisa was dead. Their daughter's life snuffed out when it had scarcely begun. How could he expect happiness, love, intimacy for himself? He didn't deserve a second chance.

'Survivor's guilt—a classic case of it,' his mother had said. His top criminal-law-barrister mother, who knew a lot about the darker side of life. She'd given him the contact details of a grief counsellor—details that still sat in the bottom of his desk drawer.

Even she had been devastated by the tragedy. She'd been very fond of Lisa and seen the birth of her first grandchild as a chance to start over. 'To be a better grandmother than I ever was a mother,' she'd said with brutal honesty.

But in these last days, spent mostly in solitude, Declan had decided there was only one honest way to handle the situation with Shelley. He had to get Princess Estella out into the open. Explain to Shelley that she had inspired his new creation. Ask her to model for him.

Not in a body stocking or a skin-tight spandex sensor suit, though his pulse quickened at the thought of it. No. In her gender-neutral gardening gear. But with her long hair let down. Maybe with a fan floating it around her face and behind her like a banner. He would ask her to pose for him so he could get the hair and face right for Estella.

There would be a generous modelling fee, of course. It would all be above board and without any hint of exploitation. He could draw up a contract. Maybe include a share of royalties—he could afford it.

He didn't want dishonesty between them. Outing Estella was the only way to go.

Buoyed by the idea, he had asked Shelley to come to the house so they could discuss it asap.

At the sound of the bell at the front door he took the elevator Lisa had had installed—'*for when we're old and can't make the stairs*'—down from his top-floor office to get to the door more quickly.

*He would put things right with Shelley.*

But the Shelley who stood on the porch outside was not the Shelley he was expecting. The only thing he recognised about her was her smile—and even that was a subdued version of its usual multi-watt radiance.

His gardener was no longer an amazon but a glamazon.

Gone was the ugly, khaki uniform, replaced by a stylish, elegant outfit that emphasised the feminine shape the uniform concealed. Narrow trousers clung to long, slender legs, the shirt unbuttoned to reveal the delectable swell of her breasts, and the high-heeled boots brought her closer to him in height and gave her hips a sensuous sway.

Subtle dark make-up emphasised the beauty of her eyes, and the lush sensuality of her mouth was deepened by lipstick the colour of ripe raspberries.

For a too-long moment he stared at her, struck dumb with admiration—and an intensely masculine reaction that rocked him.

'You wanted to see me?' she asked, with a puzzled frown.

*He could not keep his eyes off her.*

He had to clear his throat before he spoke. 'Yes. Come in,' he said as he ushered her through the door.

'I hope there's nothing wrong,' she said with a quiver in her voice.

'Of course not,' he said.

*But everything had changed.*

He needed time to collect his rapidly racing thoughts.

He led her through the grand entrance hall, her heels clicking on the marble floor, to the small reception room where he'd first interviewed her. Light slanting through the old lead-light windows, original to the house, picked up the gold in her hair. *She brought the sunshine with her.*

Immediately they were in the room she went straight to the window. 'What a beautiful view of the garden,' she said. 'It's starting to take shape. In a few weeks that wisteria arch will be glorious. I've trimmed it but it will need a good prune when it's finished flowering. You have to cut it back well and truly before the buds form for…for the next season's flowering.'

Her words trickled to a halt and she didn't meet his eye. Did she sense his heightened awareness of her as a woman, his ambivalence? She moistened her lovely, raspberry-stained lips with the tip of her tongue. The action fascinated him.

The full impact of his attraction to her hit him like a punch to the gut. He fisted his hands by his sides. He'd been kidding himself from the get go.

This wasn't about Princess Estella.

It was about Shelley.

It had always been about Shelley—warm-hearted, clever, down-to-earth, gorgeous Shelley. Even in the drab uniform with her charmingly eccentric interest in rusty old rakes and broken-down fountains she had delighted him from day one.

He could no longer kid himself that his attraction to Shelley was because she sparked his creative impulse. She sparked male impulses a whole lot more physical and urgent. She was a beautiful woman and he wanted her in a way he had not imagined wanting another woman after his wife had died.

*He could not ask her to pose for Estella.*

No way could he invite her to spend hours alone with him in his studio while he sketched her. It would be a kind of torture. That idea had to be trashed.

But he found he had to say something else to justify him calling her into the house. 'I wanted to tell you I had a note from the neighbour thanking me for getting rid of the *ficus benjamina*.'

Now that full-beam smile was directed at him.

'It wasn't to…fire me or anything?'

'Of course not.' How could she possibly think that? He realised that under her brightness and bravado lay a deep vein of self-doubt. That although she seemed so strong she was also vulnerable. It unleashed a powerful urge to protect her.

'That's a relief,' she said. 'I was racking my brains to think of what I'd done wrong.'

He had to clear his throat of some deep, choking emotion to speak. 'You've done nothing wrong.'

He ached to take her into his arms and reassure her how invaluable she was, how special. But that was not going to happen. He recognised his attraction to her. That did not mean he intended to act on it.

He now could admit it to himself. Admit the truth that welled out from his subconscious and into his dreams. Now, when he was battling the insomnia that had plagued him since the night his wife had died, in those few hours

of broken sleep it wasn't Lisa's face that kept him awake.
It was Shelley's.

*And that felt like betrayal.*

'That's great news about the neighbour,' she said.
'Makes it all worthwhile, doesn't it? And, hey, you spoke
Latin. Uh, instead of computer speak. That I don't speak at
all. I mean, I can use a computer, of course I can, but I—'

'I get it,' he said. There she went—rabbiting on again.
He found it charming. He found *her* charming. And way
too appealing in every way.

He realised she was nervous around him. Was he looking particularly *forbidding* today?

She twisted the strap of her handbag in her hands.
'Thank you for telling me that but, if that's all, I have to
go. As I said, I need to take a longer lunch hour today.'

'A date?' he blurted out without thinking.

Jealousy speared him again. Who was the lucky guy
who would be seeing her dressed up like this?

'Not a date,' she said with a perturbed frown.

Of course she would be perturbed. He had no right to
ask about her personal life. She would be quite within her
rights to tell him to mind his own business.

He could not deny his relief that she wasn't going out
with a man. But if it wasn't a date, why and where was
she going?

He forced his voice to sound casual, unconcerned.
'Lunch with a friend? It's quite okay for you to stay as
long as you like. I know what hours you've been putting
in out there in the garden.'

Her mouth twisted downward. 'Nothing as nice as lunch
with a friend, I'm afraid. I have to look for somewhere to
live. I share with my sister but she's just got engaged and
her fiancé wants to move in.'

'There's no room for you?'

'No. It's a tiny apartment.' She sighed. 'Now I'm heading off to inspect a place in Edgecliff. Along with all the other people desperate to find somewhere with reasonable rent close to the city. I want to stay in this area.' She held up both hands with fingers crossed. 'So wish me luck.'

She turned on her high-heeled boot. 'I'll be back as soon as I can.'

Declan followed her to the door, opened it for her, watched her start down the steps. 'Stop,' he called after her.

She turned. 'I'm sorry, I'll miss the inspection time if I don't leave now. I have to find parking and—'

'Don't go. You don't need to. You can stay here, in the apartment.'

He didn't know what had possessed him to make that offer. It was all kinds of crazy. To have her actually living on the premises would do nothing for his resolve to keep things between them strictly on an employer-employee basis. He should rescind the offer immediately.

'You already have the key,' he said. 'Just move in.'

Shelley was so taken aback she stood with one foot on the bottom of the step, the other on the pathway.

'Are you serious?' she asked.

He shrugged those broad shoulders. 'You need a home. The apartment is empty. It makes sense.'

'But I… I shouldn't… I couldn't—' Excitement fluttered into life only to be vanquished by caution.

'It's there for staff. You're staff.'

'Yes, I am, but…'

How to express her feelings that she was scared of living in such close proximity to him? She found him too attractive to be so near to him twenty-four-seven. Now she could go home, go out, try and forget the Rapunzel incident and how it had made her feel. Living here, knowing he was on the other side of a wall, might not be so easy.

As far as she knew Declan lived alone in the enormous house. A team of cleaners had come in on the last two Tuesdays and stayed half the day. The delivery van of an exclusive grocery store had also swept up the gravel drive several times. But no one else had come, not during the day anyway.

His house would become not just her place of employment, but also her home. Just her and him—the man who sent shivers of awareness through her no matter how she tried to suppress them.

Right now he towered four steps above her, dark, brooding and yet with something in his eyes that made her think he would be hurt if she knocked back his offer of the apartment.

The apartment that would solve her problem of where to live.

*A solution that might bring more problems with it than it solved.*

He shrugged again. 'Of course, if you'd rather live in a cheap apartment in Edgecliff…'

'No. Of course I wouldn't. I'd love to live in the apartment. It's beautiful. The poshest staff quarters in Sydney, I should imagine. Your lucky housekeeper—she must have been thrilled when she saw how it was decorated.'

He fell silent for a moment too long. 'It was prepared for our nanny,' he said. 'The wonderful woman who used to be my nanny when I was a child. But…but she never moved in.'

'Oh,' she said. *Classic Shelley foot-in-mouth moment.* He looked so bleak that if he had been anyone else, she would have rushed to hug him. But she stayed put on the step.

'I'm sorry,' she said.

The history of her working relationship with Declan would be punctuated by endless repeats of the word *sorry*. 'I need to think before I speak.'

'You weren't to know,' he said. He shifted impatiently from one foot to the other. 'So what's it to be? Yes or no?'

'I want to say yes but I need to know what the rent is first. I… I might not be able to afford it.'

No *might* about it. She almost certainly *wouldn't* be able to afford the rent and the realisation brought with it a fierce regret. She would love to live in that apartment.

'No rent,' he said.

'But—'

'No buts.' The words were accompanied by a dark, Declan scowl.

'But—I mean *not but*. I mean…*if* I don't pay rent I—'

'This is staff accommodation. You're staff. End of story.'

'I have to pay my own way.' She had never been able to accept a gift that might have been tied with invisible strings.

'If you insist on a monetary transaction I will rescind my offer.'

She had no doubt he meant it. 'No! Please don't do that. I'll work on Saturdays. For free. Well, not free. My labour in return for accommodation.'

'There's no need for that. However if you insist—'

'I insist. When can I move in?'

'Whenever you want.'

'Saturday. This Saturday. I'll start the extra work next Saturday.'

'It's a deal,' he said. 'Just remember not to use the door into the house—it's the one in the kitchen.'

'Of course not. I don't have a key, anyway.'

'The key you have operates both doors.'

'I'll respect your privacy,' she said. 'I promise.'

He nodded.

'I don't have a lot of stuff to move in,' she said, bubbling with excitement now that she could accept the reality of the situation. 'Most of my possessions are stored with my grandmother at Blackheath in the mountains. I hope you don't mind if my sister gives me a hand to move in.'

'So long as I don't have to meet her,' he said.

'I'll make sure of that,' she said. 'Thank you, Declan.'

He acknowledged her thanks with another nod.

She looked down at her smart outfit. 'Now I'm all dressed up with nowhere to go,' she said. 'I just might drive on down to Double Bay and treat myself to a café lunch.'

She bit down firmly on words that threatened to spill and invite him to join her for lunch. The fact that he was her boss didn't stop her. There was no law that said work colleagues couldn't share a bite to eat—she did it all the time.

No. She didn't voice the invitation because it would sound perilously close to asking him on a date. *And that was never going to happen.*

She thanked him again and walked down the pathway, happy with the unexpected outcome of her meeting with Declan. She had a beautiful home until her contract here came to an end and she flew away to fulfil her dreams.

For her heart's sake she just had to keep well clear of Declan in the hours that were hers to spend as she pleased.

# CHAPTER EIGHT

DECLAN DID NOT want to meet Shelley's sister. Or her sister's fiancé, who was helping with the move. Meeting her family would be a link he did not want to establish. But he felt compelled to watch—perhaps to make it seem real that Shelley was going to be living here from today on.

With typical Shelley efficiency, she'd arrived early in the morning with her crew. Feeling uncomfortably as if he was spying on them, he watched from his office window. A tall, very slender young woman with short brown hair, who must be the sister, and a red-headed guy helped Shelley bring in her stuff.

Just a few boxes and suitcases appeared to constitute her possessions. Shelley herself had a laptop computer slung over her shoulder and some clothes still on their hangers to take in.

It was still a shock to see her out of her gardening gear. Today she wore faded, figure-hugging jeans, a long-sleeved T-shirt and the ugliest running shoes he had ever seen—practical, no doubt, but a shocking contrast to the sexy, stiletto-heeled boots she'd worn earlier in the week. Or Estella's thigh-high boots.

Could the bespoke shoemaker in Italy where he bought his shoes make a pair of moss-green suede boots in Shelley's size?

He pushed the crazy thoughts aside. Both of ordering

the green boots—and of imagining Shelley wearing them, and very little else.

Shelley's helpers were in and out of the apartment within an hour. He wondered if she had so few possessions because she didn't want them or because she couldn't afford them.

He realised he was paying her over the odds for the gardening work. And he didn't begrudge her a cent of it. A horticulturalist was not the highest paid of jobs, which seemed at odds with the incredible depth of knowledge Shelley seemed to have. Again he thanked whatever lucky chance had sent her to him.

His only regret was he could not ask her to pose for him. Princess Estella had stalled on him, still missing that final extra detail that might make her viable as the character on which he could base a new game. But he had to put the thought of Shelley posing for him alone in his eyrie office out of his fantasies. Especially when he spent way too much time thinking about her—as a beautiful woman who attracted him, not as a mere muse.

However, he now had his duties as not only an employer but a landlord to consider. Once she'd had time to settle in, he would go down to the apartment—now *her* apartment—and see if there was anything he could give her a hand with. *That was not making excuses to see her—it was obligation.*

But before he could do so, he saw her heading out—and had to smother a gasp of stunned admiration. She was obviously going horseback riding. Shelley the equestrienne wore tight cream breeches that hugged every curve of her enticing behind, and a black, open-neck shirt that emphasised her slim, toned arms. She wore shiny black leather knee-high riding boots and carried a black velvet riding helmet under her arm, along with a leather riding crop.

Shelley had mentioned she rode horses as a teenager, jumping over snakes in typical warrior manner. Seemed as if she rode them still. But where? Certainly not around here, just minutes away from the heart of the city.

Who knew horseback riding gear could look so hot?

But then Shelley looked good in anything she wore—even the drab khaki. He wouldn't let his mind travel any further along the path that might have him speculating on how she would look in nothing at all.

He watched her as she paused to look at the fountain, now under repair, then continued around the corner of the house to where she parked her so-old-it-was-practically-an-antique 4x4 in the driveway. The multi-car garage was filled with his collection of expensive sports cars that rarely got an airing these days.

But he was not just watching in admiration of how well she wore equestrienne mode. His stalled creativity was also firing back into life.

Now he knew exactly what was needed for Princess Estella.

A horse.

He turned back to his drawing board, his brain firing with so many ideas his hand holding the charcoal could scarcely keep up with his thoughts. As it always did when he was driven by creativity, time seemed to come to a halt as he got lost in the world of his imagination. Hours, days could go past.

He sketched Princess Estella astride a magnificent white horse with a flowing mane and tail that echoed the Warrior Princess's glorious tresses.

But it was still not enough.

He paced up and down, up and down, coming back to the drawing board again and again. It was good but still not right.

Then it hit him. Estella was fantasy. Shelley was earthy, warm, reality.

Shelley rode a horse. But Estella was not bound by human and earthly constrictions.

Princess Estella would ride a unicorn.

Again he went back to his drawing board. It wasn't difficult to transform the horse into a unicorn. He added a silver horn to the centre of its forehead. Made its eyes look less horse, more mythical creature whose gaze gleamed with knowledge and wisdom. Attributes that would help the warrior princess in her epic battles for good.

This time when he finished and stood back to look at his work he was buzzing.

Gorgeous Princess Estella with her long limbs and sensual curves was a young man's fantasy. But it was more than that. He was convinced Estella and her magical unicorn would appeal to female gamers as well. Hadn't even outdoor-orientated Shelley admitted to playing a girly dragon game?

He wished he had someone to share his jubilation with. But he had distanced himself from his friends since his bereavement. Only his mother hadn't given up on him—which never failed to bemuse him as she had scarcely been a presence in his childhood.

His online colleagues these days were working with him on games that had little to do with entertainment and everything to do with education. They would have no interest whatsoever in Princess Estella and her unicorn.

It was with Shelley he wanted to share Estella. To let her know how she had inspired him. But he couldn't. Not now. Not when he had gone this far without letting her in on the secret that she was his muse.

He went back to work, this time on his computer. The creation of a character was only the first step in the long process of producing a new game.

# CHAPTER NINE

SHELLEY HAD SPENT both Saturday and Sunday mornings on horseback—the sport she'd loved since she'd been two years old and first begged to be lifted up onto a pony. Horticulture was both her interest and the way she earned her living. Riding a horse was pure pleasure—physical, emotional and spiritual.

A rented horse at a commercial stable could not compare to the joy of riding her own horse. But she was lucky enough to live not too far from Centennial Park, the inner eastern suburbs park that stretched out over four hundred and fifty acres and had extensive horse-riding facilities.

She had a deal with the owner of a beautiful thoroughbred chestnut gelding named Flynn that she rode every weekend. Flynn was loved by his owner, who couldn't exercise him as much as the horse needed, so it worked out well for both of them.

One day she would have that countryside cottage with enough land for a horse. And a dog. In the meantime she made the best of riding Flynn.

She didn't know when she'd get to ride him again on a Saturday now she had committed to working in lieu of paying rent. Most likely she'd saddle up very early before she started work.

It was worth adjusting her working hours to live in this apartment, she thought, looking around her with intense satisfaction. Yesterday she'd finished unpacking her stuff. She had her priorities right—she'd first unpacked the kitchen things. Not that she'd really needed to—the apartment kitchen was completely equipped with every tool and gadget she'd ever need, and more. This afternoon she'd decided to christen the top-of-the-line oven and cooktop.

One of the other things she loved to do in her own time was to bake. On the way back from Centennial Park she'd gone shopping and stocked up on everything she'd needed for a bake-fest.

The oven timer went off and she pulled out the two pies she had baked from scratch. There was something particularly satisfying about making pastry—she got a kick from kneading, crimping edges and forming pastry leaves to put on top. She set the pies to cool on a rack and stood for a long moment critically examining them.

Should she or shouldn't she? She had baked the extra pie with Declan in mind. One for him, the other to share with Lynne and Keith. But she'd assured him she would respect his privacy. Would he consider a text to ask him could she deliver a 'thank you' pie a breach of her promise?

While the pies were cooling she showered and washed her hair to get out the smell of horse—she'd groomed Flynn after their ride. She adored the earthy warm smell of the big animals she loved. She suspected Declan might be rather more fastidious.

Once dressed in pink jeans and a pale pink shirt with a cream sweater slung around her shoulders—all gifts from Lynne, who was always trying to get her to dress in a more feminine manner—she texted Declan.

Can I see you?

His reply took a few minutes to come back.

Sure—come to the back door.

She wrapped the pie with its golden, buttery pastry crust in one of the beautiful French tea towels she'd found in a kitchen drawer.

It was only when she stood at his back door waiting for Declan to open it that she seriously began to question the sanity of baking a pie for her boss.

Declan was surprised to hear from Shelley so late on Sunday afternoon. He was not long awake, having had to catch up on some sleep after the Estella marathon. He'd only just started his workout in the basement gym and normally wouldn't tolerate interruption.

He threw on a sweatshirt over his bare chest. Perhaps it was an emergency in the apartment that needed his attention, he told himself as justification for breaking his no-interruptions rule. As an excuse for the brightening of his spirits when he'd seen her name flash up on his smartphone.

He was even more surprised to see her at his door bearing the most amazing home-made pie. Apple, he guessed, if the enticing aroma was anything to go by.

She held it out to him on both hands like an offering.

'I wanted to thank you for letting me live in the apartment it's fabulous and I can't believe my luck to be living there,' she blurted out.

'You don't have to cook for me,' he said and immediately regretted it when her face fell.

'I wondered if it was…appropriate,' she said, biting her lower lip. 'You mentioned you liked mulberries. Mulberries aren't in season so I couldn't get you mulberries. I'm hoping apple and raspberry might be acceptable. I had to use frozen raspberries because they're not in season either but they're very good and—'

'Shelley,' he said. 'Stop. I'm delighted you made me a pie. It was just…unexpected.' He took it from her hands. It was warm to the touch. 'Thank you.'

'Just out of the oven,' she said. 'An oven that's a very good one, by the way.'

'Come in,' he said.

'Oh, no, I shouldn't, I—'

'Please,' he said. The realisation he had no one to share the creation of Princess Estella with had made him feel… lonely.

He was also surprised to see Shelley all dressed in pink. Pretty, girly pink. She even wore jewellery, a chain holding a silver horseshoe that rested in the dip of her cleavage. *Lucky horseshoe.* He didn't know why he had assumed she would always dress in mannish clothes. Perhaps he'd forced himself to think too much about Shelley as warrior instead of facing up to his attraction to Shelley as woman.

'Okay,' she said and followed him inside.

During the major renovation of the house the back had been opened up and a family room and what the architect had insisted on calling a 'dream kitchen' had been installed.

'Wow,' she said as she unashamedly looked around her. 'This is an amazing space.'

'It's hardly used,' he said.

'Shame,' she said. 'That's truly a dream kitchen for someone who enjoys cooking.'

So the architect had got that one right.

Most of the house wasn't used and was quiet and still with air unbreathed. He couldn't bear to go into the rooms he'd shared with Lisa. They'd been closed off for two years.

He'd never gone into the nursery they'd prepared with such hope. But he wouldn't let anyone clear it. His life in this house was confined to his top-floor workspace, the turret room and the gym with occasional forays into this kitchen.

And now Shelley had brought a shaft of her particular brand of sunshine with her into this too large, too empty, too sad house.

He carried the pie over to the marble countertop and put it down.

'I'm going to have a piece right now while it's warm,' he said. 'You?'

She shook her head. 'I baked another one to share with my sister and her fiancé. I'm having dinner with them to-night.'

Any thought of asking her to join him for dinner—to be delivered from a favourite restaurant he hadn't actually set foot in for two years—was immediately quashed. It was a stupid idea anyway. He reminded himself it was more important than ever to establish boundaries between them now she was living on site, so to speak.

He took out a plate, a knife to cut the pie and a fork with which to eat it, and served himself an enormous slice. Then pulled up a stool at the breakfast bar. Shelley took a seat two stools away.

'So I get to eat this pie all by myself,' he said, circling the plate with his arms in exaggerated possessiveness.

'You could put half in the freezer,' said ever-practical Shelley.

'Believe me, there won't be half left to freeze,' he said.

He bit into his first mouthful, savoured the taste. 'Best pie I ever had,' he said with only mild exaggeration.

She laughed. 'I don't believe that for a minute.'

'Seriously, it's delicious.'

'My grandma's recipe,' she said. 'Trouble with learning to cook from your grandmother is I tend to specialise in old-fashioned treats.'

'This is a treat, all right,' he said. 'It's been a long time since someone baked for me.'

She looked around the room. 'So who uses this kitchen?'

'I do. But only for the most basic meals. I'm useless at anything more complex.' Declan had never needed to learn to cook. He'd moved out of home at age eighteen, already wealthy enough to eat out or hire caterers whenever he wanted.

Shelley leaned her elbows on the countertop. 'Was Lisa a good cook?'

He was so shocked to hear her mention Lisa's name he nearly choked on his pie. But why shouldn't she? It was a perfectly reasonable question. Shelley didn't know of his guilt over the deaths of his wife and daughter and his determination to punish himself for their loss.

'She…she did her best—but we used to laugh at the results more often than not. We ate out a lot. I think she was hoping this kitchen would transform her into a culinary wizard. She used to talk about doing classes but… but she never did.'

'She… Lisa…she sounds lovely.' He could tell Shelley was choosing her words carefully.

'She was. You…you would have liked her and she…she would have liked you.'

He realised it was true. The two women were physically complete opposites; Lisa had been tiny and dark-haired. But there was a common core of…he hesitated to use the bland word 'niceness' but it went some way to articulating what he found almost impossible to articulate.

'I… I'm glad,' Shelley said. He could see sympathy in her eyes. But not pity. He wouldn't tolerate pity.

Even two years later he still found it difficult to talk

about Lisa. It was as if his heart had been torn out of him when she'd died.

But if he were going to talk to anyone it would be Shelley. There was something trustworthy and non-judgemental about her that made him believe he could let his guard down around her. If only in increments.

'Lisa was…vivacious. That was the word people used about her. When I was young I was a quiet kind of guy, awkward around girls. Females ran a mile from me when they learned what a geek I was.'

'I don't believe that for a minute,' Shelley said with an upward tilt to her lovely mouth. 'You're a very good-looking guy. I imagine you would have been beating girls off with a stick.' Was that acknowledgement of a fact or admiration? Whatever it was he liked the feeling her words gave him.

'Not so,' he said, with a self-deprecating shrug. 'I probably spent way too long in front of a screen.'

'But Lisa saw something in you?'

'Lisa grew up with brothers, knew how to handle boys. She took me out of myself. I was an only child of parents too busy to take much notice of me.'

'I'm sorry to hear that,' she murmured.

'They'd decided not to have children. I came as a shock to them.' He tried to make a joke of it but his bitterness filtered through. 'I don't know how many times I heard the words "Declan was our little accident" when I was growing up.'

Her eyes widened. 'Surely they said it with fondness,' she said.

'Perhaps. I didn't see much of my parents anyway. My mother was too busy defending criminals or doing pro bono work for underprivileged people to realise there might be someone at home who needed her time too. Thankfully she shunted me off to her mother for the school vacations.'

'The one with the mulberry tree?'

He nodded. 'The very one. She was an artist and took great delight in passing on her skills to me—to defy my parents, I sometimes think.'

'And your father?'

'Let's just say "typical absentee parent" and be done with it.'

'I… I feel sad for the little boy you were,' she said.

'Don't be. I put that behind me long ago. Who knows, if I'd grown up in a happy household with a boatload of siblings I mightn't have got where I did so fast.'

'That's a thought,' she said, but didn't sound convinced.

'At least they had the sense to hire a wonderful nanny for me. She more than made up for it.'

Until he'd turned twelve and they'd terminated Jeannie's employment, citing that a big boy like him didn't need to be looked after any more. Jeannie had never given up on him, though. She'd stayed an important part of his life.

'Jeannie was going to live in the apartment to…to help you with…?'

He had to change the subject. 'Yes,' he said abruptly. 'What about you? Sounds like your childhood might have been less than ideal.'

'It was very ideal until my father decided he preferred another family to us,' she said. It gutted him to see her face tighten with remembered distress.

'You and your sister?'

She nodded. 'And my mum—none of us saw it coming. He met a younger woman with a little boy. She got her clutches into him and that was the end of it. For us anyway.'

'So why did you have to leave your home?'

'He's a real-estate agent. He said our little farm needed to be sold. Then he pulled some tricky deal and moved right back in with her.'

Declan could think of a few words he'd like to use to describe her father but held his tongue. 'That's terrible.'

'He tried to make it up to Lynne and me. Wanted to keep seeing us. I was allowed to keep my pony, Toby, there. He said it was a good way to make me visit.'

By the tight set of her face Declan doubted the tale would have a happy ending. 'Makes sense,' he said.

'Until the day I got there to find she'd sold my beautiful Toby. And my father had done nothing to stop her.'

This time Declan did let loose with a string of curse words. 'That's cruelty. How old were you?'

'I'd just turned fourteen. It's a long time ago but I still remember how I felt.'

'Did you get your horse back?'

'We tracked down the new owner. But…but…' Tears welled in her beautiful eyes. 'He'd panicked when they were off-loading him from the horse trailer at the other end. My darling boy must have known what was happening to him wasn't right. Apparently he reared and thrashed around and…and broke his leg.' Her voice became almost unintelligible as she fought off tears. 'It wasn't the new owner's fault. They didn't know Toby was…was stolen. But he…he had to be put down.'

'And what about your father?'

'He made me hate him,' she said simply. 'And it never really went away.'

Something deep and long unused inside Declan had turned upside down in the face of her grief. To comfort her became more important than the inhibitions he had imposed upon himself.

He reached out and clasped her hand in his. Her hand was slender and warm but he felt calluses on her palm and fingers. Warrior calluses.

'I'm sorry,' he said. 'Not just about your horse but about

your father too.' He suspected the pain of losing her horse was inextricably tied up with her father's betrayal.

She returned the pressure on his hand, not knowing what a monumental gesture it was for him to reach out to her. For a very long moment his eyes met with hers in a silent connection that shook him. *What he felt for her in this moment went way beyond physical attraction.*

In the quiet of his kitchen, with the ticking of the clock and the occasional whirring of the fridge the only noise, this one room of many in the vast emptiness of his house suddenly seemed welcoming. Because she was there.

'I'm sorry to lose the plot like that,' she said. 'I know that my loss is nothing—absolutely nothing—compared with your loss. I know he was only an animal but—' She sniffed back the tears that obviously still threatened.

'But you loved him.'

There'd been no pets in his childhood household, despite his constant clamouring for a dog. Then Lisa had been allergic to pet hair. One day he might get a dog. It was a new thought and one immediately rejected. He did not want to take the risk of loving anything, *anyone* again.

'Yes,' she said. 'I adored Toby. There's an incredible bond between horse and rider, you know. It's not quite the same as loving a cat or a dog. Two become one, horse and human, when you ride. There's a kind of mutual responsibility. It's very special.'

'Do you still ride?' He couldn't admit how he had observed her heading out of the house dressed in her breeches and boots.

'Fortunately Centennial Park is so close by I can ride each weekend. Riding a hired horse is nothing like riding your own but I'm fortunate enough to ride the same lovely big boy every week. His owner is so grateful to have someone competent to exercise him and groom him, she only charges me a pittance.'

'Sounds like a deal,' he said.

'It's another reason I really wanted to stay in this area rather than moving out further where rents are cheaper. Again, thank you for the apartment. I love it.'

'Thanking me with a pie was a great idea,' he said.

'I make a mean chocolate-fudge cake too,' she said. 'Unless you'd prefer something more savoury.'

'Cake is good,' he said. The strict exercise regime he followed let him eat whatever he wanted.

He realised he was still holding her hand—and he didn't want to let it go. She seemed in no rush to relinquish his grip either.

'Tell me the type of treats you like so I can keep you in mind when I'm baking,' she said with her generous smile, leaning closer, so close he breathed in her sweet, flowery scent. 'If it isn't in my repertoire, I'll find a recipe.'

It was a thoughtful offer. But right now there was only one treat that was tempting him. Before he could rustle up a reason why he shouldn't, he leaned across and kissed her. Her lush, lovely mouth was soft and full under his.

She stilled at first, startled, then relaxed against him, her lips parting for his with a soft murmur as he traced their warm softness with his tongue.

He had not kissed a woman other than Lisa since he was nineteen. The feel of Shelley's mouth under his was both familiar and different at the same time. The thought of Lisa was both poignant and fleeting—then his mind was filled only with Shelley and how much he wanted to keep on kissing her. She tasted of cinnamon and apple with a fresh tang of mint as her tongue tangled with his.

As she kissed him back this kiss became unique, special like nothing he had ever experienced. Shelley. Beautiful Shelley. *It was all about her.*

Her mouth was soft and warm and generous, their hands still linked on the table between them. It started as a gentle, exploratory kiss but very soon escalated into something more passionate as she kissed him back with equal ardour.

They strained towards each other—awkward on bar stools but she didn't seem to care and he certainly didn't—he just wanted to be as close to her as he could possibly be.

But she was the one to break the kiss, her face flushed, her eyes bright.

'That was a surprise, Declan,' she said. He could see a pulse beating rapidly at the base of her throat. 'Of the nice kind. *Very* nice, actually.'

He took a deep breath in an attempt to steady his breathing.

'Much more than nice,' he said.

His thoughts were filled with Shelley. But he felt disloyal that he hadn't given thought to his late wife. Yet from nowhere came the insistent message: *Lisa would approve.* If he had been the first to go, would he have expected her to lead such a desperately lonely life?

*But he wasn't ready to move on to someone else—might not ever be ready.*

'You know this can't lead to anywhere,' he said, his voice husky. 'I have nothing to give you. Nothing. It…it all drained away when—'

Shelley put her finger on his mouth to silence him.

Her face was flushed, her voice throaty when she finally spoke. 'It was just a kiss. A very nice kiss but just a kiss. Does it have to lead anywhere?'

'I guess not,' he said, somewhat taken aback. Shelley was so different from the predatory women on the hunt for the wealthy widower.

It hadn't entered his head that Shelley might not be interested in him.

'*Men are more trouble than they're worth.*' Her earlier words echoed through his brain.

Her mouth was pouty and swollen from his kiss—which made him just want to kiss her again.

'I'm aware you might not be ready for…for anything serious.' Her stumble made him realise that perhaps she wasn't as indifferent to him as it might appear. 'And I don't want to risk opening myself to…heartbreak. I've just got over an almighty dose of that.'

He hadn't been planning on *heartbreak*. In fact that was just what he wanted to avoid. Not just for himself but for her too.

'The guy in Melbourne?'

She nodded. 'He was dishonest and he—well, he was a liar and completely untrustworthy and… Never mind, you don't want to hear the details.'

She was right. He didn't want to hear about her with another man. But was he ready to win her for himself?

'*It's been two years, Declan. Lisa would not expect you to grieve for ever.*' Now it was his mother's words borrowing his brain.

'I have plans,' Shelley continued. 'I don't want heartbreak and angst and all that stuff that seems to come with relationships—or they do for me anyway—to get in the way of achieving my goals.'

'Plans?' he said. *Goals?* He realised he might be guilty of underestimating Shelley. Had he given a thought to her life beyond his garden and her unwitting role as muse?

'Serious goals I've put on the back burner for years—derailed by relationships gone wrong.'

'I'd like to hear those goals.'

'Let me start,' she said. 'I want to visit some of the great gardens in Europe. Gardens that have had such an influence on the way people design gardens even here on the other side of the world. Some say the English perennial border isn't suited to most parts of this country—I'd love to see it at home in England. Then there's Monet's garden at Giverny, near Paris—who doesn't want to see that?'

Declan could think of far more interesting things than a garden to see in France but he was too stunned to interrupt her flow of words.

'And the Gardens of the Alhambra in Spain.' She smiled. 'Lots of fountains.'

He cleared his throat. 'When do you go?'

'As soon as your garden is done. Four more weeks, according to our agreement. Then I'll be flying off to Europe.'

'When will you be back?'

'Who knows? I'm booking an open-return ticket. My father was born in England and I can stay for as long as I like. What I really, really want to do is work as a horticulturalist in the gardens of one of the grand stately homes in England.' Her eyes shone with enthusiasm. 'I apply for every job I see—they advertise through agencies on the internet—and I'm hoping one of them will stick.'

'Sounds exciting,' he said lamely.

He realised that since he had nearly kissed her in his garden when he had unwound her hair, the thought had been quietly ticking away in the back of his mind that one day, if he was ever able to move on, Shelley might be the one. It was a shock to find she had no intention of being here, of giving him time to come to terms with the change her presence in his life might entail.

'So, you see, you're a grieving widower—and I totally understand that, I can't imagine how dreadful it's been for you—and I don't do meaningless flings.'

She leaned across and kissed him lightly on the mouth. Even it had impact, sending want coursing through him.

'So, lovely as that kiss was, I don't think we should do it again.'

Declan was too speechless to respond.

Shelley got up from her stool. 'I have to get going to meet my sister. I can pick up the pie dish when you're done with.'

'Let me see you out,' he said, getting up to follow her.

She put up her hand to halt him. 'No need.'

She strolled out, and suddenly the room seemed very, very empty indeed.

Shelley stood outside the house near the fountain, lit up by the sensor lights that had come on automatically when she had stumbled out of Declan's back door. She hoped the cool evening air would bring her to her senses. She shivered and tugged her cream sweater tightly around her shoulders. Her mouth ached from both the effort of continual smiling and appearing nonchalant—and the unaccustomed dissembling. She wasn't a liar. Yet she had lied and lied and lied to Declan.

*'It was just a kiss'* was the first lie. She touched her fingers to her mouth, shuddering as she remembered the powerful effect of his lips on hers, his tongue exploring the soft recesses of her mouth, the desire that had ignited and raced through her body. It was so much more than a mere pressing of two mouths together. Of awakened passion.

But the biggest lie of all was that she didn't want him kissing her again. There was nothing she wanted more than to be in his arms and kissing him. *More than kissing him.*

But the lies had been necessary. Because they were overwhelmed by the one big truth. *She didn't want to risk heartbreak.* And everything Declan did, what he said, pointed to massive heartbreak down the line if she let down the guard on her emotions.

Her wounds from Steve were still too raw and painful to risk opening them again. She still hadn't completed that long climb back out of the black pit of distrust that her father's betrayal and rejection of her love had flung her into.

Dating decent—if unexciting—men had set her on the first rungs of finding her way back out until Steve had kicked the ladder out from under her in spectacular fashion. Coming back to Sydney and away from anything that reminded her of Steve had started her recovery.

She had to protect herself from falling down again. Denying that Declan's kiss had affected her was one way to do it.

Although, in doing so, she was actually lying to herself.

# CHAPTER TEN

SHELLEY LOOKED LONG and hard at the door in her kitchen that, she now knew, led straight through into Declan's kitchen. The door she had promised never to use. The key was in her hand. All it would take would be to slide it into the lock and—

She put the key—which she had attached to a pewter horseshoe key ring—back down on the countertop with a clatter.

It was five-thirty in the morning. She had been awake since four o'clock. Tossing and turning and unable to get thoughts of Declan from her mind. How it had felt to kiss him. To want so much more than a kiss. More than he could give. *More than it was wise to want.*

She looked at the key again gleaming on the countertop. *Tempting her.*

At four a.m. it had been way too dark to go out and start work in the garden. She'd tried to read a book—a new one on Enid Wilson she'd ordered from a specialist gardening bookstore—but could not concentrate. Television offerings at that time of morning had not been able to engage her interest either.

So she had baked muffins. Banana and pecan muffins with a maple-syrup glaze. She could have made a pie—she had apples aplenty arranged in a fruit bowl on the table. But both of her pie dishes—enamel ones given to her by her grandma—were not here. One was with Lynne and

Keith. The other was with Declan still, from when she had last seen him three days ago.

Would it be a terribly bad thing to sneak into his kitchen, retrieve the pie dish and leave an offering of some warm banana muffins on the countertop for him?

She wanted that pie dish. She wanted it *now*. She was helping Lynne with the catering for her engagement party on Saturday night. Pie was on the dessert menu. The problem could easily be solved by asking Declan for the pie dish. But she didn't want it to look like a pathetic excuse to see him.

He did not want to see her; that was obvious. But he was here in the house. Last night she had seen the light on in the window high on the second floor she assumed was his office. With that preternatural awareness of his presence she had developed, she knew he was there even without the light as proof.

She picked up the key again. It turned easily in the lock.

Still in her pyjamas, heart in her mouth, she crept into the kitchen of the big house. It was silent, it was creepy, it was almost dark—with only the faint lights on the stove and the computer-controlled fridge to lead her way. She searched for the pie dish in drawers that glided out silently. She found her dish in the third drawer she tried, quite possibly put there by the cleaners.

*Mission accomplished.*

She eased the plate of muffins down onto the marble countertop so it wouldn't clatter. Then immediately berated herself for such an idiotic move—and blamed it on her lack of sleep. She doubted Declan would notice the absence of the pie dish. But the sudden appearance of a plate of freshly baked muffins? There would be no doubt who had left them there and that she had trespassed.

She picked them up again, and then the pie dish, and

made to tiptoe back to her door and then to her rightful side of it. Then she heard the music. A faint pulsing, driving rhythm coming, it sounded like, from somewhere on this floor.

*Curiosity killed the cat—remember that, Shelley.*

Another of her grandmother's sayings flashed through her mind. Advice that in this case she really should take. But the house was otherwise dark and deserted. She'd been wondering about Declan's secret life inside this house since the day she'd first met him. She could not resist this particular temptation.

Trying to be as quiet as possible, she tiptoed out of the kitchen and down a very short corridor. She guessed that in the old days this might have led to a scullery or cellar. Just a few silent steps from the kitchen she saw a door with a glass pane at the top—it was only the dim light coming through the glass that let her recognise it.

The music was coming from downstairs. Was Declan there? What would happen if he saw her prowling around where she had no right to prowl?

She could not resist sidling up to the glass panel and looking through.

Not a cellar but a full-size basement gym filled with serious-looking workout equipment.

And Declan was working out.

She nearly dropped her pie dish at the sight of him.

Her breath caught in her throat and her heart started hammering so loudly she could hear it.

Declan, wearing only tight black gym shorts, his upper body completely bare save for a pair of grip gloves. Declan, doing pull-ups on a terrifyingly high multi-step pull-up bar. Declan doing 'salmon pull-ups', so called because they involved not just pulling *himself* up to the bar but pushing the actual bar up with him to the next step, like salmon swimming upstream against the current. It took incredible strength in both upper body and abs to master. Strength and willpower and endurance. And courage. One slip and he'd crash to the ground taking the metal bar with him.

Shelley went to the gym when she could. But she had never seen anyone actually do salmon pull-ups.

She watched in awe as, muscles straining, he pulled both himself and the bar to the very top step without pausing. Then, again without pausing, he hooked his legs over the bar and executed a series of sit-ups punching the air as he jack-knifed his body into a sitting position—upside down.

His cut, defined muscles gleamed with sweat as he grimaced with the effort of the unbelievably tough workout he was forcing his body through.

*So that was where the muscles came from.*

Mesmerised, she could not tear her eyes away from him, even though she knew she risked discovery. This was a guy who described himself as a *geek*?

Declan working out was the sexiest thing she had ever seen. She was getting turned on just watching. Her whole body was taut with hunger for him. With pure and simple lust. She nearly fainted as he turned in mid-air to show his tight, powerful butt, the straining muscles of his broad back.

*'I don't do meaningless flings.'*

Her words of three days ago came back to haunt her.

She wanted him more than she had ever imagined she could want a man.

If she could stumble down those stairs and push herself against all that hot, hard muscle she wouldn't be thinking about *meaning*. She had to cross her legs at the thought of it.

The force of her desire for him made her tremble and her knees go suddenly weak. She leaned against the door to support herself just as Declan dropped to the ground from the top of the bar to land with total control on a thick, foam mat. He looked up and her breath stopped but he immediately rolled into a series of alternating one-arm push-ups. *He hadn't seen her.*

But she knew the longer she stayed there, the greater the risk of discovery.

Her heart started an even more furious pounding and she found it difficult to breathe. Not just with her overwhelming longing for him but with terror at the prospect of him catching her spying on him.

With one last look at his incredible body, she turned as quietly and as cautiously as she could and tiptoed back to the door that would send her through to her very short-term leased part of the mansion. The staff *downstairs* to his billionaire *upstairs*.

Once safely back in her kitchen, she stood with her back to the connecting door and braced herself against it, urging her heart to slow down, her breath to steady from short, urgent gasps to a more regular pattern.

How could she ever forget how Declan looked working out in that gym? *How much she wanted him?* Wanted this man who had made it so very clear he had nothing to give her.

Actually, when she thought back, even a meaningless fling was not on offer. He had kissed her. *That was all.* But it had been such a wonderful kiss, of course she had thought further to what that kind of kiss could lead to. *Making love with Declan.* If that one kiss had given her so much pleasure, what would—?

*She could not go there.* That would be dreaming an impossible dream. Declan was still deeply entrenched in his marriage—even though his wife had passed away two years ago, Declan had not moved on. The only outcome of letting herself fall for him would be heartbreak. And she had had more than enough of that. *She had to keep reminding herself of that.*

The grey light of dawn was starting to filter through the blinds of the apartment. She knew there was zero chance of getting back to sleep now. A quick, very cold shower and then get out into the garden.

She had a big day planned—and a surprise for Declan that he might like, or hate so much she'd never be able to face him again.

Mid-afternoon and Declan was surprised to get a text from Shelley asking him could he come down to the garden as soon as he could.

From his observation point in his office, he'd noticed a lot of activity in the grounds. A delivery of plants. Lots of digging on Shelley's part. And the pool guys were there again.

He heaved himself up from his desk. He was tired and grumpy. He hadn't slept at all the night before. But then what was new about that?

He'd worked right through. Burying himself in work was a better alternative to angsting about Shelley. Thinking about the difference she had made to his life. Not just because of Estella. In fact Estella seemed somehow peripheral now.

He realised now he had used Estella as a block to getting to know the real Shelley, not his imagined version of her. Estella had been self-protection.

There could be no doubt his attraction to Shelley made him see a glimmer of hope in the dark reality of his grief, a thawing of his long-frozen emotions. The kiss had made that very clear.

But the consequences if things went awry were huge—

not just for him but for her. Shelley was an exceptional woman in every way—and he didn't want to hurt her because he'd taken a step towards her too soon.

Perhaps she sensed his ambivalence and that was why she was determined to keep him at a distance, to concentrate on her plans for a career far away from here—and from him.

Before dawn he had gone down to the basement gym and driven his body through a punishing regime. Extended his body to its limits in a gruelling workout so that no thoughts could intrude—just pure physicality.

Even then—on the point of utter exhaustion—he couldn't sleep. After his workout he had showered in the gym bathroom, then made his way up to the kitchen.

Breakfast was the one meal he was expert at preparing. Protein and lots of it was required after such an intense workout. So why in hell had he been hit by a craving for banana muffins? He'd wanted one so badly he had sworn he could smell them fresh out of the oven right there in his kitchen.

He'd been forced to phone through an order to a local bakery and have banana muffins express delivered. They tasted nothing like how he had anticipated—dry and unpalatable. There wasn't a crumb of Shelley's pie left either. He'd bet she'd bake a muffin that would taste a hundred times better than the ones he'd had delivered and that had subsequently landed in the trash.

His unsatisfied craving had made him grumpier than ever. And that was on top of his craving for *her*.

Now Shelley wanted to see him to show him something in the garden. Oddly enough, he was looking forward to it. Seeing the garden emerge from the mess it had been was more satisfying than he could ever have imagined. Shelley had vision; there was no doubt about that.

He texted her: I'll be down in half an hour.

She was waiting for him by the fountain—familiar Shelley in her khaki gardener garb. She coloured high on her cheeks when he greeted her—the previous time they'd met he'd been kissing her.

Inwardly he groaned. He wasn't good at this. The last time he'd dated a woman had been when he'd met Lisa—and there hadn't been many before her in spite of what Shelley might think.

'Notice anything?' she asked cheerfully.

*Other than how beautiful you look—even in those awful clothes?*

He nodded. 'There's water in the pond.'

'And it's not leaking away. It's been in there for forty-eight hours. I think the pool guys nailed it. Well, not literally nailed it, of course. If they had, it would be leaking more than ever, wouldn't it? I mean…' Her voice trailed away.

In spite of his grumpiness he smiled; Shelley seemed to always make him smile. 'I get what you mean.'

He inspected the pond and its surrounds, now all mellow sandstone free of grime and mould.

'It looks awesome, doesn't it?' she said, eyes wide seeking his approval.

Even if it didn't look awesome, he would say it did just so as not to extinguish that light in her eyes.

'It's awesome, all right. What about the fountain—does it work?'

'That's why I asked you down here,' she said with a flourish of her hand. 'You are formally invited to the grand ceremonial switching on of the fountain.'

She took him around to the back of the far wall of the pond and showed him a small, discreet box housing a switch. 'The pump is behind there and all safely wired up to low-voltage electricity. All you have to do is turn it on.' She paused. 'Go ahead, you do this. It's your fountain.'

'But you're the driving force behind it,' he said. 'The honour should be yours. You've put so much into it.'

Her smile dimmed. 'It's my job, Declan. This is what I do. And when I finish this job there'll be another garden somewhere else.'

He ducked down to turn on the switch, hoping she wouldn't see the sudden pain her words caused him.

Standing beside her—and noting how carefully she kept her distance—he watched as the water started to pump through the fountain, shooting up from the top and cascading down the tiers. The water sparkled as sunlight caught it and refracted off the droplets. Now he knew exactly what she meant about adding movement to the garden. And a different element of beauty. *But Shelley was the most beautiful thing in this garden.*

'It's just wonderful, isn't it?' she said softly. 'I knew it was worth saving. Sometimes the things you have to work hardest to restore become the most valuable.'

'You're right,' he said, his voice suddenly husky.

It was his garden and she a paid employee. But she had put her heart and soul into this restoration.

While he was pleased at how the garden was progressing, he wished he could slow down the progress to give him time to come to terms with what Shelley meant to him. As it was, the days were ticking away until the time she'd pack up her tools and move on.

*Unless he stopped her.*

Right now he didn't know how that was possible.

A tiny blue wren flew through the spray of the fountain, fluffing his wings as he went. He was immediately followed by his little brown mate.

'Oh, look at that,' Shelley cried in delight.

'The local wildlife seal of approval,' he said.

'I hope everything else in the garden works out as well,' she said slowly.

'I'm sure it will. It's all starting to look very civilised,' he said.

She took a few steps away from him, then turned back to face him.

'There's something else I want to show you,' she said. 'Something I… I didn't discuss with you. I'm hoping it will meet with your approval.'

He was used to her being nervous around his forbidding self. But this was different. She had paled under her light tan and was wringing her hands together. He couldn't imagine why.

'You'd better show me,' he said.

'Just before I do,' she said, 'I want to let you know that I did it with the best of intentions, no matter what you might think.'

His interest roused, he followed her to a prominent bed in an open part of the garden behind the fountain. Looking from the house, he realised it would be in the line of vision from most of the windows of the house.

The stone wall behind the bed had been cleaned and repaired and the two antique planters put back in their place and planted with some spiky-leaved plant.

But that wasn't what Shelley was showing him. The actual garden bed had been completely cleared of weeds and whatever plants had turned up their toes from years of neglect. The earth had been freshly turned over. He realised this was where he'd seen Shelley digging and planting for most of the morning.

He drew his brows together. 'They're plants, I know, but they look to me like a whole lot of brown sticks with a few green shoots here and there.'

'They're roses,' she said. 'This is a perfect aspect for roses and I hope they'll thrive here. I've planted two varieties of roses here. In late spring they'll be glorious.'

'Yes?' he said. What was the big deal here?

She looked up at him, her eyes a little wary. 'At the back I've planted a vibrant orange and pink rose called "Lisa".'

Declan's heart seemed to stop beating and he felt a cold sweat break out on his forehead.

Shelley didn't seem to expect any response from him as she continued. 'The smaller bushes in the front have an exquisite pale pink bloom with a sweet scent. The rose is called "Miss Alice".'

Declan felt as if his throat were swelling to choke any attempt at speech. The grief he'd felt at the loss of his wife and daughter came flooding back. But with that grief came a new emotion of gratitude for the woman who had made this gesture.

'Thank you,' he finally managed to get out. 'It was very…thoughtful of you.'

Shelley expelled a great sigh of relief and he realised the tension she had been holding. 'The "Lisa" rose is probably what you could call a…a vivacious rose. Like Lisa herself, you told me.'

Shelley's eyes were misting with tears. His tears had long run dry.

Her voice was so low he had to lean down to catch it.

'This was Daphne's garden and the daphne she planted remains a memorial for her,' she said. 'Then it was Lisa's garden and I hope the roses will be a beautiful tribute to her and…and to baby Alice.'

Declan was astounded at how thoughtful Shelley had been. It was something his billions could never have bought. But it was almost too much for him to be able to deal with.

'Thank you. What you've done is…extraordinary. I won't forget what you've done for me. And for honouring Lisa and Alice in this way.'

He didn't mean for those words to sound so final but it was the best he could do. His remembered grief was all mixed up with his gratitude for what Shelley had done for him. Something that was so utterly *right*. He honestly couldn't think of anyone else he knew who would have the heart, the compassion and the imagination required.

He started to shake and before he knew it Shelley's arms were around him and he was holding her tight.

Shelley closed her eyes and leaned against Declan's hard strength, loving the feel of those powerful arms around her. During those secret, stolen moments watching him work out this was what she'd been wanting.

Was he hugging her—or in his memory was he hugging Lisa?

This was a man who had genuinely loved his wife. So devastated by grief at her loss he was unable to move on.

She had not believed in such love. Certainly had not experienced it. But now she'd seen it, she wanted it for herself.

*She wanted it from him.* She couldn't deny that any longer. The lying to herself had to stop.

But was Declan's love all used up?

It would be a tragedy if that was the case. Not just for him but for her.

Because she was falling for him in spite of the very real risk to her heart.

# CHAPTER ELEVEN

*WAS SHE IN any way envious of her sister and her fiancé's happiness?* Dressing for her sister's engagement party, Shelley couldn't help but question herself about love, life and relationships. Her answer? *Maybe.*

Not that she wished she had Keith for herself—he was a very nice man but she wasn't the slightest bit attracted to him. He was perfect for Lynne—they complemented each other's strengths and weaknesses. Above all they were head over heels in love. Keith was a jeweller and had given Lynne a lovely ruby ring he had designed just for her.

It wasn't the engagement ring that Shelley envied. The envy thing happened when she'd witness her sister and her guy planning their wedding, the family they intended to have, their future together. They were so darn committed to that future. So certain of each other.

And her? Teetering on the edge of falling in love with a man who had said point-blank he had *nothing to give her.*

Her sister's joy brought Shelley's own situation into focus. She was twenty-eight. Marriage. Children. They were something she'd always thought would happen in the future. When her career was established. When she'd met the right man. But that man had proved to be elusive.

There'd been one proposal—from a guy she had dated during her final year at university. He'd come from a prominent horse-training family and they'd met through their common love of horses. She'd been very fond of him but she'd known *fond* wasn't enough even though he'd been what her grandmother had called *good marriage material*.

More recently there had been Steve—the married man she hadn't known was married. Afterwards she had beaten herself up for having been so easily deceived. But it had certainly seemed like love at the time. And it had hurt.

And now there was Declan. Not married. But—in a way—still married.

Maybe she needed to have a good long look at herself—did she have a thing for unavailable men? And what could she do about it? Accept steady, nice Mark's long-standing and often repeated invitation to dinner?

She sighed. How could she when she was already in so deep with Declan even though it seemed impossible? How could she give another man a thought? Declan eclipsed anyone she'd ever met. And it wouldn't be fair on Mark—or any other man whom she might date.

Her hopes for the future did include marriage and children. But not for the sake of it. No settling for second best, no settling for *fond* because she feared time was running out. Women had children well into their thirties, their forties even. There was no need to panic. But children were definitely on her wish list, which brought to mind another question. Would Declan ever want to have another child?

But she couldn't have Declan and she'd better get used to the thought. Even though every time she closed her eyes she saw him bare-chested down in that gym, his powerful muscles, the look of intense concentration on his face she found so sexy. *She ached for him.*

Lynne was right: she should get out and have some fun.

She viewed herself critically in the mirror, twisting and turning to see the back of her new dress. The cobalt-blue colour alone drew attention but it was the cut of it that

had her wondering was it a tad too sexy for an engagement party.

High-necked in the front, it swooped outrageously low
in the back, secured by two heavy silver chains that started
from the back of her neck and fixed to each side. Thankfully it had a built-in bra, otherwise she'd be too nervous to move in it—let alone dance and party. The stretch
jersey fabric was ruched and shaped and *very* figure-
hugging.

But Lynne had insisted she wear it to her engagement
party, which was to be held at the luxurious harbourside
home of one of Keith's school friends. 'There will be lots
of single guys there,' her sister had said. 'Wear that sassy
dress and get your mind off that reclusive boss of yours.'

Shelley had protested but Lynne had spoken over her.
'Don't try to hide your crush on Devastating Declan from
me.'

Shelley had protested that she did not have a crush. And
she hadn't been lying. She had way more than a crush on
Declan.

For a passing moment, she wished Declan could see her
in this dress. It wouldn't hurt for him to see she was more
than a down-to-earth gardener in khaki work clothes and
an old-fashioned homemaker in an apron who baked pies.

Tonight she didn't want to look in any way like that
person. The dress was a start. Now she had to get her hair
right. She ended up with a low side ponytail, secured with
a glittery holder, that rested over her left shoulder and left
her back uncovered.

With such a bold dress, she took more care with her
make-up, darkening her eyes, slicking on deep pink glossy
lipstick. She usually wore fairly low heels so she didn't
tower over many of the men she met. But her sister's engagement party was certainly the occasion to christen

the silver stilettos she had bought on a whim but had never worn.

She had promised Lynn she would be early. So she wrapped a light shawl around her bare back and shoulders and picked up a silver evening purse.

Cautiously, in her spiky-heeled shoes, she picked her way over the gravel to where she had parked her car in Declan's driveway. She muttered a curse when she saw there was a car parked behind it, blocking the way out to the street—a new-model luxury coupe that put her ancient 4x4 to shame. Her car was not just second-hand, it was more likely tenth-hand and the other car made it look like every one of its years.

In the weeks she been working in Declan's garden she had never seen a car parked here except when the cleaners came. Who drove this car?

Cranky that the delay was making her late, she teetered on her high heels around to the front door of Declan's house. No time to text. She just wanted him to ask his guest to move that car immediately.

Declan answered the door. She lost all the words that she had prepared to politely ask could his visitor help her out and move the car. It was all she could do not to gawk at him in blatant admiration. Her heartbeat kicked into overdrive and her knees felt distinctly wobbly. How could she have ever imagined she could talk herself out of her attraction to him?

Declan looked hot in his black jeans and cashmere sweaters. He looked especially hot in those gym shorts. But he had never looked more darkly handsome than now in a more formal charcoal wool double-breasted jacket over a black T-shirt and black trousers, clean-shaven and hair brushed back.

She felt a moment of feminine satisfaction that he was

getting to see her in the gorgeous blue dress, looking more womanly than he had ever seen her. Reading other people might not be her greatest skill but she was sure he had noticed.

*But who was he so dressed up for—the owner of the coupe?* She heard a feminine voice from behind him and her heart fell to the level of her silver stilettos.

A wave of nausea made her want to double over. Declan had a woman there? This man who had said he was closed to any feminine presence in his life? *He had lied to her.* He opened the door wider, stared at her for a long moment before he seemed to find his voice.

'Shelley,' he said, hoarsely, then glanced over his shoulder. Glanced *furtively* over his shoulder, it seemed to Shelley.

She still couldn't see who was there—but his action made it very clear he did not want that woman, whoever she might be, to see *her.*

She gritted her teeth, injected ice into her voice. 'There's a car parked in the driveway that's blocking my car. Could you please ask your guest to move it?'

The voice from behind him called out, 'Who's at the door, Declan?'

A woman came into view behind him. She was older, elegant in a simple wine-coloured dress, with her hair cut in a short grey bob and a expression of curiosity on her face. Declan opened the door further.

He cleared his throat. 'Come in, Shelley. I'd like you to meet my mother. Judith Grant.' He turned to the older woman. 'Mother, can I ask you to please move your car as Shelley can't get her car out?'

*His mother!* Shelley was so relieved she had to hold on to the doorframe for support. The action made her light shawl slip to her waist. Rather than make a big deal about putting it back on again, she gathered it up and tucked it over her arm. She shivered as the chilly evening air hit her bare back. But was then met by toasty centrally heated air as she took the few steps she needed to take her into the entrance hall.

Declan's mother took in her appearance with interest and frank curiosity.

'Mother, this is Shelley Fairhill, my gardener,' Declan said.

The older woman's eyebrows rose in such a similar way to Declan's, it made Shelley smile. She could see the resemblance between mother and son—the same deep blue eyes and lean face. Though the mother didn't have Declan's very masculine cleft in his chin.

Shelley put out her hand. 'It's nice to meet you, Mrs Grant.'

His mother's handshake was brisk and firm. Again Shelley felt self-conscious about her callused hands—but they were a badge of honour of her job. 'Nice to meet you, Shelley.'

Mrs Grant looked accusingly at Declan. 'You didn't tell me the gardener who is doing such wonderful work at this place was a beautiful young woman.'

*Because he doesn't recognise me as such,* Shelley thought with a pang.

*Maybe because I wanted to keep her to myself,* Declan thought. He was finding it difficult to think straight he was so knocked out by the sight of Shelley in a short, tight blue dress that accentuated every curve and showed off her sensational legs. *Legs that went on for ever.*

Shelley turned slightly to better face his mother. Declan gasped in admiration, which he quickly had to disguise as a cough. The dress was backless and revealed all of the toned, smooth perfection of her back before swooping so low it was practically indecent. The fabric was softly shaped and had some kind of central seam in it so it clung intimately to the gorgeous curves of her bottom.

*Was she wearing underwear?* He had to swallow very hard. And keep his hands fisted by his sides to stop him from reaching out to her and pulling her close to find out.

*If his mother weren't here, he might have done just that.*

His mother addressed Shelley. 'I'm sorry I blocked your access in the driveway. I had no idea who owned the old workhorse of a 4x4.'

'It is old but it serves me well and I can keep all my equipment safely in it,' Shelley said.

Declan sensed the defensive note in Shelley's voice and in turn felt immediately protective of her—he did not want his mother criticising her in any way.

But his mother was smiling. 'Shelley, of course you need a tough car in your line of work. You're doing an absolutely amazing job on the garden. Who knew that something so superb was hiding under all that mess?'

'Thank you,' Shelley said.

But Declan could sense the anxiety underlying her politeness. Then she glanced up at the big grandfather clock standing beneath the stairs.

'Mother, Shelley has to get going somewhere,' he said. 'I think she needs you to move your car right now.'

Shelley shot him a grateful look. 'I don't mean to be rude, Mrs Grant, but I'm on my way to my sister's engagement party so I can't be late.'

'Skip the Mrs Grant, call me Judith,' his mother said, much to Declan's surprise. 'I'll go get my keys and move the car for you.'

Then his mother paused and her eyes narrowed. She snapped her fingers. 'I've got a better idea,' she said. 'You can't drive a battered old 4x4 wearing that gorgeous dress and looking like you just stepped off a catwalk.'

His mother directed her gaze back to him. 'Declan, let Shelley drive one of your sports cars. Heaven knows, you've got a garage full of them.'

Declan automatically went to say *no*. Why would he let anyone drive one of his valuable European sports cars? But this wasn't just anyone. This was Shelley. And her eyes were lit with a gleam of excitement. Of course she would be the type of woman who would love to get behind the wheel of a performance car.

He took a deep breath. 'Good idea, Mother.'

Shelley did a little jig of excitement in her sky-high heels. 'Really, Declan, you'd let me drive your car?'

He rolled his eyes in a pretence of reluctance. 'There are conditions,' he said. 'The car turns into a pumpkin at midnight. You have to have it home by then.'

Shelley's eyes widened. 'Really?' she said. 'Not about the pumpkin, I mean. Well, of course, I know you're making a joke about that. But about the midnight thing. I mean, it's Lynne's engagement party and I have to stay to the end. She and Keith are party animals so heaven knows what time they—'

Declan smiled. 'Relax. You can bring the car back any time, as long as you drive it carefully—'

'Because it's so valuable?'

'There is that,' he said. 'But it's a very powerful car and I don't want you injured either.' *She was way more valuable than any car.*

She smiled. 'I'm a good driver. I grew up in the country, remember. I was driving around the property when I was twelve, long before I legally got my licence at seventeen. I'll take extra-special care with your car, I promise.'

'I'm sure if you can drive that beast of a 4x4 of yours you can drive anything.'

She nodded in acknowledgement of his words, then turned to his mother. 'Thank you, Judith, for suggesting this. How did you know how much I would love to drive a sports car?'

'A princess can't drive a pumpkin,' said his mother.

Shelley did look like a princess—even more of a princess than Estella—glamorous and enticing. 'I'll go get the car key,' he said.

When he returned it was to find Shelley laughing at something his mother had said—and his mother laughing too. He didn't know how he felt about them getting on so well.

He jangled the keys in front of him. 'I'll take you out to the garage and introduce you to the car,' he said.

'How exciting,' said Shelley, her eyes gleaming. 'I can't wait to see my sister's face when I drive up in it.' She turned to his mother. 'Thank you again, Mrs... I mean, Judith, this is going to be such a treat,' she said.

'It's my absolute pleasure,' said his mother with speculative eyes as she looked from Shelley to Declan and back again. 'And remember, I'll be coming over during the week for a guided tour of the garden. With my son's approval, of course.'

Shelley flung her shawl around her shoulders as he led her through the connecting door to the garage. He was tempted almost beyond endurance to slide it off her. Her back view was sensational and he would have been more than happy to admire it for longer.

He stood back and let Shelley enjoy her first sight of the sleek silver sports car that was to be hers for the evening. She was unable to contain her excitement and made throaty little murmurs of pleasure as she walked around the car admiring it from every angle. She actually stroked the bonnet. *He couldn't be jealous of a car.*

'I can tell you like it,' he said.

'Oh, yes,' she said, her eyes shining, her cheeks flushed.

'The black device opens the garage door,' he said as he handed her the key ring.

She stood close by, her high heels bringing her closer to his eye level. Her sweet scent filled his senses. 'Declan, this is really good of you,' she said. 'I hope you didn't feel pressured into letting me drive the car.'

'I don't get pressured into doing anything I don't want to,' he said hoarsely.

Their eyes met for a long time. 'I wish…' she said wistfully, her voice trailing away.

'You wish what?'

'I wish you could come to the party with me,' she said. 'Of course, you could drive your car if…if you were able to come with me.'

Declan had a sudden, fierce desire to say yes. He sure as hell didn't want her to go to her sister's party alone where she would be a magnet for any red-blooded male in the room—he wondered if she had any idea how outrageously sexy she looked. He had the urge to take off his jacket, fling it over her shoulders and tell her she had to keep it on all evening. *He wanted her for his eyes only.*

'If I could come—and I can't—you would be driving, not me,' he said.

She pulled one of her endearing faces. 'But, of course, you have your mother with you. Who seems very nice, by the way.'

Declan sucked in a quick breath. *Nice* wasn't the word he would ever use to describe his barracuda barrister mother.

'She's okay,' he acknowledged. 'She insists on bringing

her laptop over every few weeks for me to help her with it when I know very well she doesn't need help.'

'No doubt she wants to see if you're okay on your own,' she said. 'My mother checks in with me at least once every few days.'

'Perhaps,' he said. He didn't want to waste time talking about his mother. Not when Shelley's shawl was slipping off her shoulders again. This time he reached over and took it right off, sliding his hands down her bare arms. She trembled—from the cold in the garage or his touch?

'One more thing,' he said.

'About the car?' she asked, eyes wide.

'About this,' he said. He kissed her, hard and hungry and demanding—making sure she went to that party branded by his kisses. With a throaty little murmur of surprise and pleasure, she opened to him and met his tongue with hers, tasting, exploring, pressing her body to his—until want for her ignited through him in a flare of need. He broke away from her mouth, pressing hot kisses down her throat, tasting her, breathing in her sweet, arousing scent, sliding his hands to cup the enticing side swell of her breasts.

She moaned and wrenched herself away from him. 'Declan. No. Stop. If…if it was anything other than Lynne's party I wouldn't go, I'd stay here and we—'

'Don't say it,' he groaned. 'Go. Just go.'

She stared at him for a long moment, her breasts rising and falling as she struggled to control her breath. 'I wish… No. I have to go.' She planted a quick kiss on his mouth and went to step back but he snaked out his arm to tug her back and kiss her again. Only then did he wrest back control of his willpower and release her.

'Whatever time you get home, let me know,' he said, fighting to regain his breath in great, tearing gasps.

'Even if it's three in the morning?' Her lipstick was

smeared from his kisses, the pupils of her eyes so dilated he could scarcely see the colour, a pink beard rash around her chin. Good. Those other guys at the party would know she'd been thoroughly kissed and be warned off his woman.

*His woman.* When had he allowed himself to think of her as that?

'I'll be awake and waiting for you,' he said.

She slid behind the wheel of his car, as if she drove a high-performance sports vehicle every day, her dress sliding tantalisingly high up on her thighs. She laughed in exhilaration as the car started with a low, throaty roar.

'I am so going to enjoy this,' she called out to him.

He watched as she drove his favourite car, which no one else but he had ever driven, out of the garage and into the night, then he slammed his fist on the wall of the garage. He wanted to be with her. But here he was, surrounded by expensive cars in the garage of his multimillion-dollar mansion but cold and alone.

Only then came the full realisation of the prison he had created for himself.

Declan knew the second he got back in the house, his mother would grill him. She did not disappoint.

'Who is Shelley Fairhill and where did you find her?' she demanded, getting up from the sofa in the formal living room that was only used on her visits.

Declan shrugged. 'She found me,' he said. 'She knocked on the door and asked could she help me with the garden.'

'And you didn't glower and send her on the way?'

'Yes, I did,' he said, tight-lipped. 'But she persevered.' He added *glowering* to the list of words people used to describe him. *Forbidding* was still his favourite.

'I would have liked to have been a fly on the wall for that encounter. Did she—?'

'Long story.'

'And one I'm unlikely to hear the details of,' said his shrewd mother. 'She's beautiful, Declan. And obviously very talented at what she does.'

He nodded. What he felt about Shelley was his own business—he did not want to discuss it with anyone, certainly not his mother.

'Have you even *noticed* how beautiful Shelley is?' She put up her hand. 'Don't answer that. I saw the way you were looking at her—and the way she was looking at you.'

'What do you mean, the way she was looking at me?'

His mother laughed. 'I'm sure I don't have to tell you that. I haven't seen you smile so much for…for a long time.'

'You're imagining things,' he said stiffly.

'No, I'm not,' she said. 'I didn't get to be where I am without being able to read people. By the way, why was her car parked in your driveway?'

Reluctantly he replied. 'Because she's living in the apartment.'

'Oh,' said his mother with raised eyebrows.

'Nothing like that,' he said too hastily. 'She just needed somewhere to stay.'

His mother sighed. 'I believe you. But for your sake I wish it were otherwise. She's lovely, Declan—warm, open and she has kind eyes. I had a really good feeling about her.'

Declan gritted his teeth. 'She's all that and more,' he said. 'But what is it to you?'

His mother stilled. 'Despite what you think, I'm desperately concerned about you. Lisa was the best thing that ever happened to you, to the family. But she's gone, Declan. You're young. You can't let yourself just shrivel up and die inside because we lost Lisa. She would never have wanted you to lock yourself away like this.'

Declan gritted his teeth so hard his jaw ached. 'You know I—'

'You blame yourself. But it wasn't your fault. Lisa died of a sudden embolism. Nothing could have predicted it or prevented it. And baby Alice? That precious little girl was just born too soon. You mustn't let the tragedy of their loss cut you off from happiness in your future.'

Declan shifted from foot to foot. 'It's not like that.' He had convinced Lisa to get pregnant when she'd wanted to wait and she'd died in childbirth. *His fault*.

'Isn't it?' His mother persevered, much as she must do in court. 'I know I didn't love you enough when you were that fiercely intelligent, questioning little boy who had his own agenda from the word go. I didn't know how to be a mother. I'm doing my best to make up for it. You need love more *now* than you did when you were that little boy.'

He shook his head. 'I don't want to talk about this.'

'But you must,' she said. 'Don't close yourself off from the possibility of love. I saw how you looked at Shelley. I saw how she looked at you. You deserve love, no matter what you might think.'

Her voice caught in a tremor and he realised how difficult it was for his mother to be talking to him like this. He also saw how sincere she was.

'I'll take that on board,' he said, relenting.

'Whatever you might have thought in the past, whatever mistakes I've made, I'm on your side and I always will be. But I don't want to grow into one of those old women protecting her sad, middle-aged son who never got over his wife's loss. There's a beautiful young woman there who might help you move on. Shelley won't wait for ever, you know. Not a girl who looks like she does.'

'It's not just the way she looks,' he muttered. 'She's kind, honest, good. So much more than just beautiful.'

He decided to tell his mother about the new bed of roses Shelley had planted in honour of Lisa and Alice.

'What an incredibly sensitive and inspired thing to do.' His mother's voice was choked and she paused to wipe tears from her eyes. 'The tragedy of it comes rushing back. I wish they were both still with us. I loved Lisa like a daughter. But this Shelley, she's a rare one, Declan. Don't let her go. Trust me, it will be like another little death for you if you do.'

Declan thought about what she'd said long after his mother left to go home. All through the long, lonely evening as he worked on the background of the Estella portrait and waited for the sound of his car bringing Shelley back home.

# CHAPTER TWELVE

SHELLEY RECKONED SHE could have gone home from Lynne's party with the phone numbers of at least three good-looking, single—or so they said—eligible men. And that wasn't counting the television producer—she'd actually given him her number after ascertaining he was the real deal.

There was something to be said about a backless dress. Or maybe it was the reckless confidence that came from being so thoroughly kissed by the man she wanted before she'd sashayed on to the party. The power of pulling up to a party in a sports car probably did something to enhance her desirability to the male population, too.

But she didn't collect any phone numbers. There was only one man who interested her and she was on her way home to him. Well, not technically home to him. He lived in the mansion, she lived in the housekeeper's apartment and she'd be wise to remember that.

It was well past midnight when she pulled into the garage—the party was still in full swing but she'd only stayed as late as she did for Lynne's sake. Before she could think about texting Declan that she was back, the connecting door from the main house opened and he was there. He still wore the same jacket, but his hair was dishevelled as though he had been pushing through it with his fingers as she'd noticed he tended to do. Dark shadows under his eyes indicated he hadn't slept. His face wore an expression of strained expectancy. *Was that for her?*

A surge of desire for him swept through her so powerfully she had to remain seated in the driver's seat and grip the steering wheel so tightly her knuckles went white and press her knees together hard. Not just sexual desire—although there was certainly that in spades—but an intense yearning to be with him, to help ease his pain, to feel his arms around her, for him to be *hers*. Her heart seemed to physically turn over in her chest with longing for this darkly handsome man who had become so important, so quickly.

She took her time to gather her evening purse and shawl, slide out of the car, lock the door, to give herself a chance to collect her feelings before she faced him. Right now, a cheerful recounting of the assets of his superb car did not seem possible.

But words did not seem to be required as he strode towards her and opened his arms. 'You're home,' he said. She went into them with a great, choking sigh of relief and shut her eyes in bliss as they closed around her and enveloped her in his strength and warmth.

He held her tight, his chin resting on the top of her head. She could feel the rise and fall of his chest, the thud of his heartbeat, strong, steady, reassuring and she let herself relax against him.

For a long, enchanted moment she stood there like that, unaware of her surroundings, the concrete walls and floor of the garage, the other cars shrouded in grey covers, the intermittent *ping-ping-ping* sounds the sports car made as its engine cooled down. She was aware only of Declan—and the joy that flooded her heart at being so close to him, the certainty that this was where she was meant to be. *That everything that had come before in her life had led to this.*

'Declan,' she finally murmured, loving the sound of his name in her voice.

He pulled her even closer. She could feel the strength of his thighs, rock hard with muscle. 'I spent all evening wishing you were with me,' she murmured, then pulled back in his arms, needing to see his face.

His arms dropped from around her, leaving her bereft. Then he cupped her face in his large hands, hands she noticed were stained with traces of paint—blue, green, white all mixed in together—and smelled vaguely of turpentine. He caressed the little hollows in front of her ears—such a simple gesture yet it sent shivers of pleasure to her deepest core.

'I spent all evening regretting I wasn't,' he said hoarsely.

She met his gaze. 'I'm glad. I mean, I'm glad I'm not imagining this…this thing between us. These…these feelings.'

Declan groaned and her heart gave a painful lurch. *He was going to fight it all the way.* 'I…don't know what to do about…about you. I wasn't expecting, didn't—'

'Didn't *want*…' she supplied the words for him.

'That's right. I didn't want the life I'd made for myself disturbed. Then you burst into it, flooding light into the shadows in which I existed.'

She swallowed hard against a sudden lump of tension in her throat. *She didn't know how to reply.*

He looked deeper into her face. 'But eyes that have become accustomed to the dark can…can be dazzled by too much light too quickly. They blink and wonder what hit them.'

'Like a bat,' she said.

Shelley stilled, mortified. *Where had that idiotic comment come from?*

Declan stilled too. His eyes widened as he stared at her.

And then she realised he was shaking with laughter he was fighting a losing battle to suppress.

'I… I'm sorry,' she stuttered. 'I can't believe I just said that.'

'First a vampire, now a bat. You really do see me as a creature of darkness, don't you?'

He let go his laughter and she couldn't help but laugh alongside him though it felt forced. But when the laughter spluttered to a halt, stopped, she berated herself. 'Why do I say things like that? Why don't I think before I speak? I've been told often enough.'

'Because you're *you*, delightful and unique and I wouldn't have you any other way.'

She sniffed back threatening tears. 'Really?' A niggling voice deep down inside her prodded her—was that ill-timed comment her way of deflecting emotional confrontations she wasn't at all sure she was equipped to handle?

'Yes,' he said. 'Really. I've laughed more since I've known you than I have since…since heaven knows when.' He sobered. 'Don't change—promise me?'

She nodded. 'I… I promise.'

'Now how about we go inside out of this chilly garage?' he said.

'Yes,' she said. She went to add: *It's hardly the most romantic place on earth* but bit down on the words. There had been no mention of *romance* between them.

He put his arm around her shoulder and steered her towards the door. 'You can think of some other dark creatures to compare me to. Maybe something that lives under a rock.'

Of course she took him literally and started to think of actual creatures that lived under rocks before she realised that was not what was required. 'Not for one second will I compare you to a centipede or a slug.'

'And I so appreciate that,' he said. 'Vampires and bats have a certain black glamour that slugs definitely do not.'

They laughed again as he walked her, with his arm still around her shoulders, into the house. Lights switched on automatically ahead of them but she immediately felt oppressed by the stillness, the vague mustiness of unlived-in rooms. She wanted to extend her time with him this evening but not here, not in this place so marked by tragedy and loss and dreams unfulfilled.

'Did you…are you going to bed now?' she asked, immediately wishing she'd said *sleep* and not *bed* with all its unspoken connotations.

'No. You?' He tightened his grip on her shoulder.

She shook her head. 'I'm still way too wired up from the party. Can I…can I interest you in a herbal tea or coffee—I don't drink coffee at night but you might want coffee—and perhaps a muffin? I baked banana muffins the other day and have them in the freezer. I just have to heat—'

Those dark brows drew together. 'Did you say banana muffins?'

She nodded, wishing now she hadn't brought up the subject. Not when she never wanted to admit how she had snuck into his house in her pyjamas and spied on him as he'd worked out.

'Strange, that,' he said. 'I thought I could smell banana muffins in my kitchen. That inter-connecting door is meant to be odour, sound and light-proof.'

She froze. 'Maybe…maybe you'd better get the door checked—the seals might need attention,' she finally managed to get out.

'I will,' he said.

'Let's go through,' she said.

'I don't have a key. The apartment is your private place.'

She'd wondered if he'd maintained access to the apartment, was glad that he hadn't.

'I... I have the key on the key ring in my purse,' she said.

The apartment seemed a sanctuary but somehow smaller with Declan's tall, broad-shouldered presence taking up so much room. She stood near him in the living room, suddenly very conscious that they were alone in complete privacy.

*A meaningless fling.* The words echoed through her head and her body tingled in all sorts of places at the thought of what that might entail. He hadn't offered one, why shouldn't she?

Not *meaningless* but *without commitment*—commitment she very much doubted Declan was prepared to make, despite the kind words he'd said about her lighting his darkness. *She wanted him so much.*

She turned to face him, thrilled to the desire for her she saw smouldering in his eyes. Her shawl was long gone and she knew from all the compliments she'd fielded at the party that she quite possibly looked the best she ever had in the blue dress.

But she'd been the one to deny the possibility of a fling. She would have to be the one to suggest it. She took the few steps needed to close the distance between them. She wound her arms around his neck, drew his face close and kissed him, her lips parted in a sensual invitation he accepted with a hard, hungry possession.

Pleasure and anticipation throbbed through her as she welcomed his mouth, his tongue, his passion. His hands slid around to her back, hard and exciting on her bare skin. She slid her hands from his neck so she could push off his jacket, tug his T-shirt from his belt with impatient fingers, splay her hands flat against the warm, solid muscle of his chest, feel the rapid thudding of his heart.

Her breath was coming in short, ragged gasps echoed by his. She wanted him so badly it was an ache. Every physical instinct she had screamed at her to proceed. To let Declan caress her—and her caress him back. To rid themselves of their clothes. To stagger into the bedroom locked in each other's arms and fall together on the bed. To bring each other's body to the peaks of ultimate pleasure.

But her instincts for common sense, for self-preservation, overrode them and begged her to stop this before it went any further. It was too soon—not just for her but for him.

She'd never been one for sex without emotion, without love. And she sensed that would never develop if the physical took over while the emotional lagged so far behind. Oh, but she wanted him so much she burned with it.

But as his hand grazed the side of her breasts, as her nipples tightened to hard points and hunger for him throbbed through her body she knew she couldn't go through with a fling of any kind. That way lay certain heartbreak and she should have realised it before it got this far.

*Meaningless would never be for her, no matter how you masked it.*

She broke away from the kiss, panting. It was an effort to speak. 'Declan. No. I mean… I mean… I mean stop.' *That sounded like such a cliché.* 'I don't want you to think I'm a…a tease but I can't go further than this. I thought I could. I want you. Want you more than I could ever have imagined but—'

He pulled away immediately, his breathing ragged and harsh. 'But you're not ready.'

She struggled for the right words. 'Are you? I would make love with you in a heartbeat but I don't think either of us is ready for that…that complication. Not now. Not yet. Some time I hope if you…when we…' She did not want him to think she was assuming they would work towards being a couple—though there was nothing she wanted more.

He paced the width of the room and she could see it was an effort for him to restore his equilibrium. 'You're right. It's too soon. I'm only just getting used to the thought of another woman—you—in my life. I don't want to hurt you.'

He took the few strides necessary to bring him back to her. Then groaned in a wrenching anguish of frustration that called to her too and planted a hard, hungry kiss on her mouth. 'But be in no doubt how much I want you. How difficult it is for me to stop.'

This was a man who knew how to love. She was prepared to wait until he felt able to love again. No matter how long that took.

She stepped back before her resolve broke and she flung herself at him and begged him for anything he was prepared to give. Another deep breath restored the beating of her heart to something less erratic.

'How...how about that muffin?' she asked, desperate to change the subject.

'Satisfy a different kind of hunger, you mean,' he said with a wry twist of that mouth she wanted so much to kiss and kiss and kiss again.

'That's one way of putting it,' she said.

Declan watched Shelley move around the small kitchen with the same efficiency of movement she gave to her work. A warrior who could cook—and cook well. She'd put the frozen muffin in the microwave and a delicious—and familiar—aroma was wafting its way to his nose. He was hungry. All his appetites had diminished in the intensity of his grief after Lisa died. But Shelley had awoken them and they came raging back. Especially his hunger for her.

She'd kicked off her shoes before she went into the kitchen. But she still wore that tantalising blue dress. He had to stop fantasising about stripping it off her, of releasing those chains that were all that held it together. She was wearing panties under the dress, he'd ascertained that in his first explorations. But no bra. Unhook that chain and the dress would fall to the floor leaving her in just panties and her silver stilettos—and then not even them.

He forced himself to think thoughts other than of undressing Shelley and carrying her into the bedroom. He leaned against the countertop.

'Tell me about the party,' he said, though he had no real interest in it. She'd come home to him and that was all that counted.

'I met a television producer. A friend of a friend of Keith's. He was really nice.'

Jealousy speared him. 'I'll bet he was.' What male wouldn't be nice to Shelley in that dress?

'Not in that way,' she said, shaking her head. 'He was there with his wife, and she was really interesting too. He produces a lifestyle show for one of the cable channels. As soon as he heard what I did he asked me would I be interested in being their gardening presenter. They want gardening to be seen as younger and…and sexier.'

Declan couldn't help his growl of possessive jealousy. 'What do you mean "sexier"?'

'Not me. Well, yes, maybe me, in that I'm young and female compared to the older guy they already have who is retiring, but they want to appeal to younger viewers who might think of gardening as something for their grandparents. He said he was excited about me because I was… well…attractive but also authoritative and knew my stuff.'

The growl subsided. 'Fair enough.'

'I was really flattered that he was interested in me.'

'Of course he'd be interested in you. Why wouldn't he? He must have thought all his Christmases had come at once. What did you say to him?'

'I told him about my plans to go visit the gardens in Europe.'

'So you'd put those plans on hold if you were to take him up on the offer?' Which would give him more time with her.

'I'd have to audition first before there would even be an offer,' she said.

'You'd be a natural for it,' he said.

'That's what he said,' she said with a delighted smile. 'He also said they could work around my travel plans if need be, that I can pre-record a series of segments filmed at those famous gardens. It would be like bringing them into the viewers' homes.'

'You obviously like the idea,' he said, knowing he sounded stilted but unable to do anything about it. She would leave here no matter what he did and he couldn't stop her. Not until he had something to offer her.

'I do,' she said. 'Gardening is really hard physical work. I don't know that I could do it for ever. This could be a really wonderful opportunity to still do what I love but in a different way.'

'It's certainly worth considering,' he said. Anything that might delay her departure would be worth considering.

He helped her to carry the chamomile tea and plate of muffins to the coffee table. Then sat down beside her. She kept a polite distance away from him but he pulled her close and she snuggled in next to him with a contented little sigh that pleased him inordinately.

'Aren't you going to have a muffin?' he asked as she sipped her tea. 'Mine is absolutely delicious.'

She shook her head. 'Too tired to eat,' she said. 'The

muffins are for you and I'm glad you like them. I thought you might.'

The muffins were everything he'd hoped his ill-fated muffin delivery would have been, and more.

She put down the pretty old-fashioned teacup that he doubted was part of the apartment's inventory. 'I'm even too tired to drink the tea—which is fine as it's meant to help you sleep and I don't think I need any help. I was digging and moving shrubs all day and it's way past my bedtime. It's suddenly hit me.' She stifled a yawn with her hand.

He pulled her closer and she snuggled her head against his shoulder. He could not resist dropping a kiss on her hair, inhaling the fresh, sweet scent of her. It was intoxicating.

'Tell me more about what the television producer said,' he asked.

'Well, the studio is in Sydney but they shoot at gardens all around the country. The producer was really interested when he heard how familiar I was with Victoria. There are some really beautiful gardens in Victoria, South Australia too. I reckon some of my former clients would love to have their gardens showcased. Or just used as a location for me to demonstrate gardening techniques.' She yawned again and her body relaxed against his. 'People don't know... don't know...about pruning and...and stuff,' she murmured and her voice trailed into nothing. Her breathing became deep and even and he realised she had fallen asleep.

He held her there for a long time until he started to get sleepy too—blessedly sleepy. Carefully he shifted on the sofa, planning to slide off and help her lie down. 'No. Don't want you to go. Stay with me,' she whispered. He wasn't sure she was even awake. But he didn't want to leave her either.

Declan tried to get comfortable but both he and Shelley were tall and the sofa wasn't long enough. His leg started to cramp.

There was only one thing to do. He got up from the sofa, despite her sleepy protests, then swung her effortlessly into his arms and carried her through to the bedroom. He pulled back the quilt and laid her on the bed, her honey-blond hair spilling out over the pillow. She shifted and opened her eyes, though they were unfocused and again he wasn't really sure she was awake. She held out her arms. 'Stay with me. Please.'

He would stay just until she fell into a deep sleep—a luxury that had been denied him for too long.

Cautiously, he took off his shoes and lay down next to her. She immediately burrowed close, pressing the length of her body against his.

*I'm sorry, Lisa,* he said in his mind, feeling as if he was betraying her memory, but immediately had the feeling that she wouldn't mind at all, that Lisa was giving him her blessing.

He held Shelley close as he in turn drifted off to sleep.

Declan awoke to morning sunshine filtering through the blinds to find Shelley spooning into his back, one arm wrapped around his waist, the other resting above her head on her pillow.

He was aroused. How could he not be with her breasts pressing into his back, her long, slender legs entwined with his, her sweet womanly scent heady and exciting? He placed his hand on her bare shoulder and she murmured throatily in her sleep as she pressed herself even closer. But it would not be right to stroke her into arousal to wake her by—

He rolled onto his back, gently disengaging her arm. The sunlight picked up glints of gold in her hair and her make-up was smeared dark around her eyes. Her lips were slightly parted as she breathed deeply and steadily. He had never seen her look more beautiful.

It was the first deep, refreshing sleep he had enjoyed for two years. He felt deeply content and…he sought to describe the feeling that overwhelmed him as he lay there so intimately close to Shelley, but could only come up with *happy*.

# CHAPTER THIRTEEN

SHELLEY LOVED EVERYTHING about Declan's garden and was immensely proud of the restoration work she had done. Spring was taking over—the crab apple tree in a froth of delicate pink blossom, daffodils that had naturalised over many years coming up in golden drifts in the lawn, the scent of daphne replaced by that of old-fashioned white freesias.

The restored dry stonewalls and hedges delineated the concept of separate garden 'rooms' that made the space such a delight. She had even uncovered a small kitchen garden with an espaliered lemon tree growing flat against a wall, a rosemary hedge and herbs, including sage, tarragon plus three different varieties of thyme. She would plant annual herbs like basil and coriander if she thought anyone would use them in their one season of growth. Declan? He'd told her he rarely cooked but he might have use for fresh herbs. She must ask him.

In the front of the garden, the climbing rose 'Lamarque' was covered in hundreds of white buds ready to burst into glorious bloom—as she had promised Declan it would. Those higher rooms in his house must now be flooded with light and soon the delicate scent of the roses. *But would she be here to see it?*

The more she worked on the garden, the more she appreciated its design, and the work of the gardeners who had come before her. The original design certainly paid homage to Enid Wilson, which was perhaps one of the reasons she'd been so drawn to it.

But on Sunday morning—the day after Lynne's party—even though she wasn't officially working, she decided to spend the morning sorting out the shed.

It was a late start. She'd awoken to the surprise of finding Declan in her bed. Well, technically *on* her bed and fully clothed—as she was too. She'd only vaguely remembered him carrying her into the bedroom the night before. He'd stayed while she'd cooked him breakfast then he'd gone back to his part of the house.

But before he'd gone he'd kissed her and said he would catch up with her later in the day. She'd been itching to ask *when* but had resisted. Declan was coming from a dark place—if anything important was going to develop between them, it wouldn't be overnight. Hope, like the spring garden, had blossomed in her heart.

She'd rebelled at wearing her gardening uniform on a Sunday. After all, it was officially her day off and she was going to fit in a ride with Flynn if she could. And, yes, if she *was* going to catch up with Declan she'd rather be seen in something other than khaki.

She didn't want to look too eager, either, so compromised with slim-legged blue jeans and a shirt with fine stripes of blue and lavender. Eye make-up and lipstick for working in the shed? Why not? With her hair in a long plait down her back instead of jammed up under a hat. And her favourite French rose perfume liberally sprayed on her pulse spots.

Over the last weeks she'd managed to get some semblance of order into the shed and turned it into a useful workshop. She'd sorted out many of the wonderful old tools and garden implements. Having a wide, clear workbench made it easier to strike cuttings, plant seeds in trays, change the soil and trim the roots of potted plants and was especially useful in wet weather. But there was a large, weatherproof metal chest she hadn't yet tackled.

Wearing her sturdy gloves, she'd brushed off the dust and cobwebs from the chest and was just about to force open the rusted lid when she heard the door opening. She turned and her heart leapt in delight to see Declan. He came over and dropped a kiss on her mouth. 'I've come down to give you a hand,' he said.

Shelley was stunned. Never had she expected that Declan would help her in the garden, the billionaire descending from his tower. 'Thank you,' she said. She hadn't expected the kiss either; casual as it had been, it was a real turning point.

He was wearing jeans and a faded grey T-shirt with sleeves that rolled up to his biceps and showed off his impressive pecs and broad shoulders. She wondered if he had left her after breakfast to do one of his gruelling workouts. He had not shaved and she decided she liked the dark stubble on his jaw, the graze of it on her skin.

'What can I do to help?' he asked.

'I'll think of something,' she said.

Shelley could think of a number of things she would like to direct Declan to do. None of them had anything to do with gardening. Just looking at him brought a flush of desire.

But she hadn't changed her mind since the previous night. When she'd woken up next to Declan, she had been relieved they hadn't made love. It took the pressure off getting to know each other, to take small steps instead of leaping in head first. To be certain.

'What's in the chest?' he asked. It still bemused her that he owned this wonderful garden and yet knew so very little—and cared even less—about the treasures it contained.

'I have no idea,' she said. 'If I can get the lid off we'll find out.'

'Let me do that,' he said. With one firm wrench he had the lid up.

They were met with the musty scent of old paper. She peered into the depths of the chest. There was a number of what looked like old diaries and a bundle of papers wrapped in oilskin and tied firmly with sturdy string.

She didn't need Declan's warning to watch out for spiders. Tentatively she reached into the chest and pulled out two of the diaries, flipped through their pages. 'They're garden diaries,' she said, unable to keep the excitement from her voice. 'Can you get the rest, please?'

Declan pulled out all the diaries and put them on the desk. It only took him a few minutes to stack them in chronological order. 'They date right back to pre-World War Two,' he said.

She picked one up randomly and flicked through the pages. Then another. And another. 'This is gardener's gold,' she said. 'Daphne and before that her mother, Lily, kept meticulous dairies about their work in the garden. What they planted, what worked, what didn't. When the first tomatoes ripened. When they sprayed for bugs. How they dealt with water restrictions in times of drought.'

She turned to Declan. 'It's the history of your garden. One of the grand old gardens of Sydney. A hidden gem.'

'That's quite a find,' he said.

'Aren't you just the littlest bit excited?' she asked.

'Why would I be?' he said. 'But I'm glad you're excited.'

'Of course I'm thrilled,' she said. 'I can't wait to read through them all.'

'Remember, it was Lisa's garden not...not mine. She... she would have been excited.'

Shelley gripped the edge of the diary in her hand. *Lisa.* Lucky Lisa in one way as she had had Declan's love, yet so very tragic that she had died so young in such sad circumstances. Yes, Lisa probably would have been excited to find the diaries. If things had been different she and Lisa might have been working together on the restoration of this garden with doting husband Declan occasionally dropping by to check on the progress of his wife's project. Vivacious Lisa, remembered now in the garden with a planting of roses that would every year in late spring be a blaze of vibrant colour.

But Lisa was gone and, no matter how he grieved, Declan could not bring her back. Shelley as a gardener knew only too well about the cycle of death and renewal of life. The shrivelled autumn leaves making way for the fresh green shoots of spring. The perennial plants that died right down in winter only to shoot gloriously to life when the days got longer. The caterpillars she let chew holes on some of the leaves so they survived to transform into butterflies. All around her in this garden she was witnessing that everyday miracle.

From what she had heard about Lisa, she doubted she would have wanted her husband to spend the rest of his years alone, to live a shadowy half life with a shrivelled husk of a heart.

Shelley made a silent vow to the dead woman: if she had the chance she would rescue Declan from his blighted life, make him happy and— She fought against using the word *love*. Not now. Not yet. She had jumped too soon into *love* before and suffered heartbreak. But if she were granted a future with Declan, she would allow herself to love him and cherish him. *He'll be in good hands, Lisa.*

But if she and Declan had any chance of that future together she had to ask. 'Declan, why do you blame yourself for Lisa's death?'

The colour drained from his face, leaving it as grey as his T-shirt. 'Because I should have got her to the hospital quicker. The doctors said it wouldn't have made any difference but I've asked myself over and over if those ten minutes I took to complete my work might have made a difference. I let my work come before her.'

'Wh… What exactly happened? I know you said she… she died in childbirth but…how exactly?'

She had never seen him look so bleak and drawn. 'The baby was premature but that apparently wasn't what caused it.'

He paused and she waited to let him gather his thoughts, stomping down on her usual urge to fill a blank silence.

'Tiny Alice had to be put on a ventilator—her lungs weren't properly developed. I went with the doctors to see what was happening. But while I was in the neonatal intensive care unit with her one of the other doctors came to find me. Lisa had complained of feeling faint. They were concerned. By the time I got back to her bed she… she'd slipped away.'

Shelley closed her eyes. She wished she hadn't asked. Could scarcely comprehend his anguish and pain. But she had to know.

'How? Why?'

'An embolism. A blood clot. It lodged in her heart. There was nothing the doctors could do. There was no warning.'

She put her hand on his arm. 'Declan, I am so, so sorry. Thank you for telling me. It…it helps me to understand you better.'

'I wish I could understand it better myself,' he said savagely, his mouth a bitter twist.

She had to tread lightly. 'But seems to me that there can be absolutely no blame attached to you.'

'So they told me. But I *should* have been able to stop it.'

'How? If a team of highly trained doctors couldn't have saved her and your baby, how could you have?'

'I know all that,' he said. 'But I... I... Lisa wanted to wait a few more years. If I hadn't cajoled her into starting a family earlier it...it wouldn't have happened.'

'How can you say that? Something else might have taken her. An accident. Disease. Anything. It was out of your hands.'

In response he made some inarticulate sound that speared her heart.

A millionaire at age eighteen. A billionaire in his twenties. Here was a brilliant man used to making things happen his way. Yet he had not been able to save his little family. And had turned it all back on himself.

Was Declan really ready to move forward? Would he *ever* be ready? And did she have the strength to be the one to help him? To keep on shining her light—as he put it—into the shadowy recesses of his soul?

*She would darn well try.*

She put her arms around him and was mightily relieved he didn't push her away.

'It's dusty in here,' she said. 'Let's go outside. Maybe I can make you a coffee.'

His face was set like granite. 'I don't need to be babied, Shelley. I've been living with this for two years. I can deal with it.'

*Yes—if locking yourself away from the rest of the world meant dealing with it.*

'If you're sure you're not letting misplaced guilt—'

'Maybe I am.' He looked deep into her face. To her relief there was a softening of his features, a dawning warmth in his eyes. 'But…but for the first time I'm beginning to believe I can forgive myself. You. My mother. You're helping.'

'And you're letting yourself be helped. That's the first step.'

'But I have to do it at my pace. I don't want to talk about it any more. Not now. Not ever.'

Shelley shook her head so vehemently her plait flew around to the front. 'There you go, being so black and white about it. You *can* talk about it. You *should* talk about it. And when you're ready I'm here to listen.'

She held out her arms to him and he came to her, holding her close against the solid wall of muscle that was his chest. She felt him take a deep, shuddering breath. 'Thank you, Shelley. I'm glad you're here,' he said simply.

Her heart soared at this first recognition of her place in his life. 'I'm happy to be here for you.'

They stood like that for a long time until Shelley pulled away. She looked up at him. 'I'm not going to talk about bats or vampires, I promise.'

He smiled. 'I don't mind them. It's the slugs I don't like being compared to.'

'And rightly so,' she said. 'It's plants I'm thinking about—plants that thrive in the shade. If you dig them up and plunk them straight away into the bright sunlight they shrivel up and die. Moving them from the shadow to sun is a gradual process. It might be the same with you—too much light too soon might mean—'

He tilted her chin so she looked straight up into his face 'If you're the light, Shelley, I don't think I could have too much of you,' he said.

She met his gaze for a long moment as the import of

his words ticked through her. 'That…that's good,' she stuttered. 'You don't mind being compared to a plant? I'm talking plants that can live indoors like *hosta* and *spathiphyllum* and—'

There she went, deflecting anything emotional when it came to her. *Why did she do this?*

'Baffling me with Latin again,' he said.

'You might know a *spathiphyllum* as a peace lily. At least I'm not comparing you to mushrooms,' she said. 'They love living in the dark and they feed on sh— Well, they feed on manure.'

Declan laughed and she loved the sound of his rare laughter. 'I'll add mushroom to the list of my attributes,' he said in a voice choked with mirth. Then he sobered. 'You really are adorable, Shelley. Don't change.'

She looked up at him. 'Just be honest with me, Declan, that's all I ask. I… I so want to be the light in your life.'

He pulled her to him and kissed her. For a long time they kissed in the filtered sunlight coming through the dusty windows of the old shed. Kissing, touching, exploring.

The pile of papers wrapped in oilskin would have to wait.

Nothing was more important than this.

# CHAPTER FOURTEEN

A WEEK LATER, Shelley stood in the spring sunshine in front of the fountain, tapping her foot impatiently. She could hardly wait to tell Declan the news that was consuming her but he was taking his time coming downstairs to the garden.

*Deep breaths, Shelley, deep breaths,* she told herself. She concentrated on the soothing splash of the water falling down the three tiers of the fountain, admired her plantings of purple and yellow Louisiana iris unfurling into bloom. The goldfish had doubled in size since she'd set them free into the waters of the pond, adding welcome flashes of gold as they flitted in and out of the plants. There were plenty of places for them to hide from interested kookaburras and other fisher birds.

She was struck by a sudden flash of déjà vu. Hadn't she stood at the site of the derelict fountain and imagined just this scene—right down to the goldfish?

Back then she couldn't have predicted how important this place would become to her. Most of all she could never have imagined how close she would become to Declan. Then Mr Tall, Dark and Grumpy, now…well, now he was everything she could ever want in a man.

The last week had been an accelerated getting-to-know-you process. She'd gone from teetering on the edge of falling in love with Declan to preparing to dive on in head first.

*He got her.* He accepted her for the way she was, didn't just put up with her foibles but actually seemed to like them. She could relax and be herself around him as she'd never been able to before. It was an exhilarating feeling.

She was ready to take the next step. Tonight she was cooking him dinner at the apartment. Sex would change the dynamic between them but it was getting more and more difficult to stop at kisses—for both of them. But she judged she was ready for that change—and she suspected he felt the same.

Then she saw him, heading towards her with the smile that seemed to have replaced his perpetual scowl. *Because of her.* She had made the difference—she made him smile with her encouragement, her support, her not-going-to-call-it-that-yet love. Oh, and the gaffes and blunders she still made in spite of her best efforts. But they made him laugh.

'You in a pink dress, the fountain, the flowers—I wish I had my camera on me,' he said. 'You make a beautiful picture.'

She was still getting used to this Declan, still surprised at the man who was revealing himself by gradually peeling off layer by protective layer. 'Thank you,' she said.

He swooped her into his arms and spun her around. 'So what's the big excitement that couldn't wait?'

Declan wished he could pause that moment of Shelley standing in front of the fountain with a look of anticipation on her face as she'd lifted her head from something she was examining in the fountain to see him. Not just anticipation. Affection too. *For him.* She was giving him the second chance he'd thought he hadn't deserved.

He wanted to paint her like this. Not Estella. *Shelley.* Not a mythical warrior woman created from his own imagination but the real woman whose warm heart and generosity of spirit were slowly thawing his own frozen emotions.

He swooped her, laughing, back to earth, set her on her feet and waited for her reply.

Her eyes were wide and sparkling. 'First I went to see the television producer and he's very interested in progressing the presenter role with me.'

'That *is* good news,' he said. 'Well done.' He hoped she would get the job. And that it would keep her here in Sydney.

She pulled out a large envelope from her tote bag. 'But the mind-blowing news is this,' she said. 'Though of course you might not find it as mind-blowing as I did. After all, I know you—'

'Get on with it,' he said with a smile that he knew she would see as indulgent. The day Shelley didn't rabbit on was the day he'd be concerned.

'Do you remember when we opened the old chest in the shed last week and found the diaries?'

'Of course.' How could he forget that time with her in that darned shed she liked so much? Although it was memories of her in his arms that came to mind rather than the set of old notebooks that had caused her such pleasure.

'I went back into the shed the next day to look at that bundle of papers that were wrapped in the oilskin.'

'I remember them,' he said. He'd been thankful she'd forgotten them and he could keep on kissing her. If there'd been somewhere more comfortable in that shed than a wooden work bench there might have been a whole lot more than kissing going on in there.

Shelley tapped the envelope. 'These are those papers.' Reverently, she pulled out a sheaf of the old documents, yellowed and faded around the edges, and pointed to the hand-drawn illustrations. 'These are original plans by Enid

Wilson for this garden. Look, there's the fountain, the walls, everything. Can you believe it?'

Declan took the plans from her hands, held them up to the light, looked at them critically. 'The plans certainly look like this garden. They're beautifully rendered in watercolour.' His grandmother's favourite medium had been watercolour. 'These are good. Very good,' he said, judging them as paintings rather than horticultural plans.

'Of course they are. Enid Wilson was an artist. Her plans were works of art and so were her gardens.' Her voice rose with her excitement. 'Your garden wasn't just inspired by her designs, it was actually designed by her.'

She waved her hand to encompass the garden. 'This is an undiscovered Enid Wilson garden.'

She seemed disappointed that he didn't pick up on her excitement. He'd told her often enough he had no real interest in gardening—the interest for him in this garden was her. 'Well, that's great,' he said, forcing interest into his voice for her sake.

She smiled. 'I get that you don't see what I see in these amazing plans.'

'Tell me what you see,' he said, prepared to stand back and listen to her enthusiastic explanation.

'As I uncovered the garden I had my suspicions. It seemed such a fabulously good imitation of a Wilson garden. There are later additions, of course, like those dreaded *ficus benjamina*. But more and more I came to think it had all the hallmarks of her designs.'

Declan frowned. 'Why is it such a big deal?'

'Most of Enid Wilson's gardens were in Victoria. She designed some gardens in this state but to my knowledge they were all rural. I didn't know if there were any city gardens in Sydney. That's one reason I didn't take my hunch too seriously. It seemed unlikely and there was no proof.' She flourished the plans. 'These are proof. It's the most amazing discovery. *My* discovery.' Her eyes shone.

He frowned. 'How can you be sure? Couldn't the plans be imitations too?'

'That's what I thought. That's why I didn't tell you until I could get an expert to look at them for me and confirm their authenticity. I scanned the plans and sent them to one of my professors in Melbourne.'

'You *what*?'

'Yes, wasn't it fortunate he was available? He's validated them as genuine. He's excited too. I hope he can get up here and see the garden for himself. I didn't say anything to the television producer, of course, but wouldn't it be the most amazing story? To reveal this hidden masterpiece?'

She kept on and on and didn't seem to realise that his enthusiasm had dwindled to zero. In fact he was furious.

'No,' he said.

She pulled up, stared at him, obviously shocked at his abrupt tone.

'What do you mean "no"?'

'There will be no visiting professors. Or any other experts. And certainly no television people.'

He felt as if he were under attack. And she—the woman he had grown to trust—was the one who'd punched a hole in the barricades to allow access to the invaders of his privacy. For so long this house had been his refuge and his haven. He would not tolerate people tramping around the place, investigating, reporting, no doubt expecting interaction from him. He wouldn't allow it. He *couldn't* allow it. *How did Shelley not get that?*

'But, Declan, this is such a find. People will be so excited about this discovery. Personally, it's so important to me, important to my career.'

He kept hold of the papers. 'These plans belong to me. You had no right to take them out of this house. To show them to other people. To invite so-called experts onto my property without my permission.'

He hated the way her face crumpled at the harshness of his words. 'I didn't realise. I honestly thought you'd be pleased,' she said.

Her mouth twisted in a cynical way he hadn't seen before and certainly didn't like. 'Your neighbours will be pleased. A heritage garden like this will add value to the street.'

'I don't give a damn about my neighbours. You should know that by now.'

Her eyes flashed. 'What do you give a damn about, Declan? Certainly not me. You won't even consider what this could mean to my career.'

'Give me the rest of the papers,' he said, reaching out for the envelope. Reluctantly, she handed them to him.

One part of him wanted to climb down. To compromise. To say she could be recognised as having discovered the lost garden. To possibly invite her professor for a private visit just the one time.

But that would be opening the floodgates. And he wasn't ready for that. Not by a long shot.

'Don't discuss this with me again,' he said over his shoulder as he strode back to the house.

Still shaking from Declan's abrupt change of mood, Shelley walked around the garden to calm herself down, to let the tranquillity of this beautiful place soothe her and work the kind of magic only nature could.

He was right; she'd overstepped the mark. How could she have let her enthusiasm for her discovery override her caution in dealing with Declan?

When it came to emerging from the shadows of his isolation she'd decided he needed to walk before he could run. So she'd darn well dug in the spurs and tried to force him to gallop.

He was still too damaged to face public scrutiny of any kind—especially on his own turf. Why hadn't she seen how far from ready he was to let down his guard and face the world? Instead she had just gone blundering in there, as was her way.

She sighed out loud, knowing there was no one to hear her. *Was Declan too much for her to manage?*

Her walk around the garden brought her back to the fountain. She thought about how hopeless a project it had seemed at the beginning, all damaged and dirty, unable to fulfil its function as a garden ornament, let alone a working water feature. Even she had quailed at the difficulty of restoring it. Had considered just pulling it down and filling in the pond. But she'd persevered—helped, of course, by Declan's generous budget—and look at it now.

Declan was still broken. But she was prepared to work with him. These last weeks she'd been given glimpses of the extraordinary man he had been—could be again. *And beyond all reason she wanted him.*

No matter how angry he was with her, she intended to hang around. It would take time, more time than she might have imagined. But she could postpone her trip to Europe. When this garden was complete, she could find another job in Sydney. Her old employer had said he would welcome her back. And then there was the television opportunity. Declan might be convinced to let her remain in the apartment. She would be there for him. For however long it took.

*He was worth it.*

Her gaze went automatically up to the top-storey window where he worked. She could text him now and ask him to come down to her again. So she could apologise. Explain. State her case. *Let him know how much she cared.*

But no.

She had her key that opened the door into the kitchen of his house. She would not give him a chance to think up excuses to put up his barriers against her again.

She would brave him in his house. Surprise him. Tell him exactly how she felt. Even if the thought terrified her.

# CHAPTER FIFTEEN

SHELLEY'S HEART WAS pounding so hard she imagined Declan could hear it—even from two floors above her. She tiptoed down his hallway in stockinged feet, holding in one hand the metallic pumps she'd worn with her pink dress to the interview with the television producer.

She paused before the elevator, decided against it. Too uncertain. What if she got trapped in it? It would have to be the stairs.

Cautiously she made her way up the flight of marble stairs with its ornate iron balustrades, past the silent floor of doors closed on what she assumed were bedrooms and bathrooms. Sad, unlived-in rooms.

She paused at the next landing to look out of the lead-light window at the view of the garden laid out below. All the structures perfectly matched the plan. The design was classic Enid Wilson—how could she have ever doubted it? But her discovery would remain private—she had to respect Declan's wishes on that. Much as she wanted—deserved—the recognition.

The top floor had another smaller flight of stairs she assumed led to the turret. The rest of the floor might have been servants' quarters in the days when a grand house like this would have employed them.

Now dividing walls had been pulled down and it had been modernised into a sophisticated living space furnished in tones of grey and black leather. Declan's domain. Beyond the living room was a door she could only assume was his office and others led to a small kitchen and a bathroom. Framed black-and-white photos of an attractive young woman with a cap of dark hair, a small, sharp face and a huge smile lined the walls. *Lisa.*

As she knocked on the door to Declan's office Shelley realised her hands were trembling. He had been so angry, so dark—as black in his mood as the storm clouds that gathered over Sydney before a violent summer storm.

Yes, she was a little afraid. Afraid of the man she was falling in love with. Afraid of the man she had planned to seduce this evening. No. Not *afraid.* Not in a million years would Declan hurt her. She was *nervous.* Nervous of his reaction when he realised she had broken her promise to him and invaded his sacrosanct, private space.

There was no reply to her knock. But she was convinced he was in there. An earlier quick glance through the window to his basement gym had shown it to be empty.

She turned the handle of the door and pushed it open.

Declan sat intently in front of an enormous computer screen, a black headset over his head covered his ears. He wore large black-framed glasses. They were hot—made him appear even more attractive to her. But they also made him look like a stranger.

*This was a bad, bad idea.*

She turned to leave, to scurry back down those stairs as fast as she could. But her movement must have caught Declan's eye. He turned. For a long moment their eyes met—his dark and shuttered, hers no doubt wide with terror.

'Shelley, what the hell?'

He took off his headset and his glasses. But even then he looked dark and forbidding.

'I'm sorry. I didn't mean to intrude on you in your... your bat cave.'

He frowned. 'My bat cave?'

She looked around her at the banks of computers and high-tech equipment. 'It does look like a bat cave—a movie–super-hero bat cave, not a real bat cave. If it was a real bat cave it would be dirty and smelly and...' Her words dwindled to a halt. She turned again. 'I'm sorry. I'm going.'

Declan leapt up from his chair. 'Shelley. Don't go. Don't apologise. I'm the one who should be apologising for the way I behaved down there. I—'

When he said 'down there' her eyes went automatically to the window, which looked over the fountain and the sweep of the back garden. There was a large artist's easel standing there, poised to catch the light, and a drawing board with a series of charcoal drawings clipped to it.

She took a step further towards the windows and she dropped her shoes with a clatter. Her hand went to her mouth but that didn't stop her gasp. 'What's this?' she said. 'Who is this?' Her heart thumped even harder and her mouth went dry.

'It's—'

She stepped closer. 'It's *me*. Paintings of me. Drawings of me. What does this mean?'

In the large canvas on the easel she rode bareback astride a white unicorn. She wore something so skin-tight it was practically nothing, and long green boots with her hair flying behind her like a banner against a background of a forest. The painting was magnificent. Breathtaking. But she felt...violated.

She turned to the drawing board. The sketches were of her too. Declan was talented; she recognised that through her shock. Just a few lines and some shading brought to life the curve of her jaw, the sweep of her hair and an action series where she was lassoing something outside the image.

'It's not you, Shelley,' he said. 'It's…it's Estella.'

'Estella? Who the heck is Estella? The only Estella I know is the character in *Great Expectations*. Is that the link? Miss Havisham. This creepy house.'

'Princess Estella is a character for a computer game.'

'*Princess* Estella? So where do I come in?'

'You're…you're my muse. My inspiration for a beautiful, kick-ass warrior princess.' He closed his eyes, shook his head from side to side in a gesture of deep regret. When he opened his eyes again it was to look deep into her face. 'I should have told you. Wanted to tell you.'

She looked to the screen where an animated character—who didn't look as much like her as the painting did—was on her unicorn and fighting an army of some kind of mutant creatures.

She turned on Declan. 'You were *using* me. So that's why you…you made friends with me. Why you…why you let me think we could be more than friends?'

She had to swallow down hard on a sickening sense of betrayal that made her want to double over. *Thank heaven she hadn't slept with him.* Having shared the intimacies of love with him would only have intensified his treachery.

He took her arm but she shook him off, unable to bear the touch of this man who was suddenly again a stranger. She had trusted him to be honest and straightforward with her but he'd thrown her back deep into that dark pit of distrust as brutally as the other men who had hurt her.

'Not true, Shelley,' he said. 'I couldn't let myself near you—though I realise now I wanted you from the get go. Maybe…maybe that's why I created Princess Estella. As a device to keep you at a distance.'

Bitterness and disappointment made it difficult for her

to speak and she had to choke out the words. 'You mean so you could make even more millions.'

His face contorted in anguish. 'No. You can't believe that.'

She didn't care if her words hurt him. 'Why not? Was this why you hired me? To…to use my image behind my back? Not for the garden at all.'

Now she began to doubt the veracity of everything he'd told her. He had lied and misrepresented himself the way Steve had told her he was single, the way her father had denied his mistress was anything more than a work colleague. She had thought Declan was different. *She had believed in him.*

'Was there really a complaining neighbour? Or did you invent all that to observe me for that…for *her*?' She pointed at the painting with a finger that wavered and trembled despite her best efforts to make a dramatic gesture.

'No,' Declan exploded. 'The neighbours' complaints were only too real. I needed you to do the garden. But unwittingly you unlocked my creativity. *Just by being you.* Your strength, your beauty, like a modern-day warrior. You inspired me like nothing or no one ever had.'

His blue eyes blazed with sincerity. She wanted to believe him. If she wasn't feeling so angry and betrayed she might even have felt flattered. But he should have told her all that long before this. Before her blundering into his bat cave had forced the issue. Had he ever intended to tell her? Or to just wave goodbye when the garden was finished?

'And yet you didn't say a word to me,' she said.

'You have to believe me, Shelley. I wanted to but…but I couldn't. I hadn't invented a game since…since…'

He didn't have to say the words. *Since two years ago.*

Would it always come back to that—the tragedy he could never put behind him?

Her shoulders sagged as she felt overwhelmed by the inevitability that she was fighting a battle she could never win—even if she were to be mounted on a unicorn and armed with a magic lasso.

He deserved a second chance at love and she yearned to give it to him. But she was ill-equipped to bring down the barriers he'd built around his heart to punish himself for the loss of his wife and baby.

She couldn't risk losing *her* heart in a futile battle for *his*.

She took in a deep breath and forced herself to speak normally—or as normally as could be expected under such circumstances. 'So if you haven't been inventing games, what's all this for? Why do you spend so much time up here all by yourself?' She spread out her arms to indicate the banks of equipment in the room.

It was obviously an effort for Declan to get his words out too. 'I haven't worked on commercial games until Estella. Instead I've worked on non-profit educational games to help train surgeons, to help save lives. There's also work for government defence departments on games that simulate terrorist attacks to help train the military.'

'Th... That's very noble of you.' She hadn't been expecting that. He was a good person—had proved himself to be kind and generous to her. Why couldn't he be good to himself?

'Not noble,' he said with that wry twist of his mouth. 'Trying to give back. To make amends.'

'To assuage the guilt you heaped upon yourself.' *For something that was not his fault.*

'Yes,' he said. 'But also because I have more money than I need and I want to contribute not just with dollars but also with my skills.'

'So what happens to Princess Estella?'

'She could be the next commercial big thing for me. Estella has a strong environmental focus, which is timely.'

Shelley shook her head. 'I don't get all this, though I like her green message and…and her green boots. But what I *do* get is I thought we had something special happening between us. I don't mind arriving second in your life after Lisa—she was your first love and I respect that. But I won't be *second best* for you. And I certainly won't compete with…with *her*—a cartoon character.' She couldn't help her voice from rising.

He looked as grim as she had seen him. 'I should have told you about Estella.'

'You're darn right you should have. I would have posed for you, you know. Not in that…that body stocking. But it could have been fun.' Her voice diminished to barely a whisper. 'Something for us to share.'

Those impossible hopes of a life with him had started to feel possible but now they slipped away like the water draining from the cracks in the old fountain.

'You still could,' he said, his voice low and urgent. 'We could develop Estella together.'

She shook her head. Her voice still came out as a half-choked whisper. 'Too late. Too late for you and me, Declan. I could never trust you again—and trust is vital to me. You were dishonest with me—from the word go, it appears.'

He groaned. 'Shelley, I—'

She spoke across him. 'I don't just mean about Estella. I guess she's the way you earn a buck—or two or a billion. You probably couldn't help yourself from…from using me.'

'You've got it so wrong,' he said through clenched teeth.

'I don't think so,' she said. 'What's worse is that you've been dishonest with yourself. You're not ready for me or for any other woman. You're lying to yourself if you think you are.' *And she couldn't deal with it.*

'That's not true,' he said, his face dark and contorted with anguish. 'I care for you, Shelley.' He took a step towards her, went to take her in his arms but she quickly sidestepped him. How could she bear to be close to him when she knew it would be for the last time? *She had to guard her heart.*

Slowly she shook her head. 'But not enough. Not enough to truly step out into the sunshine with me. You seem to need the shadows. I can't exist without the light.'

Her heart ached as though it were being torn in two, broken and bleeding. She took a final look around the grey room where this man she had come to care for so much had locked himself away and didn't seem to be able to free himself—despite her best efforts.

The warrior princess Estella would probably never give up on the battlefield. But she, Shelley Fairhill, humble gardener and heartbroken woman, conceded defeat.

She'd thought she could slash through the overgrown forest and scale the fortress Declan had erected around his heart but she'd scarcely breached the outer walls. To keep on fighting would be futile and only lead to further devastation.

With willpower she dragged from some deep, inner resource she refused to let tears fall, forced her voice to be firm. 'I'm going, Declan.'

He took a step towards her but she put up her hand in a wavering halt sign. 'Don't follow me. Please.'

She picked up her shoes. Somehow she stumbled down the two flights of stairs, holding on to the railings for support, and did not break down until she got to the privacy of the apartment.

Declan had a tormented, sleepless night high up in his solitary bedroom in the turret. Looking back at the way he had behaved since Shelley had come into his life, he realised he had made mistake upon mistake.

Especially the Estella thing. No wonder Shelley had found what had seemed like gross deception impossible to forgive.

In the grey light of early morning, he stumbled down the stairs to his studio and stood in front of the painting that had caused so much trouble. He picked up a palette knife intending to slash the canvas to shreds. But he couldn't do it. Estella had too much of Shelley in her. He could not hurt even her image. *Had never wanted to hurt her.*

How bitterly he regretted all the hours he'd spent up here creating Estella instead of spending more time with Shelley. His creation had become a barrier between him and the real woman he was falling for. Had the memory of Lisa become a barrier, too, long after he should have let his memories rest?

He hated to admit it, but his mother had been right. If he was to survive, it was time for him to move on. He would never forget Lisa or their baby. But Shelley had to come first now if he wanted a future with her. When she had told him he made her feel *second best* it was as if he'd been kicked in the gut. How could he have hurt her like that?

*He could not lose her from his life.*

He paced the floor of the studio, back and forth, back and forth, raking his hair with his fingers, working through possible solutions. Shelley was right. He didn't know how to get out from under the shadow that was blighting his life.

Professional help. It was an avenue he hadn't tried. He burrowed in his desk drawer for the card with the name of the counsellor his mother had suggested he see after Lisa's death. He hated the idea of revealing himself to a stranger.

But if he wanted Shelley it would have to be done. *And he would have to finally leave this house to find that help.*

He had to make amends to Shelley. Tell her what she'd come to mean to him. Seek her out in her apartment. Admit she was right, he couldn't climb out of the shadows on his own. Ask her to wait for him.

But when he got downstairs it was to the shock of finding her key to the apartment on his kitchen countertop. And a note in her bold handwriting. He picked it up, dreading what it might contain.

> *Don't try to find me, Declan, because I don't want to be found. There are a few boxes of my possessions in the shed that I couldn't fit into the 4x4. Could you please give access to Lynne when she comes around to collect them for me?*
>
> *I've arranged for Mark Brown to finish the last work on the garden—it's nearly done. I suggest you hire him for ongoing maintenance. It would be a tragedy to let the garden go again.*
>
> *I could have loved you, Declan. I hope your heart can heal enough for you to find love again one day.*
> *Shelley*

He stared at the words in utter disbelief, then crumpled up the piece of paper and threw it on the floor with a massive roar of pain that echoed through his empty, lonely house. For a long time he stood, focusing on the forlorn piece of paper, white against the dark-stained wood of his floor, that had destroyed his hope of making amends to Shelley.

Finally with a great shudder of agony and grief he picked it up and smoothed it out again. There were echoes of her sweet scent on the paper—he shut his eyes and breathed it in. Then he folded her note and put it into his pocket, next to his heart.

His mother's words came back to him. *Don't let her go. Trust me, it will be like another little death for you if you do.*

Why did his mother have to be so damn right?

But Shelley hadn't died. This didn't have to be final. The grief he felt at her loss wasn't the hopeless kind of grief he had endured before. He had it within his power to find his beautiful warrior and win her back.

*No matter what it took.*

# CHAPTER SIXTEEN

*Two months later*

SHELLEY KNELT AT the edge of the perfectly maintained lawn of one of the most famous gardens in England as she precisely planted bulbs that would flower next spring—paperwhite jonquils and blue hyacinths. She couldn't help but wonder where she would be when they bloomed.

She was glad she'd packed her knee pads with her when she'd left Australia. Autumn was well and truly under way in Kent and, although there had been crisp, sunny days, today the ground was wet and cold. The head gardener was exacting and she was determined to do the best job she could. She considered it a privilege to work in a garden planted by Vita Sackville-West, one of the most famous garden designers of her time and a contemporary—and idol—of Enid Wilson.

At first, it had felt disconcerting to leave Declan's spring garden and arrive in autumn for her tour of the European gardens she had longed to see but she had loved every second of it. No books or videos could give the experience of actually being in a garden like this one.

This was what she wanted—to see gardens that had influenced designs all over the world, even in climates as inhospitable to an English-style garden as Australia could be. To actually work as a horticulturalist in one was the icing on the cake.

But she was lonely and there wasn't a day that went by she didn't think about Declan. In protecting her heart she feared she'd doomed herself to a lifetime of her heart crying out for him.

She'd met a nice guy in the village where she was living—a farmer who had invited her out to ride horses on his property. Now he was pressing for a proper date. But she still longed for Declan like a physical ache. He was an impossible act for any everyday kind of man to follow.

She paused, trowel in her hand. Thinking about Declan was making her imagine things because suddenly she had that preternatural feeling she used to get in Sydney when he was nearby.

Slowly she turned around to face the lawn. A tall, broad-shouldered man with black hair and wearing an immaculately cut black coat was walking towards her. Was she hallucinating? Had she wanted him so badly she'd somehow conjured him up out of nowhere? Or was it like the other times during the previous months in England, France, and Spain when her heart would skip a beat at the glimpse of a man she thought was him only for it to be a stranger?

She blinked. Took off her glove to scrub at her eyes. But when she looked up again he was there, looming over her, a quizzical expression in his deep blue eyes. *Declan.*

She stumbled to her feet and he caught her elbow to steady her. Of all the words of greeting she could have chosen, words to let him know of her longing and regret, all she could blurt out was: 'How did you find me?'

'Mark Brown. He took some convincing to give me your contact details. But he eventually caved.'

Shelley took off her other glove to give herself time

to think. 'So why are you in Kent? In town for a gaming convention? Or a gathering of billionaires doing billionaire things? There's certainly enough wealthy people living around here for you to be in fine company.'

He smiled that familiar, indulgent smile he gave her when she was talking nonsense. 'None of those.'

'Actually, *how* are you here when I thought you could never leave that house?' she asked.

He stood very close. 'I'm here to tell you I love you, Shelley.'

She nearly fell over backwards on the slippery ground. 'Wh… What?' She managed to right herself—but her thoughts remained topsy-turvy.

Her first impulse was to blurt out *I love you too* but she suppressed it. In the two months since she'd last seen him she'd gone through too much heartache and pain to dive back in so easily.

'I love you,' he said again, slowly. 'I don't know how you feel about me, but I hope you might feel in some measure the same.' His eyes searched her face, seeking her answer.

'I might do…' she said slowly. 'Well, I did back then, now I'm not so sure. It…it's been so long.' She had told him not to seek her out, but somewhere deep inside her she had hoped he would—and been disappointed when he hadn't.

Now he was here.

'Two months I needed to sort myself out, to…to heal. You were right. I wasn't ready for you. I needed help and I went out and found it.'

'What kind of help?' she asked, amazed that he would unbend enough to admit it.

He shifted from foot to foot. 'It's difficult for a guy like me to say I saw a counsellor but that's exactly what I did.'

She frowned. 'You mean you didn't see a professional after Lisa and the baby died?'

'I did not.'

She shook her head. 'You should have. No wonder you were such a mess back then.' She slammed her hand to her mouth. 'I'm sorry,' she said. 'There I go again.'

He smiled. 'I've missed that.'

'You mean my foot-in-mouth blunders?'

'Your plain speaking and telling the truth as you see it,' he said.

'That's one way of putting it,' she said, smiling in spite of herself.

He placed his hands on her shoulders. Even through the bulk of her down jacket she could feel their warmth. 'You were right,' he said. 'I wasn't ready to give or receive love and I'm sorry you were collateral damage along the way.'

She looked up at him into those remarkable blue eyes that were now free of the shadows that had haunted them, the handsome lean face that had lost the lines of tension around his mouth that had always been there. *His mouth.* That looked as kissable as ever. 'But…' She couldn't remember what she was going to say next, too distracted by the thought of claiming his mouth for herself again.

Declan continued. 'I had to come to terms with grief and loss and guilt and to stop blaming myself for what was out of my control.'

'All…those things I couldn't help you with. And…and I had my own trust issues to deal with.' She'd had a very long talk with her mother before she'd flown out of Sydney that had helped immensely.

'Maybe neither of us was ready then,' he said. He slid his hands from her shoulders, down her arms, and pulled her closer.

'But now?' she breathed.

'I'm ready to love you like you deserve to be loved, Shelley Fairhill.'

This time she didn't hesitate. 'I love you too, Declan. So much.'

Shelley pressed her mouth to his. His lips were cold but didn't stay that way for long. She put all her hope and longing and love into the kiss. Until they were rudely interrupted by a loud wolf whistle from one of the other gardeners.

She pulled away, flushed. 'Oh, my gosh, I could get fired for that.'

'Would you care if you got fired?'

'Yes. I like this job. It's only a temporary contract but it's a delight to work in this place. Even in winter the bare bones of the garden will be inspiring. Did you know about the famous white garden? It was a radical planting in its time—only white flowers. Apparently it looks amazing dusted in snow. Truly white.'

Declan put his finger on her mouth to silence her. 'I'm sure that's fascinating stuff. But can it wait until later?' He stamped one foot, then the other. 'I'm freezing here and I'd rather talk about us than gardens.'

'Us?' Her breath caught in her throat.

'You. Me. Where you want to live. I can live anywhere, any country, for my work as long as there's electricity and internet. I don't want to live in the Bellevue Street house again—it had become a prison. I'm thinking of donating it to a heritage trust. Your professor in Melbourne is working on a proposal with me.'

'My...my professor?'

'Yes. With full recognition to you for having discovered the heritage garden.'

'You did that for me?'

'Yes,' he said simply.

She kissed him again. 'Thank you. That means so much.' There was no need to elaborate further. His actions proved his love for her and it was enough.

She didn't want to live in that house where Declan had been so unhappy either. Though she'd like him to retain control over the garden. It would be criminal for it to slide into neglect again or, worse, be ripped out.

'What about your television career?' he asked. 'Have you given up on that?'

'No way. The current presenter decided he wanted to do one more season before he bowed out so that gives me another few months before I'd have to start. The producer likes the idea of him introducing me to the viewers when the time comes.'

'So that means you going back to live in Australia?'

'Not yet. Maybe not permanently. But it's too good an opportunity to pass up.'

'I agree.'

'But I'm conflicted. I love it here,' she said wistfully. 'The ideal would be if I could somehow live between Australia and Europe for a few years at least.'

'That's entirely possible,' he said. 'First-class flights make the long flight bearable. Private jets even more so.'

'I wouldn't know about that,' she said with a rueful smile. 'It's cattle class all the way for me.'

'Not when you fly with me,' he said.

He silenced her gasp with a quick kiss. 'And if you want to live here, I've found a wonderful manor house nearby,' Declan said. 'The house is perfect but the garden is crying out for the Shelley touch to make it *your* garden.'

'Sounds promising,' she said, cautiously, not really certain of where he was going.

'It also has a stable and a few acres of pastures for a horse.'

'Sold!' she said. She drew her brows together and looked up at him. 'What did I just agree to, Declan?'

He cupped her face in his hands in the possessive way she loved. 'I hope you've agreed to be my wife,' he said.

'Your wife,' she said slowly. 'I… I like the idea.'

'Good,' he said. 'I'll take that for a yes.'

'Not so fast,' she said, taking a step back, her heart feeling like a parched plant that had just been watered. 'I want a proper proposal, please.'

He laughed. 'Why does that not surprise me?' He looked down at the mushy ground that surrounded them.

'I don't expect you to go down on bended knee or anything,' she said with a catch in her voice.

He took both her hands in his. 'Shelley, will you do me the honour of marrying me?' he asked very seriously.

She took a deep breath to steady her voice. 'I would love to be your wife. And…and the mother of your children. That is, if you want—'

He closed his eyes for a moment. 'Yes. I do,' he said as he opened them again. 'When…when the time is right for both of us to take that step.'

Shelley pulled him close and kissed him. She realised that might become another challenge. With past tragedy in mind, she could imagine how overprotective Declan would become if she were to fall pregnant. But they could face that challenge together when it came.

'I supposed you'd like a proper engagement ring too?' he murmured against her mouth.

'Well, yes,' she said. 'But I guess you mightn't have had time to buy one. I mean, what if I'd said no to your proposal? Not that I would have said no. I love you so much and couldn't imagine anything I'd like more than to be your wife.'

Declan smiled and her heart missed a beat at the love for

her she saw shining from his eyes. He pulled out a small box from the inner pocket of his overcoat.

'Oh…' was all she could manage to get out.

The ring was a huge sapphire flanked by two enormous diamonds. 'The colour of your blue dress, the one that isn't much dress at all,' he said. 'It suited you so well I thought a sapphire might too.' He slipped it onto the third finger of her left hand.

'It's perfect,' she breathed, looking down at her hand and admiring the way it caught the light. At the same time she caught sight of her watch. 'It's nearly time for me to finish. I'm sure they'll let me go a little earlier on the momentous occasion of my engagement.'

'I've already cleared it with the head gardener,' he said. 'You can come straight home with me.'

'Home?'

'I bought the manor house just on the off chance you'd like it,' he said.

'As billionaires do,' she said, laughing.

'You'll soon be the wife of a billionaire so you can do billionaire things too,' he said. 'The income from Estella will be all yours as well. One hundred per cent of it.'

Shelley pulled back from his embrace, looked up into his eyes. 'It's not about your money—you know that, don't you?' It was suddenly very important that he was aware of that. 'I love you, Declan. I'd love you even if we were going to live in the garden shed.'

'That's one more reason I adore you,' he said. 'We'll have a wonderful life together, Shelley.'

'I know,' she said, kissing him again.

\* \* \* \* \*